✹ Apalachee

Apalachee

JOYCE ROCKWOOD HUDSON

THE UNIVERSITY OF GEORGIA PRESS

ATHENS AND LONDON

To Kathy
With Best Wishes
Katherine Joyce Hudson
6-03-00

Published by the University of Georgia Press
Athens, Georgia 30602
© 2000 by Joyce Rockwood Hudson
All rights reserved

Designed by Erin Kirk New
Set in 10.5 on 13 Minion by G&S Typesetters
Printed and bound by Maple-Vail

The paper in this book meets the guidelines for permanence
and durability of the Committee on Production Guidelines
for Book Longevity of the Council on Library Resources.

Printed in the United States of America
04   03   02   01   00   C   5   4   3   2   1

Library of Congress Cataloging-in-Publication Data
Hudson, Joyce Rockwood.
Apalachee / Joyce Rockwood Hudson.
    p.   cm.
ISBN 0-8203-2190-7 (alk. paper)
1. Apalachee Indians—Fiction.   2. Indians of North
America—Florida—Fiction.   3. Florida—History—Spanish
colony, 1565–1763—Fiction.   I. Title.
PS3558.U295 A86   2000
813'.54—dc21   99-045911

British Library Cataloging-in-Publication Data available

To my husband, Charles Hudson

Presiding spirit of the house in which I have written

ACKNOWLEDGMENTS

For their contributions to this work I wish to thank Miriam Chaikin, Karen Orchard, Phil Williams, John Worth, Dave Stern, and most especially Charles Hudson.

PROLOGUE

The Apalachee people were the aboriginal inhabitants of that part of the eastern Florida panhandle that includes and surrounds the present-day capital city of Tallahassee. Although their homeland was not extensive, their reputation was, and their name was conferred to several geographical features in eastern North America: to Apalachee Bay, south of Tallahassee; to the Apalachee River in Georgia; to the Appalachicola River, which empties into the Gulf of Mexico near the town of Appalachicola in Florida's western panhandle; and to the faraway Appalachian Mountains.

The Apalachees reached the apex of their cultural achievement in the fifteenth century, when an estimated sixty thousand people lived in towns and farmsteads across an area approximately fifty miles in diameter. They were ruled by hereditary chiefs who traced their lineage from the Sun, their principal deity. The Apalachees built large, flat-topped, pyramidal mounds to serve as platforms for their temples and for the homes of the highest ranking of their ruling class. They carried on an extensive trade in exotic goods with other native peoples in the interior of North America. Renowned for the fierceness of their warriors, they were widely feared as a strong and formidable society.

In the sixteenth century, Spanish explorers invaded Apalachee and then moved on, leaving wreckage and disease in their wake. In 1608 Spanish missionaries established a permanent presence there. Spanish soldiers and ranchers followed. Although European diseases continued to ravage the native population in years to come, Spaniards and Apalachees co-existed in a relatively stable mission culture. But in 1670, England founded Charles Town on the southern Atlantic coast, and the colony of Carolina began to rise. Bitter hostility reigned between the two colonial powers, and by 1704 the future of Spanish Florida, and of the Apalachee people, had grown dark.

Part One

MISSION APALACHEE

1704

CHAPTER ONE

In the Apalachee mission town of San Lorenzo de Ivitachuco, in a small, round Indian house that stood close beside the convento of the resident Spanish priest, Hinachuba Lucia knelt beside the low-burning fire in the open hearth. Death had now come so near that she could feel the boundaries dissolving between This World and the next. Time had ceased to move. Stirring up the coals, she added more wood against the winter wind. Firelight rose and illuminated her face, its high cheekbones and brown skin framed by a black sweep of hair knotted behind her neck. Her skirt was made of deerskin and her bodice of coarse Spanish cloth. A medicine bag made of the white-feathered skin of an egret was attached to her belt, and from each ear dangled a tear-shaped, blue-green glass pendant—the tears of Mary.

Lucia sat back on her heels and watched the flames, numb to the grief that she knew would overtake her after the burial, after the presence of death had receded, when time began to move again. On one of the pole-framed beds that stood against the circular wall of the house, her grandmother, Hinachuba Isabel, slept lightly. On another her aunt sat weeping.

And on another Lucia's mother lay dying. Nothing would save her. Lucia's own medicines had been of no avail, nor had those of her grandmother, nor had the Christian prayers of her aunt. For three days, with little sleep, they had been waiting for death to come. And now, in the night that had just passed, Hinachuba Sun in the-Mist had sunk deeply into unconsciousness. The waiting would soon be over.

The old grandmother awakened and stirred. "Lucia," she said softly, sitting up. "You should sleep."

Lucia turned her head and watched as Isabel got up, stiff and arthritic, and came shuffling across the room to the hearth, a worn blanket clutched about her shoulders. Her body was bent and shrunken with age, her hair white and thin. She came up to the fire and stood before it, rubbing a hand slowly across her face, as if gathering her strength. Then she reached out and touched Lucia's shoulder.

"When did you last sleep?"

Lucia shook her head without answering.

"There is nothing more we can do," said Isabel. "She does not even know we are here now. Go ahead and sleep."

Lucia heard a muffled sob and looked over at her aunt, Hinachuba Ana, a handsome woman with an intelligent face, whose eyes were now red from crying. Ana's fingers absently stroked a small silver cross that hung from a string of dark burgundy beads around her neck.

"Ana, you are tired, too," said Isabel. "Both of you should sleep."

Ana made no reply. She took a deep breath, composing herself a little, and got up and walked over to where her sister lay. She stood for a moment with tremulous breath, looking at her. Then she reached down and stroked her hair. "Why was she so stubborn?" she said quietly. "To die without God."

Lucia's jaw stiffened and she looked away into the dark recesses of the room. Ana never saw the world exactly as it was. She was grieving for her idea of things as much as for the loss of her sister's life.

"She is not dead yet," the old grandmother said curtly.

"But she is gone from us," said Ana, turning away from the bed with a deep sigh. Then she closed her lips tightly and straightened her shoulders, as if willing herself to be strong. She walked back to her own bed and picked up her worn Spanish cloak. "I am going to the convento for a little while. Father Juan has been three days without a servant in his house."

"You should rest now," said Isabel.

"I should tend to my work," said Ana, putting the cloak around her shoulders. "Later I will sleep." She ducked through the door and went out.

"No one listens to me," muttered Isabel.

Lucia stood up and put a reassuring hand on Isabel's shoulder, her own tall height making her grandmother seem even smaller. "I cannot sleep now," said Lucia. "When it is over, I will sleep."

✴ When Ana returned, the priest was with her, Father Juan de Villalva, a brown-robed friar past the middle of his life, a man of medium height, dark hair going to gray, his flesh thin and his face gaunt from a wracking cough that had plagued him for as long as Lucia had known him. She looked up at him from where she was sitting at her mother's bedside and nodded courteously. He had been kind to her since she and her mother and grandmother had come to live in Ana's house in the mission town. Ana was the priest's house servant, and more, and she was a Christian in her heart, not merely in appearance as Lucia and Isabel were. The priest's kindness was for Ana's sake, Lucia supposed, for she herself had never tried to earn it. She was indifferent to him, though not impolite, and though she never looked for it and therefore never saw it, she assumed there must be goodness in him, for Ana herself was good at heart and would not attach herself to a man whose own heart was evil. The fact that he had come to their house seemed to her a kindness, and she accepted it as that.

"You want sofkee?" her grandmother said to the priest. The old woman spoke Spanish only haltingly, sometimes mixing in Apalachee words. She went over to the fire and looked into a clay pot of thin hominy gruel. "Plenty sofkee."

"Thank you," said Father Juan, nodding absently.

Isabel picked up the gourd dipper that lay near the pot, then reconsidered and put it down again. "I get bowl from cocina," she said and headed toward the door. The kitchen was a separate building on the other side of the yard.

"Don't trouble yourself," said the priest, waving his hand at her.

"I get bowl," said Isabel. "You want bread?" The cocina was her own domain—she was the cook.

"No," said Father Juan. "No bread."

Isabel went out.

Lucia rose and moved away from her mother's bed, making room for the priest. "She is sleeping," she said, her own Spanish fluent. She had picked up the language as a child, and not even Ana could speak it as well as she could. As she watched the priest approach the bed, she was glad that her mother had made it safely into unconsciousness before he came. Sun-in-the-Mist had always hated the priest along with everything else that was Spanish, including the language, which she had refused to learn at all. The only reason they had come here to live with Ana was because Lucia's father had died, leaving them with no one to hunt for them in the little homestead where they had lived before, and no one to protect them from the growing danger of slave-catchers. But Lucia's mother had never reconciled herself to living in the mission town. She was an Apalachee and a daughter of the Hinachuba clan, the clan of the ancient White Sun chiefs, and she had never wanted a Christian name nor any part of a Spanish life. Lucia also was a Hinachuba—clan membership came through the mother. But though she honored the old ways, she had grown up with Spaniards in her world and she could live with them. She had to live with them. To refuse that was to refuse life.

A fresh draft blew in from the door.

Lucia turned and saw Usunaca Carlos, the priest's assistant, a tall, large-boned man, his flesh lean and strong, his manner serious beyond his years. He nodded to her and she gave him a reserved nod in return, wondering why he had come. Perhaps he was here for Ana's sake, for he hardly knew Lucia's mother. Although he was Apalachee by birth, he was too much a Spaniard, too much like the priest, for Sun-in-the-Mist ever to warm to him.

It was because Carlos had been raised in the priest's own house that he seemed almost to be a priest himself, and almost to be a Spaniard. But all the schooling that the priest had given him had not been able to wipe away the brown color of his skin, nor make his dark eyes more round, nor fill his veins with pure, clean Spanish blood. To Spain he was still an Indian. His clothing reflected his place between the two worlds—his shirt, breeches,and stockings were Spanish, but his moccasins and the red blanket he wore about his shoulders were Apalachee.

Lucia had never been comfortable with Carlos. His eyes were more penetrating than Father Juan's and more likely to notice her indifference to things Spanish and Christian. But today she felt cautiously welcoming. Let him come in and fill the house with his presence so that her mother might die in the midst of mourners. That was as it should be when a person lay dying, even if the friends who came to mourn were not the person's own. Sun-in-the-Mist had no close friends in Ivitachuco. Like Lucia, she had always been content to be alone.

Lucia moved back to the fire as the visitors clustered beside the bed. Ana reached down and smoothed her sister's blanket. Carlos said something in a low voice. Lucia did not catch the words, but she saw Father Juan nod in reply. Carlos turned aside and squatted down on his heels to put a small box on the floor, a wooden chest with brass hinges and lock. Lucia's heart quickened. He had carried it beneath his blanket when he came in and she had not noticed it. Stepping closer, she watched him open it. Inside was a silver bowl, a small linen towel, and a corked vial of water for baptizing.

Lucia's anger flared. Her mother had not wanted this. "It is too late," she said, directing her words to all of them together. "She is sleeping now. She will not awaken again."

Ana and Father Juan seemed not to have heard her, but Carlos glanced up, then turned and lifted out the silver bowl.

"It is too late," Lucia repeated. "You cannot wake her. And if you could, she would not let you baptize her."

Father Juan turned and looked at Lucia with weary eyes. "It is not too late," he said. "She is still alive."

"But unconscious!" said Lucia.

He looked wordlessly at Ana, seeking help. Ana stepped around him and put a hand on Lucia's arm.

"It is better that she sleeps," Ana explained quietly. "Then she cannot renounce the vows. We take them for her, Carlos and I, her godparents, as we would for an infant. Be happy, Lucia. We are sending her to God."

Lucia pulled away from Ana's hand. "She did not want that," she said fiercely. "You cannot do it."

She looked over at Carlos. He was standing with the vial of water in one hand and the silver bowl in the other. The little towel hung over his forearm. He watched her soberly as the priest turned to him, ignoring Lucia.

Lucia stepped toward them, thinking only that she must stop them. Her blood pounded as she reached for the priest, grasping the sleeve of his robe. She heard no sound as Carlos spoke and felt nothing as Ana pulled her away and held her. She cried out for her grandmother to come, though she barely heard herself. Tearing free of Ana, she struck out at Carlos, knocking the silver bowl from his hand. The priest reached for her, but she hit his hand away, then struggled to free herself from Ana's grip and that of Carlos as she tried to get to her mother. She could feel herself crying.

"Let her die in peace," she begged, pulling against them. But they held her tightly. She heard Ana's voice trying to soothe her. She struggled again, summoning all her strength, trying to tear away. One arm came free. She swung with it, her fist clenched, but it was caught in a hard, thin hand, and she heard the stern voice of her grandmother say in Apalachee, "Be still, child!"

Isabel was breathing hard, having run across the yard from the cocina. Her grip on Lucia's wrist was strong for one so old, and Lucia sagged beneath it, all her strength draining away.

"They are trying to baptize her," Lucia said weakly. "Tell them they cannot do it."

Isabel pushed the hands of the others away from Lucia, then led her over to her own bed and sat down with her on the edge of it. "What does it matter?" she said quietly. Her voice was tired, sorrowful, her hand absently stroking Lucia's leg to comfort her. "She is gone from here. She does not know. So what does it matter, my child? Think of Ana."

Lucia made no reply. She stared down at her grandmother's hand, its thin, transparent skin barely covering the bones and veins and swollen joints. The others were standing together, silent, waiting for calm, for things to be easy again. Lucia knew they would have their way. But she would not stay to witness it. She rose and picked up her blanket from beside her mother's bed, and wrapping it about her shoulders, she went out into the cold.

✳ Lucia's mother died the same day she was baptized, and on the next day she was buried in the floor of the church. In the night following the burial, Carlos tossed on his narrow bed, restless and awake. Moonlight sifted through cracks in the window shutters into his tiny room off the back of the convento. He felt confined in the darkness of his room, trapped between walls he could almost touch with his arms outspread. Yet for how many years had this been his home? It was the generosity of a priest to a young orphan boy, a room built by closing in a portion of the porch which ran the full length of the back of the convento. No other Apalachee had the privilege of living so near the priest. The orphan boy had been thrilled and flattered, and still as a man Carlos was thankful when he thought of all Father Juan had done for him. The priest had raised him, taught him to read and write, schooled him in church doctrine and liturgy. He could do anything the priest himself could do, were he to seek a friar's vocation. But Carlos' future was not to be in the Church. The priest had groomed him for another purpose. Even though he was not a Hinachuba, Father Juan intended him to be chief of Ivitachuco when the life of the present chief, Hinachuba Patricio, was over.

The priest could not ordain this. The council house still governed itself. But the Hinachuba clan had almost died out in this town. The chief's closest heir was the grandson of his mother's sister and lived in a distant town. The Usunacas, themselves a noble clan, and the one to which Carlos belonged, had become the strongest clan in the council house. In these extraordinary times, Carlos' special qualities—his literacy and his intimate knowledge of Spaniards—were held in high regard by the people of the town. When it came time to name a new chief, the priest's hope for him was likely to be fulfilled. But how long must he wait? He was not a boy anymore, content to pass his days in passive service to the priest. The room had grown too small for him. Prayers no longer calmed him but gave way instead to troubled thoughts, even to doubts.

He fought back the doubts, for he still believed much of what the priest had taught him, and he wished to believe all of it with the easy faith he had once possessed. He blamed his restlessness in part on the priest, who had become remote in recent years, preoccupied with his growing illness. But he knew the fault was in himself as well. He wrestled to contain it, succeeding well enough in daylight hours, but at night he would awaken, restless and tense, unable to return to sleep.

A walk sometimes helped. He got up, wrapped his red blanket around his shoulders, and went out into the night. The cold air on his face calmed him and strengthened him. He stood for a moment before the church, looking across the moonlit plaza to the council house on the other side. The town was asleep. He could almost imagine himself chief of it. He turned from the plaza and made his way quietly among the houses, thinking what he would do to make Ivitachuco a better place. He wanted above all to lead well.

The houses were dark and silent beneath the light haze of smoke that rose from the ash-banked fires in their hearths. Here and there stood great live oaks draped in hanging moss, ragged like the town in its poverty. Even in the darkness he could feel the destitution. There were too few men for all the women here. Not enough meat was being brought in, not enough deerskins, too much illness and misery. As he moved away from the town's center, he began to pass by houses that were empty—deserted dwellings that had fallen into ruin. A few elders were yet alive whose own parents had grown up in the old Ivitachuco and who carried stories from that time. When the first Spanish friars came, as many as fifteen hundred Indians lived here. Now there were barely six hundred. Spanish diseases had killed hundreds of them. Many others had deserted the town to live elsewhere.

Carlos tightened his blanket against the chill of the night. He felt it was God's anger that caused the people to die in such numbers from the Spanish fevers, their punishment for clinging so stubbornly to the old ways. If they could be persuaded to be better Christians, surely the diseases would diminish. But how to stop the desertions? Always there had been a trickle of people who walked away, but recently it had swelled to a flood. And not because of anything the priest had done. It was the work of the English. From their new colony of Carolina they were arming Creek Indians and sending them south against the missions to raid for slaves. The raids were sporadic and unpredictable. Sometimes there were large assaults on entire towns, but more often there were isolated ambushes, a few slave-catchers hidden near a spring or a trail, always unexpected, brutal, leaving terror in their wake. Life in Florida had become dangerous to the extreme. For some it seemed safer to join the enemy, to go north and settle among the Creeks.

Carlos looked scornfully at the stockade on the outskirts of Ivitachuco, the top of it visible above the houses, dark against the starry sky—a small wooden structure manned by four soldiers. Four soldiers. No wonder people were frightened. No wonder they deserted. Who could believe that four soldiers were enough to protect this town—and the entire eastern half of Apalachee besides? Yet the governor at San Augustín refused to send more. Last year the English had attacked San Augustín itself and razed the presidio town. The only safety there now was in the great stone fortress. The presidio was more important to the governor than the people of Apalachee were. But if Carlos were chief, he himself would journey to San Augustín and make a forceful case for more soldiers.

Still in the old ruined section of Ivitachuco, he came to a house that had not yet been abandoned. The light of a freshly stoked fire shone through the cracks in the plaster of the wattle-and-daub wall. The shaman Usunaca Salvador lived here, a kinsman of Carlos, both men linked to the same clan through their mothers. But unlike Carlos, Salvador was a thorn in the side of the priest. Neither repeated whippings nor threat of hanging had ever induced him to give up his sorcery. He had been baptized as a Christian and attended Mass regularly, and Father Juan, in truth, could not hang him nor even banish him from the town, for Salvador's following among the converts was far too large to risk such a rupture in the mission. Carlos hoped as chief to wean away some of Salvador's supporters. He knew the struggle would be a long one. Father Juan had spent himself in that battle. Yet as Carlos stood in the dark shadows and watched the light flicker through the cracks of that dilapidated house, he felt that his own way would eventually prevail over the pagan way of his kinsman.

He walked out to the edge of the town and then began circling its periphery, passing beneath the walls of the stockade without challenge from the sleeping sentry. The dogs who awoke in the yards of the houses watched him without alarm, for they were accustomed to his nighttime wanderings. He wondered if they would recognize a Creek slave-catcher, or if they would just lie there and watch an enemy as passively as they were watching him. When he became chief, security would be tighter. No one would pass without challenge.

As he came around to the convento again, he could feel the tug of sleep. Dawn would soon lighten the sky, and with it would come the clanging of the waking bell and the preparations for the morning Mass. He hoped for a few moments of rest. He could almost feel the warmth of his bed.

Then, as he started around the corner of the convento, he saw a movement in front of the church door. Thinking of slave-catchers, he stepped out of the bright moonlight into the shadow of the churchyard wall and let his blanket slide to the ground. He waited a moment, listening, and then slipped quietly along the wall until the area in front of the church was in full view. He crouched, scarcely breathing, his eyes searching the moonlight and shadows until he saw the figure of a woman, blanketed, walking slowly away from the plaza. She paused and looked back at the church as if giving a parting glance to someone she was leaving behind. As the moonlight caught her face, he saw that it was Ana's niece, Lucia, her hair flowing loose in mourning for her mother, who was now interred with so many others in the floor of the church.

He should have known who it would be out here in the night. If ever there was a strange one, it was this woman, so alone and yet not seeming lonely, always busy with her curing. But it was more than her curing that made her strange. Her Hinachuba clan was the ancient chiefly lineage, whose glory had been greatest in the old days of Apalachee, before the Spaniards came. Something of that time lingered in her old grandmother,

as it had in her mother, more pagan than the rest, and it seemed also to
have passed into Lucia. She came to Mass, but she was no real Christian. A
real Christian would not have tried to stop her mother's baptism, nor come
to tend her grave in the secrecy of night. He could see the two pottery
vessels that she carried, and he knew what she had done. Earlier in the night
she had slipped into the church and hid them in the darkness near the new
grave so that her mother could take nourishment on her way to the Other
World. Now she was removing them before daylight, concealing her stubborn paganism from the priest.

Carlos leaned against the cold wall of the churchyard. He should report
her. But as he watched her walk away in the moonlight, he knew that he
would not.

CHAPTER TWO

Lucia led the way along the edge of the field until she came to the faint
animal trail that ran into the woods. She stopped and glanced back at Isabel.
"It is in here," she said, motioning toward the trees.

The old woman came up beside her and looked dubiously at the heavy
undergrowth that screened the entrance of the forest. Then she looked back
toward the town, a long distance behind them. The field was green with
Father Juan's crop of winter wheat. Above, the sun shone brightly in a clear
blue sky, warming the open air. But the floor of the canopied forest was in
shadow, a cold place and a dangerous one. "What is it worth to us to have
this root?" asked Isabel. "Is it worth being caught by slave-catchers?"

"I am not worried about slave-catchers," said Lucia. "I will go in and get
the root myself. You wait for me."

"We will both go," said Isabel. "But you should have sense enough to be
afraid."

Lucia started into the woods without concern. She was sure no slave-
catchers would be lurking here, for no one from Ivitachuco ever came here.
She herself had come only once before. Last summer she had stolen away
from work in the field, which was planted then in corn, and had gone back
into the cool shade to take a moment's rest away from the overseer's relentless gaze. She had seen the button snake-root then, an important plant, not
easy to find, and she had noted its surroundings so that she could return
for it when she needed it.

It oppressed her now to remember that time, the miserable labor of summer, those endless rows of corn beneath the blazing sun. Soon another

spring would arrive and the great fields would have to be broken up again and planted and the weeds chopped, the work rolling forward endlessly. And for what? For a life of dreary monotony, waking up every morning to a clanging bell, shuffling into the church for Mass and then out to the fields for a long day of toil, and then back to the church for evening prayers, and then to bed to sleep until the next morning bell. It was no life. She remembered her girlhood years in the cornfield of her mother's homestead. That, too, was hard, sweating toil, but it had been woven into a cycle of seasons that were filled with ritual and stories and laughter. Their lives had been their own.

Lucia pushed through the underbrush into the tall open forest and stopped for a moment to look around. Isabel followed and stood beside her.

"Winter changes things," the old woman said. "It should not surprise you if you cannot find it again. That is often the way it is, unless you leave a mark."

"The mark is here," said Lucia, tapping her head, her eyes studying the forest, reconstructing and remembering. After a moment she moved forward again, leaving the animal trail and picking her way through a stand of young oaks. Near the base of one of the oaks, she knelt down with her digging stick and began to probe gingerly into the soft ground, until finally she laid the stick aside and dug down with careful fingers to pry loose the root from its hold in the earth. When at last she held it unbroken in her hand, she glanced up at Isabel, looking for the medicine bundle that her grandmother was carrying. Isabel handed her the little clump of frayed blue cloth that had been given to them by the relatives of the sick child for whom the root was intended.

"I do not know why I bother to come along with you anymore," said the old woman. "I have taught you everything I know about curing. You are better at finding medicines than I am. You have become a better curer, too."

"There is still more to learn," said Lucia.

"But that will always be true," said Isabel.

Lucia unwrapped the cloth and spread it on the ground, revealing a piece of green bark already in it along with two other roots, none of them as rare as this last medicine that she placed now on the cloth—the fourth, the completion of the circle. She blew her breath softly upon them, then wrapped them up and slipped the small bundle into the egret-skin medicine bag that hung from her belt.

"I want to show you something," she said as she rose to her feet.

"Show me something where?" asked Isabel.

"In here." Lucia nodded toward the depths of the forest.

"We should go back to town," said Isabel. "This place is too dangerous."

"Just let me show you this," said Lucia, and reaching out, she took the old woman's arm to bring her along.

Isabel allowed herself to be led, but she was clearly unhappy.

"It is not far," said Lucia, letting go of her arm. She walked quickly through the trees, Isabel following more slowly, putting her hand to her back now and again as if all this danger were making her arthritis more painful. They went on deeper into the forest until finally Lucia stopped and pointed ahead. "Look there," she said.

"Ah," Isabel said quietly, coming up to stand beside her. Before them was a flat-topped earthen mound as high as a house, covered with trees, almost invisible in the forest. "I had heard there was one of these around here."

"What is it?" asked Lucia.

"The ancient people built it."

"Yes, but what is it? What was it for?"

"Before the Spaniards came," said Isabel, "this was a town, all open and clear. One of the White Suns lived in a house on that mound. The White Sun himself or his sister, the White Sun Woman. It could have been either one. It meant something in those days to be a Hinachuba. It was more than being a chief in the council house. Not like today."

Lucia nodded. "I thought it must have to do with the White Suns," she said quietly. She stood in silence for a time, looking at the mound. Then they turned and started back through the woods.

"These were only little White Suns," said Isabel as they walked along. "The great White Suns, the brother and sister above all the others, lived north of here in the ancient days. At first they lived in the Great Town near the lake. But then that place was abandoned and another town close by it became the center. That one was not so grand as the Great Town. They say the Great Town was something to see. There were many mounds there. The temple, the council house, the houses of important people, all were on mounds. The White Sun and the White Sun Woman were on the highest one of all, above the rest. They were the son and daughter of the Sun."

"You used to say that you are the White Sun Woman," said Lucia. "When I was young, I thought you meant that because our clan is Hinachuba, all the women of our clan are White Sun women. But that was not what you meant, was it? You meant that you are the one above the rest."

"Yes," Isabel said quietly.

Lucia glanced at her and saw how thoughtful she had become, her eyes fastened on the ground. Lucia kept silent, waiting to hear what else she would say. They had reached the edge of the woods and were coming out into the warm sun of the wheat field.

Isabel suddenly stopped and turned to Lucia. "Why did you take me to the mound?"

Lucia shrugged. "I wanted you to see it. We had come so close to it to get the root."

"But why today?" asked Isabel. There was urgency in her voice. "It is strange that it would be today."

"Why strange?"

Isabel began walking again, Lucia falling in step beside her. "Yesterday I had a talk with Salvador," said Isabel, "and he told me something that has been on my mind ever since. I could not decide what to make of it. But now you have shown me this and asked me these questions and it all becomes clear to me. Something important has happened, my granddaughter."

"What do you mean?"

"It is true what I used to tell you. I truly am the White Sun Woman. When the very first Spaniards came, it was the uncle of my grandmother's grandmother who reigned. After him, it was my grandmother's grandmother herself. Then it came to my grandmother's uncle, who was the White Sun when the first friars came. He had two sisters. My grandmother's mother was the older sister, but she had only a daughter and no sons. The younger sister had a son, and when the old White Sun died, the Hinachubas passed over my grandmother and named the younger sister's son as chief." Isabel paused and looked at Lucia. "Do you follow this?"

"Yes," said Lucia.

"In the old days the succession would have passed to my grandmother," said Isabel, "but now the people wanted a strong man to stand up for them to the Spaniards. Maybe they were right. Since the friars have come, things are not the same as they used to be. Now a White Sun is only a chief. He leads the councils and deals with the Spaniards, but much of the old way has been put aside. In the old days the succession would have gone from my grandmother to my mother's brother and then to me, as his sister's oldest daughter, because my mother did not have a son. But instead it went down the other line to Don Patricio. It is just as well. Don Patricio is a good chief." She paused and shook her head. "So much has changed. So many people have died, and so much of the old way has been forgotten. I know that in a certain way I am the White Sun Woman. But to me it has never meant anything. It has only been a memory passed down from my grandmother. But now Salvador has had a dream."

"About the White Suns?"

"Yes, and I want you to hear him tell it. You are as much a part of it as I am. You are the one who would be the White Sun Woman after me."

"It should be Ana. She is next in line."

"No," said Isabel. "You know it could never be Ana. Ana has turned away from the old ways."

Lucia walked in silence for a moment. Then she said, "It is dangerous to talk to Salvador. If we are seen with him, we could be accused of being witches. The priest could say we are curing for Satan instead of God."

"The priest is a fool," muttered Isabel.

"But he can make us stop our curing."

They had almost crossed the field now and were nearing the road. Not far in the distance a rider approached at a leisurely pace, a Spaniard coming not from the ranches, which were in the opposite direction, but from the river just east of the town, where the royal road entered Apalachee territory. From that river it was a two-week journey east to San Augustín. All of the missions were located along the road, and a traveler was not an uncommon sight.

"I suppose I will have to cook for him," Isabel said irritably as she peered at the rider.

Lucia glanced up at the sun, still high in the sky. "No. It is early. Whoever it is, he will only stop for a rest and then go on."

Isabel shook her head. "It looks like Don Manuel Solana to me. He will stay the night, and Father Juan will want a feast for him."

Lucia looked again. The rider was closer, and now she could see that it was indeed Manuel Solana, a friend of Father Juan's. Until recently Don Manuel had been deputy governor of Apalachee, the highest official in the province. He lived in San Luís, two days further to the west. "When was he here before?" asked Lucia. "Two moons ago, at least. He was on his way to San Augustín to visit the governor. Now he is coming back."

"It means I will be in the cocina for the rest of the day," said Isabel.

"But he will keep Father Juan busy tonight."

Isabel smiled. "Yes, it would be a good time to meet with Salvador."

Salvador looked up without rising as Lucia and Isabel entered his house. "You have come," he said formally.

"We have come," Isabel replied.

"Here is sofkee," he said, motioning with his hand toward the pot of hominy gruel near the door.

Lucia and Isabel each politely dipped out a little of the gruel with the gourd dipper that was in the pot. They drank it and then seated themselves beside the fire.

The shaman's house was cold, the winter air moving freely through the cracks in the clay plaster of the walls. But it was warmer here than it would have been in the canebrake outside the town. That was where they had first arranged to meet Salvador. But those plans had been changed by the events of the evening: a woman and her son taken by slave-catchers while drawing water at the spring. Despite the reassuring presence in the town of Don Manuel Solana, fears were heightened all around, and the meeting at the canebrake became out of the question—they would have to risk coming to Salvador's house, the lesser of two dangers. And so Lucia and Isabel, having finished their labors in the cocina, had waited in their beds until the dead of night, until those hours before dawn when nothing stirs and even the dogs sleep deeply, and then they had slipped out through the stillness of the town and come unseen to the house of Salvador.

Now silence settled over them. It was Salvador who presided over the silence as he sat cross-legged on a soiled cane mat, a tattered piece of blue blanket clutched around his shoulders. He stared into the fire as the light rose and fell upon his face. He was an old man, but not extremely so—not as old as Isabel. His hands, one holding his blanket and the other resting motionless upon his knee, were still strong, though marked with his years.

Lucia looked around at Salvador's sparsely furnished quarters. There was nothing Christian in this house. Nothing Spanish. Salvador might go to Mass every week to appease the priest, but he was a man of the old time. In his youth he had been apprenticed to an elderly shaman who could remember the time before the missionaries came, when the Spaniards were only a distant presence to the east, in Timucua and San Augustín. And Salvador's teacher had in his own youth known old ones who remembered the ancient days when there were no Spaniards in the world at all. Lucia had learned this from Isabel, who often conversed with Salvador in the plaza or in the churchyard, daring the priest to challenge an open exchange between two supposed Christians. Lucia herself did not know the shaman well, separated from him as much by age as by the risk of earning the priest's disfavor. She was facinated now to sit at his fire. If anyone still knew the old Apalachee way, it was Salvador.

The old man began at last to engage them. He looked at Lucia, his eyes intense but cordial, and nodded slightly. Then he busied himself lighting a stone tobacco pipe carved in the shape of a peregrine falcon, and he blew smoke to each of the Four Ways. The peregrine falcon was an animal held sacred by the ancient people.

"I have had a dream that concerns you," he said, his voice strong, pleasing in its tone.

"I have heard," said Lucia.

"The White Falcon came to me," said Salvador. His fingers moved on the stone pipe, absently caressing its polished curves. "She came down from the Sun, the light so bright in her feathers that I could hardly look at her. It was the Sun who sent her."

Lucia gazed at the pipe as he spoke, at the falcon it portrayed, the swiftest bird and the best hunter, beloved of the Sun. Their love for each other went back to the beginning of This World, when animals ruled and people did not yet walk the earth.

"She sat across the fire from me," said Salvador, "as you are sitting now. She spoke as clearly as I am speaking. She told me that the Sun is angry with the people of Apalachee."

Lucia nodded. Everyone knew that. How else to explain the Spaniards in the land? The fevers and death? The English and their slave-catchers? Of course the Sun was angry. She had turned her face away from the people of Apalachee years ago, long before Lucia's birth, even before Isabel's.

"She says we, who are her kinsmen, have turned our faces from her."

"She turned away first," Lucia said, glancing up at him.

"It is the Hinachubas she holds responsible—they who are her blood kinsmen, her progeny, who have always been loved by her above all the other Apalachee clans. And especially she blames the White Sun Woman, who stands closest to her above the rest, so close that the Sun calls her 'Daughter.'"

Lucia glanced at Isabel, but the old woman's face was closed as she watched the fire and listened.

"The White Falcon told me this," said Salvador, his voice becoming more resonant, filled with the import of his vision. "Hear me now. She said the White Sun Woman must turn her face to the Sun as her White Sun ancestors did in the days before the Spaniards, when all was well in the land of Apalachee. The peace that our people knew then is coming back to us, as spring returns after the bitterness of winter. It is the White Sun Woman who must welcome the Sun as she returns. The White Sun Woman must be as one who awaits a beloved guest and goes out each day along the trail to see if the honored one is yet approaching."

Salvador paused and relit his pipe, blowing the smoke once again to each of the Four Ways. "Hear me, now. This is what the White Sun Woman must do. She must arise each morning at dawn and greet the Sun as she makes her appearance on the Red Way of the East. It is the trail by which she comes to us, and the White Sun Woman must go out to meet her. This is the song she must sing." Salvador raised his hands and held them, palms up, in a gesture of reception as he stared into the swirling smoke.

"You have come, my beloved White Mother.
You have come to be among us again.
This is the way to my house.

There is sofkee for you here.
There is dancing.
There are little ones whose faces you have never
 seen.
Come sit by the fire, my beloved White Mother.
Stay with us and grant us your light."

Salvador dropped his hands. "That is all," he said, his voice suddenly normal again. "The White Falcon flew up into the heavens and the dream was over."

Lucia smiled. She liked this man, and she liked his vision, so full of hope, so simple in its demands. A song in the morning. Who would not gladly give that to the Sun? She looked at Isabel. "Are you going to do it?"

"Why would I not?" said Isabel, and her eyes, too, were happy. "I have never known what to do as the White Sun Woman, but now the White Falcon has told me. Today is the beginning. I will greet the Sun as she rises, and I will continue to greet her each day for as long as I remain in This World. And when I am gone, you will do it."

Lucia nodded. "It is a good song."

"It brings hope to Apalachee," said Salvador. He got up and went to the door and opened it and looked out toward the east. There was a dim light along the horizon. "Dawn is coming," he said.

Isabel adjusted her blanket against the cold air that came in from the open door and moved a little closer to the fire. "It is not time to sing yet," she said. "We must wait for the Sun's face."

"We cannot stay here until it is light," said Lucia. "We will be seen as we leave."

Isabel looked up at Salvador, as if this detail had escaped her. "She is right. We cannot forget the danger."

Salvador nodded. "Go now while the dark is still with us. I will watch here, and when I see the Sun lifting her face above the earth, I will know you are singing to her."

Lucia was already on her feet, holding out her hand to help Isabel get up.

"You are afraid," Isabel said quietly to her.

"The light is coming," said Lucia. "We should not have stayed so long. We will be seen."

"You have time," said Salvador. "The town still sleeps." His voice was strong and reassuring, and Lucia let herself be calmed by it.

☀ It had been another night of little sleep for Carlos, this one worse than others because of the woman and her son who had gone to the spring at the edge of nightfall and never returned, only their cries drifting back in the evening chill. The men of Ivitachuco had chased after the slave-catchers, their courage buoyed by the presence of Don Manuel Solana. But the slave-catchers got away with their prizes, two more Christians to be sold into bondage to the English heretics in exchange for guns and cloth. And the fear in Ivitachuco had deepened.

Carlos had gone to bed weary from the chase, and for a time he had slept. But then he was awakened by the old unease, stronger now than ever, and he had come outside to walk, the only remedy he knew. Passing through the old part of town, he heard a soft murmur of voices from the house where Salvador lived alone. Carlos paused in the shadows of the nearby ruins and watched as the door suddenly opened and Salvador appeared, looking out at the eastern sky. Then the shaman turned back inside and more words were spoken with his unseen guests. Then an old woman appeared in the door, small and round-shouldered, huddled in a blanket. When she came out into the faint light of dawn, Carlos recognized her as Isabel. Then Lucia appeared behind her, tall and straight-shouldered, following her grandmother into the yard.

Still watching, Carlos pulled back into the black depths of a ruined house. The chickens that were roosting inside cackled uneasily, and Lucia glanced toward the sound, though only briefly and without alarm, for this dark moment of gathering dawn was the very time when chickens would be astir. As Carlos caught that fleeting glimpse of her face, he puzzled about her. The old man and the old woman he could understand. They were too advanced in years to see the new way. But this young one. What was it that made her hold so stubbornly to the ways of the past? The question nagged at him as he stood in the darkness and watched her.

※ Ana was awake when Lucia and Isabel arrived home. They heard her sit up in her bed. "Where have you been?" Ana asked in the darkness.

Lucia did not even try to think of an answer. She waited for Isabel to do it.

"With Salvador," Isabel said bluntly.

Kneeling by the hearth, Lucia stirred up the fire and listened to the silence that came from Ana. She blew gently on the glowing embers, and in a moment a flame came up, casting its dim light into the room. She glanced over at her aunt, who sat now with her feet on the floor, her cloak drawn around her as she looked at the two of them with exasperation.

"Why did you have to tell me?" she said at last. "It would have been better if I did not know."

"I will not lie to my own daughter," said Isabel.

"What am I to think?" asked Ana. "Salvador is a servant of Satan."

"The time got away. And now you are making me even later." She turned away and began walking quickly toward the plaza.

"If it happens again, you will answer for it," Lorenzo called after her, and she heard him lash his whip against the earth. Isabel's sharp voice rebuked him. Lucia quickened her step and reached the church just as the priest was about to begin.

CHAPTER THREE

Father Juan de Villalva faced his flock from the altar of the chapel of San Lorenzo, a looming barn-like structure with vertical plank walls and a thatched roof. He held his arms out in a gesture that he had once meant as an invitation to worship but that now was no more than an habitual stance before the beginning of a mass. For a moment he gazed out at the ragged, dark-haired young people who were the bulk of his congregation. All felt the absence of the boy who had been captured last night, who only yesterday had been standing here among his friends. Juan could imagine the boy's despair at this very moment as his Creek captors marched him north to Carolina to be sold as an Englishman's slave. God's mercy be upon him—and upon all these others who remained. He could feel their restlessness, even their sullenness, though as always they were silent, obedient if not devout. They only came each morning because he made them come. No lifetime habits were being formed in them. They would marry as soon as they could, and having thus stepped into the acknowledged world of adulthood, they would make their appearances only on Sundays and feast days, if at all. Their catechisms would be forgotten and their eyes would turn from God to the old shaman Salvador. Only a few would remain loyal.

He looked over at Don Manuel Solana, fellow Spaniard, friend of his heart. His bond with Solana went back many years to the time they both arrived together in Apalachee, Juan as a missionary from Spain, Solana as a soldier from San Augustín assigned to the Ivitachuco garrison. They were enemies at first, priest against soldier-rancher, competing for control over the Indians and their labor. But in time the two of them had learned to yield, and where they could not yield, they had learned to forgive. Solana had long since moved on to San Luís, there to rise through the ranks of officialdom until for a time he had held the highest post in the province. But always the bond remained strong between them, a friendship based on the years they had shared. Juan's spirit rose as he contemplated it, and he drew in his breath to begin the Mass.

His chest convulsed. A violent spasm of coughing seized him, and he
turned away toward the altar, drawing out a handkerchief from the sleeve
of his brown robe and pressing it tightly against his mouth. When at last
the coughing subsided, he drew away the handkerchief and looked for a
moment at the red stain spreading through it, and then he folded it and
tucked it away. For a moment longer he leaned against the altar, staring at
the embroidered linen cloth, waiting for his strength to return. Then he
turned and raised his arms and began again.

The familiar words slipped away through his lips, their recitation dulled
by twenty-five years of endless repetition. Some days he would say the
words without hearing them at all. But this morning Solana was here. A
Spaniard. Juan could feel the difference his presence made. The commu-
nion of Spaniards. It was almost sacred. The words of the Mass, as he spoke
them now, gradually took on more meaning until they began to seem new
to him, as if he had never uttered them before. The presence of God, so
rarely felt, welled up within him, and he partook of the Sacrament with
tears in his eyes. When the service was finished and the young people were
filing out, he dropped to his knees and offered a private prayer of thanks-
giving that such a moment should have returned to him yet one more time
in his undeserving life.

The emotion had exhausted him, and he labored so in rising that Carlos,
his assistant, stepped in to take his arm and pull him to his feet. As Manuel
Solana came forward, Juan looked at him and smiled, embarrassed by his
weakness.

"It is the weather," he said, trying to shrug off his illness. "My cough is
always worse in winter. Sometimes I can barely get through the Mass. But
when spring comes—." He puffed out his chest and playfully flexed his
biceps. He turned and looked at Carlos. "Is it not true, my son? In spring I
am a lion!"

Carlos gave a half smile and nodded. The priest could feel Solana's distance, not from himself but from Carlos. Even now, when Juan was drawing Carlos into their conversation, Solana refused to acknowledge the Indian's presence, treating him as a mere footman, a piece of furniture. Juan's
spirit began to fall. It was one of the things he had learned to forgive in
Solana, this contempt for the Indians, and yet he regretted it and hoped
always for a change in Solana's heart.

Carlos excused himself, his eyes hard as he gave a parting glance at
Solana, a direct look that the Spaniard had to shift his own eyes to avoid.
Carlos walked out of the church and left the two of them alone.

"You have made him a brazen fellow," Solana said gruffly. "Too forward
for an Indian."

"He's a good man," said Juan, taking off his chasuble and handing it to the sacristan, who was clearing the altar. "He'll make me a strong chief."

"He'll make you trouble," said Solana.

Juan looked at him. The light was dim in the church, but still he could see the lines around Solana's eyes, deeper than ever, and the last few wisps of graying hair that clung stubbornly to the shining crown of his head. He could see himself aging in Solana. They had been young together.

"I have enough real trouble without worrying about possible trouble," the priest said. "I have hardly any young men left here and few at all whom I can trust. But Carlos is like a son. If the English attacked tomorrow, he is the only one I could be sure would not go over to the enemy. Of the rest, some would go and some would stay. But which ones? I cannot say."

"Not even of your chief?"

"He would stay, of course. Most of the older men would. It is the young ones I'm unsure about. I pray they're never put to the test."

Solana looked away, remembering something, and seemed about to speak but then did not. Juan got his cloak from a bench against the wall and began walking with him from the church.

"You were going to say that you passed through Pilihiriba on your journey from San Augustín," said the priest. "I am not so ill that I cannot hear bad news. Tell me how it goes with them."

"The pagans burned the entire mission," said Solana. "The church, the convento, the houses, everything. No one knows how many Christian Indians were captured or how many simply deserted. More than a hundred are missing. And as many again are dead. They are sure of that. They found the bodies."

"Will they rebuild?"

"Yes," Solana nodded grimly. "They are fools. Only a handful remain, and they are raising themselves another church. What hope will they have if the Creeks come back?"

"What hope do any of us have?"

"Here you have plenty. You have the stockade."

"And was there ever a smaller fort in the whole Spanish empire?" Juan spoke with more irony than bitterness. "Four soldiers. Tell me what good four soldiers would be against hundreds of Creeks? Not even half of my people would fit inside the walls of that stockade." He shook his head. "In our lifetime we've seen all the Guale missions destroyed on the coast above San Augustín. Spain spent more than a century building them up, and in little more than twenty years the English heretics destroyed them. What makes us think our fate will be different?"

"Spain should never have let the English settle Carolina," said Solana. "The king should have sent an army to stop them."

They had come out into the entryway, where the morning light was brighter, the front door standing open. The air was cold. Juan tightened his cloak and led the way out into the plaza.

As they started in the direction of the convento, Lorenzo came walking quickly toward them, his whip swinging in his hand. He was an unpleasant man with a wide nose and small, sharp eyes. But he was a zealous Christian, entirely trustworthy, and for that, Juan was thankful.

"They send me to tell you," said Lorenzo in his broken Spanish. He bowed to the priest and then to the former deputy governor. "Spanish rider comes. They see from stockade. Rides fast." Lorenzo made a motion of swiftness with the hand that was holding the whip.

Juan sighed, already weary though the morning was not half gone. "Tell them to bring him to the convento. I'll receive him there."

"Yes, Father," said Lorenzo, bowing again as he left them.

They walked to the convento in silence. It was a large wattle-and-daub structure, rectangular in shape, its long wall running exactly parallel to the church. On both the side facing the church and on the opposite side were porches running the length of the building. Juan looked for Carlos, who was nowhere in sight, and felt a vague regret at the rudeness with which Solana had treated him.

Ana met them at the door, her dark eyes sweeping briefly over the priest as she took his cloak. It was her habit to be always assessing his health, as if she alone were the guardian of it. Keeping the silence of a servant, she went back into the room and set two cups of white and blue Mexican majolica on the table.

"We expect another," said Juan. "A rider is coming in." He watched her as she went to the rude cupboard beside the window and brought out another cup. She too was aging, the wrinkles deepening around her eyes, her flesh gradually giving up its firm smoothness. But her body had not gone to fat as with so many women. She was still slender and attractive, her hair rolled and knotted neatly behind her neck, the scattered strands of gray still lost in its darkness. She moved to the small charcoal fire that glowed in the brazier and stirred the dark tea that was simmering in an Apalachee clay pot.

"You want cassina now?" she said in Spanish. "Or you wait for the other?"

As she was speaking, a commotion arose outside, the snort of a horse and voices.

"He is here," said Juan.

Ana went over and opened the door, and they saw Don Gaspar de Velasco jump from his horse and hand the reins to one of the soldiers from the stockade. Juan watched him without pleasure. Don Gaspar owned the largest of the Spanish ranches near Ivitachuco. A crude man, he lacked the wisdom of Solana, the talent for giving ground and finding compromise. He did everything as he was doing now, bursting into the friary as if he owned it, brushing past Ana, who stood ready to take his cloak.

"So it's you, Don Gaspar," said Juan, rising to greet him with a pretense of cordiality. Solana also rose and reached out to shake his hand, but Velasco dispensed with formalities.

"They've come," he said abruptly. "They're besieging Ayubale. Father Miranda is making his stand in the church, but there are more than a thousand Creeks and fifty Englishmen. The man at their head—Moore is his name—he's the same son of a whore who led the siege against San Augustín two years ago."

For a moment Juan only stared at him.

"Holy Mary preserve us," said Solana, sitting down heavily in his chair.

"What do we do?" asked Juan, turning desperately to Solana, surrendering all authority to him as former deputy governor of the province.

"Call in your chief," said Solana. "Tell him to round up his warriors and bring his people in from the homesteads outside the town."

The priest stepped outside. His thoughts were clear, though his legs felt weak as he ordered the soldier who was holding Velasco's horse to summon the chief. Returning inside, he looked at Ana, and she met his eyes with fear.

"We'll have cassina now," he said to her softly, almost tenderly. Then he offered Velasco his chair. But Velasco declined it and went to stand with his back to the fire. Juan sank down into the chair.

"They'll not stop at Ayubale," said Velasco. "It's only a league and a half from that place to this one. Not even two hours on foot."

"The question is, how long can Father Miranda hold out?" said Solana. "How many are with him in the church?"

"Only the ones from the village," said Velasco. "They were caught by surprise at dawn, and the ones from the homesteads never had a chance to get in. The only hope for those on the outside will be the woods, but the pagans are sweeping the area. The man who gave me this news saw his sister and nephews taken."

Juan stared at the cup of steaming cassina that Ana placed before him. He thought of Miranda fighting for his life inside the walls of his churchyard, no soldiers to help him, fewer than a hundred Indian men with a few rusty matchlocks and a small stock of arrows, their women and children huddled in the corners. He could imagine their terror.

"God's mercy be on them," he whispered.

"We have to think of ourselves," said Velasco. "I've sent runners to the ranches. Our people are on their way here. We'll take shelter in the stockade until this is over."

Juan looked at Solana. "Can we hold the stockade?"

"It's stronger than a fenced churchyard. You have artillery. There's a chance you can defend it. A chance."

"You'll stay with us, surely," said the priest, alarmed at the distance in Solana's voice.

His old friend shook his head. "I have my family at San Luís. My ranch."

"But San Luís is invincible. A great strong blockhouse, fifty soldiers. They'll not attack it. Your sons are men. They can take care of things. But here we have nothing. Four derelict soldiers. A handful of ranchers. We need you, my friend."

Solana stared into the fire.

"The father is right," said Velasco. "And besides, there is too much danger in setting out now for San Luís. The country is filled with the enemy."

Still Solana made no answer. He got up and walked over to the window and looked out.

There was a rap at the door and Ana hurried to answer it. Hinachuba Patricio, the chief of Ivitachuco, stepped into the room and stood near the door with his battered felt hat in his hands. He was an old man, though not ancient, politely subservient and yet with features that were strong and eyes that did not go meek when he bowed. He was a Hinachuba, but he cared little for traditions of ancient privilege. His authority came from the strength of his person. He was the only chief in Apalachee whom the Spaniards addressed as "Don." Now he looked from one Spaniard to another, seeing clearly that something was wrong.

"Your hearts are on the ground," Don Patricio said in his own language. "There is trouble."

"The English and their pagans are attacking Ayubale," said Juan. "More than a thousand strong."

"Holy Mother of God," murmured Don Patricio, crossing himself. Then in clear and perfect Spanish he said, "We must bring in the people."

"Yes," said Juan.

Don Patricio shook his head, still trying to absorb it. "More than a thousand Creeks," he murmured. "And the English themselves come to lead them. Like the siege of San Augustín, except we have no stone fortress here."

"You have the stockade," Solana said irritably.

"And we have you to help us," said the chief, bowing slightly. "God be praised."

Solana looked at Don Patricio, then turned away without acknowledging his words, obviously agitated, pacing from the window to the fire, staring for a moment at the glowing coals and then turning to stalk back to the window. Again he stared out, and Juan knew that his thoughts were in San Luís with his wife and two sons. Solana clenched his fists and pressed them down hard against the rough sill of the window.

"It is here I must stay," he said tightly and turned to face the others. "How many warriors do you have?" he asked brusquely of Don Patricio.

"More than a hundred. With the young ones, perhaps a hundred and fifty."

"But how many of them can you depend upon?"

The chief shrugged. "More than half. Who can say?"

Solana glanced at Juan, acknowledging the irony of their conversation of not even an hour ago. Then to Don Patricio he said, "We need food and water hauled to the stockade and to the church." He looked at the priest. "We must make the church our second fortress. There is not room in the stockade for all your people."

Juan nodded grimly.

"The cattle must be brought in," said the chief. "And the horses."

Solana began pacing the room again. "Gather all the muskets together, in whatever condition. We'll repair as many guns as we can."

"The church vessels and ornaments must go into the stockade," said Father Juan. He turned to Ana. "Call Lorenzo. And Carlos. I need the two of them immediately."

Ana nodded, her face ashen as she hurried away.

Juan leaned back in his chair and tried to quiet his fear. The hour had come. Above all, he must be calm.

☀ Lucia was among the first to leave the church when Mass was over. She went home for her water jar and then joined the women who were gathering at the edge of town to go together to the spring. She would have preferred her usual solitude, but the danger of slave-catchers was too fresh in her mind, and so she followed along with the others as they moved out onto the path, all carrying their jars, she keeping a little apart while the others talked and laughed among themselves. The capture of the woman and boy the night before was making everyone more vigilant than usual, but no one was really afraid, for the two who had been taken had been alone.

The spring was a sinkhole of crystal-clear water in a grove of evergreen live oaks and magnolias. The women grew quiet as they approached it, but once they were in among the trees and could see there was no danger there, they began to talk again.

Lucia moved among them to the edge of the spring and knelt down, setting her water jar on the bank beside her. For a moment she was still, quieting her mind and watching the water, so clear she could see fish swimming deep within it. She put her hand into the water and felt how warm it was in contrast to the winter air. The water was icy cold in summer, but in winter it felt warm. Springs and rivers were portals to the Under World, that strange realm where seasons were opposite the ones in This World. She brought up a small bit of water and tipped out part of it on her forehead and then put the rest against her breast. It was not a simple act of bathing, but the ceremony of Going To Water. She repeated the washings, four times in all, a circle of power drawn up from the Under World.

She straightened herself and sat back on her heels, turning to lift her water jar from the bank to fill it. Then the bell in the town began to ring.

The conversations of the women ceased and all of them looked up, the motion of their jars frozen. They turned as one to look toward the town, but from where they were, they could see nothing, and after the briefest moment looked instead at each other as the bell continued ringing.

"Slave-catchers," someone said quietly, and immediately they were in motion again, hurrying now to scoop up the water and swing the jars up onto their heads, glancing anxiously into the woods around them, seeing nothing, but worried nonetheless.

"Perhaps a house is burning," someone said, but no one answered her, for all could see that the sky was clear, no cloud of smoke arising. They hurried away from the spring. Lucia did not see so soon as the ones in front of her that someone was coming toward them on the path. But she heard the others.

"Who is that running?"

"What man is that?"

"One of ours."

"Carlos."

As the women stopped and spread around him, Lucia could see how serious Carlos was. He had the grim calmness of someone performing in a crisis. His running had barely winded him.

"Ayubale," he said, looking beyond them for stragglers. "The English are attacking it with Creek cutthroats. A great many. Hundreds. Maybe a thousand. They are sweeping the countryside. We will be next."

The women began to murmur. He held out his hand to calm them. "There is no danger now, except out here." He looked around at the spring and the fields and groves. "They will sneak around where they can, but they cannot come up on the town itself in daylight. For that they will wait until night and use the darkness to take their position. Then in the first light of dawn they will strike. But we will be ready. We have the stockade, the artillery, the soldiers, a hundred men of our own with guns and bows. And we have warning. Ayubale had none."

There was a moment of silence.

Then someone said, "I have a sister in Ayubale."

"My son is there," said another.

The sorrow in their voices was painful to hear, and Lucia looked down at the path.

"We have not heard that it has fallen," said Carlos. "Perhaps they can hold it."

Lucia glanced up at him, doubting that he himself believed what he said. His eyes, sweeping over the women, fell on her and stopped. For an instant they looked at each other. She was startled by the interest in his eyes, and curious to know its meaning. But she looked immediately away.

"We should get back to town," said Carlos, and he turned and started with the women down the path.

Lucia waited, letting the others go ahead, and then followed a few paces behind them. Alone she could think, and she needed to think, so much happening in so short a time. The visit in the night with Salvador. Isabel restored as the White Sun Woman, and she herself named to succeed her. And now this. Ayubale under attack. The English. A siege like San Augustín, except here there was no fortress. She looked around, trying to feel the danger, but everything looked as it always had, the fields stretched out in the morning sun, the cold breezes scattering the smoke above the town, carrying it away in light, hazy trails. There was only the ringing of the bell to make the danger real, and all the women hurrying home to safety.

She noticed then that Carlos had dropped back from the others and was only a short distance in front of her. Slowing her step, she let a wider gap spread between them. But now he glanced back at her and stopped altogether, so that unless she too would stop, she had to walk on past him. There was something unnerving about him today, an attention to her that made her uneasy, as if he might know that she had been to Salvador's, dealing in pagan things. She kept walking, but she did not look at him. As she drew up even with him, she walked a little faster, anxious to get by him, but he fell in step beside her, and though he did not look at her, she knew that he meant to be walking where he was. She quickened her step, but he kept pace with her. It was awkward, and she decided that her very silence made her seem as if she had things to hide from him.

"Who would have thought this would happen today?" she said, her words falling clumsily into the cold air. He made no response. "It could be the end for us," she added quietly.

He turned and looked at her, and she let her eyes meet his, searching again for what it was in him that had to do with her. She saw nothing and looked away. Blood was rising in her cheeks and she resolved to ignore him and retreat into silence.

He continued on beside her, an oppressive presence, taller than she— not all men were—large in his features, broad-shouldered, his head massive and dark, his face in shadow. She shifted the water jar slightly on her head, steadying it with her hand.

"One has to wonder why such misfortunes fall upon us," Carlos said suddenly from the silence, his voice low and directed to her alone.

"It is God's will," she said in pretended piety, her eyes still fixed ahead.

"His wrath, you mean."

She made no answer.

"There are so many in Ivitachuco who call themselves Christians, but are servants of Satan instead. I am forever amazed at their numbers."

Still she was silent, giving him nothing.

"It is hard to understand why anyone would risk God's wrath, having once learned of His mercy." He was walking more and more slowly as he spoke, widening the distance from the others, keeping his words for her alone. "Yet some will persist. They will go into the church with food for the dead as if they were pagans who had never heard God's word. They will visit the shamans in the dark of night. They think they are not being seen, but they are wrong."

Lucia's heart was pounding. Was it possible he had seen all of this? She knew she should feign ignorance, pretend she had nothing to hide. But she said, "Are you blaming me, then, for Ayubale?" Her voice was low and defiant.

"No," he said curtly.

She walked with long strides, her eyes fixed straight ahead. They had almost reached the town, the bell ringing, ringing.

"I am only warning you," he said quietly, and then he turned abruptly from the path to cut diagonally across the field toward the stockade.

Lucia watched him go, his red blanket flaring out behind him. What did it matter if he knew those things? The English had come to Ayubale. People were dying there. And tomorrow it would all be happening here. She felt a sudden chill and folded her arms against herself. Fear was coming through to her at last.

✹ The town was in chaos, the bell tolling endlessly, the plaza, streets, and yards of the houses swarming with people whose numbers were swelling as the Christian Indians poured in from the nearby homesteads. Pigs, cattle, and horses were being driven in, adding to the confusion. A family of Spanish ranchers had arrived, the first ones, their oxcart piled high with possessions as it lumbered slowly toward the stockade.

Lucia made her way across the crowded plaza, stopping once to help a young boy head off a calf that had escaped from his care. There was something of a festival air, as if the next thing would be music starting up and the people clearing the plaza for dancing. But there was the tolling bell, that was the difference, and the anxiety on the faces of women who scanned the crowd for their children.

When Lucia got home, Ana and Isabel were not in the house, so she crossed the yard to the cocina and found Isabel inside at the hearth, her thin legs tucked beneath her on a cane mat, her hands busy with the making of bean bread. She looked up as Lucia came in, and then she turned back to her work, scooping up a handful of cornmeal dough with beans in it and patting it into a thick cake.

"The priest wants food to take into the stockade," Isabel said flatly. "I'll be working here until the arrows start to fly." She took two brown corn leaves from a pot of water where they had been soaking and wrapped the bean cake in them, tucking in the edges until all was secure, then dropped the cake into a copper kettle of boiling water. A second pot on the fire, one made of clay, was already filled with leaf-wrapped cakes.

Lucia sat down and began to help. A grim silence filled the cocina, broken only by the sound of their hands patting the cakes, the crackle of the fire, and the soft plopping of the water boiling. And outside, the clamor.

"What do you think?" Lucia said at last.

Isabel hesitated a moment, and then she said, "Does it seem strange to you that this has happened on the very day I first sang the song to the Sun? At the very moment I was singing, the English were falling on Ayubale. Think of it. If we had strained to listen, we might have heard them."

Lucia paused, a half-shaped bean cake in her hand. "Do you think these things are connected?" she asked, her anxiety rising, as if they had unwittingly started something that could not be stopped.

Isabel shrugged. "There is a circle, perhaps, that goes around it all. Perhaps the song was given to save us. Perhaps I only sang it just in time."

"But not in time for Ayubale," said Lucia.

"No, not for them." Isabel fell back into silence. Lucia knew she was thinking of all the people she knew in that beseiged town.

Lucia's own thoughts drifted back through the morning. She wondered if she should tell her grandmother about Carlos. But with everything else that was happening, there seemed little point in it. So she kept her silence, and reaching for the long-handled strainer of woven cane, she began lifting the cooked bean cakes from the boiling water.

CHAPTER FOUR

Father Juan de Villalva lay awake in the darkness, unable to sleep, yet too exhausted to be up and about like Solana, who was out with the men in the stockade. Thank God for Solana. Thank the Blessed Jesus and his Holy Mother and all the saints of heaven.

The convento was quiet. He could hear voices from the stockade and from the fires close around its walls and around the church. He could hear the cattle in the churchyard and a child crying. Everyone was waiting. In a few hours, when the night was almost over, they would pack themselves into the crowded safety of the stockade and into the fenced churchyard between the convento and the church and brace themselves for the attack that would come in the moments before dawn. Turning over on his side, the priest kept to the same warm spot in the straw mattress, tucking the blanket around his chin and closing his eyes, hoping for a moment of sleep.

The door latch clicked softly. He opened his eyes and raised his head and saw Ana in the moonlight. She closed the door and it was dark again, so that she was barely visible as she crossed the room. He held open the blanket and wrapped it around her as she slipped in and nestled close against him, seeking his warmth. He held her tightly and rested his face against her hair.

"It must be that I come," she said softly. "People are everywhere. Maybe they see me, but I come anyway. This night is too lonesome. I am afraid."

"It doesn't matter anymore what they see," said Juan. He reached beneath her shift, a cast-off garment of a rancher's wife, and caressed her breasts, seeking comfort in her, not passion. There could be no passion tonight, not with the wolf at the door, with Ayubale fallen into the hands of the pagans.

Ana pressed against him. She too wanted to be comforted. "You think they come here at dawn?" she said.

"Perhaps."

"You think they kill everyone there? At Ayubale?" She was asking if she would be killed.

"Not the women," he said.

"I'm too old to be a slave. My breasts are hanging."

"You're not old," he whispered. "They don't hang. Not much." He could tell she smiled at him. He kissed her neck and rubbed his cheek against her hair. "We have artillery. And soldiers. And a stockade with strong walls.

Ayubale had no defenses. And they were taken by surprise. Let's sleep a little while."

"Do you think they kill the priest at Ayubale?"

"Shh," he whispered and changed to her language. "Sleep now. Sleep a little bit."

She grew silent and still, not asleep but resting, while his own eyes stayed open and stared at the slits of moonlight in the shutters. Was this the last night, like Christ in the Garden? Dearest God, how far he had come from Christ, how far from the pious disciple who had come here so many years ago, the young friar who had spread his pallet on the floor and cooked his own food and shared his friary with the sick and the old, who had prayed all the prayers of the Divine Office each day and repeated his vows each night. How far from the penitent young sinner seeking solace in Our Lady for his despair and loneliness, seeking strength from her Son in his struggle against the flesh, a struggle he often lost alone with himself, though he never touched a woman. Not until Ana.

Ana had come when he was weary of struggling, after he had watched too many of his converted and baptized children grow into recalcitrant adults. He had begun to use the whip more often. More and more he had concerned himself with the church fields, with the cattle, with the profits of trade at the port of San Marcos on the nearby Gulf coast. He had stopped repeating his vows except on the anniversaries of his ordination. His house was no longer a hospital, and he allowed himself a servant, an old woman at first, and then a younger one. And then Ana.

From her breathing, Juan knew she was sleeping now. He moved gently to pull free his arm, which was growing numb beneath her, and when she did not awaken, he turned carefully to lie on his back, his leg touching against the back of hers, and his hand on her hip. He stared up into the darkness. . . . *Hail, holy Queen, Mother of mercy, our life, our sweetness and our hope. To thee do we cry, poor banished children of Eve.*

But he did not repeat his vows. They were broken beyond repentance. His Christ-life had slipped away, and God had slipped away with it. He seldom felt Him anymore, though sometimes He came near, as at Mass with Solana this morning. And sometimes God was there when Ana was there, and he took it as a blessing on their marriage, a secret marriage in his heart, never spoken of. He was wed to her now, not to the Church. And tonight he arrived at his Gethsemane wholly a man, a mere man, unable to keep awake at the watch.

Was the priest at Ayubale dead? Perhaps they had put him to the torch. Perhaps even now they were torturing him while his brother in Christ lay abed not two leagues away and caressed the warm flesh of a woman. *Do not despise me, O God my Savior.*

He knew he should be praying, as Christ prayed in the Garden. He
should be praying for the priest and captive Christians in Ayubale, and for
Ivitachuco, for his people, for himself, for deliverance from the terror of
dawn. *Be not far from me, O God.* But the effort of prayer was too great and
he drifted into fitful sleep.

✳ Lucia was summoned from sleep by the gentle shaking of Ana's hand.
"Wake up," Ana said quietly. "It is time to go into the stockade."

As Lucia opened her eyes, a vague fear sharpened within her, growing
stronger as she came fully awake. It was dark, no light of dawn filtering in
through the roof-thatch. No bell was ringing. She sat up and could barely
see Ana moving around in the darkness and her grandmother rising from
her bed, wrapping herself in her blanket. The fire remained cold in the
hearth.

"How long until dawn?" asked Lucia, pulling her blanket over her shoulders as she rose.

"A little while," said Ana.

"I am taking my kettle," said Isabel. "I do not want the pagans to get my
kettle." Lucia saw her dim outline by the hearth as she stooped slightly for
the copper kettle she had brought in from the kitchen the night before. But
then she straightened up without reaching it, her hand on her stiff back.
"Here, Lucia. Come pick it up for me. I cannot bend over so early in the
morning."

"No, my mother," said Ana. "Only Spaniards can bring their belongings. Indians are to bring blankets and weapons, that is all. You know how
crowded it will be. We are lucky to be let in at all."

"But I will not leave my kettle," the old woman said irritably. She
stooped for it again, bending stiffly.

Lucia went over to pick it up.

Ana sighed. "Try taking it then. See what they will do."

Isabel took the soot-covered kettle from Lucia, pulled her blanket more
tightly about herself, and went out the door.

Lucia followed her. The town, though silent, was filled with people, dark
forms moving by low-burning fires. A steady stream of blanket-wrapped
women and children shuffled into the church, their faces lit briefly by the
torch at the door. The men stood at the fires, their bows strung, arrow
quivers on their backs. Here and there one held a musket. Some of the men,
notwithstanding the cold, were naked except for their breechcloths. Others
wore ragged shirts or pieces of tattered blanket. All were silent.

Lucia went with Ana and Isabel to join a smaller number of people going toward the stockade. These were the Christian stalwarts, trusted Indi-

ans with whom the Spaniards were willing to share their strongest walls. These, too, were silent, glancing often at the eastern sky, fearful of the coming light.

As the three women entered the gate of the small stockade, no one noticed Isabel's kettle. The yard was already crowded. The Spaniards from the ranches had been there through the night and had claimed more than half the space for themselves, much of it taken up with their carts piled high with belongings. Ana led the way to a small open space not far from the western wall, and the three of them settled there, sitting on the corners of their blankets. The yard continued to fill until at last there was no more room and the gates were pulled shut. Lucia looked anxiously at the eastern sky, which seemed faintly lighter. Shivering with cold and fear, she strained to hear a signal from the sentries, some warning of the enemy's approach.

Dawn came unmistakably now, the stars steadily disappearing until only the morning star remained. In the growing light the robed figure of Father Juan could be seen pacing the parapet high up on the eastern wall, watching, waiting for the enemy to flood over the land and surround their tiny fortress.

A soft hum began to drift through the cold air, indistinct at first so that Lucia barely heard it at all. But gradually it nudged at her consciousness, a rhythmic chant. The song to the Sun. She turned and looked at Isabel and saw her hands raised surreptitiously to the light spreading above the stockade wall. Then a shout rang out from the guard tower, and Lucia's heart crashed against her chest.

"Scout coming in," a sentry called from above.

And now they waited to hear the cry that the enemy, too, had come in sight. Isabel had finished her song, and the stockade was utterly still. In her mind Lucia could see beyond the walls—the deserted town, the road stretching out through the fields, the scout flying along it, solitary, all the land empty around him—and still empty—no cry going up—still empty. There was a turning of eyes to the stockade gate, hers with the rest. Still no enemies. Only the scout on the road, and he must be close now, almost here. No other cry was ringing out. Nothing.

The gate opened just enough for a man to slip through, and as it closed again, a murmur of anticipation spread.

"What could it a be?" Lucia asked quietly.

Ana raised the palm of her hand to the sky. "It is day. Would they attack in full light?"

"How can we know?" murmured Isabel. "Englishmen are leading them. How can we know what Englishmen would do?"

Near the gate people were getting to their feet, smiling and laughing.

"Something good!" Ana exclaimed. Others were rising, talking, smiling and shaking their heads. The word passed over the crowd like a wave, drawing people up, and in a moment's time Lucia was hearing it: Help had come, an army from San Luís, Spanish soldiers and Apalachee warriors, several hundred strong. They had fallen on the enemy at Ayubale. At this very moment a battle was raging. Ivitachuco was spared.

☀ Father Juan de Villalva tried to sit calmly on one of the three narrow beds in the barracks room beneath the eastern wall of the stockade—but he was too excited, too filled with relief. Even his health seemed suddenly better. He got up, went jubilantly to the door, looked out for Solana, and not seeing him, came back in and sat down again. He should be sober and reflect on God's mercy. He was unworthy of this deliverance. Yet so glad of it. He rose again and was walking toward the door when Solana appeared. "Manuel, my friend," Juan said joyfully, holding out his arms to embrace him. But Solana looked soberly at him and the priest lowered his arms.

Solana came in and began to pace the small room, circling the table and bench in the center. "I should be fighting beside them," he said grimly. "I am certain my two sons are there. The deputy governor is a horse's ass. He'll lead them into trouble."

"Do not think like that," said Juan, but Solana made no reply, and Juan looked away, knowing that Solana was right. The present deputy governor was a lesser man than Solana by far and had only been given his office through the foolishness of politics. Juan felt his ebullience fading. He sat down on the bench beside the table.

"I want to take our men out to reinforce them," said Solana.

"And leave Ivitachuco undefended? You know that is impossible. We are undermanned as it is."

Solana turned and glared at the priest. "My sons have come all the way from San Luís to fight this battle for you, and I, for one, do not intend to cower behind these walls while they perish from want of support."

Juan met his eyes without flinching. "You have seen all the women and children we have here. Do you think our men would leave their families unprotected while the enemy is at our very doorstep? You know they would not go with you even if we both commanded them to go."

Solana stood in silence.

"You know it is true," Juan said again.

Solana nodded grimly and turned away.

"You'll not go out there alone?" Juan asked quietly.

"That would be folly," said Solana, his voice more subdued now. "I need a force to lead. What good would one more man be to them if the tide is against them?"

"And why must you think that it *is* against them? Only an hour ago we were waiting for our own end to come, and now God has spared us. Are you so mistrusting of His gift to us that you look for trickery in it?"

Solana rubbed the back of his neck wearily. "We will put our hope in God, then," he said without conviction. He turned and started toward the door. "I'm going back up to watch for word."

Juan rose and went with him to the door and stood watching him leave. His chest felt constricted and uncomfortable, the earlier improvement in his health now fading. He turned back wearily into the room, closed the door behind him, and moved slowly to the nearest of the beds.

Solana returned at noon. Juan was alone in prayer when he heard the knock at the door, and before he could call out an answer, Solana entered. The priest rose slowly from his knees, his eyes on Solana's distraught face.

"Is there word?" asked Juan, trying to hold in his voice the hope to which he had clung throughout the morning.

"Routed. Our people were routed. They are retreating toward San Luís."

Juan dropped his head.

The former deputy governor went to one of the beds and lay down. Folding his hands on his chest, he stared up at the ceiling in silence.

"What will happen now?" Juan asked.

"They will come."

"With the next dawn?"

"Probably."

"And there is no more help for us?"

"None at all."

Juan sat down at the table, leaning against it, feeling a convulsion rising in his chest. He kept silent until the urge to cough had passed. Then he said softly, "I pray your sons are among those retreating. May the Holy Mother grant that it be so."

Solana made no reply, and Juan rested his head in his hands and closed his eyes.

The priest moved through the crowded stockade, stepping carefully in the light of the torch that Carlos held for him. At each huddled form he stooped and heard the whisper of a brief confession, then pronounced absolution and moved on. The night was half spent, but most people were too cold and anxious to sleep. Two fires burned, one on the Spanish side of the yard and one on the Indian side. As Juan leaned down and spoke in whispers to a woman, a wolf howled in the darkness, and Carlos turned his head to listen. It came again, closer now, coming clearly from the road outside the village.

"A scout is coming in," Carlos said.

Juan straightened up and stood for a moment listening. Then he said, "Go meet him and bring him to me. Tell Solana and Don Patricio to come as well." He turned and made his way back through the crowded darkness to the barracks room. After a few moments Don Patricio and Solana arrived, and the three sat in silence in the candlelight and waited. Then there was a rap at the door, and Carlos came in with a young woman, dishevelled and frightened, clutching a ragged bit of blanket around her shoulders.

"Who is this?" asked Juan, an edge of irritation in his voice.

"One of the scouts found her and brought her in," said Carlos. "She escaped from Ayubale."

"Ayubale?" said Manuel Solana. "How long since she was there?" They were interested now.

Carlos spoke to the woman, who looked at the floor, her lips trembling slightly. Then she whispered in her language, "I left there tonight, after it was dark."

The priest got up and went to her, reaching out to put a hand on her shoulder. She shrank toward Carlos.

"Do not be afraid," Carlos said to her softly.

"Come sit, my child," Juan said gently in Apalachee. "You are safe now. We will talk." She nodded, still looking at the floor. He guided her to one of the beds. As she sat down, she glanced at the men around her and began to tremble even more.

"Bring her something to eat," Juan told Carlos.

Carlos left the room, the young woman watching him, her fear rising as he disappeared.

"Do you speak Spanish?" Juan asked her.

She shook her head, looking down again.

"It is all right," he said. "We speak your language."

She nodded but would not look up.

"What is your name?"

"Maria," she said softly.

"A lovely name. The mother of our Lord."

She nodded and then glanced up as Carlos returned with a gourd dipper of hominy gruel. She looked at it without enthusiasm and seemed only to take it because she did not know how to refuse.

"Stay with us," Juan said to Carlos. "She is less frightened when you are here."

Carlos closed the door and came over and sat beside her.

They waited while she sipped at the gruel, but it was clear she had no appetite. After eating only a little, she handed the gourd to Carlos, who set it on the floor. Juan looked at Solana and asked, "Where do we begin?"

"Ask her if the enemy is still at Ayubale."

Juan asked her in the Apalachee language, and she nodded. Then she mumbled something in words too soft for them to hear.

"What did she say?" asked Solana.

"She says they are torturing people there," said Juan. "The pagans are torturing people."

"What people?" Solana asked anxiously. "Spaniards? Ask her if she knows about the battle this morning. Ask her if there were Spaniards taken."

"Tell us who they are torturing," Juan said to her. "Do they torture soldiers? Spanish soldiers?"

"Indians," she said softly. "They tortured the chief of San Luís."

Don Patricio murmured and stared away.

"And another Indian from San Luís," said Maria, her voice stronger. "They say he was a principal man there."

Agitated, Solana began to pace the room. "They were taken in the battle," he said. "How many others were taken?"

"Those two they burned slowly," said Maria. She closed her eyes, her face drawing up in anguish. "All afternoon, a little at a time. They cut them all over and put fatwood splinters in the cuts and set them afire."

"Did they die with courage?" asked Don Patricio.

"Yes," she said, opening her eyes but still not looking at them. "They spoke about God as they died. They said that death would not kill them. They said they went to God and those who burned them would themselves burn forever in hell. They were very brave. The Spaniards encouraged them to be strong."

"What Spaniards?" asked the priest, sitting forward. "Are there Spaniards there?" He glanced at Solana, who had stopped his pacing and turned to the woman.

She nodded. "Soldiers taken in the battle. In the morning. Many warriors from San Luís were killed in that battle. And a friar. And some soldiers. Two, I think. The deputy governor was shot in the leg and captured. And some others were captured."

"How many Spaniards were taken?" Solana asked.

Maria shook her head. "Maybe five. Or six."

Solana sat down heavily on the bench. "The deputy governor wounded

and captured. God knows, he was an idiot to have come out against them.
But what else could he do? If my sons have been taken . . . Ask her if she knows any names."

Juan asked her, but she shook her head.

"The priest who was killed?" said Juan. "Do you know which mission he was from?"

"They say he was from Patale," she said.

"Father Parga," said Juan, feeling sick inside. For a moment he could not speak. Then he asked weakly, "Was he tortured?"

"No. It is like I said, he was killed in the battle. I heard about it. I never saw him."

"What about the priest from Ayubale? Is he alive?"

"Yes. He walks about freely. So does the deputy governor, except that he cannot walk very well. The other soldiers are bound. The enemy took their clothes, but they have not hurt them. It is only Indians they are killing. They are burning them."

"How many?"

She shook her head. "Very many."

"Ten?" said Juan.

"More."

"A hundred?"

"I cannot say. How could I count them? They are my kinsmen, my neighbors. They are not burning these so slowly as the first two. They die quickly. My brother was one." She stopped for a moment and raised her hand to her cheek, her eyes fixed on the floor in front of her. "I ran away because I could not watch. No one saw me go. I just ran. I do not know how I got away. I just ran."

There was silence as each of them took in the picture she had drawn.

"Holy Mary, help us," Solana said at last.

"Will it be us tomorrow?" murmured Juan.

"They can take the church," said Solana. "And if they are willing to suffer losses, they can take the stockade. There's nothing in all of Florida that can stop them except the walls of the fortress at San Augustín."

"Then we should go there," said Juan.

"It's too late for that. This is where we make our stand, here in this stockade. We have no other choice."

"These tales of torture," said Don Patricio, looking slowly from one person to the next. "They must not leave this room. Too many would be frightened and desert us for the enemy."

Carlos looked up at him grimly. "It is too late to conceal it. The scout who brought her in is already among the people."

"Dear Jesus," said the priest, clenching his fists and feeling himself near tears. "Is God so far from us?"

✻ Lucia stood horrified among the people in the crowded darkness of the stockade, listening to what was being said. Those who loved the Spaniards best were made to suffer most: the chief and one of the principal men of San Luís. And the others being burned, were they also special friends of the Spaniards? Some were women, it was said. The one talking was the scout who had found the young woman of Ayubale and brought her to the stockade. He had seen the light of the Ayubale fires, and he was frightened. He spoke of surrender, of going over. He said that all the Indians here in the stockade were favorites of the Spaniards and would be known as such because there were Apalachees among the enemy who would recognize them and point them out. Their only hope was to surrender, to separate themselves from the Spaniards.

Lucia moved away through the frightened throng. There may be hope for others, but for Ana and Isabel and herself there was none. Everyone knew that Ana was the mistress of the Spanish priest, and that Lucia and Isabel were her family. Her stomach felt as if it would cave in and bend her double. Never had she known such terror. She struggled to shake free of it, turning her eyes to the sky to seek the comfort of the stars. Her death would not change them. Her end would not be the end of all. That calmed her, and she drew in her breath as if life itself had returned.

She moved in among the Spanish carts that separated the Indian side of the yard from the Spanish side. From here she could see the Spaniards, less tightly packed. An old man near the Spanish fire played his guitar as if he had not heard of the torture at Ayubale. And perhaps he had not: it was an Indian scout who was giving out the tale, and the Spaniards were keeping to themselves, away from the Indians.

Beyond the fire and the guitar player and the tight groups of men and women, she could see the barracks room, a small lean-to shed where the soldiers of the stockade usually slept, now the headquarters of the ones in charge of the defense of Ivitachuco. The door opened and for a moment she glimpsed the candle-lit interior, the men standing motionless in the dimness. A woman's dark figure appeared in the doorway, and behind her loomed the tall, broad figure of Carlos.

Lucia watched them come out into the yard and make their way among the Spaniards, who paid them no attention. Carlos walked close beside the woman as if to protect her from danger. Standing back against one of the carts, Lucia watched, unseen in the darkness. As the two approached the carts, Carlos reached out and took the woman's arm and pulled her to a halt. On the far side of the line of carts was the crowd of milling Indians, astir now with the news of Ayubale. Carlos murmured to himself and stepped up on the tongue of the nearest cart and looked out over the heads of the people. There was a fire in the midst of the Indians, but it was smaller than the Spanish fire and the light went no further than those standing close around it. He stepped back down to the ground.

"I cannot see her," he said quietly to the woman. "Let me go look for her. You wait here for me. When I find out where to go, I will come back and take you there."

The woman looked around to see exactly where it was that he proposed to leave her. There was fear in her manner, an unmistakable distress. Her eyes fell upon Lucia's dark form in the shadows and the sight startled her.

"Who is that?" she said in a low voice, pointing toward Lucia.

Carlos turned and looked, but in the darkness, with the massive cart obscuring Lucia's silhouette, he did not recognize her.

"It is I," said Lucia, without moving.

"Ana's niece?" asked Carlos. He took a step toward her.

"Yes."

"We are looking for Ana," he said. "This is Maria. She escaped tonight from Ayubale. She has had a bad time."

"I have heard," Lucia said. She felt Carlos looking hard at her.

"What have you heard?"

"Enough to know my life is over."

"That is not true," he said soberly.

"How can you say that? The same way you said yesterday morning that Ayubale might hold?"

He made no answer, and she fell silent, remembering the woman Maria who stood beside them in obvious pain. Lucia reached out and touched her arm.

"My heart is on the ground for your sorrow," she said softly.

Maria nodded silently.

"Father Juan told me to ask Ana to take care of her," said Carlos.

"Then come with me," said Lucia. "I will show you the way."

She crossed over the tongue of the cart and stepped into the milling crowd, setting her course toward the western wall. Several times she looked back to make sure that Carlos and Maria were still with her, and each time she saw the change in the crowd as recognition spread and people began to follow after them. Carlos drew Maria close to him, shielding her, she seeming smaller than ever as she shrank against him.

"Tell us what happened," someone called out.

Maria put her hands against her ears.

Lucia no longer had to push her way ahead. The crowd was opening before her now, until at last she reached the place where Ana and Isabel were sitting. They rose to their feet as the commotion reached them, Isabel grunting with her stiffness.

"What is all this?" said Ana.

"We have a guest," said Lucia, reaching out to take Maria's hand. Maria stepped toward her, trembling, and Lucia put her arm around her. "Her name is Maria. She is the one from Ayubale."

"My child," Ana said softly. Then she turned to the people pressing around and raised her voice: "What is it that you want? Go back to your blankets."

"We want to hear what happened," someone said.

"The scout has told you what happened," said Carlos. "Who would want to hear more?" He stepped in among them and began moving them away, not forcibly but with the authority of one who would one day be chief.

Ana turned back to Maria. "Come sit with us," she said. "What is your clan?"

"Hinachuba."

"Ah," said Ana with a smile. "Then we are of the same blood. All of us. I am mother to you, and Lucia is your sister, and this one, Isabel, is your grandmother."

The young woman nodded in acknowledgement, and Lucia could see that her face would be beautiful were it not for so much grief.

"She can sit on my blanket," said Isabel, moving her kettle aside to make more room in their crowded quarters.

"You need that blanket for yourself," said Ana. "We can get some straw for her."

As the stricken woman submitted to their ministrations, Lucia was suddenly overwhelmed with sadness. Turning away, she returned to that place of stillness and solitude she had found earlier among the carts.

The night air was not terribly cold, but the wind was blowing, pushing small, scattered clouds across the moonlit sky. She pulled her blanket more tightly about herself and sat down on the ground, leaning back against a high cartwheel. The Spanish guitarist was singing a sad lament. Drawing up her knees, she rested her head in her arms, and gradually the world softened around her. She closed her eyes. The guitar grew distant and the murmur of voices dimmed almost to silence.

Then the softness of a footstep reached her ear. Opening her eyes, she saw Spanish stockings and dark woolen breeches, and behind them the softly billowing hem of a blanket. She raised her head to see Carlos standing above her, tall and solid, like a great pine tree, shutting out the stars. She made a move to rise, but he put out his hand to stop her and then sat down beside her, leaning back against the cartwheel, his knees partly raised with his forearms resting upon them. Only the hub of the axle separated him from her. She shifted uncomfortably.

"All we can do now is wait," he said.

"Yes," she answered and could think of nothing more to say.

She leaned her head back against the cartwheel. His presence was faintly comforting. There was a calmness in him that strengthened the calmness she was feeling in herself. Let him stay then, if he would not trouble her with his Christian righteousness. She turned her head slightly to look at him. He was staring away across the yard at the bright flames of the Spanish fire, his thoughts elsewhere, not on her or on anything around him.

He is in Ayubale, she thought. He is seeing all the terrible things of which that woman spoke.

She studied him in the starlight, his head large, his features broadly angular as if carved roughly from a heavy block of wood. His black hair hung loose like the hair of a Spaniard and reached almost to the breadth of his shoulders. He looked like a chief. Everyone knew the priest had groomed him for that. She wondered how he felt about it, whether he grew impatient as he waited for Don Patricio to die. But then she remembered the news from Ayubale, and she turned away and leaned back, closing her eyes again.

The silence went on unbroken. She slept a little, consciousness fading in and out, weaving fleeting patterns with fragile threads of a dream in which her mother stood in a field outside a distant homestead, hoeing weeds from a new planting of corn, and Lucia walked toward her, the spring sun warm on her neck and shoulders. But then all of that faded away, and she became aware again of the stockade, of the cartwheel rough behind her shoulders, of the numbing of her buttocks against the hard ground. She opened her eyes, and as she moved to shift her weight, she glanced at the place where Carlos had been and saw that she was alone.

CHAPTER FIVE

Once again dawn came to Ivitachuco without bringing the enemy. Yet another runner appeared, a boy this time, and he carried a letter in his hand. The people greeted this new development with silence, exhausted now by the long ordeal. Carlos himself felt numb as he led the boy to the barracks room where Father Juan, Don Manuel Solana, and Don Patricio were waiting to receive him.

"What is this?" the priest asked the boy, holding out his hand for the letter.

The young messenger did not give it to him but held it firmly down at his side. He seemed proud of his mission and unwilling to be rushed, aware that he was entitled to protocol.

"I am from Ayubale," he said formally. "My clan is Chinacossa."

Father Juan closed his lips with tight impatience, but Don Patricio, the chief, nodded courteously to the boy and said, "Then you are of my wife's clan. You have come."

"I have come, señor."

Again the priest extended his hand for the letter, but still the boy held it close, as if he expected a pipe of tobacco to be smoked and a pot of cassina drunk all around, as was done when men sat in council.

"Give us the letter," said Manuel Solana in a weary tone that was full of the authority he carried from his years as deputy governor of the province.

The boy glanced at him, his eyes wavering, but still he would not be intimidated or hurried past the formalities he knew to be his due.

Carlos smiled slightly, admiring the boy's spirit. He nodded to him. "My clan is Usunaca."

"Then I am a cousin to you," said the boy, returning his nod. "My father is Usunaca."

"Our hearts are heavy because we have no tobacco to offer you," Carlos said solemnly. "Nor any cassina to drink." He swept his hand about to indicate their poor circumstances. "Things are not as they should be with us. But we hope that when all is well again, you will return and let us entertain you in our council house and show you proper courtesy. It would lift our hearts."

The boy seemed satisfied. "I will come back and smoke with you," he said. Then he raised the letter as if he were just now bringing it to their attention. "The English colonel told me to deliver this. It is for the chief of Ivitachuco."

"I am the chief," said Don Patricio. The boy gave him the letter, and Don Patricio turned it in his hand, inspecting the seal and the words of address written on it.

"I cannot read this," he said. "The words are not Spanish."

"The man is English," Solana said impatiently.

"I can read English," said the priest, and Don Patricio handed the letter to him. For a moment Father Juan studied the address, and then, looking up, he said dryly, "To the King of the Attachookas."

The boy shook his head. "We tried to tell him the name of this place. He could not get it right."

Father Juan broke the seal and there was silence while he read the letter slowly and with obvious difficulty, his lips moving to shape the unfamiliar words. At first his face brightened and he glanced up with a smile at Solana. But then, as he read on, his expression slowly changed, the light fading from his eyes, dismay settling over his features. As Carlos watched him, he noted how drawn and worn the priest had become from these two days of terror. It showed more on him than on Solana, whose sons had been in yesterday's disastrous battle. It showed on him even more than on Don Patricio, who faced the prospect of the hideous torture that had been inflicted on the chief of San Luís.

Father Juan sagged. The hand that held the letter dropped loosely to his side, and he looked about, disoriented. Spying the bench beside the table, he moved to it and sat down, his hands lying limply in the skirt of his robe between his knees.

"They will bargain with us," he said in a low voice.

Carlos felt his hopes begin to rise.

"They fear the stockade," said Solana, he too showing relief. "That must be it. They have decided they cannot afford the losses it would cost them to storm it."

The priest's breath was loud, rasping in his lungs. "They want ten horses loaded with booty. Guns, blankets, whatever we have. They want everything."

"That is not so bad," said Carlos, puzzled at Father Juan's dismay. "They rob us, yes, but we have our lives. It is better than anything we have dared to hope for."

"They want the church silver," said the priest in a flat, emotionless voice. "The candlesticks, the holy vessels, everything. They warn us to hold nothing back."

"Mother of God," Solana said angrily. "That English son of a whore! He burned San Augustín to the ground, all that we had built for over a hundred years. And now he comes here where we have almost nothing and takes away what is most sacred to us."

"Of course, we cannot do this," Don Patricio said calmly. "The ten horse loads we could give. But we cannot deliver the holy vessels into the hands of heretics. It would be a sacrilege."

Father Juan looked at him. "You would die for this?"

"If I must."

"And let all the people of Ivitachuco die with you? Let all we have built here perish?"

"If I must."

The priest shook his head and looked down at the letter in his hands.

"Not I," he said hoarsely. His chest began to convulse and his coughing slowly rose up and consumed him until he was gasping so desperately for breath that Solana stepped over to him and put a hand on his back. The priest fumbled in the sleeve of his robe for his handkerchief, already stained brown with blood, and raised it with a trembling hand to his lips, spitting weakly into it. The coughing began to subside, until finally he lowered his head and rested it on his arms on the table, his breath slowly returning.

Carlos watched him, thinking of the pictures of the saints that were tacked to the walls of his small room in the convento. He thought of the stories of the martyrs told to him since boyhood by this very man. He was relieved at the decision the priest was making, and yet something in him was slipping away as he watched this, something he had been straining to hold onto for a long time. He watched the humped shoulders, the backbone sharp against the brown robe, no flesh between skin and bone, and he knew that when this was over he would go back to his room in the convento and take down the pictures of the saints.

Solana leaned over and spoke to the priest in a low voice. Father Juan nodded without raising his head. Solana turned to the boy from Ayubale, who had been watching everything with large eyes.

"Tell the Englishman," Solana said grimly, "that we accept his conditions." Pausing, he turned back to Father Juan and asked, "How are we to make the delivery?"

The priest raised himself up, resting his forehead in the palms of his hands, his elbows on the table. The letter lay in front of him. "We are to meet him tomorrow at noon at Oldfield Creek."

Solana turned back to the boy. "Tell the Englishman we will follow his instructions. We will meet him there tomorrow."

"And you will bring all that he demands?" the boy inquired boldly.

Solana glared at him. "Everything!" he snapped. "Be on your way!"

The boy turned without further ceremony and let himself out the door.

Solana looked irritably at Don Patricio and Carlos. "Go tell your people what has happened. Turn them out of this stinking fort."

Carlos met his eyes. "Don Patricio is chief of this town. Is this entire matter to be decided without a word from him?"

"He said he would give the ten horse loads," Solana said curtly. "The church silver is for the priest to decide."

Carlos looked to see if Father Juan concurred, but the priest seemed not to hear them as he sat with his head in his hands. The old chief reached out and touched Carlos' arm.

"It does not matter, my son," he said in their own language. "Let us go."

Carlos turned away without looking again at Solana and began to follow Don Patricio from the room.

"Carlos." Father Juan's voice was barely more than a whisper. 49

Carlos paused and looked back at him. The priest's face was like that of an old man, his defeated eyes sunk deep in their sockets.

"Tell Ana to come to me," Father Juan said softly. Closing his eyes, he put his head back into his hands.

"Yes, Father," Carlos said tightly, and turning away, he went out into the crowded yard.

🔆 It took longer to empty the stockade than it had taken to fill it, and Lucia's euphoria gave way to weariness as she walked slowly along in the crowd with her grandmother and the woman Maria from Ayubale. Ana had been called away by the priest. Lucia could see out through the gate to the checkpoint just beyond, where the priest's man Lorenzo was stopping each person. She would have to give up her blanket there, a small enough price for her life. But even if they all put in everything, it was going to be difficult to raise ten horse-loads of goods from the impoverished people of Ivitachuco.

As they moved through the high, wide gate and left the timbered walls behind, Lucia drew in a deep breath. Alive and free. She slipped her blanket from her shoulders and folded it across her arm, letting herself get used to being without it. In front of her Isabel held hers tightly about herself, clutching it as if she would never let it go. Her copper kettle bulged beneath it.

They waited now while a man in front of Isabel handed Lorenzo his musket and his blanket and then proceeded to take off his worn Spanish shirt. Lorenzo took the shirt and threw it on top of the pile of blankets where other pieces of clothing were already mixed in. The man moved on his way, clad only in a breechcloth, leggings, and moccasins, his chest naked to the cold.

Now it was Isabel's turn, but she still clutched her blanket tightly about herself and took on a pitiful air. "I am an old woman," she pleaded. "I will freeze."

Lucia knew it was the kettle that she cared about, not the blanket.

"Winter is almost over," said Lorenzo without a trace of compassion. "Go home and sit by your fire."

"Let me bring it back to you," suggested Isabel. "I will go home and find a rag to put around my shoulders and bring the blanket back to you."

Lorenzo looked at her coldly. "That is not the way we are doing it. Give me the blanket." He reached out to take it from her.

She pushed his hand away. "Watch how you treat me," she warned. But she was relenting, loosening her blanket, no fool to reality. "Who taught you to treat old people so rudely?" She turned slightly from him and lowered the kettle to the ground behind her in a vain attempt to keep it from his notice. She took off the blanket and handed it to him. "Where were you raised? In the swamp with alligators?"

He nodded toward the kettle. "I will take that."

"You will not." She spoke matter-of-factly, as if her authority in the matter was beyond question. "It belongs to the priest. But here, take this." She slipped off her bodice of Spanish homespun and held it out to him, moving all the while to stand more firmly before the kettle. Her bare breasts hung shrivelled against her chest. She showed no sign of chill. "I never liked this thing, anyway," she said. "All my life before I came to this mission, I could bare my chest the same as any man. There was no shame in it."

Lorenzo was shaking his head with disapproval, pushing back the bodice.

She looked down at her withered breasts and smiled wryly. "They were beautiful when I was young." She lifted one in her hand. "Men would always take a second look."

"Cover yourself," Lorenzo commanded. "You are a sinful woman. Pray God will forgive you for this."

Isabel shrugged, taking back the bodice. "I only want to help," she said, and without putting the bodice back on, she turned and picked up the kettle and started to move away. Lucia stepped up quickly into her place and pushed her blanket into Lorenzo's hands. Then she took off her crucifix and gave that to him as well. But he would not be diverted from the kettle.

"Bring it back!" he ordered.

Isabel turned around and innocently offered the bodice again.

"The kettle, woman! Give me the kettle!" He grabbed up his whip. Isabel only glared at him. He struck out, the lash snapping against the ground, the end of it hitting her foot, causing her to jump back. Lucia reached out and seized the lash and wrapped it around her hand. Lorenzo gave it a fierce jerk, pulling Lucia toward him, but still she hung on, glaring angrily at him.

"To treat an old woman so," she said sharply. "You are no Apalachee!"

Then suddenly Maria was there beside her, taking hold of the lash above Lucia's hand, and together their strength matched his. It was a stand-off, neither side able to pull the whip free. People began to back away. Some were laughing, others talking excitedly. Lucia kept her eyes on Lorenzo, not knowing what was going to come of this, nor when or whether she would let go. She did not see Carlos until he stepped in between them and put his hand on the whip.

"Give it to me," he said calmly. She looked at him for a moment and then began to unwrap her hand. She and Maria both let go and stepped back. Lorenzo still held his end.

"Give it to me," Carlos said again, and this time he looked directly at Lorenzo.

There was a moment of surprise in Lorenzo's eyes, then anger again. But he let go of the whip. "It was that old woman," said Lorenzo. "Ana's mother. She would not give us her kettle."

"It belongs to the priest," Lucia said quickly. Looking around, she saw that Isabel and the kettle were gone.

Carlos had the whip and was coiling up the lash. His appearance had changed since Lucia had last seen him. Not only was his red blanket gone, but also his shirt, his breeches and stockings. He wore a breechcloth of faded blue wool and a pair of torn deerskin leggings, too short for him, which someone must have just given to him. His broad chest was bare, the muscles firm and smooth. She looked away, fearing that her interest would be noticed.

"It is true that the kettle belongs in Father Juan's cocina," he said, laying the whip down on the ground on the far side of the pile of muskets. "I will speak to him and see what he wants done with it." Then he looked at the people who had been held up all this time in a line that stretched back into the stockade. "Come on," he said, motioning to a woman and her small son who stood near the front of the knotted crowd.

"I am next," said Maria, taking her ragged piece of blanket from her shoulders and offering it to Carlos.

He shook his head. "The English would laugh at that," he said. "It is just a rag. You keep it."

"We are taking everything," Lorenzo said sternly, reaching around Carlos to take it. "Ten horse-loads, where will we get it if we do not take the rags? Not everyone has so fine a blanket as that red one of yours."

Carlos pushed his arm away. "Go ahead," he said, motioning for Lucia and Maria to move on.

"You are letting them go?" said Lorenzo. "After what they have done?"

"I will speak to Father Juan about them."

"They should be whipped," grumbled Lorenzo. "And the old woman, too." But Carlos had turned his attention to the people still waiting in line.

Lucia led Maria away, and when they had gotten some distance from the others, she reached her arm around her and hugged her.

"It was good of you to stand with me. My heart is full."

Maria shrugged. "You are my sister. She is my grandmother."

Three children from the stockade ran past them, exhilarated at their freedom. Lucia smiled, relieved that no enemy had stormed the walls at dawn, and relieved that she had evaded a whipping for having defied Lorenzo. Isabel's triumph seemed all the sweeter for it. "She kept her kettle," she said happily, glad for the company of this woman beside her.

"Badly," said Juan.

"Then I speak the language of Spain," Moore said gallantly, showing his command of Spanish to be more than adequate. He nodded toward Don Patricio. "He is the king?"

"He is the chief of Ivitachuco. His name is Don Patricio Hinachuba. I am Juan de Villalva."

The Englishman ignored the priest, putting out his hand to the Indian. "I am glad we do not fight," he said to Don Patricio. "It is better to be friends. In my land of Carolina I have many Indian friends. For you and your people to come to my land is good."

Don Patricio nodded politely, but made no answer.

Juan glared at the Englishman. "What are you saying? That you will make them go with you to Carolina? They have brought you all they own to ransom their freedom according to your word. Is this nothing but a trick?"

"I speak of free will," said Moore, his voice strong and arrogant. "If the king meets our demands, he is free to come or stay. But someday he comes to us. The nations move like the tides, my friend. Spain ebbs. England rises. The Indians are not blind. They see this."

"You presume too much," Juan said tersely. His eyes moved beyond Moore in the direction of Ayubale where the English and their Indian allies were still encamped. What right had they to come into God's vineyard killing and destroying? All the efforts of his life, poor as they were, were being swept into oblivion. He looked back again at the English colonel. "God has not forsaken us. In His own time He will give us strength to stand against your forces of heresy."

"Heresy does not defeat you," Moore said with a condescending smile. "Commerce defeats you. You offer them salvation. We offer guns and cloth. They choose guns and cloth. Salvation be damned!" He laughed at his own clever words.

The priest looked away in disgust.

Don Patricio's jaw was firmly set, his eyes unwavering. "It is not so with my people," the chief said calmly. "We give up all that we have for the sake of our souls. We turn our backs on your guns and cloth. We denounce your way of torture and murder. We keep our feet upon the way of Blessed Jesus and his Holy Mother. We ask you to take what we own and leave us in peace."

"You own little," said Moore. "The Spaniards give you nothing. They have nothing. Once they had much gold and silver from the Indies. But— how do I say it? No commerce. Gold makes commerce. But not for Spain. Gold is gone and no commerce. Come live with the English and you will be amazed. Our goods are cheap. For a few deerskins you fill your house with riches."

"We choose to stay in our own land," Don Patricio said stubbornly. "If
you do not wish to give us our freedom for what we have brought, then we
will return with it to our town and fight you from there."

"Let me see," Moore said to him, nodding toward the pack horses. "Do
you have the church silver?"

"It is not his to give," said the priest. "I bring that myself, though it
sickens me. It is only for my Indians that I do this."

"And for your own skin," Moore said offhandedly.

Juan looked at him without response. Then he turned and nodded to
Carlos, who unlashed the wooden chest from one of the horses. Juan took
it from him and for a moment he held it, his back to the Englishman as he
stared down at the box that contained everything his life had been, twenty
years of baptisms, masses, and last rites, using these sacred vessels. And
now he was handing them over to a heretic.

"This is a grave sin," he said as he turned and put the chest on the
ground, opening it for Moore to see. "May God forgive us both."

Moore looked the contents over carefully and then motioned to one of
his Englishmen to pick it up. Juan watched as the man closed the lid, picked
up the chest, and carried it over to his horse. Then the priest turned away
and walked back across the field toward the black waters of the swamp.
Without a struggle he had let a door close against him. It was the door of
his church in Ivitachuco. The door of his seminary in Spain. The door of
the kingdom of heaven. His battles were over, and he had lost. At the edge
of the swamp he stopped and sat down on a fallen tree and waited for the
Indians to hand over the rest of the ransom.

✳ On the floor beside the fire, Lucia laid out rabbit skins, making a
block of them to see what they would look like sewn together. Her mouth
crooked into a smile as she looked up at Maria. "One shoulder," she said
and began to laugh at the ridiculousness of ever thinking they could make
a blanket from them. "We could cover one shoulder at a time."

All morning they had been at work softening the few skins that Isabel,
ever thrifty, had saved in a moth-eaten pile beneath her bed. It was more
than a year's worth of skins, and yet not enough. They were able to snare a
few rabbits from time to time, but there was no man to hunt for them, that
was the problem. No one to bring in meat and skins. And now no Spanish
blankets either.

"It will be just the thing for whichever shoulder is away from the fire,"
said Maria. The humor in her voice was good to hear.

Lucia put the skins back into a pile. "Is it even worth sewing them
together?"

Maria shrugged.

Isabel appeared in the doorway. "Lucia," the old woman said without coming inside, her small form silhouetted against the light outside. "I need you in the cocina."

"Where is the awl?" asked Maria, reaching to pull the pile of skins closer to her. "I will work on them while you are gone. They make the start of a blanket, at least."

Lucia gave her the awl and a ball of sinew and then went out and followed Isabel across the yard and into the cocina.

Salvador was there. He was sitting away from the firelight, quietly absorbed in a dish of sofkee. Lucia hesitated inside the door, distressed that he should endanger them by coming here.

"You have come," she said stiffly.

"I have come," he answered.

Isabel took a seat on a cane mat by the fire, and Lucia walked slowly over and sat beside her. Salvador was running his finger around the inside of the dish, cleaning up the last traces of the sofkee. He set the empty dish in front of him and looked up at Lucia.

"Do not worry," he said. "Our time in this place has ended. Let them see everything we do. Let them say what they will."

Lucia glanced at Isabel to see if she followed Salvador's meaning, but evidently she did not, for she, too, was regarding the shaman with reservation.

Salvador had picked up his pipe and was tamping down the tobacco with his finger. Isabel found a twig and held it into the fire. Then she passed it to him, the small flame lasting barely long enough to light the tobacco.

"Your meaning is not clear to us," she said gravely.

He slowly smoked his pipe, blowing smoke to the Four Ways. Then he put the pipe in front of him beside the empty dish and said, "I have had another dream. We are to leave this place."

"Who is to leave?" Isabel asked in a cool voice that Lucia had not heard her use before with Salvador.

"All those who will become the new Apalachee people. Those who will live alone in the old way, with the White Suns to lead them."

Isabel shook her head. "This is no time to try something like that. They will not let us live alone. The Spaniards will hunt us down as rebels, and the English will hunt us down for slaves."

"I have been told otherwise," Salvador said patiently.

"By whom?" Isabel reached out and stirred the fire, a shimmer of sparks rising with the smoke. The blanket that Maria had given her slipped from her shoulder and she reached quickly to catch it and pull it back again.

"By the Water Cougar," said Salvador.

"A dream from the Under World," said Isabel, her tone noncommittal. "What did it tell you?"

"To go to the place where the Great Town once stood and wait there until the Englishmen and Spaniards have driven each other from the land. Then Apalachee will be ours again. The White Suns will lead us as in the days of old. There will be peace in the land and great harvests. All will be new and reborn."

"The Great Town," said Isabel, her voice still subdued. She would not look at him. "Do you know where it is?"

"North of here, near the lake of the Ancient Ones."

Isabel nodded. "And what sense does it make to put a camp that much closer to the slave catchers?"

"I have spoken of this to others," said Salvador. "To men who have recently hunted there and to some who have even hidden there, in small camps. It is shielded by deep forest. Slave catchers seldom go there because there are no people living there."

"But if you settle there, that will no longer be true. You will give them a reason to go there. They will come and kill your men and carry your women and children away." She shook her head. "It is too dangerous. Our only safety is this stockade." She pointed with her thumb over her shoulder in its direction. "It is the only thing that saved us. Ayubale had no stockade and Ayubale was lost. I do not love Spaniards, my brother, but as long as they can offer me protection, I will cling to them as tightly as if I were a Christian saint."

Salvador shrugged, seemingly undisturbed. "There are many from this town who are coming with me." He looked at Lucia. "You, my child, will you join us?"

Lucia looked at him directly. It would be comforting to believe in this hope that he offered. But she shook her head. "I cannot leave my grandmother."

Salvador nodded, as if he had expected this. He picked up his pipe and Lucia gave him a splinter of pine with which to relight it. "Will it ruin your plans if the White Sun Woman is not with you?" she asked.

He lit the pipe without answering and smoked a few moments, taking pleasure in it. Nothing they had said seemed to discourage him.

"The White Sun Woman will be here in Ivitachuco," he said, "singing her song to the Sun. So long as she remains in Apalachee, the people in the Great Town will prosper."

"I will sing every morning," said Isabel, letting him know that she meant no break with him. "And if there ever comes a day when the danger is past,

I will come and join you. I would like to have the life that you see for us. I would like to have it for a little time before I die. But I am old. Perhaps Lucia will have it."

"You are not that old, my grandmother," said Lucia, trying to lighten the tone.

"I am at least that old. Maybe older." She looked at Salvador, good humor in her eyes. "We wish you well, beloved man."

"We will not be apart," he said. "There will be messengers back and forth, though they will have to move in secret." He looked at Lucia. "We will wait for you, my child. You will be welcome when it is time for you to come."

Lucia smiled slightly and nodded. She doubted she would ever go, and yet she did not want to say so and disappoint him or make things strained between them. She watched as he tucked his pipe into the pouch on his belt and rose easily to his feet.

"We leave tonight," he said. "When I see you again, it will be in another place."

"In another place," answered Isabel, and they watched him as he left. For a moment there was silence. Then Isabel said, "If the White Falcon had come to him in his dream, it might have been different. But I do not trust the Water Cougar." She spoke in a low voice so that Salvador would not hear her as he walked from the yard.

Lucia gave a little sigh. "It would be good to live in the old way again."

"I will still sing the song," said Isabel. "That seems to be the right thing. But this other seems wrong to me. I did not know this about Salvador. He has visions, but he cannot tell the good ones from the bad ones."

"Maybe it is we who cannot tell," said Lucia. She picked up the pine splinter that Salvador had used for his pipe and tossed it into the fire.

CHAPTER SEVEN

The news came with the morning light that the Englishman Moore was taking his army west to raid towns on the road to San Luís, leaving Ivitachuco untouched as he had promised. Solana, hearing the news, rose from his chair at the table in the convento and began to get ready to leave. The priest watched him soberly.

"You move with too much haste," Juan said. "There will be pagans on the way. Stay with us until it is safe."

"It is safe enough," said Solana. "The scouts say the enemy is taking the lower road. God help all the missions along the way. I'll take the upper road and be waiting for them at San Luís."

"But San Luís is safe without you. They'll not storm the blockhouse. It's ten times stronger than our stockade." Juan knew it was unreasonable to ask him to stay, but he no longer cared to be reasonable. Reason had led him to surrender the holy vessels, reason and fear, and he was sick of it, sick of the cold emptiness of his soul. His only comfort was the company of this good Spaniard.

"I must go back to my family," Solana said simply. "I need to know that my sons are safe."

"Yes, you need to know that," said Juan, relenting. "You've been waiting since the morning of the battle. What do we know of what happened in the fighting except that Father Parga was killed? One priest, at least, with courage." He looked down and studied his hands. "I'll go with you as far as Ayubale. I must find his body and bring it here to bury in the church. He died a martyr's death."

"Yes," said Solana, lifting his bundled belongings to his shoulder. "You should do that. His body is sacred now."

Juan got slowly to his feet and picked up his hat and cloak. Then he stared down at them, trying to remember why he wanted them, what it was he had decided to do. It took him a moment, wading through all that was swarming in his mind, until at last he remembered Ayubale—the martyr's body. He put on his hat and drew the cloak over his shoulders. Then he glanced at Solana and saw him watching, and he made himself smile, trying to dispel the concern that he saw in his friend's eyes. Solana looked away and moved toward the door, going outside into the morning light with an air of relief. Juan followed after him.

The town was astir with activity. The people from the homesteads were breaking camp to return to their homes, some already strung out along the road, more women than men, more children than adults. They went without the blankets they had come with, without their rosaries. They were poorer than poor, and their ears rang with stories of English riches, of red wool and silver buttons, of cloth and guns without end. Many would walk past their homesteads and not stop until they reached Carolina. Juan watched them grimly. Lorenzo had come to him at the break of dawn to tell him that the old devil Salvador had deserted in the night. At some other time Juan might have felt pleasure at the news. But now there were too many who would follow.

He turned to Lorenzo, who lounged near the door of the convento, tending Solana's horse. "Get four men to go with me to Ayubale. We will need a litter to bring back the body of the priest."

"Yes, Father," said Lorenzo, bowing dutifully. "Blessed be the memory of the dead father." He crossed himself and headed across the plaza toward the council house.

"Lorenzo!" Juan called after him.

"Yes, Father."

"Find Carlos and send him to me."

"Yes, Father," said Lorenzo, bowing another time.

Juan leaned against the hitching post where Solana stood with his horse. "Some of them are loyal. I praise God for that. They take my teachings to heart and live as Christians. My despair would be even deeper were it not for the ones like Lorenzo and Don Patricio and Carlos. And Ana of course." He coughed suddenly, red flecks appearing on his lips and chin.

Solana looked away, pretending to check his horse's cinch. "I think you should ride my horse to Ayubale. To walk there and back in one day would be too much for you."

"No," said Juan, wiping his handkerchief over his mouth and smiling ruefully. "A Franciscan does not ride like an earthly lord, but walks humbly as Christ walked. I've not been on a horse since the day I entered the Order. That's the only vow I've managed to keep, and God help me, I'll not break it now."

"We are a long way from the seminaries of Spain, my friend. Those vows were not meant for a place like Apalachee."

"I will walk," said Juan.

They waited in silence until the four bearers arrived, one of them carrying a cane-mat litter rolled up on its two poles. Carlos came up behind them.

"At your service, Father," he said, bowing as Lorenzo had bowed. Juan regarded him with affection, but for a moment he could not think of why he had sent for him. Then he remembered—the martyr's body.

"I want you to come with me to Ayubale. To find Father Parga. I want you to help me bring him home with the honor he is due."

"As you wish," said Carlos, turning to put his back to the wind, for he had no blanket to keep away the cold.

Solana handed the reins of his horse to Carlos. "Bring him along. I'll walk with the father."

"Is he nothing but a servant to you?" Juan said sharply to Solana, stepping over to take the reins from Carlos and giving them instead to one of the litter bearers. "I want Carlos beside me." He motioned for Carlos to join him, and the three started out abreast toward the edge of the village. "You are a son to me, Carlos," said Juan, emotion straining at his voice. He saw Solana look away, but he ignored him. "You are the same to me as Don

Manuel's sons are to him. Is that not true, my friend?" He looked over at Solana. "They are even close in years. How old are your sons now, Don Manuel?"

"Juan is twenty-two," Solana said stiffly. "Manuelito is eighteen."

Juan forgave the disdain in his voice. Solana did not know what it was to be a priest, to be a father to these poor, wretched people. "This son of mine is older," he said, putting his hand on Carlos' shoulder. Carlos held his dark head erect, and Juan felt tension in his muscles. "I remember the night he was born. I was a young priest, new to the field. Do you remember, Manuel, how I was so full of blessed hope? God was always beside me then, just as the two of you are with me today." He paused, sorting through the memories now tumbling through his mind. He knew that Solana was uncomfortable and that his own words were strained, but something had gotten loose in him and could not be contained. "His mother was a good Christian Indian, an obedient woman, devoted to the Virgin. Her husband summoned me that night to confess her. The midwife had declared her condition hopeless and said she would die in her labor. But to a young priest with faith, there is nothing that is hopeless. I prayed with her through the night and gave her an image of the Virgin to hold and kiss, and just before dawn the baby was born, this one, this Carlos. It was a miracle. His mother lived, but in a few short years she died of a fever and her husband after her. I took little Carlos in. I felt like a father to him and have always treated him so, raising him up in the love of the Blessed Savior." He turned to Solana, pleading for understanding. "He was a miracle, Manuel. I used to see miracles."

"Of course," said Solana, softening. He took the priest's arm, offering support. "And still we see them every day. God's hand is everywhere,"

Juan leaned on Solana's arm and said no more.

✸ The putrid smell of Ayubale came to them on the cold wind while the village was yet beyond view. Juan steeled himself, summoning what strength of heart was left in him. As they came within sight of the charred ruins, the stench grew so strong that he drew out his handkerchief and held it to his nose and mouth. The familiarity of the scene was dreadful to him, the road he had traveled so many times, the fields and trees that in happier days had spread so pleasantly before his gaze, the crisscrossing paths where children used to run and play. Now the church and all the houses of the village were burned to the ground. Great live oaks towered over the empty yards, their wide limbs charred by the flames. At this distance they could see no bodies in the blackened rubble. But they could smell them. As the party drew near the edge of the village, the four men who had come to bear the litter began to murmur among themselves, until at last one of them announced in Spanish, "We wait here."

Juan stopped and turned to them, moving his handkerchief from his face. "There is no danger," he said, gasping as he tried to avoid breathing the foul air. "The pagans are gone."

"There are many dead in there," said the bearer, lapsing back into Apalachee. "We will wait here. When you find the dead father, you call us. We will come for him."

"Very well," said Juan, too low in spirit to argue. "We'll summon you." He turned to Carlos. "What about you? Are you afraid of ghosts, too?"

"No," said Carlos, giving him a hard look.

"Then come along," said Juan, and putting the handkerchief back to his nose and mouth, he led the way into the village.

Scavenging birds flew away as they approached. The dead were everywhere, in the ruins of the church and in the plaza, tied to stakes and trees. Some had been burnt and some shot through with arrows. Some were women, mutilated, pierced with arrows and half roasted. And worst of all were the small children impaled on poles about the plaza. They were the ones who were too young to walk to the slave market in Charles Town.

Juan walked with his free hand clutched against his stomach, fighting back nausea. Solana had turned away and was staring back toward the fields with clenched fists. But Carlos did not take his eyes from the carnage. Tears welled up as he looked slowly about at every man, woman, and child whose life had been torn away. Juan and Solana moved on and left him there to grieve for his own.

The two Spaniards crossed the village and went out along the road that led toward San Luís, looking for the battleground where Parga had met his death. They found it easily, upwards of fifty bloating bodies scattered in a field, some of them partially consumed by wolves, others by the crows and buzzards that were even now at work, taking flight reluctantly as the two men moved among them inspecting each frightful body. But all they could find were Indians, Apalachees from San Luís, until at last, as they walked near a canebrake at the edge of the field, a buzzard arose from within, and the priest parted the canes and looked down upon the headless body of his brother in Christ. Parga's robe was gone and his body was torn and bloated, but Juan recognized him by his boot—a single boot, for his other leg had been hacked away.

He and Solana crossed themselves and Juan murmured a brief prayer. Then they both began a search through the canebrake for the missing head and leg. But Juan's heart was not in it. He did not want to find the gory parts. He followed Solana, looking absently in places already searched.

Then he stopped. Solana had come upon a human foot protruding from a place where the cane was thick. The foot was bare and bloated, with round, unnatural toes. But it was not the leg of the priest. Juan knew this immediately from the way Solana was looking at it. There was a recognition in Solana's face that was horrible to see. Solana knew this leg. Even in its bloated state, he knew the shape of the foot, the hair on the ankle, the length of the calf, the knee, the thigh. And the body attached to it. Pushing back the canes, Solana knew all of it, though the face of the dead man was turned away. He bent down and with trembling fingers grasped the hair of the head and lifted it, turning the face toward him. Scarcely had he glimpsed it when the hair came loose and the head of the corpse fell back with a thud against the earth. Solana gasped and staggered back, shaking his son's hair from his hand in horror. He turned away and fell to his knees.

Juan stood helplessly, his heart caving in, crushed by this final blow. He was a priest and should give comfort, but he could not remember any words that a priest should say, any knowledge that a priest should have. He could not remember God or hope. He could not remember faith. He was in a field of dead men with buzzards picking at their flesh. He began to cry. He stumbled to Solana and sat down beside him, weeping piteously. He wept for Solana and for Parga and for Apalachee itself, all crushed and mangled. He wept for his own defeat, for the relentless consumption that was stealing away his life, for the elusive faith that had lured him from Spain and abandoned him in this place beyond reach of prayers and comfort.

Then Juan felt Solana's arm about his shoulder. "There," Solana said in a voice that was strong in its grief. "Look here at these angels lying together, my Juan and Father Parga. Juan was defending him. He died defending the faith. How many have wished for such a holy death?"

The priest could not find words.

"My Juan is with the Virgin now. He will be our advocate in heaven, yours and mine. Even now he is beseeching her to comfort us and lead us from despair."

Solana's words were the ones Juan had lost, and he was comforted by them. His tears slowly ceased. "It is you who should be the priest," he said, straightening himself. He sat back on his heels and closed his eyes. The dull pain of his breathing was greater than it had ever been before. Yet his mind was growing calm. His soul was stirring. Perhaps even yet it could be restored.

He opened his eyes to see Carlos standing before them, tall and massive, looking down at them in their grief. There was a hardness in his eyes that Juan had never seen before.

"Call the bearers," Juan said to him.

Carlos turned away without a word and walked stiffly back across the field.

"This carnage has been a shock to him," said the priest, feeling unsteady and light-headed as he rose to his feet. But his mind was easier now. "It has been a terrible thing for all of us. Especially for you, my friend. May God continue to give you comfort." He stood for a moment looking down at the body of young Solana. "We'll take him with Father Parga and bury them together in the church."

Solana shook his head. "I want him in San Luís. I'll have the bearers dig a grave for him here. Deep enough to keep him from the wolves. When the pagans are gone from the country, his brother and I will come back and take him home where he belongs."

"Whatever you wish," said Juan.

He looked away through the pines and tried to think of the days just past, of all that had moved and changed in so short a time. Only four days since the first word of the English attack. It seemed as long as all the rest of his life before it.

CHAPTER EIGHT

It had been one of those days of early spring when the fragile sun soaks the open places with its warmth and yet remains too weak to take away the chill from the cool, closed places. And now in the dusk the inside chill sharpened, and Carlos moved quickly about his little room, piling his few belongings on an old deerskin that was spread open on his bed. He heard footsteps come onto the porch outside his door, but recognizing them as Lorenzo's, he did not bother to look around until he had finished tying up the bundle. When he turned and saw the shock on Lorenzo's face, he smiled. "Perhaps Father Juan will let you have this room," he said.

Lorenzo stared speechlessly. Then he said, "Does he know? I just came from him. He does not know. What are you doing? You will kill him."

"What do you think, that I am deserting? I am moving out of the convento, that is all. I am tired of living here."

Lorenzo studied him, unable to absorb it. "He is sick in bed. Do you want to kill him? Why have you not spoken to him about this?"

Carlos shrugged. "He will soon be up and about. Then he will see. What will it matter? Just one more change among so many. How long has it been since he took to his bed? He has not been up since the martyr's funeral. He has not seen how empty this town has become, how many have left."

"He knows all of that. You have told him yourself. But of this you have said nothing—changing your place. What does it mean? He put you here to wait. Will you still be chief when the time comes?"

"You take the room, Lorenzo," said Carlos, picking up the bundle from the bed. "You be chief when Don Patricio is dead."

"Now, there!" said Lorenzo, his voice rising in agitation. "Now there it is. What are you saying? You will not be chief? You are the one they would choose, not me. I am not a Hinachuba or even an Usunaca. I am not the one they look up to. This room is nothing. What matters is all he has taught you, all he has done for you. You will kill him! That is what you will do. He will die when he hears this. You are his hope, the one he loves most."

"Do not worry yourself. He will not die for an Indian. For a Spaniard, perhaps, but not an Indian. And think about it now. If it is not the room that makes a chief, then what does it matter if I move across the plaza? All of this amounts to nothing. So be easy. Do not alarm him about a thing so small. Let it be."

"Then you will be chief," said Lorenzo.

Carlos shrugged. "Don Patricio is a healthy man. Old age improves him. So who will die first? The chief or the priest? Or will it be the town? Or Apalachee itself? I am tired of waiting. You take the room. I will live from now on as an ordinary man. And if some day they need a chief and I am the one they want, I will decide then what to do." Tucking his bundle under his arm, he started toward the door. Lorenzo stood still for a moment, blocking his way, but then moved aside to let him pass.

Carlos stepped out into the evening air, welcoming the warmth that could still be felt there. The western sky was red with the lingering sunset and all the town reflected its fading light. A breeze ruffled over the plaza. There were few people about because there were few in the town, less than half the number there had been before the attack on Ayubale. The rest had fled—to the English or to the woods. And who could blame them? Who could say what was the best thing to do? No one felt safe anymore.

The move Carlos himself was making was not precipitous. More than a month had passed since his trip to Ayubale and the death he had seen there in the fire-blackened plaza. The vision of it still woke him in the night, and he would lie with it in the dark, sweating in his cold room, and remember how the priest had viewed that carnage with eyes that were perfectly dry— only to weep like a woman at the sight of two dead Spaniards. In that he had seen the real truth of things. It had worked on him gradually, night after night, until the room in the convento and all it represented became unbearable to him. It sickened him to think how he once had gloried in it. But that was over now. He was out of that room and would never go back.

He walked lightly across the plaza, passing close by the ball pole in the center of it, reaching out to touch it as if to reconnect with his Apalachee soul. He felt good. There was a growing energy in his step as his eyes scanned the newly abandoned houses up ahead. There were plenty to choose from. He would find a small house with a good roof and tight walls. And perhaps tonight he would sleep through until morning without waking.

☀ The dawn was cold and clear, the sun rising brightly into a cloudless sky, promising another day of warmth. Carlos trudged out from the town into the field, joining the straggling ranks of women and children and old men. At first no one paid him any mind, though some may have wondered about the hoe that he carried. Yet no one suspected his purpose and no one looked twice until he actually swung the iron blade into the earth. Then Lucia and the woman Maria from Ayubale, near whom he had taken his place, straightened up from the work they were beginning and looked at him with surprise. When he smiled at them, they looked away, not knowing what to think, and went back to their work. He heard Maria speak softly to Lucia, who answered with humor in her voice, though he could not catch the words.

The morning was beautiful to him. He felt rested and reborn, breathing the cold air like a prisoner set free, swinging the hoe like a man whose arms had been loosed from their chains. Across the field the word of his presence was passing and heads turned to look curiously at him, the priest's favorite, the one who would be chief, working like a common laborer in the church fields. Last of all the word reached Lorenzo, who was serving as overseer. Lorenzo came striding across the field, his whip in his hand, anger in his eyes.

"Now what?" he asked as he came up beside Carlos. He was trying to talk softly but he was too excited to do so, and people all around were listening, the motion of their hoes slowing almost to a halt. "What is this you are doing?" His tone was more pleading than demanding, for who was he to demand anything of Carlos? "What am I to do? Shall I summon Don Patricio?"

"For what?" asked Carlos. "So he can tell you what I am doing? I am hoeing the field, getting it ready for planting." He turned and looked at Lucia. "Is that not what we are doing?"

She nodded, keeping silent. It was a fine day. Carlos could not remember when he had felt so good.

"I am going," muttered Lorenzo. "This is not for me. It is for Don Patricio. He is the chief." He turned and started away.

"Leave it be," said Carlos, his voice suddenly stern. "You are right, this is not for you. So leave it alone. There is work to be done and not enough people to do it. Perhaps you should take up a hoe yourself."

Lorenzo stiffened and turned to see the smiles on the faces of those who had heard. He raised his whip to them. "Get to work," he said sullenly, and they swung their hoes, though their smiles remained. Lorenzo gave Carlos a last hard look, and then, with a sigh of resignation, he wandered back to his duties, barking commands more fiercely than before.

The sun climbed and the day warmed. The work became wearying. Carlos' muscles, unused to such labor, began to ache, and for a time he contemplated the fact that while he himself could lay down his hoe and walk away, no one else could do that, not the oldest, most venerable man in the field, not the youngest child, not Maria who had survived the destruction of her people, not Lucia who was the niece of the priest's own mistress. None had any privilege. All were virtual slaves beneath the lash of Lorenzo, by order of the priest, by order of the King of Spain. Only he could walk away, and the muscles of his body begged him to do so. But he worked on, enslaving himself, tasting in it a new freedom from a worse kind of service to the priest.

After a while the pain in his muscles began to pass, and his strength seemed to increase. When Maria lagged behind, weaker, or perhaps more dispirited, than the others, he stepped over and quickly worked ahead for her. Maria thanked him shyly, which added an erotic twinge to the already peculiar pleasure of the day, and he worked on with the sun warm on his back, enjoying being close to her, and to Lucia. They both were beautiful women, though different, one small and exquisite and appealingly vulnerable, the other tall and magnificent and possessed of a curious strength of heart that drew him to her. They did not talk to him, nor he to them, and yet he enjoyed their presence, and they seemed to have no objection to his.

A break came at midday, the women and men segregating themselves on the grassy margin of the field. Carlos had neglected to bring food for himself, but several of the men shared what they had, and the time was passed pleasantly with small talk that avoided the real question in everyone's mind: What was he doing out here? When the food was gone, he lay back on the grass and felt the sun on his face as he watched the small clouds drifting in the high blue sky. What was he doing out here? He closed his eyes and sleep stole in briefly until the sobbing of a child dispelled it and he sat up to find himself almost alone.

The workers were moving back across the field to their places, leaving him to sleep, for who were they to tell him to go back to work? The only others who remained were a woman and the child that was crying, a boy barely old enough to swing a hoe, who refused to get to his feet and would not stand when his mother, growing ever more desperate, repeatedly pulled him up. His weeping grew more insistent, and Lorenzo, who had been following the others across the field, turned around. The woman bent over the boy, pleading with him to get up. "You can rest tonight," she told him. "Just a little longer and you can rest."

"What is this?" said Lorenzo as he came striding toward them. "Get back to your places. I can make him mind if you cannot."

"No," the woman said quickly. "I can do it." And again she pulled at the boy. Lorenzo prodded him with the handle of his whip.

"Perhaps he is sick," said Carlos, walking over to them.

"He is," the woman said softly. "He tires so quickly. He must be sick."

"Is he sick or not?" said Lorenzo. "Does he have a fever?"

"No," said the woman, defeat in her voice. "But he is weak."

"Did he eat?" asked Lorenzo.

She nodded. "He ate some bread."

Lorenzo scoffed. "Then he is playing the devil with you. Let him taste my whip. That will raise him."

"No," murmured the woman, bending over her son. "Get up, Eugenio," she said, pulling at him again. He had stopped crying, and this time he rose to his feet, standing uncertainly beneath her hands.

"There," said Lorenzo. "What did I tell you? Now get to your places."

The woman took the boy by the arm and began leading him into the field, following after Lorenzo. Carlos walked behind, and he could see the boy's legs swaying, until at last he stumbled and went down on his knees, too weak to catch himself. He began to cry again, though softly now.

"He is sick," Carlos said loudly to Lorenzo. "Bring someone to look at him."

Lorenzo looked back and was about to argue, but the command in Carlos' voice was too strong for him, and he turned away in silence and walked ahead to the other workers. In a moment he was back again, bringing Lucia with him. He stood by sullenly while she examined the boy, looking into his mouth and feeling his joints and his abdomen and speaking to him in a low voice, asking him questions to which he nodded or shook his head.

At last she stood up, half a head taller than the mother who looked anxiously at her. "It is the spring sickness," said Lucia. "His gums are bleeding."

"I did not see it," said the woman, shaking her head, ashamed of her apparent neglect. "I should have seen that."

"They are only just starting to bleed," said Lucia. "He will be all right. Give him dried persimmon pulp, if any can still be had. And give him pine needle tea. The fresh new tips. Do not worry. Green things are beginning to grow now. He will soon be well."

"I should have seen it myself," said the woman, seeming distraught, exhausted by the tension of the incident and the long morning of work.

"Take him home," Carlos said. "Give him persimmon pulp and tea, as she said."

"What do you mean?" said Lorenzo. "She is not sick. Let the boy go home alone. She can give him tea when she has finished her work."

"I will finish her work," said Carlos. "The work I do for the rest of the day will be hers." He smiled at the confusion in Lorenzo's face. "I do not have to be here, do I?"

"All right," said Lorenzo. "But I am going to Don Patricio tonight. We will get some of these things straightened out."

"What things?" said Carlos with a shrug. He looked at Lucia. "We had better go back to our work."

She turned and walked with him across the field, no words passing between them until they were almost to the others. Then she said, "Will you work again tomorrow?"

"Yes," he said.

"Why?"

"Because I am tired of waiting."

There was a pause while she thought that over. "Tired of waiting to be chief?"

He did not answer.

After a few moments she said, "This is a hard way to pass the time, sweating like a slave in someone else's fields."

"What would *you* do?"

Again there was silence. She seemed to be thinking, trying to understand who he was now. Finally she shook her head, unable to find an answer for him. They had come to the place where she had left her hoe. Stretching ahead was a strip of unturned ground left for her by the others, who were back at work.

"You go and join them," he said. "I will catch you up." He was looking around now for his own hoe and saw it tossed aside, no one having believed that he would return.

"No," she said. "I'll do this. You have that to do." She nodded toward another strip halfway across the field where the woman and her son should have been working.

Carlos stretched the muscles in his shoulders, which had begun to ache again with the rest he had taken. He watched Lucia start to work, her hoe chopping quickly into the burned stubble of the field, turning up the earth, chopping, turning. She could work faster than he could. Her muscles were hardened to it. But so would his be before long.

CHAPTER NINE

Father Juan de Villalva pushed back his blanket, which was making him too hot now that the sun was streaming in through the open window. The fresh smell of the outside air invigorated him. Moving slowly, he swung his feet to the floor and sat for a moment on the side of his bed, then rose and walked on unsteady legs to the window and leaned on the sill to look out. His strength was returning. For more than a week now he had felt the improvement. Soon he would begin to get out, a little each day, and by the time the corn was up he would be there to see it. It was the winter weather that had brought him so low—that and the strain of the English attack. But now it was spring. He had lived to see new growth again, and if he could do that much, he could do more, perhaps set things right in the mission and entice the deserters back. And solve the problem of Carlos and his alarming behavior. Though even that did not seem so terrible now with the spring breeze brushing gently at his face.

Ana's footsteps, bare feet on the packed earth floor, padded quietly to his doorway, and he turned to her as she put her head inside.

"You are awake?" she said. "Don Gaspar is here to see you." She rolled her eyes at him, knowing his antipathy for the rancher.

He smiled. "Bring him in. It's a fine day for visitors." And he too rolled his eyes, making her laugh a little as she came in to pull a bench away from the wall and position it near the bed at a suitable distance for conversation. He returned to bed and arranged himself for company, sitting back against his pillows and smoothing the blanket over his lap.

Ana went back and ushered Velasco into the room.

"Don Gaspar," said Juan, reaching out a thin hand to the rancher. Velasco shook it without warmth and would not keep Juan's gaze. He glanced about, looking things over, for he did not come often to the convento and this was the first time he had ever been in Father Juan's private chamber.

"It is a splendid day to be out," said Juan. "You must have enjoyed your ride through the countryside."

Velasco shrugged, walking slowly to the small rough table near the window, inspecting what was on it: a breviary; a water jar of plain Apalachee pottery; a damp rag spread across one edge of the table to dry; and an Apalachee potter's version of a Spanish cup, red-filmed, holding some half-wilted wildflowers.

"I have much on my mind these days," Velasco said slowly. "Much that weighs me down." And then, as if remembering simple courtesy, he turned to the priest and said, "And how is your health, Father? Better, I hope."

"I will soon be up," said Juan. "Though it will take time to recover my strength. Lying in bed weakens a man as much as illness does."

"Yes," said Velasco, nodding absently. He was turning away again.

"Take a seat, Don Gaspar." Juan motioned toward the bench. "How is it with you these days? Not well, you say?"

Velasco looked at the bench but made no move to sit on it. "I saw the church fields as I rode in." He was speaking carefully. "They are nearly planted already. You have many workers."

Juan shook his head. "Not even half the number I had last year. I am leaving fields fallow that should be planted."

"I have no workers," Velasco said, looking directly at the priest. "None but my overseer and his family. All the rest have gone, deserted to the English. The last ones went yesterday. Now I ask you, what am I to do?"

Juan shook his head sympathetically. "These are hard times. With the overseer and your sons you can grow enough to eat, at least. Perhaps your workers will return. Let us pray that next year will be better."

"Next year? I will be ruined by next year. I need workers, Father." He paused, watching the priest. "You have workers."

Juan broke away from his gaze and looked down at his bony hands, smoothing the blanket over his legs. "Ask them," he said. "You are free to ask them. If any want to go with you, they are free to do so."

"But we both know how that would be," said Velasco, a hard edge on his voice. "They would never come willingly." He turned and walked to the window and looked out. "You must tell them to come."

"You know I cannot do that," said Juan. "They are the Christian flock of the Church of San Lorenzo. Their labor cannot be forced from them. They cannot be enslaved."

Velasco turned abruptly to him. "And what do you call it when you are working them in your fields? Your overseer carries a whip the same as mine."

"They are working for themselves and for God. They must eat, they must tithe. No one forced them to come here to live. No one forced them to be baptized."

"But you force them to work here, do not deny it. They grow far more for you than they eat. They eat the tenth part and tithe all the rest, and you sell it for your own profit at the port."

"They do not tithe so much as that, and I do not sell our produce for profit." Juan struggled to contain his anger. "I use it to buy the things I need for the mission. The candles and the wine. Spain does not send me half enough, and it never comes on time. Two years, three years late. I have to manage as I can."

"Candles and wine," scoffed Velasco. "What about the silver, Father? You handed over a fortune to that Englishman, paid for by the sweat of your dark-skinned Christians."

Juan looked sharply at him. "My people work for the mission that gives them life."

Velasco turned away to the window again. "I need laborers for my fields. Twenty-five or thirty laborers. I need them soon, this week, before it is too late to plant."

Juan stared at Velasco's back, wondering how he could be so bold in his demands. "I cannot force them give their labor to a private citizen. The king's law protects them."

"By that law I'll starve to death come winter. Is that what the king intends?"

"You're not asking to keep away starvation. Not with thirty workers. You're asking for a surplus of your own to trade at the port. I am sorry, Don Gaspar. The Church has no obligation to turn you a profit."

Velasco turned and looked coldly at him. "Who are you to speak for the Church? You with an Indian whore in your bed? Here you sit holding sway over this empire of yours. But what if the father superior in San Augustín were informed of your indiscretions with this woman? What if he were informed in a written complaint that could not be ignored? Then it would all come down for you, wouldn't it, Father Juan de Villalva? It would all be over."

Juan glared at the rancher with blazing anger, a surge of heat rising from his chest to his face. His thoughts were with Ana listening in the front room, and he wanted to hurt this man, to pick up the bench and knock him senseless, to kick him until his face bled, until his teeth were in his throat. His breath came quickly, and he could not find words to speak. He was almost in tears with the helplessness of his rage.

Velasco looked away. "I will settle for twenty workers if they are young and healthy. At least half should be males." He looked back squarely at the priest. "Are we in agreement, Father?"

Juan stared at Velasco as if to absorb his essence into his heart to hold there and hate. Then he nodded and leaned back against his pillows, closing his eyes.

Velasco made a move to leave in the same direction by which he had come. Juan opened his eyes. "Do not go that way," he said, his voice low and tight. "I do not want your feet to touch the holy churchyard of San Lorenzo." He pointed to the back door. "Go that way."

Don Gaspar bowed slightly and turned and went as the priest directed.

"Do not return to this house," said Juan, his teeth clenched against his fury. "Do not let my Ana see your devil face again. If you do, I'll kill you and end my life on the gallows. I swear by the Holy Virgin."

Velasco went out without replying, closing the door firmly behind him.

Juan lay quietly and listened to the footsteps fading away and to the silence of Ana in the other room. He lay in his own silence and waited, hating Velasco with a fury he had never known before. He heard Ana come quietly to stand in the doorway, but he could not make himself look at her. He had lacked the courage to defend her. She might be his mistress, but she was no whore. He could have said that much.

She came in and sat down on the bed with her back to him, and for a time she was still. Then she said in her own language, "In the way of my people there is nothing wrong with our life together. In the way of my mother and my grandmother, you are my husband and I am your wife. And that is how it seems to me to be. But in the Christian way, I am a whore and you are a fallen priest. I sometimes wonder why we choose to be Christians."

Juan reached for her and pulled her down beside him. "You are no whore," he said softly. "You are my wife before God. I should have told him that. But I have no courage, Ana. I have strayed too far from God. I am a fallen priest, but not because of you. It is because of everything else I have done. My soul is lost, but yours must not be. Cling to the Holy Mother. Stay close to her and she will show you the way to heaven."

"Do not say that your soul is lost," said Ana, turning to look into his face. "I do not want to go to heaven without you."

He smiled at her. "You'll not miss me. You'll have the Blessed Savior and all the saints."

"But you must come with me."

He shook his head, no longer smiling. "To save my soul I would have to stand up to that devil Velasco. I would have to report my own offenses to the father superior, confess and repent my life with you, resign my post, leave you behind, and spend the rest of my days praying in a monastery. I do not intend to do any of that. I'll cling to what I have for as long as I can hold it, and I'll thank God for every day He gives me."

"Then we should not be Christians anymore," said Ana. "In the Apalachee way, there is nothing wrong with you. In the Apalachee way, we can both go to the Other World together."

"Now you frighten me," said Juan, tightening his arms about her. "You must not lose your soul. When I think of what my life has been good for, I can only think that I led you and a few others to Christ. You must never turn away from him, not even when I'm gone." There was silence. "Do you hear me, Ana?"

"Yes," she said softly. "I hear you."

✳ It was a warm night. Lucia sat with Isabel and Ana and Maria near the fire in front of their house by the convento. They should have been glad to look up and see the stars and listen to the spring frogs peep-peeping in the darkness. It was always good, these first nights out, free from winter's smoky closeness and too early yet for the misery of summer's mosquitoes. But tonight there was no laughter, no idle talk, only silence. Lucia, sitting with her arms clasped about her legs, watched the stars glumly. Ana stirred softly and added more wood to the fire and then was still again. And the silence went on.

At last Isabel spoke. "What if Lucia and Maria simply refuse? Why should they go and be slaves for Don Gaspar? That man is a devil."

"We have to go," Lucia said grimly. "It does no good to talk about it. Father Juan told Lorenzo to pick twenty workers, and we were chosen."

Ana nodded. "They have to go."

"There is a law against it," Isabel said stubbornly. "The Spaniards have laws for everything, but they forget them whenever it suits them."

No one answered and there was silence again.

"What if they just do not go?" Isabel repeated.

Maria looked up. "If we do not agree to go, then we must leave this place. We cannot stay here anymore. That is what we have been told."

"They will throw us to the slave-catchers," said Lucia, and she picked up a twig and tossed it into the fire.

"Father Juan would not turn you out of here," said Isabel.

"Lorenzo said that he would," Lucia said quietly. "He said he spoke for Father Juan. Father Juan has said nothing to contradict him."

Isabel shook her head. "I am afraid for you. You will be too far away, and there will be no one to help you. They can treat you as they please, like slaves."

"If it is very bad," said Maria, "I will run away to the English." She reached up and brushed a strand of hair from her face. "I will not be a slave."

"And you?" Isabel said to Lucia. "Would you run away, too?"

"I will not leave Apalachee."

Isabel nodded grimly. "You are the next White Sun Woman. If you leave, the Apalachee people will die."

Ana looked up at them, and for a moment it seemed she would scold

them for their heresy, but then she dropped her eyes and stared at the fire 75
again. Don Gaspar had made no secret of how he had pried the workers from the priest. Everyone knew it. And though no one blamed Ana for it, the weight of it lay heavily upon her.

"It is not right to make the White Sun Woman a slave," Isabel said morosely. "It is not right what the priest is doing."

Ana got up without looking at her and went into the house.

Lucia gave a sigh and looked across the fire at Isabel. Why was she so insistent? The lines in the old woman's face had deepened and her eyes had sunk back in dark sockets. She looked older than ever.

"There is the matter of the song," Isabel said quietly. "You are to sing it when I am dead. But if we are not together, you will not know if I die."

"I will not be gone forever," said Lucia. "One moon, that is all."

"You should sing it while you are away. We will both sing the song. Then we will be sure."

Lucia nodded. "If you think that is what we should do." She glanced at Maria and gave her a little smile. "Do not be surprised when you see me doing strange things." But Maria's seriousness made Lucia grow sober again. "Would you really run away to the English?" she asked.

"I might," said Maria. "One of my brothers left for the Creek country two winters ago. He tried to persuade me to go with him, but I was afraid. I wish now that my heart had been stronger."

"But to live in another land," said Isabel, shaking her head. "To be a stranger there."

"Could it be worse than this?" said Maria. She looked away from them into the fire.

"It can always be worse," said Isabel.

CHAPTER TEN

Never had they worked like this, not in all of Lucia's life, never under such a relentless driver nor with so much weariness and despair. Work in the mission fields had always been hard, but the discipline had been restrained by others above Lorenzo who would hear about it if he drove the workers with too much cruelty. The priest and the chief had a measure of concern for the people. But here there was no concern but for the land, for the planting to be done, for the time slipping away. The whip was the way of the overseer, and in the weeks since they had come to this place, Lucia had several times felt the sting of the lash.

The overseer was Pedro, a mestizo. His father was Don Gaspar himself, his mother an Apalachee house servant long dead. Pedro was merciless in his driving of the Indian workers, as if he hated that portion of his blood that had darkened his skin and forbade him access to the front entrance to Velasco's house. He used the whip as casually as others would speak. There was no looking up from work in his fields, no glancing behind to see how much had been done, nor ahead to see what remained, nor to the sky to see how long before the sun would go down and bring the day's work to a halt. There was no talking in his fields, no pausing to wipe the sweat from one's eyes. Twice during the day the workers were allowed to stop for a brief time, and only then could they eat whatever food they had, quickly chewing and swallowing and swilling down some water.

In the early mornings Don Gaspar would come riding out to survey their progress. Always he complained that the work went too slowly. He would sweep his arm impatiently at what remained to be done, and the extent of it kept growing. The more they did, the more he wanted from them, and they had only the assurance given them by the priest before they left Ivita-chuco that there would be an end to their labor—a month's work and they could return home again.

When Don Gaspar was in the field, he would walk his horse slowly in front of the line of workers, just out of reach of their hoes. His presence was unnerving, and they would work faster, fearing the whip. It began to be part of his routine to stop directly in front of Lucia and Maria, who always worked side by side, and he would wait there until their hoes came dangerously close to his horse before he would move on. At first Lucia would not look at him, but each day her eyes rose further—to his horse's knee, and then to its flank, to Don Gaspar's hands on his leather saddle, to his paunch hanging over his sweat-stained belt, to his chest rising and falling beneath his dirty homespun shirt. There seemed to be no punishment for looking up at him, no whip falling across her shoulders. So the day came when she glanced fully into his face, and she saw then that his eyes were on Maria, and only on Maria, moving slowly over her with vacant pleasure, with the suspension of thought that accompanies a man's desire.

In the evenings work went on until there was no more light by which to see. At Pedro's word, the workers would drop their hoes and stumble wearily over the rough ground to the cluster of ragged huts in which they lived. There was little food, nothing but corn, and they were too weary to pound it into meal for bread. They would crack it and boil it and eat it as a coarse gruel. And now, after two weeks, Lucia could feel her clothes sagging on her body from the slow starvation.

She sat down heavily beside Maria at one of the fires that had just been lit in the yard outside the huts. What if when their time was over, Don

Gaspar did not let them go? That question was always in her mind now.
What if this went on forever? She leaned back on one elbow, exhausted,
looking up at the stars that were brightening against the growing darkness
of the sky. The frogs droned loudly in the cane swamp by the nearby
stream. She closed her eyes. How could it have come to this? What could
she have done to have made a difference in her life? Perhaps if she had
believed Salvador's vision and gone with him to the Great Town. His camp
there was prospering, she had heard.

She drifted with the night sounds, almost sleeping, though she still heard
the murmuring voices of those gathered at the fire. At last she sat up and
ate the gruel that Maria had saved for her in a broken gourd cup.

Carlos was there, always among the ones who sat at this fire, though he
was a silent presence, seldom speaking at all. He had come of his own will
to work with them, the only one for whom there had been a choice. But
once he arrived here, all privilege was gone. Don Gaspar cared nothing for
the way Carlos was regarded in Ivitachuco, and the overseer cared even less.
Carlos was nothing to them but a laborer, and a prized one at that, for he
was big and strong, and they drove him hard, trying to make him set a
faster pace for all the others. He quickly lost that cheerfulness he had
brought to the drudgery of the mission fields, and he began to brood, growing ever more silent, avoiding contact with others. It was hard to remember
him now as the man who would be chief.

"Tomorrow is Sunday." A man named Antonio spoke, his voice dulled
by exhaustion. No one else cared enough to respond. They ate their gruel
slowly, making it last as long as possible. There was not enough of it to
satisfy their hunger.

"What of it?" Lucia said at last. "We work on Sunday. Have you forgotten that?" But she regretted the sarcasm in her voice. Antonio did not
deserve it.

"The last time was the only time," said Antonio. "Don Gaspar said we
would not have to work on Sundays anymore."

"Don Gaspar is a pig," said Maria, whose hatred was making her strong.
"He says anything. He lies. He is the devil's own pig."

"Was there anything said today about working tomorrow?" asked another woman. "Did you ask the overseer, Antonio?"

"Who can ask him anything?" grumbled Antonio. "A man who throws
a whip like that? You cannot say a word to him. But tomorrow is Sunday.
Someone should have asked." He glanced at Carlos, as if Carlos should have
been the one.

Carlos looked at him a moment, his mouth set tight. "Why have you
stayed in the mission, Antonio? Why have you not gone north to the
English?"

"I have a wife in Ivitachuco," Antonio said defensively. "She will not leave. And I have a sister there."

"Wives and sisters are left behind every day," said Carlos. "What stops a man from getting out? You could go to the woods. There are whole camps of deserters in the woods. We have all heard about them."

"I have told you," Antonio said sullenly. "Perhaps other men can leave their wives. Perhaps they care little for them. But I do not feel that way."

"Antonio is a good man," said one of the women. "Leave him alone."

Carlos nodded. "I meant nothing." He retreated back into silence, and that silence spread to all of them now, no one looking at anyone else, all of them staring dejectedly into the fire. Voices still came softly from the other fires, but there was no laughter in the camp.

Then from the darkness came the sound of footsteps. Lucia turned to listen, glancing about to see if anyone else was hearing it. Carlos and Antonio were also listening. Soon the others caught the sound, their bodies tensing as they turned and looked toward it. Antonio put out his hand for silence, though there was no need. In the stillness the footsteps could now be plainly heard. They were strong and deliberate and came from the direction of Velasco's house.

"Pedro," Antonio said softly. "He comes to tell us there is no work tomorrow."

Lucia watched the darkness until she could see the dark form of a man in the starlight. Antonio was right. It was the overseer. Her spirits lifted and she began to think of a morning spent sleeping, of an afternoon for pounding corn and making bread and catching fish in the stream.

Pedro stepped into the firelight, loosening the lash of his whip so that it fell to the earth and trailed behind him in the dirt. Approaching the fire nearest the one at which Lucia sat, he walked slowly around it, peering down at the faces of the people there. She began to grow uneasy. The camp was in complete silence, everyone waiting, the drone of frogs loud in the darkness.

Still without speaking, Pedro turned away from that fire and came to this one, and here, too, he walked around, looking at the people who were there. No one looked up at him. He stopped, the tail of the whip lying still in the dust behind him. "Don Gaspar wants to see you," he said quietly.

Lucia raised her eyes and saw him standing above Carlos on the far side of the fire. But it was Maria to whom he was speaking, looking down at her across the flames. She had not looked up and did not know she was the one. Carlos made a move to rise, but the overseer shoved roughly at his shoulder, and Carlos settled back and waited.

"You," Pedro said in a louder voice. "I am talking to you."

Now Maria looked up. When she saw she was the one to whom he was
speaking, her face went blank with shock.

"What is your name?" Pedro demanded. "Don Gaspar wants to know."

Maria dropped her eyes. Her knuckles were white as she clasped her
hands together in her lap.

"Someone tell me," said Pedro, looking at the others. "What is her
name?" No one would look at him now. No one spoke.

He looked down at Carlos and kicked his leg. "Tell me, goddamn you."

"Maria." It was Maria herself who spoke, and her voice was strong. She
was staring straight ahead, her face hard.

"Good," said Pedro. "You are a smart girl. Now come along with me.
You will like Don Gaspar. You will see."

Carlos rose suddenly to his feet, and Pedro stepped back, changing his
whip to his left hand and drawing a long-bladed knife with his right. Carlos
opened his hands and held them out. "I have no weapon," he said. "We
will talk about this like men in council. There is no need to fight."

Pedro smiled. "Men in council? Where do you think you are? Gaspar
Velasco is the council here. The girl comes with me, or tomorrow she gets
the whip. Will you earn her a beating? I think she would rather come with
me than have you bring it to that."

Carlos glared at him. Lucia could see that he was weighing it, thinking it
all the way through. And as she watched his face, she saw defeat stealing in
at the edges. She put out a steadying hand to Maria, gripping her leg. Maria
put her own hand on Lucia's and pressed it, then rose to her feet.

Carlos looked over at Maria, shaking his head to tell her to stay where
she was, but she paid no attention to him. Her face was hard and deter-
mined, not sorrowful like the night she had come to them after her escape
from Ayubale.

Looking again at Pedro, Carlos said, "The priest will not allow this.
He will call the workers home if he hears of it. And we will see that he
hears of it."

Pedro shrugged. "Don Gaspar is not afraid of the priest."

Carlos' anger was rising. Lucia was afraid of what he might do. But then
Maria moved away from the fire and began walking into the darkness in
the direction from which Pedro had come—toward Velasco's house.

"Maria!" Carlos said sharply.

Pedro started after her.

"Come back here, Maria!" Carlos' voice was stern and commanding, as
if he still were the man who would be chief.

She looked back at him, though in the darkness they could not see her
face. "There is nothing you can do," she said in a hard voice. "Do not

make it worse for me." Then she turned away and walked with Pedro into the night.

The camp was completely still. No one spoke or even moved. When Maria was out of sight, Lucia rose to her feet and walked through the silence to the tiny hut where she and Maria lived crowded together with five other women. It was empty now. She made her way through the darkness to her cane mat on the floor, dropped to her knees and then lay back, crossing her arms over her face. She moaned softly.

Someone else came in and she thought at first it was one of the other women. But the footsteps were not those of a woman. She looked up in the darkness and saw Carlos standing over her, tall like a tree, as she had seen him once before, by the carts in the stockade on the night when Maria first came. She sat up, but said nothing.

"What could I have done?" he said. His voice was low and tight with despair, and it drifted down to her from his great height as if from the sky itself. She shook her head. She could feel his helplessness and did not know how to respond. Tears sprang into her eyes, and she pressed her hand against them, not wanting to cry in front of him.

"I know you care for her," she said softly. "You would have stopped it if there had been a way. But we are slaves here. All of us." She could not hold back the tears. She turned away from him. "Leave me now," she whispered. "Please leave me alone."

She did not hear him go, but she knew she was alone again. Weeping, she lay back down in the darkness. After a while the other women came in softly and went to their beds without speaking.

Lucia lay awake into the night, waiting for Maria to return. Once she slept and then awoke with a start and reached out in the darkness and found Maria's mat still empty. She did not sleep again after that. When dawn came at last through the open doorway of the hut, Maria still was not there.

✷ Don Gaspar came as usual to the field at mid-morning. The sun was hot, almost like a summer day. A pale yellow butterfly fluttered for a moment above Lucia's hoe and then flew away as the legs of Don Gaspar's horse came into her narrow view. The rancher stopped in front of her, and she looked up boldly and saw the displeasure on his face as he looked at the workers around her.

"Where is she?" he asked irritably. "What does she think? That she does not have to work anymore? I never told her that."

Lucia looked at him closely, considering his words. "She did not come back to us," she said. "We thought she was still with you."

"What are you saying? I sent her back to the camp. Is she going to hide from me now? Tell her I won't have it. I will make her pay, and you with her. Tell her that her friend will be the first to feel the whip. If she hides, I will take it off your back, do you hear?"

Lucia straightened herself and looked directly at him. "You are mistaken, Don Gaspar. She never came back last night. If she is not with you, then she has run away. You can beat me until I am dead and nothing will change. I do not know where she is."

"Run away?" Don Gaspar sat back in his saddle. The other workers had moved on ahead, leaving Don Gaspar and Lucia on a little strip of unturned earth. "Where would she go? Back to the mission? I will send my man tonight to bring her back."

"And if she is with the priest?" Lucia spoke without considering her impudence, that she was the slave, he the master. He glared down at her, turning his riding whip in his hand. But then he smiled and shrugged, mellowed, perhaps, by his night of pleasure.

"What would the priest want with her?" he said with a chuckle, reaching down with his whip and prodding Lucia's stomach, as if to force her to share his joke. "Tell me that? What would he want with her? He already has a woman of his own!" He laughed and turned his horse and started off across the field. "We will bring her back," he said over his shoulder. "You'll see. My man will bring her back tonight."

✹ Pedro left at nightfall, when the workday was finished, and took the road to Ivitachuco as Velasco had instructed him. As soon as he was out of sight, Carlos also set out, staying off the road until he was well past the overseer, and then, with the firmness of the trodden road beneath his feet, he hurried on through the night toward the mission town, running as much as he could, but more often walking, for Velasco's driving work had worn away his strength.

It was near midnight when he reached Ivitachuco, and the convento was dark. As he stood before the door and waited for an answer to his loud knocking, he looked about the town and felt oddly displaced, as if he were a stranger here. The priest himself answered the door, a candle in his hand, his face sleepy and haggard, his ungirded robe hanging loose.

"I didn't know who it could be," the priest said as he stepped back and let Carlos inside. "I could not think of anyone ill enough to call for confession. That is usually what it is in the middle of the night." He spoke easily, as if Carlos had just come from his old room in the back of the convento.

Glancing toward the darkness of the priest's chamber, Carlos wondered if Ana were lying there in the silence. Father Juan put the candle on the table and motioned for him to sit down.

"I am not the only visitor you will have tonight," Carlos said as he seated himself on the edge of the chair, the priest taking the chair on the opposite side of the table. "Is Maria with Isabel?"

Father Juan drew back his head and gave him a puzzled look. "Maria? The one from Ayubale? She went with the others to Velasco's ranch." And then, as if only now remembering that Carlos had gone there, too, he added, "She went with you."

"She has run away," said Carlos. As he told the story, Father Juan sat motionless, staring off into the darkness beyond the candlelight. His lips stiffened with anger, and for several moments after Carlos had finished, he did not speak. Then his old resignation returned.

"I am glad she escaped," he said quietly. "But she never came here. I have no idea where she could be."

Carlos watched him in silence, wondering himself where Maria could be if not here. A long night's journey for nothing. And tomorrow he must work the same as if he had slept. The priest would not act. He was sick and weak.

"I must go back, then," said Carlos. "When Velasco's man comes, do not tell him I was here. It will go easier for me if he does not know."

The priest looked up. "Are you afraid of him? That is not good, Carlos. I wish you would not go back. I did not bring you up to grovel at the foot of some scum of an Indian overseer."

"Pedro is half Spanish," Carlos said tightly. "Does that make it more tolerable?"

The priest shook his head. "You twist my meaning. I have prepared you to be the leader of your people, a nobleman above the common sort. But if you keep on as you are, it will all be undone. Do you think a nobleman of Spain would ever lower himself to live like a common laborer? I don't know what you are thinking. It baffles me. But you must not go back there."

Carlos looked hard at him. "Bring home the others and I will stay. Velasco is working us like slaves, and whoring on our women besides. Who will be next for him? Lucia?"

The priest looked down, and in the silence Carlos heard a soft rustling in the back room. He was sure that Ana was there.

"It is almost over," the priest said quietly. "Two more weeks. I told him he could have them for a month."

Carlos rose to his feet. "When the time is over, you will have to come yourself and make him let us go."

"When the time is over, all you have to do is leave. What can he do to stop you?"

"It is not what he can do to us, but what he can do to you. Has that not been the issue all along?"

The priest shook his head. "We have a bargain, he and I. If he breaks his part, I will break mine. I will have him sent to the galleys for forcing labor from Christian Indians."

"Do they really punish men for that?" Carlos asked cynically.

"It is the law."

"And who will come to Apalachee to enforce it?"

"I have four soldiers at the stockade."

"They are more loyal to Don Gaspar than to you."

The priest rose to his feet. "I will call on Manuel Solana for help, if it comes to that. Tell our people that when the time is over, they must leave Velasco, no matter what he says. And when you have told them that, Carlos, you yourself must come back home. I never meant for you to be a slave."

"I will come home when the others come." Carlos felt the distance between them, wider now than ever. "It is as you said, only two more weeks. Almost over." He turned and started for the door.

The sound of movement in the back room grew more distinct, and then Ana called out his name. He turned and saw her standing against the darkness, barefooted, in a rumpled homespun shift with the priest's blanket about her shoulders.

"Is Velasco giving you enough to eat?" she asked simply.

Carlos shook his head. "He gives us corn, but not enough of it."

"Come with me then. We have meat in the cocina." She disappeared again.

Carlos hesitated. He could hear her going out through the back.

"Go on," said the priest, motioning for him to follow her. "Lorenzo slaughtered a cow on Saturday. Take as much as you can carry."

Carlos went into the darkness of the back room, past the empty bed, musty-smelling, out through the back door and across the moonlit yard to the cocina. Inside the small, low building Ana was raking back the ashes in the hearth, exposing buried coals which reddened in the air. She added a knot of pine, and in the dim glow of the coals she and Carlos watched the black smoke come swirling up until it was in their nostrils, pleasantly pungent. Ana blew gently and a flame came up, consuming the smoke and lighting the room with its low, flickering light. Turning to Isabel's copper kettle, she silently fished out large pieces of boiled meat and placed them in

Lucia sat back, and for a moment she watched the sun in the trees and listened to the crows flying over the fields, calling out their impatience for the corn to be planted. Then she rose and turned to start back.

Someone was in the cane!

She stepped back, shock going all the way through her, even as she saw who it was, only Carlos standing there. She put her hand against her heart, as if that would stop the pounding.

"Mother of God," she said weakly in Spanish. Then in Apalachee she said, "You should have made some noise. I thought you were a slave-catcher."

"I did not mean to frighten you," he said. "I followed you when I saw you coming in here. I thought you would want to know what I learned."

"Did you find her?"

He shook his head. "She did not go to Ivitachuco. No one there has seen her."

"Then where could she be?"

"Ana thinks she has gone north to the English."

"I have wondered about that. Perhaps she has." Lucia shook her head and looked back into the water. "I hope she can make it." Her eyes followed some white blossoms that were floating on the surface of the stream, a sign of good fortune—for Maria, perhaps. "My heart is on the ground," she said sadly. "She was becoming a sister to me, the only one I have ever had. I was all alone growing up on my mother's homestead." She closed her lips tightly, feeling foolish for speaking so intimately. In the silence the canes rustled in the breeze and the water murmured softly on its slow journey. A crayfish darted from the reedy shallows into the middle of the stream, disappearing in the waters' depths.

"You called the Sun your mother," Carlos said quietly. "Our people say she is their grandmother, but you spoke to her as mother."

Lucia turned and looked at him. At another time she would have been angry at him for spying, but Carlos had changed. He was not the same as before. "I am the daughter of the Sun," she said softly. "Or I will be when Isabel is gone. She is the White Sun Woman, and so will I be after her." She smiled and shrugged. "It is the old way. I did not choose it for myself."

"What about Don Patricio," said Carlos. "Why is he not the White Sun?"

"He is a little White Sun," said Lucia. "The Hinachubas turned away from the true line of the great White Suns after the Spaniards arrived. The only heirs left in that line were women. It seemed better to have a strong man as chief. Our line did not resist."

Carlos cocked his head and looked at her. "And if they had stayed with the first line, you would be the great White Sun Woman of Apalachee?"

"Isabel would be."

"And then you?" He smiled, as if he were genuinely pleased. "Of all the women in Apalachee, you are the one?"

Lucia turned away from him, embarrassed. She watched the stream again. "It does not mean anything. A song to sing in the morning, that is all."

"But in the old days, think of it." He came across the grass and stood beside her, and he, too, looked into the water. "Think what your life would have been if the Spaniards had never come."

"I think of it all the time," she said quietly. "Not to be the White Sun Woman, but just to be a woman who is free. To have a homestead like my mother's. You do not know. You have always lived in the mission."

"There are too many things I do not know. I can read and write and explain church doctrine. I could go to San Augustín if the occasion arose and impress the governor with my conversation. But I have never gone to water, and I have only the dimmest notion of what it means. I watched you a few moments ago and wished I had your knowledge. The priest kept it all from me. He wanted me to be a Spaniard in an Indian's skin."

"But you will be chief someday. Who is there in the town who would not trade places with you?"

"You would not."

She smiled. "How do you know that?"

"I have been watching you."

"Yes, like the cougar watches the deer. Every time I turn around you are there."

He made no response, and she regretted having said it. It was not as if she really minded that he was always there, sitting at her fire or working near her in the field.

"If you were not who you are," she said quietly, "if you were not the one who is going to be chief, would you stay here? In the mission, I mean? Or would you go to the English? They say life is better in the Creek trading towns. No one forces work from the people who live there. No slave-catchers snatch them away."

"Because they *are* the slave-catchers."

"But would you go there? If you were not who you are?"

He turned and looked at her. "Why do you ask me this?"

She shrugged. "I was only wondering what you might do. You are changing. You are not the same anymore. I heard you ask Antonio why he did not go north." She reached up and pushed a strand of hair from her face. "Maybe you could find Maria there."

He looked away from her into the stream. "Perhaps we could find her together," he said. "Would you go with me if I went?"

She looked to see if he were teasing her, but his face was grave. She shook her head. "I would not leave Apalachee. I cannot. I am the next White Sun Woman."

"You mean that."

It was not a question, and so she made no answer. But for a moment she looked at him, seeing him differently than she ever had before. He had asked her to go with him, and though she had brushed it aside so quickly, it stayed with her and warmed her. "We should go back," she said. "If we are late for the field, there will be trouble." She turned and started away, but he reached out and took her arm to stop her.

"What about Salvador?" he said, a strange urgency in his voice. "Why did you not go with him? He never left Apalachee."

"My grandmother would not go." She looked down at her arm and he released it. "She did not trust the dream that sent him there. She was afraid of the danger."

"But they say he is doing well."

She smiled. "You hear those things, too?"

"I hear people talking. They say he is somewhere to the north of here."

"He said he was going to a lake near the ancient Great Town. His dream told him that was the place."

"But Isabel said the dream was no good?"

"It came from the Under World. The Water Cougar brought it. With the Under World, you never know. There is power there, but danger as well. It is not like a dream from the Upper World. You can never be sure."

"You seem to understand the pagan way," said Carlos, still a bit skeptical, but with a growing respect in his voice.

"It is not so difficult."

"I will come tomorrow," he said. "I want you to explain some of these things to me. I want to know about going to water."

She looked at him and saw that he was serious. "It is not as if you can just come and watch me do it. There are ways of learning. You must fast and prepare yourself."

"Fasting is no problem. We are all fasting at this place."

"But you must do it properly. No food until just after sundown. No salt. No meat."

He smiled ruefully. "I have just brought us meat. A basketful. Ana sent it."

"Meat!" She put her hands to her stomach. "Then you should eat. We are all starving here. You can start your fast when the meat is gone."

"I ate a little of it on the way. That is enough. My fast starts now. And how long must it last? Four days?"

She smiled at him. "You do know a little."

"Every Spaniard in Apalachee knows as much. Four is the pagan number."

"That is what they say," she said. "Four will take you to hell, but three will take you to heaven—Father, Son, and Holy Ghost. Come on now, or it will go badly for us. I am afraid we have been here too long." She turned and started away, and this time he followed after her, the cane rustling softly as they passed.

☀ It was the last day of their month of labor in Velasco's field, and Carlos felt the tension as dusk settled over the workers. They were all on edge as they planted and covered the seeds. Their bodies did not sag so wearily as on previous evenings. Yet the overseer seemed oblivious to it all as he strolled among them with his whip. The field they were working had been turned and smoothed, but only a little more than half of it had yet been planted with seed.

The dusk deepened. They could no longer see the seeds they were planting, but still they worked steadily on and waited. Then at last Pedro gave the signal to stop. Those with hoes let them fall to the ground, and those wearing seed bags slipped them from their shoulders and set them down. For a moment they looked at each other uncertainly.

"Let us go," said Carlos, and he began leading them away, not toward the huts of their camp but toward the path that led home to Ivitachuco.

"Where are you going?" demanded Pedro in surprise. When no one turned to heed him, he came striding after them. "Where are you going?"

Carlos stopped, motioning to the others to keep on their way. "We are going home," he said to Pedro. "We have finished here."

"Finished? What are you talking about? Look at all that is left to be planted!" He pointed with his coiled whip to the field.

"You will have to plant it yourself. Let Don Gaspar come help you." Carlos turned and started away.

"Tell them to come back," Pedro commanded, following along behind him. "Don Gaspar will come to the camp and talk with them."

"Let him come to Ivitachuco. He can talk to the priest."

"Call them back, you son of a whore!" Pedro's voice rose in anger. "That field is not planted, goddamn you!"

Carlos heard the sound of the whip and turned, trying to leap away, too late as the lash struck his legs and wrapped tightly around them. But before the overseer could follow through and pull him to the ground, Carlos grabbed the whip and jerked it from his hands. He disentangled his legs and brandished the whip at Pedro, who promptly retreated to a safe distance. Then Carlos strode away to join the others, Pedro standing still and watching him go.

When they were almost out of sight, Carlos looked back, barely able to make out the overseer's form in the gathering darkness. "Señor!" he called. "Here is your whip!" And he hurled it away as far as he could into a dark field of weeds.

CHAPTER ELEVEN

As he walked among the people in the meadow by the town, Father Juan felt strengthened by the night's festivities, by the laughter and the dancing and the plentitude of summer. It was the Feast of Saints John and Peter, and his Indians were celebrating with as much joy and revelry as he had ever seen among Spaniards in the streets of Seville. It was good to be up from his bed. He felt better than he had in months. Perhaps good health was returning at last.

He stood and watched the dancing, the women shuffle-stepping in their circle around the fire, themselves encircled by the men, who were led by a dancer in a bear mask. The unpleasantness of the spring had passed without lasting damage. The workers had returned sullen from Velasco's ranch, but he had shortened the workday in the mission fields to make it up to them, and everything soon settled down again. There still were too few people in the mission, but he hoped that the deserters would eventually return. Only Carlos remained a pain in his heart. He had changed and Juan did not know him anymore. Why was he keeping to himself and refusing to attend Mass? He would not even come to the convento when bidden. The only hopeful thing about him was that he did not desert, and so perhaps with time he would come around. Juan would certainly take him back, there was no question of that. Carlos was still his best hope for the future.

The priest moved to the table where the feast was laid. Half the food had already been consumed, but still there was enough to last through the night and into the following day. He picked at the roast pig and dipped a piece of it into a dish of peach sauce and ate it contentedly, licking his fingers and searching the table for another treat. A distant shout went up from the stockade announcing a rider on the road. Someone coming late to the festival, thought Juan, and he picked up an ear of corn, sweet from the fields.

Before long, Don Patricio appeared at his side.

"Look at this feast," Juan said to him proudly. "Who would know the setbacks this mission has seen? Our Lady watches over us even in adversity. What more proof would a pagan need to turn his eyes to God?"

"We have new trouble," the chief said gravely.

Juan's ebullience began to fade. "Don't tell me unless it is important," he said. "Save it for tomorrow."

"Forgive me, Father, but it cannot wait. Solana has sent word from San Luís. The enemy has returned. They have destroyed the missions at Patale and Aspalaga. Solana is going out with his forces to meet them at Patale to keep them back from the ranches at San Luís. He sends for me to come immediately with my warriors. The four soldiers from the stockade are to come as well."

Juan put down the ear of corn in his hand, feeling no surprise, no sudden panic. It was as if he had known this all along.

"So the missions at Patale and Aspalaga are gone," he said. "We are the only ones left. This place and San Luís."

"I will call my men together," said Don Patricio. "We will leave at once."

"I will come with you," said Juan, wiping his hands on his robe.

"No, you must not, Father," said Don Patricio. "You are not well enough."

"Who are you to say if I am well?" snapped Juan. "Call out your men. And have Lorenzo saddle me a horse."

Don Patricio bowed his head. "Yes, Father."

✳ "You foolish man," Ana said angrily, pushing Juan roughly from the door. "You should be in bed, and here you say you go to war. What craziness is this?"

"Don't push me, Ana!" Juan said fiercely, grabbing her hard by her wrist. "I'll do what I must."

Tears came into her eyes and she pulled at her arm until he released her.

"You do not know the terrible way you look," she said, fighting back the tears. "You do not know you are so thin, so black around your eyes. You cannot walk nine leagues to Patale. How are you thinking? I do not understand you."

"I'm not going to walk. I'll ride a horse." He stopped to let the anger go out of his voice. Then he said, "I must go. This is our last chance, our last battle against the pagans. I feel good tonight, Ana. My health is good. I believe the Holy Mother has raised me up to give me this final opportunity to do what is right. I want to give strength to my warriors. I want to inspire them with courage and urge them on in the fight, maybe even bring them to victory. God grants miracles to men of faith. Yes, He does. And these men of mine, these loyal ones, they may be few in number but their faith is stronger than any army we've ever mustered from this place. They've stayed with us because they love God. The least I can do is go with them to fight in His holy war."

Ana looked at him, and for a time she said nothing. Her eyes moved slowly across his face and down his thin body beneath the brown robe. Moving to him, she dropped to her knees and took his hand in both of hers and kissed it. He reached out with his other hand and caressed her hair.

"God casts us down and raises us up again," he said softly. "Blessed be His name."

❋ Lucia was sleeping when Isabel came with the news. The enemy had returned to Apalachee; the warriors from Ivitachuco were going out to fight; and Carlos was outside, asking to see her. She sat up, her hand against the dull menstrual pain in her body.

"He is going to war?" Sleep was clearing from her mind, but still she felt confused. When she had gone to bed, the town was feasting and dancing, she keeping to herself because her menstruating condition made her dangerous to others, especially to men. And now while she was sleeping, war had come.

"I cannot see him. Tell him I am in my menses. I would spoil his power. Tell him . . ." She stared into the darkness. Tell him what? That she was afraid for him? That she did not want him to go? Who was she to say any of those things? Especially like this, through Isabel. She looked at her grandmother and could only see the faintest outline of her in the darkness. "I wish that I could speak to him," she said quietly. "But I cannot. Tell him I wish him well."

"Perhaps I should tell him you will fast for him," said Isabel.

Lucia lay back on her bed. "Yes. You can tell him that." She turned on her side and watched as Isabel left. Then she heard her grandmother's voice outside and the voice of Carlos coming softly in reply. She pulled up her knees against the menstrual pain. He was going to war, then. He would not go to Mass for the priest, but he would go to war for him. Though what else could he do? He could never be chief if he refused to join the men in war. That would seal it. He might as well desert then, go north and find Maria.

She closed her eyes, wishing to call out to him, to say something to him, anything, and hear him answer. But there was silence now and she knew that he was gone. She opened her eyes and stared at the empty doorway. In a moment there was a glimmer of firelight there, and it grew brighter as Isabel appeared carrying a piece of burning pine that she had lit from the outside fire. She brought in some small wood with her and dropped the pieces onto the cold hearth and then thrust the burning pine into the midst of them.

"He is gone," the old woman said.

"I know." Lucia sat up to face the fire, folding her hands between her knees, her shoulders bent forward. She did not look at Isabel.

"It is surprising to me that he came," said Isabel, pulling a cane mat away from the heat of the fire and sitting down on it. The night was already too warm and the fire was only for light, as if Isabel had a special need to see Lucia's face as she spoke with her.

"He is a friend," said Lucia, staring into the flames. "At Don Gaspar's ranch he would come with me when I went to water in the mornings. He was trying to learn the old ways."

"And you told him things?"

"I taught him a little. The kinds of things that most people already know. He barely knew more than a child would."

"Have you lain together?"

Lucia looked at her. "No. It was not that way."

"And since you have come home from Don Gaspar's? Have you still been teaching him?"

Lucia looked down at her hands clamped between her knees. The fire was making her hot. She could feel perspiration on her face. "At Don Gaspar's there was a stream and I could get away to a hidden spot. But here when I go to water at the spring other women are there, so he does not come. I talk to him sometimes in the plaza or when we are working in the fields. But it is not serious talk."

"But now that he is going onto the war trail, he comes especially to speak to you. More seriously, I think."

Lucia shrugged. "We are friends. Since he moved out of the church, he does not have many friends. People are puzzled by him. They do not know what to say."

"He said to tell you not to be afraid."

Lucia rubbed a hand over her forehead, wiping away the perspiration. The menstrual pain was growing strong again and she rocked gently to ease it.

"He said he would come back," Isabel said quietly.

Lucia nodded, slowly rocking as she stared into the heat of the dying fire. The glowing embers fell in upon themselves, and the light faded back into darkness.

CHAPTER TWELVE

The priest rode beside Don Patricio at the head of fifty warriors, who moved on foot through the silence of the pre-dawn darkness. His body ached almost beyond endurance and he clung to the saddle with both hands, while Carlos walked before him leading the horse. Through the last part of the festival night, and through the next broiling day of summer heat, and now through another long night, they had marched continuously, stopping but a few times to rest. Juan closed his eyes and struggled with his breath. If only he could lie down. Anywhere. The hardest ground would be better than this horse. But the scouts had come back reporting contact with Solana and his men. The meeting place was close at hand.

Don Patricio turned off the road through the trees, and Carlos followed after him, leading Juan's horse behind. They came almost immediately to a large, open meadow. With the faintest light of dawn upon it, Juan could see on the farther side, in dark silhouette, a large congregation of men and horses. Their own two horses snorted, anxious to join the ones on the other side. Juan reached down for the reins, and Carlos gave them to him without a word and went back to join the other warriors. The priest straightened himself, endeavoring to look well and alert. A dark form he knew to be Solana strode out to meet them.

Solana greeted Don Patricio first and then looked toward the priest.

"Holy Mary," he murmured in surprise. "Can that be you, Father Juan?"

"I've come to fight," Juan said hoarsely. Then to his dismay a violent fit of coughing seized him and bent him in agony over the neck of his horse. Solana stepped close and steadied him with his hand, and Juan looked at him with wide and helpless eyes. When the coughing eased, Solana helped him dismount. The priest stood on trembling legs, holding the saddle while he struggled to catch his breath.

"You should never have come," Solana said sternly.

Juan shook his head. "Just let me rest. The journey tired me. I've not been on a horse in more than twenty years."

"This is a battleground. What do you mean coming here like this? You are a sick man."

"I'm here for the battle. God may do with me as He pleases."

Solana looked at him for a moment and then stared out into the dark meadow. The Indian men from Ivitachuco had joined the ones from San Luís, making perhaps two hundred altogether. They stood apart from the smaller cluster of Spaniards, who numbered no more than fifty. "I have a terrible feeling about this day," he said quietly. "I wish you had not come. I think it would please God if you would get on your horse and go on to San Luís."

Juan shook his head and held himself up. "I will stay right here," he said firmly, his strength slowly coming back to him. "Tell me what is happening? How many are against us? Is Moore leading them again?"

Solana shook his head. "There are no Englishmen this time. Only Creek pagans from the trading towns. And there are rebels with them, our own people who have gone over. We are not sure of their number, but my guess is that they are twice as strong as we are. Perhaps three times."

"And our people are willing to go against them?"

"They have come with me, have they not? If we catch the pagans by surprise, there is a chance for us." Solana glanced nervously at the eastern sky where the darkness was slowly giving way to light.

"The pagans are close by then?" said Juan, feeling strangely calm.

Solana nodded. "They are camped at Patale, only a quarter of a league from here. We will go on the road until we are almost there, then spread out to encircle them. Be sure that you keep behind the fighting. Do not forget what happened to Father Parga."

"I will never forget that," said Juan. He put a hand on Solana's shoulder to send him on his way. "Get on with your work now. I will take care of myself."

Turning from Solana, Juan took the reins of his horse and was about to move away when three warriors came over to Solana. One of them began to speak in Spanish. Juan paused to listen.

"We have been talking," the man said, sweeping his arm to the rest of the warriors on the other side of the meadow. "We have been remembering the other battles we have fought for you." He paused, as if giving Solana a chance to remember them, too. "No Spaniard has ever led us to victory against the English or their pagans. Always we are killed in your battles, ten of us for every one of you. So this time we say to you, if you want us to fight, you must go on foot as we go. You must die as we die. Leave your horses and fight beside us as brothers. Or else you will fight alone."

Solana looked hard at the three men, and the conflict was plain on his face: the doom of his men if they must fight on foot, the doom of Apalachee if the Indians refused to fight. But one was more certain than the other.

"We will all fight on foot, then, and God help us," he said. "Now let us get moving before daylight brings the enemy down upon our heads."

The Indians appeared satisfied and carried the word back to the others.

"Mother of God, I hate Indians," muttered Solana. He turned and looked grimly at Juan. "What kind of army do I have? It was a curse on me when the governor made me his deputy again. I should have taken the next ship to Spain, like the last deputy governor."

"You're a better man than he," said Juan. "Apalachee is safer in your hands."

"Apalachee is doomed," said Solana, and he turned and went back to his men.

Juan took his horse across the meadow and left it with the other ones that now were to be held back from the battle. Then he went over to join the ranks of the warriors. They were clothed only in breechcloths, the skin of their faces and bodies painted red and black for war. They had feathers and charms tied to the tufts of hair that grew long from the crowns of their heads, and many wore crucifixes around their necks. Some were armed with muskets, some with bows and arrows; all carried war clubs and scalping knives in their belts. Juan made his way among them and came at last to his own men from Ivitachuco.

"The Holy Mother is with you," he said to them softly. He glanced at Carlos, who looked away. "These pagans have come into our Christian land to destroy the law of God. They hate God and love the Devil. This is a holy war. If we die, we go to God, for we have died in defense of His holy law. Remember that this life on earth is nothing but sorrow compared to the joy of heaven. Fight with courage, my beloved sons. Do not be afraid to die. I am beside you. I go with you gladly to encourage you and to beseech God's mercy upon you."

"God is our shield and our victory," said Don Patricio. The older men, standing near the chief, murmured and nodded. But the younger men had their eyes averted, some looking down, some across the meadow, and as Juan's gaze swept over them, he began to be afraid. He looked around and saw Solana putting the Spaniards in order, all of them on foot as had been agreed. This was all the strength that Apalachee had left—fifty Spaniards reduced to foot soldiers and two hundred faltering Indians.

Solana gave the signal to move out, and the company of Spaniards led the way from the meadow through the trees toward the road. Juan walked behind them in the front rank of the Indians. He fingered his rosary, but he did not pray, for his thoughts were on things of this world, on the warm moist air of the summer dawn, on the silence with which so many men were moving, such silence that he could hear the soft snorting of the horses left behind in the meadow. Ahead the Spaniards in the vanguard reached the road and then stopped suddenly, the priest and the warriors stopping behind them without knowing why. There was a pause, a silence in which could be heard the waking song of a meadow lark.

Then a musket shot exploded, and another, and the Spaniards surged forward as if to battle, though there was hesitation and confusion. Juan pushed ahead and reached the front in time to see three Indian warriors—Creek pagans—running away down the road toward Patale. Two others lay dead on the road. An advance party—the pagans themselves were on the move.

Solana's voice rang out. "Pull back! Back to the meadow, you whoreson idiots!" He began shoving at his men and they turned and surged back toward the trees. "Prepare for battle! We fight from the meadow!" He looked at Juan, who stood unmoving in the road, trying to comprehend what was happening. "Move!" Solana shouted and waved his hand at him. Juan hurried before his wrath, and Solana came behind him. "God save me from this army of fools!" Solana muttered. "They attack against my orders and raise the alarm. The pagans will be on us like a thunderbolt, and I've nowhere to make a stand except this God-cursed meadow." He pushed past the priest and ran ahead to draw up the army for battle.

Juan made his way through the trees to the edge of the meadow and stopped there, wondering what to do. This place was no good for a battle, he could see that much, but the forest-lined road would have been even worse. The surprise was spoiled, the only chance they had, and now they were not attacking but defending. Juan felt useless and afraid. The meadow was all confusion, the Spaniards and the Indians milling together, some listening to Solana, some not. He looked beyond them to the horses and briefly considered going there and seizing one of them and riding away to safety. Closing his eyes, he tried to pray. *O merciful God, aid me in my weakness. O Holy Mother, raise me from my sins.*

Then from behind came a sound that made his flesh go cold. It was the running of many moccasined feet, thudding against the packed earth of the road, and then, even worse, a crashing of brush in the woods.

"The pagans!" he cried, running out into the meadow. "Fight! Fight! For the glory of God! For the Holy Mother!" The Spaniards surged forward at his cry and he turned and charged with them, his head suddenly clear and his body filled with life. "Fight, Christians! Fight for the kingdom of God! For the Blessed Savior!" He was ecstatic as he ran toward the pagans, who streamed now into the meadow with hellish whoops and cries. He felt as fleet as a deer, as if the wings of angels carried him along. "Fight! Fight!" His voice was drowned by the cracking of muskets, and he saw a dark hole open in the chest of a pagan, who staggered, ran further, and then fell. He looked around for the Christian Indians and saw them lagging, some running toward the battle, but others moving slowly or not at all, their attention not on the fighting at the front but on the woods around the meadow.

He ran back to them. "On, Christians!" He tried waving them forward. "Fight for Holy Mary! For your Christian homes!"

He looked again to the front and was aghast to see the Spaniards falling back.

A shout rang out: "They're in the woods!"

"Fight!" cried Juan. He ran forward and then turned and ran back toward the Indians.

"We're surrounded!" cried a Spaniard whose voice rose above the din. "God help us! They're in the woods!"

The Christian Indians stopped in their tracks. A few, and then more, and then nearly all of them turned and ran back toward the horses.

"Stop!" Juan cried hoarsely, running to catch them. "In the name of God, stand and fight!" He saw Solana also running after them, and he heard the bellow of his voice.

The pagans were breaking through the Spanish ranks. Juan grew more frantic, laying hands on a retreating Indian. But the man pulled free as easily as from the snag of a briar, and Juan gave up on the Indians and turned back to rally the Spaniards.

The soldiers were retreating, turning back to fight and then retreating some more, loading muskets as they went, spilling powder and dropping balls. The pagans closed in and the Spaniards began to cry out, some using their muskets as clubs, some slashing with swords, others turning from the fight altogether, trusting only to their heels.

Juan stood in his brown robe and watched as the fighting drew in upon him. He tried to call out brave words, but his voice was gone. The pagans were taking prisoners, dragging them screaming to the woods. Some of the Spaniards were running fast enough to escape. Others whirled in narrowing circles, slashing with their swords, swinging their muskets, crying to God for deliverance.

Then the sweep of the pagans closed the Spaniards from view and rushed on toward the priest. Helpless to save himself, he fell to his knees and closed his eyes. The noise of battle faded. His lips murmured the Our Father, and the presence of God seemed near.

Suddenly he was jerked to his feet by the cowl of his robe, his neck nearly breaking, and a musket exploded in his ear. As his eyes flew open, he saw the pagans scatter before him, one falling dead with his face shattered in a horror of blood. Then came a shove with a force that nearly knocked him from his feet, and he turned to see Solana shove him again, and then again until he was running as fast as Solana, who had now dropped his musket and drawn his sword, looking back as he fled with the priest toward the horses.

The horses were in chaos, the Christian Indians swarming around them, loosening them, seizing the ones they could hold. Some had already mounted and were riding away into the woods. Solana ran for a horse that was loose, brandishing his sword at an Indian who challenged him for it, a man Juan recognized as one of his own Christians from Ivitachuco. Ignoring Solana's threats, the Indian grabbed the horse's mane and was about to leap into the saddle when Solana slashed out with his sword, severing the man's hand, which fell lifeless to earth. The man staggered back, his face white, and Solana moved in to take the horse.

He turned to Juan. "Get on," he said brusquely.

The priest stepped back, shaking his head. His whole body was trembling. His flesh was cold. "No," he said, barely able to speak. "You take it. Save yourself."

"Get on!" Solana roared, grabbing him and shoving him to the horse, half lifting him into the saddle.

Juan could do nothing but take hold of the saddle and pull himself up, struggling all the while to untangle his legs from his robe. He was barely in the saddle, his feet still searching for the stirrups, when Solana shoved the reins into his hands and stepped back and struck the horse's rump with the flat of his sword. The horse bolted out of the clearing into the woods, and Juan ducked low against its neck. When he raised his head, he thought he saw Carlos ahead, disappearing among the trees. He ducked again to keep clear of the branches overhead. Behind him were the sounds of battle: cries of Spaniards being dragged into captivity, the victorious whoops of the pagans, and above it all the voice of Manuel Solana shouting out commands.

Behind him was his martyrdom. It all grew fainter as the horse plunged through the forest. Juan clung to the mane and let the reins hang loose, knowing the horse could find its own way back to San Luís far better than he could guide it.

CHAPTER THIRTEEN

Don Patricio returned to Ivitachuco with only a handful of men, Carlos not among them. Some said Carlos died in the battle. Some claimed to have seen him escape into the woods. But if Carlos escaped, he also deserted, for he did not seek refuge inside the fort at San Luís where Don Patricio regrouped his small force of survivors before finally bringing them home again, leaving behind the priest, who was too ill to travel. The Creeks had defeated the last army that Apalachee could muster, and the Spanish forces were confined now to their two strongholds: San Luís on the west and Ivita-chuco on the east. The land in between was the free range of Creeks and rebels, and it was only a matter of time before the last Spaniards would be forced from Apalachee, and their Indians with them.

Lucia heard the news as soon as the men arrived.

"What will we do?" she asked as she sat shelling beans with Isabel and Ana in the shade of the thatch-roofed portico before the door of their house.

"How can we say what we will do?" said Isabel. "We do not know what will happen."

"What *can* happen?" said Lucia. "There are only so many ways it can go."

"We will wait and see which one it is," Isabel said. "And then we will decide what to do."

"We should talk about it now," said Lucia. She looked to Ana, hoping for some help in the discussion, but Ana shook her head and looked down at the pod of beans she was shelling. She was lifeless and sad with the priest away. Lucia knew she feared she would never see him again.

"All I can think," Ana said quietly, "is to wait for Father Juan to come home."

"But what if when he comes," said Lucia, "all the others from San Luís are with him and they are abandoning Apalachee and going to San Augus-tín? Would we go with them? That is what we have to decide."

"No," Isabel said firmly. "I will not leave Apalachee."

"Only for a little time, my mother," Ana said to her. "We will come back when things are safe again." She looked at Lucia. "Yes, we will go."

Isabel shook her head. "Not I. I will always stay here in this land."

"How?" asked Lucia, picking up a bean pod and breaking off the end, drawing down the string to open it. "Would you go find Salvador?" With her thumb she raked the beans into the basket on her lap.

"No. That dream of his was a bad one. I would not go where the Water Cougar beckons."

"They say he has a regular town now," said Lucia. "A plaza and a council house. And more people there than are living here in Ivitachuco."

"That is not so many," said Isabel.

"How could you even think of going there?" said Ana. "They are rebels. They have turned against God. It is worse for them than if they had never been converted."

"Those are the priest's words," Isabel muttered, and Ana retreated back into her melancholy silence.

"Then what would you do?" Lucia asked Isabel. "Where would you go?"

The old woman dropped her hands into her lap in exasperation and looked at Lucia. "I do not know, my granddaughter. If I knew, I would tell you. When it is time to decide, I will decide. There has never been a time like this, and there is no way for us to know what to do until things happen that cause us to act. Today I will do my work. Tonight I will sleep. And if tomorrow comes, I will get up in the morning and sing another song to the Sun. Beyond that I do not know. Nor does Ana know. Nor do you. So let us have a little peace here, a little rest for our hearts while we shell these beans."

Lucia gave up and let the silence come, and with it the emptiness that was always with her now when she was still, for then her heart would go wandering through the dying town, searching dark, empty houses, scanning the plaza where children had once played and old men had sat placidly in the shade. And her heart would wander out through the fields, through the corn and the beans and the pumpkins and melons where only women and children were gathering the harvest. And out onto the path to the spring where again there were no men. And to the stockade where there were only Spaniards, too frightened to stay in their homes now that pagans and rebels moved freely through the land. And as her heart searched, the emptiness deepened, for Carlos was nowhere to be found. He was gone, and she could not put his memory behind her. At night he came into her dreams. And in the daylight, when her heart wearied of its search for him, she would find in fantasy what the world outside would not give her. . . .

All of it foolishness. He had never been her man. Lucia emptied her basket of beans into Ana's. "Look how many we have," she said. Anything to keep her mind from him. "Here, let us have yours, my grandmother." She reached for Isabel's basket and emptied that into Ana's as well. "Now," she said, "look at all of these beans."

"And look at all of these," said Isabel, taking up a double handful of unshelled pods from the pile that remained and handing them over to her.

Lucia took them and started to work again. "Tell us a story, my grandmother. Something to entertain us."

"What do you want to hear?" asked Isabel without enthusiasm.

"Something from the old days. Tell us about the White Sun Woman who saw the first Spaniards."

Isabel smiled and settled back a little. "That is a good story. I will tell you that one."

☀ It was twilight when Lucia got up and went into the house and found the water jar almost empty. She brought it outside, hoisting it onto her head to take it to the spring to fill it.

Ana, who was building up the fire in the yard, saw her come out and glanced anxiously at the dying sunset. "It is late," she said. "You should have gone earlier."

"It will be all right," said Lucia. "The slavecatchers are busy in other places. There has been no sign of them here for a long time."

"But if no one else is going to the spring, you should wait until morning."

"She is right," said Isabel from where she sat beside the house, her back against the cool plaster of the wall. "If no one is on the path, you should come back."

"I will," said Lucia. She left the yard and walked through the town with a long, hurried stride. Most of the yards were empty, the open doorways dark, the houses abandoned. She came to the place at the edge of town where the path led out across the field to the spring. The path was empty, no one going or coming. She hesitated, glancing up at the sky. There was time enough to make it to the spring and back before it was completely dark. But Isabel and Ana had made her say that she would not go out there alone. She felt she should keep her word to them.

As she turned to start back into the town, she saw a young boy emerge from the shadowed yard of a nearby empty house. This part of town suddenly seemed dangerous to her, the child vulnerable in the growing darkness.

"You should be home," she said as she approached him, her voice loud in the silence.

The boy stopped before her and peered up to see her face. She recognized him as Eugenio, the boy who had been ill in the fields on the day when Carlos had first come out to work.

"You are the one I am looking for," Eugenio said, and he seemed quite satisfied by that fact. "There is a man who wants you to come to the spring."

"A man?"

Eugenio nodded. "He told me to tell you to come when no other person is there."

"A man?" Lucia said again. "Do you know him?"

"It is Carlos," the boy said.

Lucia slipped the jar from her head and set it on the ground. "Carlos?" She looked hard at him to see if he were joking. "Where did you see him?" She clasped her elbows as if suddenly chilled.

"At the spring," Eugenio said impatiently.

"How did you see him there? Were you alone?"

"No. My mother and two of my aunts were by the water. I was playing. And he was there."

"Did they see him?"

"No. I was in that big magnolia tree. Do you know how the branches grow down near the ground?"

"I know," said Lucia, nodding. She turned her head and glanced out across the field. The treeline of the spring was dark against the sky, the evening star shining bright above it.

"He was on the other side of the magnolia tree. He motioned for me to be quiet and come over to him. We walked away a little and then he told me what to tell you. You and no one else." He drew himself taller. "You are the only one I have told."

Lucia smiled. "I believe you, Eugenio. I will tell Carlos how good you were, how you waited so late for me."

"I thought you were not going to come. I walked by your yard, but you were with Ana and your grandmother."

"You did very well," said Lucia, glancing again across the field. "Now run home. Your mother might be worried."

"I *know* she is," he said dramatically, looking up at the darkness of the falling night. He smiled broadly at Lucia, pleased at his conspiracy with her, and turned and ran back into the town.

Lucia stood for a moment and looked at the path stretching out into the darkness. More stars were appearing as the last traces of daylight faded. It was like one of her fantasies, as foolish as that, to walk out into the danger of the night and find him there waiting. Her chest tightened with fear — not of slavecatchers, but of meeting him. The palms of her hands were so damp that she rubbed them against her skirt. Lifting the water jar to her head, she looked behind to make sure she was alone, and then she walked out into the darkness.

The night was warm, the breezes soft against her face. The pulsing hum of the locusts seemed to come from another time, from earlier summer nights in the fields of her mother's homestead. Her feet moved easily along the path, which stretched before her in a faint ribbon of reflected starlight. Ahead, the treeline of the spring grew closer, and she hurried her step.

When she entered the trees, she paused for a moment, trying to see into this deeper darkness. The water jar still rested on her head, one arm raised to steady it. At last her eyes picked out the dull glimmer of the water and she moved slowly toward it.

"Carlos," she said softly, and the sound of her voice sent a sudden shiver of fright through her, as if all this might be a trick. She stopped, her blood rushing loudly in her ears.

"I am here." His voice came softly, almost lost in the roaring of her blood. But she saw him now, a dark form against the glimmer of the spring, and she did not move again, but stood and looked at him. As he came toward her, she did not take her eyes from him, knowing that in the darkness he could not see how she stared. He was beautiful to her in a way that hurt her throat. When he reached her, he put out his hands and took the jar from her head. It was a gentle, thoughtful act that made her fear drop away.

"I did not know if the boy would speak to you," he said quietly. "I was afraid he would tell his mother."

She smiled. "He said he told only me. He was proud to keep your secret." She heard him chuckle, though in the darkness she could see only the outline of his face. "I thought you had gone to the north," she said softly.

"No," he said, and in the silence that followed, a pain came into her breast, a fear that she was presuming too much, for in truth she did not know why he had come. She shifted her feet, moving back from him slightly, as if to adjust a mistaken closeness between them. Her eyes looked away, down into the darkness beyond him as she waited for him to speak. In the silence she reminded herself that he had never been her man.

"The battle was a disaster," he said at last. "You have heard what happened."

"Yes. A little."

"It was lost before it began. We could all see it. I do not know why we stayed in it as long as we did." There was another silence, and she did not try to fill it. He turned away from her slightly, as if he, too, wanted to make the distance greater. "It finished me with Spaniards. I asked myself, in the middle of the fighting, What am I doing with these people? We let them be masters over us in our own land and they give us nothing. Against our enemies they are useless. We can do better without them." He fell silent again, a silence that seemed to amplify the song of the tree frogs in the warm, humid night.

"No one knew what had happened to you," she said quietly.

He walked down to the edge of the spring. "I have been with Salvador at his new town," he said. "He has brought the ancient mother town back to life. Every day more people come." He paused. "We have spoken about you, he and I. We wish for you to come there and take the place that is yours. The people are waiting for the White Sun Woman to come and live among them."

She felt her face flush, hot with embarrassment and disappointment, because of the distance in his voice. "And it is for this that you have come here?"

"Yes."

"Then you are speaking to the wrong person. It is my grandmother who is the White Sun Woman."

"But she will not come."

"And you think that I will?"

"It is our hope."

"Yours and Salvador's?"

"Yes."

She drew in her breath and let it out again, staring at his back. Then she turned away, feeling suddenly very tired and wishing for a place to sit down. She took several steps, aimlessly, then stopped and raised her hand to the back of her neck and rubbed it hard, digging in her fingers, as if that would bring clarity to her thinking. He had never been her man. How many times had she reminded herself? But going to Salvador's camp was separate from that. She must think about it separately.

The tree frog's song was harsh to her now, a shrill monotony pulsing in her ears. And beyond it another sound, scarcely audible but growing in her consciousness until at last she recognized the soft padding of running feet. She turned and peered through the darkness toward the field beyond the trees. "Someone is coming," she said softly, not looking back at Carlos, keeping her eyes on the opening in the trees where the path came in from the field. She heard Carlos come up behind her and felt his hand on her arm.

"This way," he whispered, drawing her in among the great horizontal limbs of a live oak tree. They waited there in silence and listened. It sounded like only one person, the running footsteps light. At the edge of the trees the footsteps slowed and then came completely to a halt.

"Carlos!"

The voice that came softly through the trees was that of the boy Eugenio. Lucia felt Carlos' hand relax on her arm and then drop away as he started to move out from the cover. But she put out a hand to stop him.

"Let me," she whispered softly. "There may be others with him." She moved away from him into the open.

"Eugenio?" she said. "Is that you?"

"Are you in there?" he answered. He was keeping his voice low and secretive.

"Who is with you?" she asked, walking toward him.

"No one. I have come to tell you that they are looking for you in the town."

"Looking for me or for Carlos?"

"For you."

"Who is looking?"

"Ana. I heard her asking some people if they had seen you."

"And did you tell her where I am?"

"No. But I came to warn you because they will be coming here very soon to look for you. They know that you were going to the spring. You had your water jar."

She glanced back toward Carlos but could not see him beneath the shadow of the tree. She must go back to the town, then, and give them some excuse for where she had been. Back to the dreary house beside the convento. Back to waiting with those sad, dispirited women for a hopeless future they could not bring themselves to think about. If only he had come here as her man. But he had not.

"Wait for me, Eugenio. Just a moment. We will go back together."

"Is Carlos still here?"

"Yes. Just wait for me a moment."

She turned and went back into the darkness, and now, coming close, she could see him where he had come out and was standing in front of the live oak, a dense, upright shadow against the more varied shadows of the tree. She stopped a little distance from him.

"I must go back," she said. "I have already told Salvador that I cannot come to his camp. Tell him that nothing has changed."

Carlos did not move. It was as if he were a part of the tree and she were speaking into the darkness to no one at all.

"I am glad that you came, here," she said to him. "It is a relief to know you are not dead." She paused and then added, "Do you wish me to tell it in the town, that I have seen you?"

"I wish you to come with me." His voice was low and urgent and he took a step toward her. "Come for one moon. One moon only. If it does not please you, I will bring you back."

"After a moon?"

"Whenever you wish. After a day if you are unhappy there."

She turned and looked back at the boy, who was waiting for her at the edge of the trees. Then she looked at Carlos again, at the dark shape of him standing close before her.

"Do you think there is a life for me there?" she asked softly.

"Yes," he answered. "A life with me." He put out his hand and touched his fingers against her cheek. She turned her face against them and felt their warmth, their tenderness. How had it happened? This man was part of her now. Somewhere along the way it had come to be.

She put her hand to his and gently moved it away. "Let me tell Eugenio," she said, her voice low, changed by the fullness of love that had risen up in her. She turned away and went back through the darkness to the boy.

"I am going with Carlos," she said to him. "I will not be going back to the town."

"Are you deserting?" There was admiration in Eugenio's voice.

Lucia smiled. "Yes. I am deserting. I want you to do one more thing for me, Eugenio. I want you to go to Ana's house and speak to her and to my grandmother. Tell them what has happened to you today, how you met Carlos at the spring and then found me and told me he was here. And tell them how you came back and have been speaking to me now. Tell them that I have gone away with Carlos and that I will be living now in Salvador's camp." She paused, thinking of so much else she should say to them. But for a boy so young the message must be simple. "Tell them that I will see them again."

"Is that all?"

"Yes."

"Can I tell anyone else?"

"No, it would be better if you did not."

"Then I will only tell those two."

"You are good, Eugenio. We will remember what you have done for us. We will make a song about it and Carlos will sing it in the plaza whenever there is feasting."

"In Salvador's camp?"

"Yes. There are people there who know you. They will like hearing about you in a song." In the starlight she could see the whiteness of his teeth as he smiled. "Hurry now, before they come looking for me."

"I will see you someday in Salvador's camp," he said. "When I am old enough, I am going there."

"Good. We will be glad to see you."

He turned and started back, and again there was the swift padding of his running feet. Carlos came up and stood beside her.

"It has been a day for him," she said. "And he cannot tell his friends."

Carlos reached out his hand to her again, very briefly, his fingers brushing her cheek and her hair. Then he said, "We must get away from here."

"How did you come?"

"Through the fields. We circle around until we are clear of the town. Then the road is ours. The whole country is empty."

"We should hurry then."

She followed him out of the trees and along the edge of the fields, circling wide around Ivitachuco and leaving it behind.

✳ They walked with a steady pace along the road, neither hurrying nor going too slowly. The moon had finally risen, a hefty crescent in the clear sky. After so much darkness, the moonlight seemed almost like daylight flooding down upon them. She could see Carlos's face now, and sometimes she glanced at him, although as they walked along they only spoke of the smallest matters having to do with the journey—whether to pause at a stream for water, whether to circle an abandoned mission town or follow the road through the center of it. It was the same Carlos who had sat so silently beside her against the cartwheel beneath the stars in the stockade. But she knew him now and was not so puzzled by him. Whenever his world shifted, he became silent and thoughtful, and his world was shifting now. He had come to seek her out, and here she was walking beside him, a part of him. He was no longer one person alone, nor was she. The silence was not between them. It encircled them and they walked easily within it.

Near midnight the land through which they passed began to be familiar to her. The hills were more rolling and there were places that she recognized, homesteads that were abandoned now, all the land empty.

"I have been here before," she said to Carlos as they passed by one homestead. "Before we lived in Ivitachuco, I used to come to this place with my grandmother to do curing for a woman who was always sick."

"You lived nearby?"

"Not far. There is a little road up ahead. A path. It goes off to the north. I will show you when we get there."

Again there was silence and she watched the land, pleased to be seeing it again. She tried to think ahead, to what the next hill would look like, testing her memory and surprising herself at its accuracy.

"At the bottom of this hill," she said as they came over a rise, "the path to my mother's house is there. It goes up to the top of the next hill. Then two or three more hills and you are there. Three hills, I think, if you count the one the house is on."

He looked at her and smiled. "You remember it all?"

"Everything."

"I remember when you first came to Ivitachuco," he said. "Ana had always lived alone. Then suddenly her house was full. Her mother and her sister and a girl with legs like a colt."

"I was already a woman then."

He laughed softly. "Maybe so. But a very young one, all legs."

"I felt old, like I had seen all there was in life. My father was dead and we had come through a terrible winter, and here we were in a strange place with bells ringing, and we could never go home again."

They were walking with long strides down the hill.

"Do you want to go look at it?" he asked.

"I do not think it would still be there."

"Maybe not the house. But the clearing will be there. You will remember the land."

She looked at him. "Do you want to go?"

"Yes. I would like to see it."

"Then help me find the path. I am afraid it will be grown over now. No one is left to keep it open."

"There are still cattle," he said.

Carlos was right. The path, when they came to it, showed plainly in the moonlight, angling up a hillside meadow through a scattering of trees. She went ahead of him, pointing out familiar features of the land. But as they started up the last hill, she grew silent and apprehensive, for she knew that the homestead itself would be different from her memory, and she did not know how it would make her feel.

She stopped when they reached the edge of the clearing, and Carlos came up to stand beside her. Where corn had once grown, there were young trees now, poplars and pines the height of a man, scattered among sumac and brambles.

"A good place to trap rabbits," said Carlos.

She laughed, relieved that the sight was not depressing to her. "A well-set fire would clear it out again," she said. "My mother kept beautiful corn fields. My father was proud of them. When visitors came, he would take them out to walk in them and would boast of how well my mother took care of them. She would blush and laugh and say that it was all in the way he burned and cleared the land in the spring. But they knew it was her work."

"Hers and yours."

She smiled. "My grandmother's more than mine. They would let me run off to play. But you would always see the two of them, Sun-in-the-Mist and Sparkling Water, hoeing in their fields."

"I had forgotten that Isabel's name was Sparkling Water," he said. "What about you? I cannot remember what your name was before you were baptized."

For a moment she did not answer. She looked out over the moonlit clearing, and for the first time now she felt a twinge of sorrow. "Light of Dawn," she said softly,

He started to repeat it, but she put up her hand. "Do not say it," she said. Her voice was only a whisper and tears pricked her eyes. "It is over. That time will not come again. I am Lucia now."

He reached out and took her hand, holding it in his own. He spoke her name, "Lucia," and pulled her gently to him, putting his arms around her and pressing her tightly against him. She buried her face against his neck, and feeling her tears on his skin, she clung to him and wept for the release of her loneliness, for his welcome presence and the wholeness that she felt.

After a time her tears ceased. He continued to hold her. She could hear the high-pitched clamor of the tree frogs coming as it always had from the grove of trees around the spring near her mother's house. She pulled back from him a little and smiled. But he did not return the smile. He looked at her with great seriousness, and bending his head he kissed the tears on both her cheeks, and then he put his mouth to hers and pulled her to him again. The intensity of it swept into her and weakened her legs, and she moved with him toward the earth, down into the tall, summer grass. The grass closed around them, making a place that was all their own, and he filled it. She opened her eyes and he filled it completely, the grass all around and the night sky beyond and his hands caressing her, finding their way to the smoothness of her skin, pressing her, feeling her. She arched against him, and the eagerness that was in him was in her, too. She held him tightly as he came into her, and there were tears again, not weeping, but tears from the closeness and the power.

Afterwards they lay together in their tunnel of grass and watched the stars and spoke softly of various things, of themselves and their lives before their coming together. And after a while they made love again, more slowly this time. And then they slept.

In the morning, in the earliest light of dawn, Lucia got up and wrapped her skirt around her and walked through the clearing to the place where her mother's house had been. There was nothing left of it except a slight rise in the earth, with a great thicket of sumac growing on top. She stood and looked at it for a moment, and then she went on to the spring. She waited there, and when the first rays of sunlight came breaking through the trees, she raised her hands and sang the song of greeting to the Sun.

CHAPTER FOURTEEN

The camp of Salvador lay deep within a forest laced with animal trails. Only because Carlos had been there before did they know which trails to follow. Near the camp, however, the human trail became more distinct and Lucia herself could pick it out. She joked with Carlos, saying she would lead the way, and so he stopped and let her go in front of him.

She found it good to walk ahead, almost like being alone. For two days she had walked beside Carlos or behind him through the woods and fields, and the sight of him was such an amazement to her that her mind was continually preoccupied in its effort to absorb his reality and take for granted that he was there. It was a relief to be in front of him now, not looking at him and only barely hearing his footsteps as she walked along and watched the forest, heavy and green with summer. A brown thrasher, startled from its foraging in the leaf mold, flew up into a sweet gum tree and was lost in the foliage. Beyond the leafy canopy, high above them, the bits of sky were intensely blue. The midday sun was hot out there, but here beneath the green canopy it was cool.

Then suddenly, from behind, came the loud barking of a dog, and Lucia whirled to find Carlos smiling playfully. From the direction of the camp came an answering bark that faded to a tremulous howl, as when one dog hears another in the distance and sends up a song of loneliness.

"You made that bark?" she asked, laughing with him. "That was very good. And was that a sentry who answered?"

"We keep careful watch," he said, motioning for her to go on. "Slave-catchers have never bothered us here, but there is always the danger of them."

"And of Spaniards," she said. She let him go first again on the trail, then followed along behind him.

"We are not worried about the Spaniards." He spoke without looking back. "They would not come so deep into the forest. They no longer have the strength to do that."

"But what stops the Creeks? They are strong."

He shrugged. "Why should they treat us as enemies? We are not vassals of Spain here."

"Nor vassals of England, either," Lucia said. "It is reason enough to come against us if they can enslave us and trade us for guns to the English. Me, they would trade. You, they would kill." She meant to say it lightly, but it stayed with her a moment too long. "And if I were a slave, I would die," she said softly. "I would help myself into the Other World."

"What is this?" He looked back at her. "What is all this gloom?"

"It is nothing," she said, and reaching out she rubbed her hand over his back as they walked along. "How did you learn to bark like that? The priest never taught you."

"It takes practice, that is all."

"Do you think I could do it? I liked that other bark, the one the sentry made. I'm going to try it. Are you ready?"

"No. You will confuse the sentry."

"I will do it softly."

"It cannot be done softly."

But she tried, making some yipping sounds and fading off on a wavering note. "I sound like a person trying to sound like a dog."

"It is because you are doing it softly. You cannot do it if you hold back."

"Someday when we are further away from the camp I will try it."

"I would like to hear that."

"You are not laughing, are you?"

"No. I believe you can do it."

"I know I can. At least as well as you."

"At least."

"And you do it very well."

"A dog could do it better."

She laughed and reached out and rubbed his back again.

When they came to the sentry, they stopped to exchange greetings with him. He was a young man whose eyes and complexion suggested Spanish blood, though only faintly, perhaps from his grandfather. He wore a Spanish shirt hanging over his breechcloth and was armed with a bow and a quiver of arrows.

"This is Domingo," Carlos said to Lucia. "He is from San Luís."

"We have come," Lucia said politely.

Domingo nodded and did not reply, turning his eyes awkwardly from her. Through the trees she could hear the sounds of the camp. He looked at her again and said, "I do not know the proper greeting for the White Sun Woman."

She laughed. "I do not know it either. Nor do I care about it. I liked the signal you gave, the bark with the howl on the end. I told Carlos I am going to learn that myself."

Domingo shrugged. "It is just one that I do. A dog has many ways of barking."

She looked at Carlos and said wryly, "Do you think it would be proper for the White Sun Woman to learn to bark like a dog?"

"We will ask Salvador," said Carlos. "I think he regards the White Sun Woman very seriously."

"Then we will not say anything about barking." She nodded a friendly farewell to Domingo and they continued along the wooded trail toward the camp.

"Over there are some of the mounds that the old ones built," said Carlos, pointing into the trees.

Lucia stopped at the sight of them—great flat-topped mounds, massive and silent, tree-covered, part of the forest now. They were much larger than the one near Ivitachuco.

"There are more of them further back," said Carlos. "We cannot see them all."

"Think what it must have been like," said Lucia. "All of this a great town."

Carlos shook his head. "It is hard to imagine. Our people were at their height when they lived here. Salvador chose this place for his new town because it is purely Apalachee. It had already been abandoned before the first Spaniards came. It has not been defiled, he says."

They moved on along the path toward the camp, which was soon visible through the thinning trees. As they came into the clearing, Lucia could see that this was indeed a small town with regular houses, pole-framed with round wattle-and-daub walls and thatched roofs. There was a central plaza, and beside it a conical-roofed council house, the largest building in the town. Near the council house was a quadrangle of open sheds where men could escape the summer sun. Around a tall pole in the center of the plaza young men were practicing the ball game, an Apalachee sport outlawed many years ago by the friars. But here there were no friars. Nor was there a church, nor anything that was Christian. No stockade, no soldiers, no ranchers. Lucia had never before been in an Apalachee town in which there was not a Spanish presence. Was this what life was like in the ancient days? She tried to feel it that way. She wanted it to be so. But she could not forget the world outside. This was not the time of long ago, and this refuge could not erase the world as it was now. She knew she must not forget that.

She noticed how many men were here. There were women in the yards of some of the houses, and here and there children were playing. But mostly it was men she saw, far more in proportion to the women than she had ever seen in Ivitachuco. This might look like a town, but in fact it was more a warriors' camp.

As Lucia and Carlos approached, people began to notice them, looking up from what they were doing and smiling, some raising a hand. Those from Ivitachuco who knew Lucia got up and came out to speak to her. But in all of them there was the same reserve that she had experienced with Domingo, as if they too were uncertain how to give greeting to a White Sun Woman. With Carlos they were less restrained, and some of them teased him for what they saw in the way the two of them were walking together—that she was his woman now and he was her man.

They found Salvador in the yard of his house sitting on a cane mat in the shade of a tree. He waited until they were almost to the yard, then rose to his feet and came out to greet them. He had a large white cloth folded over his arm, and there was a solemn air about him, so that the people who had come walking with them through the town fell silent and came slowly to a halt, letting Carlos and Lucia go forward alone. Lucia smiled at the shaman, preparing to give him a friendly greeting, but he lowered his eyes with great solemnity, inclining his head in deference to her, so that she did not know how to respond. Her smile faded, and for a moment she only looked at him.

"I have come," she said at last, her voice grave.

"You have come," he answered solemnly and raised his eyes. He looked at Carlos and nodded to him, not in greeting but to tell him to step back. There was a moment's pause, but then Carlos did as he was asked and moved back several steps, leaving her to stand alone. From behind she could hear the shuffling of the onlookers and could tell that their number was growing.

Salvador took the white cloth from his arm and began slowly to unfold it. It was not Spanish cloth, but the old style cloth that the women of Apalachee used to weave from the fibers of mulberry bark. As he opened it, he had to hold his hands as high as his shoulders to keep it from touching the ground. Then he stepped away from Lucia and held it up to show it to those looking on. "The mantle of the White Sun Woman," he announced.

Lucia glanced at Carlos, wishing she could convey to him the unease that she felt, but she kept her face blank because of the people watching.

Salvador came back to her now, and she stood stiffly and without expression as he put the mantle about her, hanging it over her left shoulder and tying the two corners beneath her right arm. Then with his hand lightly on her back, he turned her to face the people, and standing to one side of her, he said in a loud voice, "The White Sun Woman. She has come." He dropped his eyes, folded his hands chest high, and said, "Hu!" Then the people, seeing now the proper way to greet her, did the same. At the sight of them all with their eyes to the ground, the blood rose in her face, and she looked at Carlos and saw that he, too, had his hands folded.

"This is enough," she said very softly to Salvador. But he did not look at her. He was watching the people now as they began to look up, a few at first, and then more, and then all of them. Raising his arms in front of him, the shaman began to sing.

It was a song that Lucia had heard before, one that was sometimes sung at dances by some of the older men. It was called the Cougar Song, but it was one of those whose words had no meaning, or if there ever had been meaning in them, it was lost now. Salvador's voice was strong and vibrant, and the people smiled as he sang. When it was over, they joined with him to cry out the "Hu!" that brought it sharply to an end.

Salvador was no longer solemn. "This is a time for dancing," he announced. "A time for feasting. We will begin at sundown in the plaza."

The people nodded in approval and began to drift away, talking among themselves.

Salvador smiled at Lucia. "I am glad you have come, my child."

Lucia did not return his smile. "This is not what I expected," she said. "I do not want it to be this way. I want to live here quietly."

Carlos came over to stand beside her. He too was unsmiling.

"It is new to you," said Salvador. "You will learn to be easy with it."

She lifted the edge of the mantle and looked for a moment at the cloth. "This is very beautiful. Someone worked hard to make it. But I do not want to wear it. I do not wish to go about as the White Sun Woman."

"Only on public occasions, my child. Tonight you should wear it to the dancing. The woman who made it belongs to the Hinachuba clan, a grandmother to you. She is the one you will live with until we build a house for you."

Lucia looked quickly at Carlos and was glad to see his face hardening.

"She will live with me," Carlos said bluntly.

Salvador looked at him, surprised and not entirely pleased. "This is new," he said. "Are you the husband of the White Sun Woman?"

Carlos looked at Lucia.

"He is my husband," she said.

Salvador nodded slightly, acceding. He kept his eyes on Carlos. "Yours is a position of honor."

"So it seems," said Carlos.

"But only as a reflection of her honor. In the end you are her servant, as am I."

"In the end he is my husband," said Lucia. "If there is honor, it should go to Isabel. She is the real White Sun Woman. I am not sure I want to be what you want me to be. I will keep on with my curing and sing the song to the Sun in the mornings. But as for the rest, it is not like anything I am used to."

"And that is the only difficulty," said Salvador. "You are not used to it. But in time you will be. Everything here is different from what you have known before. Here we are in the world of our grandmothers. It has come around to us again. The circle is closing and you are in the center of it. If it were an earlier time, it would be Isabel in the center. But she is old now, almost gone. You are the one, my child. No one chose you. You were born to this, and you will learn to be easy with it." He reached out and took them both by their shoulders, a hand on each. "It is good that you are together. I should not have been surprised. I should have seen it in the way he was so willing to go back for you. It is only that I did not expect it from a man with so much Spanish in him."

"I have no Spanish blood," said Carlos coolly.

"Not blood. Mind." Salvador tapped his finger against his own forehead. "But it is good," he said. "There will be children now. They will be the new White Suns, a brother and sister to reign together as in the days of our grandmothers. It is good." He patted Carlos on the shoulder and said again, "It is good."

✸ They sat together in the dim interior of the little house that Carlos had built for himself when he had come to the camp after the battle of Patale. He was by the door looking out into the hot afternoon, and Lucia sat on the bed. It was a hard bed, only one mat spread over the surface of cane poles. The white mantle of mulberry cloth lay beside her in a heap. The air in the small house was hot and still and she could feel a light layer of perspiration over all of her body.

"If you are unhappy," he said, "I will take you back. I told you I would."

"I am not unhappy, I would never want to go back." She wanted to say that she would never want to leave him, but that was too difficult to say while he was across the room. Such words only came easily when he was close, when she could touch him as she spoke, and even then the words were not enough, her voice sounding the same as if she were speaking of food or the weather. "It is only this that bothers me." She picked up the mantle and let it fall again. "It is not right for me. I am one for being on the edge of things, off to myself."

"I did not know he was planning all this," Carlos said. "I would have told you if I had known."

"I would have come anyway. So long as you wanted me with you, I would have come."

He looked at her, his face relaxing, light coming back to his eyes. "Then it will be all right. We will work things out with Salvador."

"He has changed since Ivitachuco," she said. "His power has grown."

"Here it is in the open. He had to keep it hidden there."

"It is more than that. He is stronger now. His power is greater."

Carlos nodded. "Perhaps it is so. I hardly knew him before. You would know better than I."

"He drops his eyes as if he would serve me, but the real power is his."

"You would rather have it for yourself, then?"

"No. I would rather that he himself were the White Sun and I were out of it altogether."

"But you were born to it and he was not."

"Look what he has done to me," she said. "Here I am hiding in the dark like a rabbit. I come to live in a new town and now I am afraid to go out and look at it."

"There is nothing to fear," said Carlos.

"Not to fear, no. But it is unpleasant to go walking about as the White Sun Woman with people staring at me and dropping their eyes, folding their hands, and feeling awkward when they speak to me."

"Give it time. It will pass." He stood up and held out his hand to her. "Come on. We will go out. You have not yet seen the lake. I think it will please you."

"Is it away from the town?"

"Yes. But first we are going to walk through the plaza. I think we should let people do their staring once and for all."

She nodded, and with a sigh of resignation she got up and followed him out into the heat of the day.

The town was still, the dogs lying in the shade and the children playing quietly. Though many of the people were asleep in their houses, others sat outside beneath their porticos. When they saw the White Sun Woman, they stared and smiled, and some remembered to fold their hands and murmur, "Hu!" But the disruption that had greeted her earlier was not repeated and she began to feel better about things.

Carlos led her all the way through the town and then out to the far edge, where cornfields stretched away before them in the hazy sun. And there beyond the fields was the lake. She stopped to gaze at the scene—the green gold of the tasseled cornstalks, the wide water with sunlight bright upon it.

"It is beautiful," she said, feeling happy again. She looked at Carlos, strong and calm beside her, and suddenly she marvelled that he should be here at all in this pagan camp, he of all people, who could read and write as well as any Spaniard, who was so much of the Church that he had once seemed like a priest to her. But now here he was standing next to her in this place, the husband of the White Sun Woman.

Aware that she was watching him, he glanced at her and then went on ahead, leading her down an open path in the corn, grasshoppers flying up from their feet as they walked along.

She lifted her face into the air and breathed in the musty sweetness of the ripening corn.

"It would be good to have a homestead out here," said Carlos. "How would it be to look out your door and see the Sun rising from the lake?"

"It would be very good. I would not be so much in the center of things out here. I would only be the White Sun Woman when I went into the town."

"Not in the mornings? Not when you are singing the song to the Sun?"

"That is different. I mean I would not be Salvador's White Sun Woman. I would not be like a saint in one of Father Juan's festival processions. It would be good to live in a place apart."

"Out there," he said, indicating a distant line of trees along the edge of the fields. She looked where he was pointing, her hand shading her eyes. The sun was hot on her head and shoulders.

"And what about slave-catchers?" she asked quietly. "A dawn raid and we would be finished out there." She kept looking out, not wanting him to see her disappointment.

"That danger will be over some day," he said.

She took her hand from her eyes and glanced at him. "Do you believe that?"

"I hope for it," he answered simply.

She nodded. And so would she hope for it. How else could they imagine any future at all? "When the slave-catchers are gone," she said, "we will make a homestead out here. Shall we choose the spot for it now?"

"At this moment? In all this heat? Tomorrow morning we will come out and do that. I will even start clearing the land for you, if you want." Reaching out, he put his hand behind her neck and drew her to him and kissed her.

She laughed, pulling free. "If they see you doing that, they will tease you forever. They will say I have you too much in my power."

"Then we should go back to our house. We will do it properly with no one looking."

"In the Apalachee way," she said smiling, and she turned to start back up the path.

"If this were our homestead," he said, "we could do whatever we wanted right here in the cornfield."

She stopped and turned around, her eyes playful. "It is very much the Apalachee way to do it in a cornfield. Anyone's cornfield at all. It is only a matter of being discreet."

He looked to see if she meant that as an invitation.

She did.

"You go first," he said.

She kissed him flirtatiously and then left the path and walked into the corn, making her way among the high stalks, keeping on a long way, going deep into the field, beyond any chance of discovery. And as she walked she could hear him coming behind her, a steady rustling of the corn at a distance that was properly discreet.

CHAPTER FIFTEEN

It was the middle of the night, almost a month after they had come to Salvador's camp. Lucia awoke suddenly in a fright, her heart pounding, her eyes wide and searching the darkness. She reached out and felt Carlos in the bed beside her and then lay still for a moment, trying to collect herself. What had it been? She had no memory of a dream. A sound, perhaps, but all was silent now. The town was still, like any other night. Out in the darkness there were sentries guarding. There was nothing to fear. But her heart would not stop its pounding, and her breath came quickly. Fear was on her like a cougar on a fawn. Again she put her hand on Carlos and the fear quickened. He was leaving. Could it be that? At dawn he was going out to hunt. For a few days, he had said. But that was not unusual. In a few days he would be back again. What was this fear?

Carlos lay with his back to her and she turned to him and slipped her arm around his chest and held him tightly, pressing her face against his back. She was trembling. He stirred and reached back for her, pulling her more tightly against him, and then, waking a little more, he felt her trembling.

"What is it?" he said.

"Take me with you when you go." And with that, the fear began to subside.

He turned around to face her in the darkness, resting his hand on her hip. "You want to come hunting with me?" There was amusement in his voice, but she did not mind it. She did not want to tell him about the fear. She could not explain it even to herself.

"When I was a little girl," she said, "I used to go hunting with my father."

"And did you kill much game?"

"He did. I had no strength for the bow. But I could move as quietly as he could, and we would go a little apart, or at a stream at dawn we would wait in different places for the deer, and if I saw something I would make the sound of a chickadee to tell him."

"You can do that? A chickadee?" He was moving his hand lightly down her leg, then up again over the curve of her hip.

"Tomorrow in the woods I will show you."

"Do you truly want to go hunting?" He seemed amazed, and pleased. She felt easy now. Her fear was almost gone.

"There is much a woman can do on the hunting trail," she said. "There is meat to be dried and skins to be dressed, and she can carry the pack basket so that the man is always free with his bow."

"And what will Salvador say when he hears you are going hunting? Carrying things on your back? It is not proper for a White Sun Woman."

"I am tired of what Salvador says."

"But we will have to tell him something."

"Then I will tell him I had a dream. I will say that the White Falcon came and told me to go away for a little while. To a place alone to greet the Sun. For four mornings."

"Four? That is a long time."

She smiled. "Everything has to be in fours. What kind of dream would it be if I said three days? He would think you dreamed it. A Christian dream."

"Four, then. That is good. I would like being away for four days."

"Maybe I will have these dreams more often."

"Why not? You are the White Sun Woman. He is not the only one who can have a dream." He slipped an arm beneath her and pulled her closer.

"Be careful," she said softly. "It spoils your power for hunting if you have a woman just before."

"That is the Apalachee way," he said. "Salvador was right. In some ways I am a Spaniard."

☀ It was good to come out of the forest and see the open sweep of the land, the scrubby meadows with scattered trees where Spanish cattle used to graze. All was empty now, no sign of life, not a horse or a cow, not a Spaniard or a Creek slave-catcher. It was as empty as the forest had seemed to be. They had been hunting for three days and had nothing to show for it. The one deer they had seen had seen them first, and they had glimpsed only its white tail bounding away out of range. It might have been a small matter had they brought more food, but they had expected better luck, and their food was gone after the second day. They did not want to go back to the camp before their four days were over. They would have to tell an elaborate lie to Salvador to accommodate the one they had already told. And besides, they enjoyed being away on their own. Except for how hungry they were. The roots Lucia had dug and cooked for them on the third night had only helped a little, and now on the fourth day, with one more night to spend before they went home, they decided to try their luck at the abandoned Spanish ranches. Surely somewhere there was a cow or pig or chicken that someone else had not already stolen.

Coming out of the forest, they walked through scrub until their course intersected a small road. It was little more than a path in the meadow but they could see that two-wheeled carts had once passed over it. In one direction or another, then, this cart track would take them to a Spanish ranch.

"We will probably find one either way," said Carlos. "Where would a Spaniard go on a road like this but to visit another Spaniard?"

"You should know," Lucia teased. "You are the one with the Spanish mind."

"Then we should go this way." He pointed to the east. "Any slave-catchers coming our way will have the sun in their eyes and maybe we will see them before they see us."

Already it was afternoon and the heat was oppressive. Were it not for the hunger that was driving them on, they would have taken a more leisurely pace and lingered in the shade of the trees that they passed. But they walked quickly and nervously, looking constantly about for any sign of human life. Anyone they met would likely be an enemy, either a Spaniard or a Creek slave-catcher. Even other Apalachees could not be trusted, so many had thrown in with the Creeks.

As the afternoon wore on, storm clouds appeared in the west, first along the horizon but then rising quickly and blocking the sun, throwing a cool shade over the land.

"Where is this ranch?" asked Lucia, glancing back over her shoulder at the darkening sky. "We are going to get soaked."

"I have no idea where it is," Carlos said irritably. "Will a little water hurt you?"

Lucia said nothing. Let them get wet, then. She walked in silence beside him and thought of what a mess it was, out here in the middle of nowhere, starving to death, with a thunderstorm over their heads. It would be just the thing to stumble onto a band of slave-catchers. That would be the thing to top off four days of such marvelous luck.

She felt his fingers on her back, lightly tickling down her spine. For a moment she would not look at him.

"Next time," he said, "I will do it the Apalachee way. I will be as chaste as a priest before I go out to hunt."

She smiled. "It is a hard choice. Food or love."

"If you had to choose now, which would you take?"

"Food," she said.

"And a place to stay dry?"

"Is that one of the choices?"

"If at the top of the next hill we see no sign of a ranch or a homestead, we will head for some trees and put up a shelter. A few pine boughs would be better than nothing at all."

"It would," she agreed. She looked back again at the gathering storm and quickened her step.

When they reached the top of the hill, there was an abandoned ranch ahead, like a miracle of which a priest would speak, a Spanish homestead with a small wattle-and-daub house and a kitchen behind, and a pigsty, and beyond that a cowpen with a dungheap beside it. The storm cloud was overhead now, and in the west they could hear Thunder starting out on his eastward journey. They hurried down the hill with long fast strides. With the first large drops of rain, they began to run, dipping down into the little valley and up the next slope, pushing hard to keep their speed on the up-hill climb, Thunder coming fast behind them. They were laughing as they reached the house, but Carlos put out his hand to stop her at the door and had her wait against the wall beneath the eaves while he went inside with his hatchet in his hand and made sure that the place was as empty as it looked. When he came back for her, his eyes were bright.

"You will never guess," he said, drawing her inside. It was dark like an

Indian house, no light but from the doorway. A rough table stood against one wall and an overturned bench lay in the middle of the floor. Carlos steered her around the bench into the other room of the house, pushing her before him with his hands on her shoulders. This room was lit by another door standing open to the storm. He turned her toward a dark corner, and there, on a crude wooden bedframe empty of its bedding, chickens were roosting. Four chickens, shifting about uneasily, clucking and stretching their wings.

Lucia reached back over her head and caught Carlos' neck and hugged him. "We need a fire," she said, letting him go and moving back into the front room. Thunder had caught up with them now, booming overhead, and his two mischievous nephews were with him, fighting and playing in bright, startling flashes.

"We should have thought to bring in some wood," said Carlos. "Everything outside will be soaked after this."

"When the rain is over, I will go look in the cocina," said Lucia. "People abandoning a ranch would not take their firewood with them."

They waited near the doorway, watching the rain and feeling content with the coolness that it brought and with the dryness of their shelter and the promise of food. When they wearied of standing, Carlos righted the bench and they sat on that and watched as the storm slowly lightened. Thunder and his nephews had moved beyond them now. They could hear them rumbling away to the east.

"We should have come here on the first day," said Lucia. "This would have been a good place to spend four days."

Carlos shook his head. "A place like this is dangerous. It draws people to it, the same as it has drawn us. Probably we should not even sleep here."

"You are right," she agreed. She stood up and went to the doorway. The rain had stopped, only the water from the roof still dripping. Outside the warm earth steamed and the clouds overhead were breaking up before the late afternoon sun. Thunder was almost beyond hearing in the east.

She put her hand out beyond the dripping of the eaves to feel the air empty of rain. "I am going to look for some wood. Will you have a chicken ready when I get back?"

"It will be dead, at least."

She went out, breathing the warm earth smell. She walked around the corner of the house and crossed the yard to the cocina, a small building with the same wattle and daub walls and thatched roof that an Indian house would have. But the door was Spanish, rough split boards held together with pegged crossbars. It was slightly ajar, and she put her hand against it and pushed it open a little further. From inside came the acrid smell of old smoke. She took a tentative step, pushing the door all the way back to let in the light, and then, after a moment's hesitation, she went inside.

Suddenly the door moved, swinging back again. She turned and saw a figure in the shadows. Crying out, she leapt back toward the narrowing doorway, her hand reaching the edge of the closing door, pulling it open again, her legs propelling her toward the steamy daylight. Then her skirt was caught! She called out for Carlos. Pulling her skirt free, she tumbled out, falling to her hands and knees and rising again. Carlos came running around the corner of the house, his hatchet in his hand, his legs straining and his face fierce, desperate to reach her.

Looking back she glimpsed the figure in the doorway just as the door was slamming shut. She ran to Carlos, shaking her head, unable to speak, putting out a hand to stop him.

"Someone is there," she gasped, trying to catch her breath and turning again to look at the kitchen. "An old woman, I think. At first I could not see. But just now. I do not know. It looked like an old woman to me."

Carlos pulled her back around the corner of the house. "Was she alone?"

"I think so." Lucia leaned against the house, her legs weak. Carlos was standing by the corner looking toward the cocina.

"Was there a fire inside? Could she be living there?"

"I did not see a fire," said Lucia.

"Do you think she was alone?" he asked again.

"I think so, but I am not sure."

He turned and looked at her and smiled a little. "Are you all right?"

She nodded and tried to smile back, but she could not. "It scared me."

He looked again at the kitchen. "Should we try to talk to her?"

"Maybe we should just get away from here."

"Was she a Spaniard?"

"No. An Indian, I think. But I am not sure what I saw. Maybe there are slave-catchers in there. Maybe we should leave." But even now she could feel her hunger. "Did you kill the chicken?" she asked.

He glanced at her and laughed. "The chicken has gone to heaven." He was looking at the kitchen again. "I am going to try to talk to her." Lifting his chin a little, he called out, "My grandmother!"

Lucia put her head around the corner to look. Nothing moved. There was silence except for the dripping of water from the eaves of the buildings.

"My grandmother!" Carlos called again. "We are Apalachees." Another silence. Then he added, "I am of the Usunaca clan. My wife's clan is Hinachuba. If you are a friend of these clans, it would lift our hearts to greet you."

Still there was no response from the cocina.

"The chicken was probably hers," Lucia said softly. "Maybe we should just take it and go."

But then the door of the cocina opened very slightly. "My clan is Usunaca," a voice said. It came strong and clear through the humid air, a woman's voice deepened by age.

"Then you are indeed my grandmother," Carlos called to her. "My heart is soaring. I am Usunaca Carlos from Ivitachuco. I have come."

The door opened further and they could see her now, an old woman in a skirt of blue Spanish cloth, her gray hair straggling loose from its knot behind her neck.

Carlos stepped out from the house and tossed his hatchet onto the ground.

"You have come, my grandson," said the woman. And then to Lucia, who was coming out to stand beside him, she said, "And you, my grandson's wife. It was not my intention to frighten you."

"Nor mine to frighten you," said Lucia, smiling.

"I am not afraid of your hatchet," the woman said to Carlos. "Keep it with you, if you wish."

Carlos shook his head. "Let it lie where it is. Among kinsmen there is no need for weapons."

"But who knows who else might come along," said the woman. "Maybe we would all feel better if you had it with you."

So Carlos retrieved the hatchet, and the woman came out and met them in the yard.

"You came very quietly," she said. "I did not hear you before this one pushed open the door."

"We thought there was no one here," said Lucia. She smiled. "I thought you were a pack of slave-catchers."

"They are not unknown around here," the woman said soberly. "To me they are not much of a danger. I am too old to bring a price as a slave. And I offer them no resistance when they come. I invite them to sit down and share my fire. They have no reason to kill me. But you—" She looked at them and shook her head. "This wife of yours," she said to Carlos. "How beautiful and strong she is. What a price she would bring. And, oh, how you would fight to defend her. And they would cut you down and send you to the Other World. A man is of no use to them. A woman, yes. A child, yes. But an Indian man is too stubborn to enslave. His soul flies away from him, and he withers and dies. So they cut down the men and steal away their wives and their little ones." She shook her head sorrowfully. "What terrible grief they have brought us."

"Do you think they will ever leave us in peace?" asked Carlos.

"No," said the woman. Then she shrugged. "But who knows? I thought the Spaniards would be here forever, and now they are gone. Who would have ever thought that?"

"Gone from here," said Carlos. "But not from San Luís."

"Yes, from San Luís."

"What do you mean?" asked Lucia.

"I will tell you," said the old woman. She stopped and looked at them, considering something for a moment. Then she said firmly, "You will sleep here tonight, in my kitchen. I will cook for you. Oh, I am a good cook." She patted Lucia's arm. "Tonight there is no work for you. You sit with him and we will talk together. If slave-catchers come, I will keep you safe. They will never see you."

"Our hearts are full, my grandmother," said Lucia. "But we must confess to you that we have killed a chicken of yours. We did not know there was anyone here to claim it."

The woman waved her hand. "You saved me the trouble of killing it myself."

"But what about San Luís?" said Carlos.

"There is time for that," she said. "We have all night to talk."

She got up and went into the house and came back with cane mats, which she spread by the outside hearth. She kindled a fire and soon had the chicken roasting on a stick. The sun was setting, spreading red and purple across the sky as the old woman went cheerfully about her work, refusing to let Lucia help her. She pounded corn and made cakes that she put into the ashes to bake. She cut up peaches into a clay pot, added a little water, and put them on the fire to stew into a sauce for the chicken.

"Today at noon my son-in-law came to me," the old woman said at last. "He told me that this very morning the Spaniards abandoned San Luís. They are going back to San Augustín, all of them, and they go with much haste, afraid that the Creeks will come after them and kill them on the way. They burned the blockhouse to keep the English from having it. It is all gone, burned to rubble."

"They forced my father to help them build that place," said Lucia. "His health was never the same after that. He died too young."

The woman nodded. "Who does not have a story of suffering? I can remember when on a summer night like this these hills around us were lit by the fires of my kinsmen. Oh, it was a sight for a girl to stand in the darkness and turn in every direction and see homesteads full of people who cared for her and protected her." The woman reached over and turned the chicken on the spit. "But the Spaniards came and took this land for their ranches and forced our men to come work for them. My mother stayed here as a servant on this ranch, and I raised my own children here." She paused and craned her neck to look into the pot of peaches, stirring it with a wooden spoon. "But all that is over now. When the Creeks struck at Patale, all the Spaniards around here fled to San Luís. I myself went with them. We all went, all the servants, including my daughter and her husband. We did not know then that the Spaniards were finally beaten. But in the blockhouse we could see it. When they came back from the battle at Patale, there was no life left in them. From that time on, they were just waiting for the governor in San Augustín to send permission for them to leave. So I said to myself, What am I doing here? The homestead is mine again. And I left the blockhouse and came back."

"But your daughter would not come?" said Lucia.

"She could not. The slave-catchers are a danger to her. She is not old and ugly like I am."

"So what will she do, she and her husband? Are they going with the Spaniards?"

"The Spaniards wanted them to. They want to take as many Apalachees with them as they can to give themselves protection as they go. They have offered forgiveness to all those who have run away if they will come back now and join them. But my daughter and her husband are finished with Spaniards. They are going west to the French at Mobile. Many from around here are going there. They wanted me to go with them, but I told my son-in-law today that I am too old to start a new life. I will stay here where I have always been."

She looked into the fire, sadness settling over her. After a moment she raised her head and looked out beyond them at the low hills fading away in the darkening twilight. "To think there were once so many of us," she said. "And now I am the only one."

CHAPTER SIXTEEN

Lucia felt at peace as she walked with Carlos along the forest path toward the camp of Salvador. The four days away had been good for her and she did not mind so much going back to be the White Sun Woman again. Perhaps it was true what Salvador had told her, that in time she would get used to her new life. Certainly if she could get away like this whenever she wanted, things would not be so bad. Next time they went out, they would have better hunting, and they would take some game to the old woman.

When they had left her that morning, in the misty dawn, they had promised her they would return another time.

As they approached the point near the camp where they should give a signal to the sentry, Lucia touched Carlos' arm. "Let me try it," she said.

"Go ahead," he answered.

She raised her head a little and cupped her hands around her mouth and made the barking sound that she had been practicing all day. She did it well and was pleased with herself as she put her hands on her hips and listened for an answer. But in the stillness of the summer noon only silence came back to them. She looked at Carlos. "Was it so bad? It sounded good to me."

He seemed a little puzzled. "It was good. But perhaps not loud enough." He cupped his hands around his mouth and made his own barking sound, louder than he usually made it, loud enough for anyone to hear. But the dense green forest closed around it and nothing came back except the cawing of crows above the treetops overhead.

Fear was coming to Lucia now, slipping in quietly to press against her heart. She looked at Carlos, who was staring ahead up the path, thinking. Then he turned and led the way off the path, and they moved silently together beneath the trees. When they were deep into the forest, far from the path, they stopped beside a great oak tree, its limbs wide and gnarled. Lucia glanced at Carlos. His face was grim.

"You do not think the sentry is sleeping," she said softly.

"No."

"Nor do I. Our signals would have wakened him."

"There is no sentry," said Carlos.

"Maybe it is because the Spaniards have gone. Maybe the camp is no longer afraid." But she did not believe that herself. It had never been Spaniards that the people here had feared.

"There should be a sentry," he said.

She was staring absently into the forest, one hand on her hip and the fingers of the other hand against her lips.

"Wait for me here," said Carlos. "I will go and have a look. If everything is all right, I will come back for you."

"No. I will come with you."

He shook his head. "I want you to wait here. What can you do if you come?"

"I can see what has happened, the same as you. And if there is danger, do not worry about me. I will meet you back here."

He looked at her and smiled a little. "You think you are that smart and quick, that it would be nothing to get back here?"

She shrugged. "If we are quiet, there will be no danger. If we go carefully, there will be no need to run."

He could see now how serious she was and that she knew what would be required. "Come after me, then. A little way behind. And watch for whatever signal I might give you."

She nodded, and he turned and started away in the direction of the town. She waited a few moments and then followed. They had only gone a short distance when she began to smell the stench.

✸ Buzzards swirled overhead. The camp was in ashes and many of the bodies were burned. But even those that had not been burned could not be recognized, for the summer heat and scavenging animals had worked quickly on them and there was nothing left of them that was familiar. Lucia had tried to be strong and walk with Carlos through the carnage, but it was more than she could bear, and she had turned away at last and gone back into the forest to wait for him at the great oak tree. She lay now on the soft forest floor with one arm stretched out beneath her head and watched a file of large black ants moving over the leaves. Every now and then she reached up with her free hand and brushed away the tears that rose to blur her vision. She had seen enough to know that the dead were mostly men and old people and children too young to walk. Most of the women and older children had been taken away. The work of slave-catchers.

Carlos found her lying there when he returned. He sat down beside her and for a long time they were silent. Then he said, "I think I saw Salvador."

She nodded but did not speak.

"I am not certain," he said. "But I think it was he. I looked for some others, but I could not tell. I would have known them by their clothing, but the slave-catchers took all the clothing away."

"When do you think it happened?" she asked quietly.

"The day we left."

"The dream of the Water Cougar," said Lucia. "Isabel tried to warn him."

"And who warned you, that last night we were here? What if you had not come with me? How did you know to come?"

"Perhaps it was a dream. But I cannot remember one. Only a terrible fear. It went away when you said you would take me with you."

They were silent again, neither of them moving. They were trying to bring it all into themselves, to know it and accept it.

At last she said, "We cannot stay in Apalachee any longer."

"No, we cannot stay here," he agreed.

"Where will we go?"

"To San Augustín or to Mobile," he said. "We have our choice. To the Spaniards or the French.

"Or north to the English."

"No," he said firmly. "I will never live with the Creeks. Not after what they have done to us. I saw Ayubale and now I have seen this. I want nothing from the Creeks unless it be revenge. They are more our enemies than the Spaniards are."

"Many of our people are among them."

"They are not my people," Carlos said bitterly. "Not any more."

"Then you would go with the Spaniards?"

"Yes, that is where I think we should go. We feel nothing for the French. We do not know their language. With the Spaniards we can get along."

She nodded.

"And will the White Sun Woman leave Apalachee?" he asked.

"Yes," she answered softly.

He looked down at her and brushed his fingers over her cheek. "It makes you sad."

"Yes, but I am tired of trying to stay here. It will almost be a relief to go."

"You can still sing the song in the mornings."

She nodded. "I can, it is true. The Sun will come the same every morning no matter where we are."

"And the song is very lovely."

"Yes. Perhaps I will still do that."

There was silence all around them in the forest, the air hot and still. In the distance they could hear the raucous cries of the crows as they squabbled with the buzzards for the carrion.

CHAPTER SEVENTEEN

The day was overcast, as if a blanket of gray had been draped across the sky. Later there would be the misery of rain, but for now Father Juan de Villalva welcomed the relief from the beating sun. He lay on the jolting litter, his head turned to one side as he listlessly watched his people in their flight. Two men carried him, two Spaniards from San Luís who could have been put to better use carrying precious food that all these people would need when they reached San Augustín. That city was already starving even without this new burden of refugees. Perhaps it was a blessing that most of the Indians at San Luís—as many as 800—had gone west to join the French at Pensacola and Mobile.

The priest would have understood if he had been left behind. It would have been reasonable, a man so ill as he, with no hope of recovery, especially after the horses and cattle were driven away. That had been the final blow for them at San Luís, the sabotage of Manuel Solana's plan for an orderly evacuation. There were to have been horses to carry food and belongings and the sick and the old. And cattle were to be driven along to provide meat, both for the journey and for later at San Augustín. But then the loyal Indians, the ones with whom they had shared the walls of Fort San Luís, the ones who were supposed to be pious Christians and loyal servants, those very ones absconded in the night with horses and cattle that they themselves had been sent out to round up. That betrayal was the final blow. When Juan heard in the morning that the horses were gone, he had given up all hope of ever leaving that place. He would die at San Luís, left behind to be murdered by the pagans. Although it frightened him, he had accepted it.

Then Solana had come to the little room where the priest had lain ill for more than a month on a hard bed in a corner among a store of empty barrels. Those barrels would remain empty now and never again be filled with wheat and carried to the port to be shipped to San Augustín and—illegally, but more profitably—to Cuba. Solana had come there, to that dark little hole where the priest was contemplating his death, and had stood beside his bed and told him that two men would carry him on a litter. Juan had tried to refuse. He would die no matter what, he explained, and it would make little difference whether it were in San Luís or San Augustín. But Solana was firm, and the priest had given in at last with thankfulness in his heart.

And now he was here in the train of Spanish and Indian refugees, his suffering almost as great on the litter as it would have been at the hands of the pagans. His face was painfully burned by the sun, his lips cracked and swollen. Every part of him hurt from the sag of the cane mat litter, the sides of it pulled up tight against him by the poles on which it hung. But he would see Ana again. That, at least, was a comfort.

He watched the country go by, empty and desolate, and thought of how it had been in the beginning when they had arrived here as young men, he and Solana, to make their lives in this well-populated, fertile land. Who would have thought then that it would end this way? Solana had expected his sons, and the sons of his sons, and their sons, to always be here. They would be hidalgos, gentlemen of Apalachee into a future without end. And he himself, what had he expected? That the fruits of his mission would reseed and bear more fruit and that this would be a Christian land forever. But very soon now they would be at Ivitachuco, and when the people there had come out to join the flight, it was Solana's plan to burn the mission to the ground.

Juan felt a hand on his arm. Turning his head he saw Solana walking beside him.

"How goes it?" asked Solana.

The priest licked his lips to loosen them enough to speak. "Better," he said. "Better without the sun." His mind was clear, unlike yesterday when he had swooned in the heat.

"Even the rain will feel good," said Solana.

"At first, yes." The priest touched his fingers to his lips and then looked to see if there was blood. There was, but only a little. "Can you see Ivitachuco?"

"Not yet. Perhaps from the next hill." Solana walked in silence for a time. Then he said, "Some friends of yours have joined us."

"Who is that?" the priest asked without much interest. Ana was the only one he wanted to see now. All others he had known in his life were no longer of any concern.

"Carlos," said Solana. "And that woman who is related to Ana. The young one."

At first the priest made no response. He stared away into the gray of the sky and tried to remember things from the past. What was it that had happened to Carlos? He had become strange, left the church, and taken up work in the fields. Then there was the battle at Patale. He thought Carlos had deserted and had put him out of his mind, too ill to wrestle anymore with such things. So he was back again. But Lucia? Why would she be with him? "Let me speak to them," he said.

"I will send them to you." For a moment longer Solana walked beside the litter, and then he turned back along the line of marchers.

It was some time before Carlos and Lucia appeared. The bearers had already told the priest that they could see Ivitachuco ahead, and now he was watching familiar places go past, feeling joy at his return, even though it was not to stay. He would have Ana with him again, and wherever she was would be home to him. He began to feel expectant, as if at any moment she might appear at his side. He had almost forgotten about Carlos, and when it was he who was suddenly there beside the litter, it startled him.

"I have come," Carlos said quietly in Apalachee.

The priest licked his lips, stretching them a little. Then he said, "Do you not speak Spanish anymore?"

"Yes, Father," Carlos replied in Spanish. "I hope you are well."

"I am not well."

"But in spirit I hope that you are."

The priest was gratified to hear kindness in his voice. "My spirit is well," said Juan. "How is it you have come here? Solana tells me Lucia is with you."

"She is here," said Carlos. He slowed his step a little so that Juan could see her walking on the other side of him. Her distant smile reminded the priest that he had never really known her nor been able to speak to her beyond formalities.

"Are you together now?" he asked Carlos.

"Yes. She is my wife."

"Wife?" he murmured and thought to object, to point out the absence of Christian sacrament. But what did it matter anymore? And who was he to speak? He, too, had a wife he had never married. "That is good," he said. "God's blessing be on you both."

"Thank you, Father."

"She has been away from Ivitachuco with you?"

"We were with Salvador." Carlos spoke bluntly, without apology. "He is dead now. His camp was raided, everyone killed or enslaved. We were not there when it happened."

"Then God spared you."

"Yes."

"And so you have turned back to God again?"

"We have come back, yes. It is our wish to go to San Augustín."

"Good. That heartens me, my son. Stay by me and I will see that you go with me as my servants to the convento in San Augustín. Otherwise, life could be very hard for you. They say there is hunger there."

"Thank you, Father."

"Are we home yet?" Juan craned his head, but he could not see past the bearer in front of him.

"Almost," Carlos answered.

"Tell me what you see."

"A few people are standing out on the edge of town watching us come. They have packbaskets and bundles ready. There are two horses and some cattle."

"Do you see Ana?"

"No, I cannot see her. If you wish, I will go find her and bring her to you."

"Yes," said the priest. "Do that." Lowering his head back into the litter, he closed his eyes to wait.

✸ When Lucia and Carlos reached the edge of town, they learned that Don Patricio had already departed with most of the people, heading eastward for Timucua. He planned to stay in that neighboring province, near one of the destroyed missions. The slave-catchers had already done their work there, he reasoned, and perhaps they would not return. Don Patricio and those who followed him were more willing to take that risk than to risk a life even more unknown in the far-away world of San Augustín.

The few remaining people from Ivitachuco had already begun to mingle with the people from San Luís. Lucia moved slowly among them, searching for Ana and Isabel. But it was Isabel who found her first, coming up from behind and clasping her arm with her bony fingers.

Lucia turned to her, smiling. "My grandmother, I have come."

Isabel held her arm, squeezing it very tightly. There were tears in her eyes. "We heard what happened to Salvador," the old woman said. She shook her head, pressing her lips together with emotion. "Just this morning we heard it. We thought you were there."

"No," Lucia said quietly. "We were away when it happened. We are here, Carlos and I both." She looked around for him, but he was not in sight.

"So he finally talked seriously to you?" said Isabel.

"Yes," she said, smiling.

"And you have lain together?"

"Yes.

"And you will stay with him now?"

"Yes. He is my husband."

"Good." She patted Lucia's arm. "That is what you have been needing, a man like that. Ever since he moved out of the convento he has been a man worth having."

Lucia was happy to be with her again. "You are not angry at me for leaving you?"

"No. When I heard you went with Carlos, I was not angry. But I was worried about you at Salvador's camp."

Lucia was silent for a moment, remembering the carnage. But she pulled her thoughts away from it. "We are going to San Augustín," she said. "We will all be together."

"Except for me," said Isabel. "I am not going."

"But what will you do?" Lucia remembered the old woman of the Usu-anca clan who had fed them and guarded their sleep.

"I am going back to our homestead."

"There is nothing there. I saw it. The house is gone."

"Then I will build another. A small one. One old woman does not need very much."

Lucia looked away, knowing there was nothing she could say. The crowd had thinned now, many people having joined the line of refugees. And there was Ana coming toward them, walking quickly. As she drew near, she held out her hands to Lucia, who clasped them and held them tightly.

"I have come, my mother's sister," said Lucia.

"You have come," said Ana, tears in her eyes. "Holy Mary be praised, you have come."

"We were not with Salvador when the slave-catchers came," said Lucia.

"I know," said Ana, nodding with relief. "I have spoken to Carlos."

"Did he take you to Father Juan?"

"Yes." Ana turned and looked back toward the priest's litter. "He is dying," she said quietly.

"We are all dying," Isabel said impatiently.

Ana gave her a sharp look.

Lucia was surprised at the acrimony between them. She said to Ana, "My grandmother says she is not coming with us."

"What can I do?" Ana said in exasperation. "For two days we have argued about this. She is as stubborn as a tree stump."

"I am if I need to be," Isabel said sharply. "We all do what we must." But then she reached out and put a hand on Ana's shoulder. "Go on now, my daughter." Her voice was gentler. "Go be with your man."

Ana looked at her sadly, all her impatience gone. "It is a hard thing you ask me to do, my mother."

"Yes, but you must do it. Go on." Isabel reached with her other hand for Lucia. "You, too, my granddaughter. Go to your man." She pushed them both away from her.

Lucia looked at her, thinking of arguments to make. But she could see that it was hopeless. "When we come back," she said, "we will look for you where you said."

"I will be there."

"I will still sing the song to the Sun every morning," said Lucia.

"Good. We will both be singing it. Go on now. Your men are waiting." She turned away from them and began walking back into the town.

"There is nothing we can do," said Ana.

Lucia nodded, and they stood in silence and watched her until she disappeared among the houses.

There was no time lost at the stopover at Ivitachuco. Manuel Solana requisitioned one of the two horses for himself, and the caravan moved on, Spaniards and Indians together, all of them homeless, fleeing toward the east. As the people descended the long slope to the river, Spanish soldiers put Ivitachuco to the torch. The refugees, glancing over their shoulders,

saw the flames come up, and some of the people turned around to watch.
First the fire engulfed the pitch-laden pine posts of the stockade. Then, as it burned hotter, sparks were blown to thatched roofs close by and the fire spread quickly across the town, waves of smoke and heat rising up into the gray, heavy sky. Lucia stood beside Carlos and watched it without sadness, feeling only a detached fascination with the magnitude of the fire.

Then Carlos touched her arm and pointed past the fire to a solitary figure walking away along the ridge of a hill, almost out of sight. There was no question who it was—a small woman, white-haired, wearing a skirt of deerskin, her chest bare in the summer heat. She had a pack basket on her back, and from her hand a copper kettle swung along with her steady stride. After a moment she disappeared over the hill.

"The White Sun Woman remains," Lucia said softly. She glanced once more at the burning town and then turned with her husband and resumed the journey down the long slope to the river that marked the eastern border of Apalachee.

CHAPTER EIGHTEEN

The priest lay struggling for breath in the stifling heat of the temporary Convento de San Francisco, near Matanzas Bay. The old convento had been a substantial building worthy to be headquarters for the Franciscan mission in Florida, but it—and most of the rest of San Augustín—had been burned to the ground two years earlier when the Englishman Moore made his siege. The new convento was a collection of wretched wooden huts thatched with straw, overflowing with refugee friars who had fled their missions in the ravaged provinces. Many complained of the abysmal conditions, but Juan himself was content. His bed of straw on the floor reminded him of Christ's manger, and when he closed his eyes, he sometimes felt himself a child again, a baby even, nestled down in a stable like the Lord.

He opened his eyes briefly and watched the beam of morning light that angled down from the smoke hole and fell to one side of Father Superior Claudio de Florencia, who knelt on a cushion on the floor beside Juan and read prayers from his breviary. Juan had been drowsing to the drone of his voice, hearing it as the lowing of a cow, a Spanish cow in a Spanish stable. The Holy Mother of his stable had the dark Spanish eyes he had known from the cradle, the eyes that had seen his first steps and watched the child grow into the man and then wept to see him leave for the mission fields of God. The sunbeam did not fall on Father Florencia. Neither did it fall upon

Juan. He lay in his manger aware that his head was bare of the least trace of holy light.

Father Florencia ceased his lowing, his rigid body sinking back onto his heels. He gazed at Juan, who closed his eyes to shut him out. Only if the father superior kept up his lowing did he belong in the stable.

"Are you ready now, my son, to confess your sins before God?"

Shaking his head, Juan began to cough. He turned on his side and buried his face in his bed to keep from strangling on the bloody refuse from his lungs.

"Your immortal soul is in danger," Florencia said solemnly. "Death is coming for you. You must turn your face to it."

Juan nodded, his face still buried in the straw.

"What are we to think? That you've given your soul over to Satan? Why do you refuse God's absolution? Every mortal man has sins to confess, and you not the least. God will forgive your broken vows, my son, but you must make your confession first."

Juan lay still, struggling to draw his breath. Bits of straw prickled against his face. He knew he must confess. There was so much he wanted to repent, so much he would have done differently had he been able to find the strength. He was sorry for his weakness. He should never have been a priest. A bureaucrat, perhaps, in a government office in Spain—he might have done well at that. He was not meant to be celibate, to be a selfless servant of God. And yet he had taken the vows. He had believed in himself and spoken the words, like so many other men, mortals the same as he. How many of those others, too, had failed? They were none of them divine, none of them were Christ.

He slowly turned his face up from the straw, but still his eyes were closed, keeping out Florencia, keeping himself alone with his soul. He could feel tears beneath his eyelids. "I have sinned," he whispered.

Florencia made a response but Juan did not hear his words, only the sound of his voice. There was so much to confess.

"Velasco," he whispered. "I gave him Christians for his fields. There was no strength in me. I gave him what he asked." He lay still, thinking of how he had once been young and full of zeal. Indians then had been souls to save. When had they become nothing but hands to labor in the fields? His sins against them were more than words could tell.

Tears squeezed out from his tightly closed eyes. "I ceased to pray. I did not love God with my whole heart." He turned his face back into the straw, his tears falling, his thoughts on Ivitachuco, on the crude wooden church, the little convento, the loneliness. So many years.

He heard Florencia speaking, his words close to Juan's ear as he bent over him. "There is more, my son."

Juan lifted his face enough to uncover his mouth. "A horse," he said
faintly. "I rode a horse to battle." He buried his face again. It was useless to speak of that or anything more. His confession was made and his soul was lighter. He had not loved God with his whole heart. He had been weak. He was a man.

Florencia's voice came again, persisting. "And what about the woman?"

Ana. Juan drew comfort from the thought of her. His breath came more easily and he lay drifting with his face in the straw, drowsing in his manger again. There was nothing to confess about Ana. She was God's gift to him in that lonely place. His confession was finished.

The father superior was speaking again, a droning of words that Juan could not make out. His absolution must have been in them. He felt himself absolved. But the words themselves became again the lowing of a cow, a Spanish cow tethered in a Spanish stable. After a time the cow grew silent. Someone led it out into the bright Spanish sun and the manger was peaceful again.

Juan slept—the shallow, fitful sleep his dying body allowed him, never true rest anymore. Once when his eyes fluttered open, he saw Ana returned to her place beside him. That was good. His sleep deepened until stabbing pains in his bowels brought him back again. He lay blinking his eyes, looking at his wife before God. He would have smiled for her except that it would have been too much a lie. He breathed in shallow, gasping breaths.

"Did you rest?" she asked him.

He shook his head and reached out his hand to her. Sometimes she seemed to be his mother; the two were becoming one to him. She took his hand and held it gently in her lap. Closing his eyes, he drifted back into sleep.

✳ Lucia waited for Carlos near the drawbridge that crossed the moat of the great coquina fortress, the Castillo de San Marcos. Behind her the massive walls rose dark against the sky. Before her lay what remained of the town of San Augustín. James Moore had ended his siege the day after Christmas, 1702. The impregnable castillo had saved the Spanish presence in Florida, but as the English departed from San Augustín, they set fire to the town, and because the houses and buildings were built almost entirely of wood, virtually everything burned to the ground—the parochial church, all of the missions, the Convento de San Francisco, the houses of the Royal Governor, Royal Accountant, and Royal Treasurer, and almost all of the private homes. Only a few poor houses on the western side of the town escaped the fire. The town had been ruined, and rebuilding proceeded only slowly. Because the Creeks continued to maraud in the woods, it was difficult for the townspeople to go out and gather poles and thatch for temporary houses, much less to fell trees and saw lumber for permanent ones. Only a few of the wealthiest Spaniards had rebuilt. Everything that now stood, whether temporary or permanent, was crowded in close to the Castillo. The danger of another English attack was still very real, although it did not seem so on a day like today.

The bridge to the Castillo was as open as any street in the town, the guards paying little attention to those who entered. People of all kinds passed across it: soldiers and sailors, well-dressed hidalgos, black and Indian servants, and brightly dressed mestizos. For a little while Lucia watched them come and go, but then she turned away and looked out over the bay where the sun shone down on the water from a high blue autumn sky and seabirds flew, some high and lazy on the way to other places, others skimming low over the water in search of food. Nearby was the wide, shell-flecked sandy street that ran south along the bay toward the convento where she and Carlos and Ana were living as servants of the priest. But the priest was almost dead. And when he was gone, where would they go? That was the question that was ever in their minds now.

Lucia brushed at the mosquitoes and turned again to watch the people in the street. It had taken time for her to get used to all this, so many different kinds of people, Spaniards, Indians from all the provinces of Florida—from Guale, Timucua, and Apalachee, and from places to the south where there had been no missions for a very long time, though the slave-catchers of the English were there. There were also black people in the streets, some slaves of the Spaniards, some escaped from the English. At first she had been fascinated by them and had watched them whenever she was out. But now she was used to them and it was Spaniards she watched, though not all Spaniards—only those who appeared to have means enough to keep servants. It was one of these whom Carlos had followed into the fortress, intending to offer himself for hire.

How long had he been in there? She turned and looked across the drawbridge, but there was still no sign of him. Probably it was good that he was not back yet. Always before he had been quickly rebuffed by anyone he approached to ask for work. It seemed to make little difference that he spoke fluent Spanish. His breechcloth and leggings had been the problem. No one wanted that kind of Indian for a servant. But today he was dressed differently.

Yesterday she had been walking with him along one of the side streets past a little straw-thatched Spanish house with no fence around the yard, and there on a flimsy framework of sticks some clothes were hung out to dry—two shirts and a pair of breeches. Carlos had slowed his step, and she

had known at once what he was thinking, though he did not look directly
at the clothing.

He had stopped suddenly, raising up his foot as if he had stepped on something, a sharp shell, perhaps, in the sandy street. He turned toward the tabby house as he stooped over a little, bringing up the bottom of his injured foot for inspection and holding Lucia's arm to steady himself. As he pretended to look at his foot, he was studying the house instead, the window with its shutters open to the inside, the door that was closed despite the heat of the day, as if someone had gone away for a few moments, pulling it closed behind them.

"They hang thieves," she had said to him softly.

"Only if they catch them," he answered. Then, lowering his foot and straightening up, he said, "Go along. Go on to the convento."

"You are not going to do this," she whispered sharply.

But in letting go of her arm, he gave her a little shove. "Go on," he said firmly, "before we are noticed here."

And so she had gone, her stomach tight with fear as she walked slowly along the street, not daring to look back, but listening, listening, expecting any moment to hear the cry of "Thief!" But the cry did not come, and then she began to have other worries. What would he do with the clothing? How would he get it back to the convento? An Indian in a breechcloth with a bundle of clothing beneath his arm would surely arouse suspicion. And while she worried about this, she heard him coming up behind her. She waited until the footsteps had almost reached her and then glanced back and saw him. He was empty-handed, but smiling triumphantly.

"Where did you put them?" she asked.

"Beneath a barrel in an alley behind the house. I will go back after dark and get them."

And then she herself had smiled.

Even now as she thought about it, she smiled, standing in the shadow of the fortress walls. It was only by luck that the breeches had fit him at all. They were almost too small. But the shirt was loosely tailored and fit well enough, and this morning when they had gone out once again to search for work, he had seen a prosperous-looking gentleman going into the fortress and had followed after him with none of the guards asking any questions of him at all.

She reached up nervously and smoothed her hair. Their plan was that he would secure a position for himself first, and only then would he inquire whether his new master might also have a place for her. If not, he would still take the work, and she and Ana would continue to look elsewhere. If they should fail to find anything more, they might be able to survive, though barely, on what he earned. That would be something, however little. There were Indians in the refugee settlements who had nothing at all and were dying from starvation, and all because of slave-catchers, the same problem here as in Apalachee, only here it was many times worse. Not worse, however, than it had proved to be for Don Patricio and the refugees from Ivitachuco who had tried to start a new life in Timucua. Word had reached San Augustín that the slave-catchers had completely ravaged their encampment. So this place, as bad as it was, was their only hope.

Here the slave-catchers were thick in the country around the town. Any task that required venturing out beyond range of the guns of the fortress was an enterprise of utmost danger. Just as the sawyers could not go into the forests to get lumber without risking death, neither could the people who were hungry go out to fish or gather roots. Many went anyway because they were desperate, and hardly a day went by that the news did not come that someone else had been snatched away or slaughtered by the slave-catchers.

Carlos appeared at last on the drawbridge. He looked handsome in his homespun shirt and dark breeches, but Lucia's hopes fell away as she saw his face. He would not look at her as he approached. She moved with him out into the street, waiting for him to break the silence. They headed north, away from the street that led to the convento.

"He at least allowed me to speak to him," Carlos said at last. "But he told me that the only Indian servants he keeps now are the ones who have always been with him. When he needs someone new, he can hire a Spaniard, since there are so many of them here who have fled from the provinces and have nothing." He paused and then said bitterly, "I never thought I would stoop to ask a Spaniard to be master over me. But now that I am doing it, I can find none who will have me."

Lucia knew there was nothing she could say. She walked in silence beside him and began to wonder where he was leading them, for he did not turn down any of the side streets she expected him to take, but kept to the main street, heading toward the gate of the city. When they reached it, he still did not turn back. They walked out through the gate and a little way further, until at last he stopped and put his hands on his hips and stood looking at the shantytown that sprawled before them.

The people without Spanish blood lived in collections of hovels like this one, making a barrier between the Spaniards and their enemies. They were given nothing except the protection of the guns atop the fortress. The food from the royal storehouse did not come this far. Firewood and building materials were scarce. There was crowding and sickness. There were different settlements for different peoples—the Apalachees lived in San Luís de

Talimali; the Guales, from the coastal areas to the north, lived in Santa Caterina de Guale and Tolomato; the Timucuans, who came from the land that was between this place and Apalachee, lived in Santo Tomás de Santa Fé, San Juan del Puerto, Nombre de Dios and Salamototo. In another settlement were the black people who had escaped slavery in Carolina. The Spaniards allowed them their freedom, hoping to weaken the English colony by encouraging their slaves to run away. Lucia thought as she stood there that slavery under the English must be the worst thing in the world if life in this place was preferable to it. Here was nothing but ragged huts and crude lean-tos with emaciated, idled people sitting listlessly about. There were no trees, no grass, no dogs. Everything that could possibly be eaten or burned for fuel was gone.

For a long time Carlos stood staring out at it. Then at last he turned back to the gate, moving slowly, seeming very tired now. Lucia reached out to take his arm in comfort, but he shrugged her hand away, and she left him alone, walking in silence beside him.

☀ Through half closed eyes Juan looked up at Ana and Solana, at their two faces golden in the candlelight, hovering close before the darkness beyond. As Ana reached out with a damp cloth and wiped his forehead, he closed his eyes and felt himself in the convento at Ivitachuco, the fire glowing warmly in the hearth, Ana serving them cassina as Solana told him gossip from San Luís. He opened his eyes and looked at them again, Ana having retreated a little now, sitting back in deference to Solana.

"You know," he murmured to Solana. Then he swallowed to ease the pain in his throat. His face burned with fever. His mouth was dry.

"What do I know, my friend?" Solana asked gently.

"About Ana," Juan whispered. "And me."

Solana nodded. "I've never judged."

"I'm dying."

"Yes," Solana said quietly.

"Don't let her be alone."

Solana looked at him without replying. In the candlelight beyond, Ana dropped her eyes.

Juan gazed at her. "She is a true Christian," he said softly. "Always true. Always. Let her serve you. I beg of you. Take care of her. She is my wife."

Solana still hesitated. His eyes flickered up and stared beyond the priest into the darkness. At last he said, "Be at peace, my friend."

"Bless you," Juan murmured and closed his eyes, weary from so much talk. His breath was shallow and filled with pain.

He heard a stirring, Ana coming close again, but his eyes remained closed. He drifted to Ivitachuco and walked through a field of golden wheat. A cool cloth wiped his face and he reached up feebly for Ana's hand and drew it down and held it against his heart. His eyes fluttered open, but he could barely see her now. Darkness was swallowing her. He knew he should be taking another breath, but he only looked at her, seeing nothing but the barest outline of her in the gathering darkness. From a distance he heard her speak his name. He took a final breath. There was no more pain. The darkness closed and he felt himself receding into it, moving through it toward a peaceful light.

※ Two days after they buried Father Juan, Carlos stood before the house where Manuel Solana was staying, one of the few substantial houses in the town. At the gate in the high pole fence he pulled a dangling rope and heard the clang of the bell within. He brushed at the mosquitoes that hummed near his ears. They were bad here, but not as bad as in the Apalachee shantytown where he and Lucia and Ana had just spent their first night after having been turned out of the convento. He had not slept at all, lying there in the sorry lean-to they had built with palmetto fronds and sticks and a piece of rotten sailcloth he had found near the harbor. He had lain awake feeling the chill of the autumn night and brushing at the mosquitoes, made sluggish by the cool weather, and he had worried about the coming winter with no blankets or food or firewood. As he lay there, he had been filled with fear, a hard, palpable fear that was more for Lucia than for himself. Death was all around them in that place. Were he alone, he would not feel so much dread, for what would his own death matter in so meaningless a world as this one had become? But now he had Lucia, and the fear that was in him was the fear of losing her.

He reached for the bell rope and rang again. Just as the bell clanged, the gate in the high fence opened and before him stood an aged black man dressed in old, frayed clothing. The man's manner was hard and his eyes sharp as they rose to Carlos' height and noted the Indian features of his hair and eyes and skin and then moved quickly down to examine the shirt, the breeches, and even the shoes and stockings that Carlos had stolen that very morning to better his chances of gaining access to this place. The man could not see the pain in his feet from the terrible fit of the shoes.

"I have come to see Don Manuel Solana," Carlos said smoothly, affecting the air of a high-born Spaniard.

The man's face grew harder and again he looked him over from head to foot. "This is not the house of Solana," he said guardedly.

"Of course not," Carlos said impatiently, as if he were a man of substance with no time for the impertinance of slaves. "It is the house of Florencia. But Don Manuel has been staying here since he arrived from Apalachee. Surely you know what goes on in your own house. Tell Don Manuel that Don Carlos is here."

"*Don* Carlos?" The black man was looking closely at his face now, at the shape of his eyes and the darkness of his skin.

"Don Carlos. From Apalachee." Carlos waved his hand impatiently. "Go, man."

The black man tightened his lips and drew in a perturbed breath through flared nostrils. Then he turned abruptly and disappeared. He had not asked Carlos to step inside, but neither had he closed the gate.

Carlos stood calmly and surveyed the courtyard through the open gate. There was a well with waist-high boxing on which a wooden bucket stood, its rope, scarcely ten feet long, lying haphazardly on the ground. Small orange and pomegranate trees were scattered about, all planted since the fires of the siege. He could hear low voices coming from a place in the yard hidden from his view. Then the voices ceased.

After a moment the black man reappeared. "Follow me," he said curtly.

Carlos went in through the gate and now had a view of the newly built wooden house. His eyes traveled up to a balcony where a finely dressed woman stood fanning herself as she stared idly over the yard. As the woman's gaze turned down to him, Carlos looked away, and he saw Solana, his back to him, strolling in the courtyard along a fence of low, split palings surrounding a vegetable garden. When he reached a small outbuilding at the far corner, Solana turned back, his demeanor stern. Carlos, crossing the courtyard, nodded courteously, but Solana looked away toward the house and the balcony and the woman who was there.

Finally, when Carlos had come close enough to be greeted, Solana looked at him contemptuously and said, "*Don* Carlos, is it? Since when were you made an hidalgo?"

"Since Don Patricio's death," said Carlos. "I succeed him as chief of Ivitachuco."

Solana scoffed. "There is no more Ivitachuco. Where did you steal those clothes?"

"From the governor's house," said Carlos, as if they were friends making a joke. "Where did you steal yours?"

Solana glared at him, angered at his disingenuous bluff. "What do you want?" he said.

"I come on behalf of Ana, the priest's woman."

"As a beggar, then." Solana turned away and stood looking into the garden. For a moment Carlos expected him to order the black man to put him out. But the order did not come.

"She tried to see you yesterday," said Carlos, still attempting to be civil. "But she was turned away at the gate. It seems your man did not understand who she was."

"Why should I grant an audience to an Indian woman?" asked Solana. "Of course she was turned away. The same as I should have done to you."

"I am speaking of Ana," said Carlos, his voice hardening. "The priest's woman. The one you promised him you would care for."

"You do not know what you are talking about." Solana was still facing away. Carlos watched him and knew now why Solana had let him in. It was to lay the matter to rest. Nothing more.

"I am speaking of the promise that you made to the priest," said Carlos, knowing now that it was hopeless. "You can deny it to me and to Ana, but not to God in heaven."

"Do you think God gives special rewards to the mistresses of his priests?" He gave a mocking laugh. "Villalva used to tell me you were a theologian. I never realized the extent of it." He turned to face him. "The priest is dead. He left no family. I paid for masses to be said for him. My obligations are over. I made no promise to him. Do you hear me? I want you to tell this to the woman. I owe her nothing. I do not want her coming here again. Do you hear me?"

"I hear you. And Father Juan hears you, too. How long were you his friend? For how many years? You were the last one in this world he spoke to. With your assurance, he closed his eyes and died in peace. And now you bring torment to his soul."

"Who the devil do you think you are to speak this way to me?" Solana's voice was rising, his face turning red with anger. "Who do you think you are, you son of an Indian whore? I am sick to death of goddamned Indians! Traitors and whores! I lost everything because of you! Get out of here, you son of a bitch! God blast you to hell! Get out!" Solana turned away and walked quickly toward the house. "José!" he shouted, and the black man came running. "Throw this Indian bastard out!"

The black man came toward Carlos, agitated, muttering under his breath in a language Carlos had never heard before.

"Never mind, Grandfather," Carlos said quietly and started across the courtyard. The man followed, still muttering, and slammed the gate behind him when he went out.

Carlos stood in the street, calming himself, trying to think what to do next. That had been their one remaining hope, to prevail upon Solana to take Ana in. Had Solana done so, there may have been enough scraps from that house to keep the three of them alive. But now their last tie to the Spaniards was gone. Standing there, he began to feel again the pain in his feet, forgotten in the heat of the encounter in the courtyard. Moving into a nearby alley, he took off his shoes and stockings. He looked at them a moment, and then, wrapping the stockings around the shoes and tucking them under his arm, he went off to find someone to whom he could trade them for a bit of corn. If nothing else, then, he would be a thief.

CHAPTER NINETEEN

In the Apalachee shantytown, Lucia lay awake, listening to the wind blowing in the night, feeling its icy breath as it seeped through the thatch of the hut. The three of them were huddled together for warmth, Carlos on one side of her, Ana on the other. She thought it likely that both of the others were also awake, and yet she lay very still in case at least one of them might have found some sleep. The night was nearly over. She felt as if she had not slept at all, though surely she had—there must have been moments when she had drifted off.

The winter had been worse than they had feared. They had not been able to imagine the misery of living without a fire whenever they wanted one. It was worse than starving to endure this endless cold without relief, no warmth at all except what the Sun would send down on a clear day. No fire. No blanket but a sorry piece of sailcloth. No food except what Carlos risked his life to steal. The Spaniards hanged thieves in the courtyard of the fortress or sent them out to sea to be worked to death as galley slaves. The fear that she felt whenever he was gone was worse than the hunger he was trying to fend off. Twice he had almost been caught, twice that she knew of because she had been with him and had heard the cry go up close behind as the theft had been discovered, though both times he had managed to get rid of the thing, a length of cloth the first time and a pewter tankard the second, and they had slipped away through the confusion without being noticed or suspected. She had begged him not to try it anymore. She had wept and behaved badly, and she would do it again in spite of her resolve against it, knowing it was hopeless to protest, seeing how thin he and Ana were and feeling her own strength waning. They had to eat, at least a little. But whenever he brought something home, she would hoard it away and ration it out in the smallest portions to put off as long as possible the necessity of his going out to steal more.

Sometimes they would take their chances with the slave-catchers. They would go out with others, in a large group for safety, and dig for clams in the mud of the marsh creek that ran near the shantytown or try their luck at fishing. But because there were so many foraging together, there was never much to show for a day's effort. And those who ventured off alone were taking a risk that was greater even than thieving. Hardly a day passed that someone was not taken. A woman. A child. Two women. A man killed and his wife taken. Almost every day. Because people were starving and they had to have food. Because they were freezing and they had to have wood.

This wind. Blowing bitterly cold from the northeast. A storm was coming, and the roof would leak. Already the wind was enlarging the holes. A storm like this could last for days. And there was no wood. No food. And now in the wind the baby was crying. The baby again. That was the misery that capped it all. That dying baby in the hut beside them. Those cries that went on and on. How had it lived so long? Teresa, the mother, was very young, this child her first, and she cried when the baby cried. She had enough milk in her breasts to keep it alive, but not enough to stop the crying. It was a thin, pitiful little thing, and Teresa was thin, and Ana and Carlos were thin, and Lucia herself was thin. But at least, thought Lucia, she did not have the added agony of a child. Not a child of her own. Only that poor little sorrow in the next hut. Her own menstrual blood continued to flow, moon after moon, and she wondered sometimes if she would be like Ana and never conceive at all. But for the present she was glad she had not conceived. Because there was no wood here. No food.

Why had they come? In Apalachee there had been food. But there was nothing there to keep the slave-catchers away. Here there were the guns of the fortress, giving them a little island of safety. But there was no food. No life.

Carlos stirred beside her and she reached over and put her hand on him. He was tense, and she knew he had not been sleeping. Or maybe the baby had wakened him. But probably he had not slept at all. He lay very still, tight with thought and worry, and he did not respond to her hand on his leg or to her wakefulness beside him.

On the other side of her, Ana moved, turning from her side to her back.

"That baby," Ana said into the darkness.

Lucia reached over to make sure that Ana was still covered by the edge of the sailcloth. The wind was easing a little with the coming of the morning, but it still gusted and the air was very cold. Soon it would be raining.

"Carlos," she said quietly.

"What is it?"

"We cannot stay here any longer."

Carlos lay very still and made no reply. Lucia did not try to touch him.

She wrapped her arms about herself beneath the thin sailcloth and shivered
with the cold and the tension she felt.

"We must go north to the Creeks," she said into the silence. "It is the only place left where people can live. It is the only place where there are still towns, where people can grow corn and hunt and move around the country without fear."

"And how many Apalachees have the Creeks killed?" said Carlos, anger in his voice. "In Ayubale how many babies did I see impaled on stakes, like turkeys roasted at a fire?"

"But why do they do it?" said Lucia. Tension was squeezing her chest, making it difficult to speak. "It is the English who pay them for slaves. The English are our enemies, not the Creeks."

"There is truth in that," Ana said, speaking softly in the darkness. "When I was a child, there was no Carolina, and the Creeks were our friends. They would come down among us and trade for Spanish cloth and for knives and scissors and hatchets. Not a large trade. Not like what they have now with the English. But there was friendliness. Some of our people would go into their country, sometimes to live, and there would be marriages both ways. There were connections between us. But then the English came, and the slave-catching started."

"They have destroyed us," said Carlos.

"But not the Creeks," said Lucia. "It is the English who have destroyed us."

"It is the Creeks who have killed," said Carlos. "They are the ones who have dragged away our women and children. I have seen what they have done. You have seen it."

"But why have they done it, my husband? That is what you must consider. It is because the English pay them to enslave us. The Creeks are like hunters. A man who kills a deer has not declared war on deer. Men and deer are not enemies. Hunting is not war. It is the English who are our enemies, not the Creeks. It is the English who have turned us into deer."

"That is a strange way of thinking," Carlos said coldly.

"But try to see it. Our people have always gone in peace among the Creeks. You heard what Ana said. And the worse the slave-catching has become, the more our own people have gone up to live in the Creek country and been accepted there as friends. The only peace for anyone is in a place where the English do not make people into deer. And that is in the trading towns of the Creeks."

There was silence then, and Carlos did not say anything. Lucia was aware of Ana lying very still on the other side of her.

"What do you think, my mother's sister?" Lucia asked softly.

"It is hard to know what to think," said Ana. "I am a Christian woman. I would never want to live among pagans. But we are starving here."

"Among Christians we starve," said Lucia.

"If they had more food, they would give it to us," said Ana. "I am sure of it. But there is not enough."

"They give it first to Spaniards," said Carlos.

"Yes," said Ana.

"And if there were any scraps," he said, "they would throw them to the Indians. But there are none."

"That is true," said Ana. "But you have a hard way of saying it."

"Would you come with us to the Creeks, my mother's sister?" asked Lucia.

"Are you going?"

There was a pause, a silence. "I do not know," said Lucia. Then silence again. Lucia looked toward Carlos in the darkness. "Are we going?" she asked him softly. But still he would not speak, and the silence settled over them again.

Lucia remembered again the night in the stockade at Ivitachuco when he had sat beside her, leaning back against the cartwheel in silence. She watched him now in the first faint light of dawn and wanted to touch him. But instead she kept her distance, close but not touching, leaving him to his silence and his thought. And finally, when the light had grown so much that she could see the outline of his face, he spoke.

"The hardest thing would be to get away," he said. "To get through the circle of slave-catchers."

"But if we are going to join them," said Ana, "would they not let us go through?"

"They do not stop for conversation," said Carlos. "And they would not believe us anyhow. They would not want to. We are guns and cloth to them."

"This does not sound good," said Ana. "Where is the safety in it?"

"The safety is in being in Creek country," said Lucia. "Once we are there, we are English Indians, not Spanish anymore."

Ana made no reply. Lucia knew she was thinking of the priest and regretting that things were turning out this way. If only Solana had not betrayed her.

"We will have to go in the night," said Carlos. "And it will not be easy. We do not know the country."

"We can talk to people who know the country," said Lucia. "We can find out how to go." If only she could reach over and touch him. He was better now, not so withdrawn. But still she waited, not wanting to seem as if she had won something when all she had done was help him see what he had

to see, what he would have come to see on his own in time. He had been
awake all night. Surely this was part of what he had been thinking.

"We will need some moonlight," he said. "But not too much. The half moon. That is when we should go."

Lucia stared up into the darkness that still hung above them beneath the roof. There was no food. That was the problem. It might be better to leave now, even with the moon too dark. Except that a storm was coming. It would be foolish to go out in that.

"I will go into town again," said Carlos. "Today. As soon as it is light. I will get enough food to carry us through."

"No," said Lucia. "We can find food some other way."

"What other way?"

"Something less dangerous."

"Everything is dangerous."

"We will go hungry then. I would rather go hungry."

"That is fine," Carlos said sharply. "A good solution. We will starve to death. That will take care of everything." He pushed aside the sailcloth blanket and got up. There was enough light now to see.

Lucia pushed up on her elbows to look at him. "What do you mean, starve to death?" She, too, was getting angry. "We are not going to starve to death in a few days."

"No, probably not. We might still have the strength to crawl out of here. It would be something to see, the three of us dragging ourselves into the arms of the slave-catchers."

"Carlos!" Tears were coming now. She could not stop them. "Please! Do not go out there again. Please. Let us think of something else."

"I do not want this from you," said Carlos, starting toward the door. "It is bad enough without this." He stopped for a moment, but did not look back at her. "What else is there? You tell me that? You tell me what else I can do?"

She shook her head, trying to stop crying, knowing there was nothing else. He went out and she lay back, still crying. Ana put an arm around her and held her.

"You are too upset about it," said Ana. "It is the hunger that does this to you. You are not seeing things clearly."

"I know," said Lucia. "I cannot help myself." Then she sat up suddenly and pushed back the sailcloth. Getting to her feet, she started toward the door.

"Lucia!"

"No, it is all right. I just want to talk to him. Make it up. It will be all right."

She ducked outside into the cold, gray morning and walked quickly among the huts, winding her way toward the town, looking for him. At last she saw him up ahead and started running. He did not know she was behind him and he walked on with a long, steady stride. She watched him as she ran, his tall form dark and beautiful to her in the grayness of the morning. The wind was still blowing in gusts, rattling the palmetto thatch on the huts that she passed, but she was not feeling the cold now. Because of the wind he did not hear her following until she was almost upon him. He turned then and saw her. For a moment his face was guarded, as if he thought she had come after him to carry on the argument. But it must have shown on her that it was over because his face relaxed and his eyes smiled as he stood waiting for her to come up to him.

"My sweet one," he teased, putting out his arm to slip it around her waist and draw her along to walk beside him. "So easy-going. So agreeable."

She laughed. "Sometimes I am. In Creek country I will be that way all the time."

"Good. We are almost there."

"We are," she said. "There will be an end to all of this. Among the Creeks we will live like human beings." They were walking slowly along, the city gate not far ahead. A few other people were out in the morning, but not many yet, because of the cold.

"We should have gone long ago," said Carlos. "When Maria went."

"You asked me then. Do you remember? That morning by the stream?"

"I remember."

"But you did not mean it."

"Why do you say that?"

She shrugged. "It did not seem to me that you meant it."

"Why not?"

"Who was I to you then? It did not seem to me that you could mean it."

"I meant it."

"Maybe now, thinking back."

"I meant it then."

"Is that true?"

"What do you want from me, a Christian oath?"

"Then why did you not tell me that you meant it?"

"Because I did not think you would come with me."

"I would have."

"You say that now. But then you were the White Sun Woman. You said you would never leave Apalachee.

She nodded. "It is true. I did say that."

"So there it is."

They walked for a moment in silence. Then she said, "But if I had known you really meant it."

He squeezed his arm more tightly around her. "Will you come with me now? To Creek country? When the storm is over and the moon is half full?"

She smiled. "Now that you have made yourself clear, I certainly will."

"Good." He dropped his arm away. "Now let me go do what I have to do."

"Go on," she said. She stopped and let him go ahead. "I am very easy-going in matters like this," she said after him. "I will have some firewood when you get back. Whatever you bring for us to eat, we will not eat it raw. We will cook it."

He looked back, his face was serious again. "Be careful then, if you are going for firewood."

She nodded and stood for a moment, watching him walk on toward the gate. Then she turned and went back to Ana.

☀ A large group went out to gather firewood that day. The threat of the storm drove them to it, and as the number of those gathering at the edge of the shantytown increased, even more people came and joined them, thinking there would be safety in the midst of such a crowd. But with so many people, it was necessary to go deep into the forest, those ahead struggling under growing loads of gathered deadwood, those behind moving on empty-handed until gradually the ones in front had all they could carry, and the ones behind moved past them and began to find the wood.

Lucia and Ana were in the middle of the crowd and had their loads before some of the others behind them. Lucia, when she could carry no more, dumped her load at the foot of a tall pine. It was exhilarating to be so deep in the forest, as if a kind of freedom had been won. She felt no danger. Other people were scattered all around. She could see them in the dim light beneath the moss-draped oaks and pines, and there were others she could not see, obscured by palmetto thickets and vines, though she could hear the low murmur of their voices.

Ana came up beside her and dropped her wood next to Lucia's and brushed off her hands. Other people were going by, still gathering their loads.

"Did you see the kunti?" asked Lucia, nodding at the thin, green, briery vines growing up from the forest floor into the trees.

Ana nodded, her eyes bright. "We have come in so far. When was the last time we saw kunti? When did we last taste kunti gruel?"

"It has been a long time," said Lucia. She was searching now among the wood they had gathered, looking for sticks that would be good for digging. She found a strong one of the right thickness, long enough to be broken in two. She pulled it up against her knee, struggling hard to break it and realizing in the struggle how weak she had become from so much hunger. But here was kunti, its large, starchy tubers not yet dug by the hungry people who had scoured the places closer in.

She gave half the stick to Ana. "It is not sharp," she said, "but I think the ground is soft enough." They went to work, digging into the earth at the base of the vines, using the sticks and using their hands, prying the fat tubers loose from the soil until they had made a pile of them. Then they moved on to another place and started digging some more.

Lucia was happy now. The storm was closing in, the sky getting darker, the wind blowing in heavy gusts. But they had firewood, and if they were careful not to waste it, it would last the few days until the moon was right. And they had kunti tubers to pulverize and make into a gruel to go along with whatever else Carlos brought home. There would be plenty of food now and they could build up their strength while they waited. And then they would get out of this place.

The wind was steadily rising. It rocked the trees and whipped the palmetto, rattling it so loudly they could not hear the other people anymore. Lucia looked up. Her hands were cold and stiff from the damp earth, and she rubbed them on her skirt as she looked around. They were alone.

"Ana," she said, rising to her feet.

Ana was working hard to dig loose a large tuber. She did not hear her over the sound of the wind.

"Ana!" Lucia spoke more loudly and Ana looked up. "We had better go," Lucia said.

Now Ana, too, was looking around, becoming concerned as she got to her feet. She bent over and quickly gathered up the tubers into her skirt and brought them over and dumped them down on the ground with the ones that Lucia was stuffing into a bag of woven marsh grass that she had brought with her.

"Where did everyone go?" asked Ana.

Lucia looked around again, feeling the beginning of fear. She shook her head. It was hard to understand what had happened. The others had drifted away, but surely they were not far.

"I do not think we should go looking for them," said Lucia. "I think we should start back. Probably they are heading back, too. The storm is almost here." She tied the bag of tubers to her belt. It pulled heavily and bumped against her leg as she moved over to where Ana was gathering up the firewood. Already Ana had more than half of it in her arms.

"Let me take some of that," said Lucia. "You have too much."

"No," said Ana. "Get what is there. Hurry."

The fear was growing stronger. Lucia fumbled with the wood. Be still, she told herself. Just pick it up. Think of good things. Of the fire tonight. Of the food.

She had the load now. She motioned for Ana to go on and then followed behind her. There was no path here, no fixed way to go. But they knew they were going in the right direction. It was going to be all right. There would be a fire. And Carlos would be coming with some food. Maybe meat. How would that be? What if he came home with some meat? And they would talk about their day. And she and Ana would tell him what had happened here, how they had lost sight of the others, how there had been some uneasy moments.

Ahead of her Ana paused and then looked back and said, "Do you think we are going right?"

"Yes," said Lucia. "This is the way." But the fear was coming into her heart now, beating in her blood. Where were the others?

Ana went on, walking faster, and Lucia followed, the wood growing heavy in her arms, the bag of tubers bumping against her leg. What if this was not the way? Coming in they had had their eyes on the ground looking for wood, following others and not paying attention. But surely this was the way. The general direction. It was only a matter of hurrying along. And then they would be home.

Ana stopped suddenly, Lucia bumping against her. Ana's wood fell to the ground, and for an instant Lucia thought it was because she had collided with her, but now Ana was turning, her hands reaching to turn Lucia, too, and push her back. And then Lucia saw warriors moving out from a thicket of palmettos, their eyes fixed on the two women. Dropping her wood, Lucia turned and started to run. *Run, run!* It was all she could think. *Run! Slavecatchers! Run!* Then ahead, another painted face moved into her path. She wheeled and turned and ran. And there was another. *No! Oh, Carlos! Which way?* She wheeled and ran, wildly now. No way to go. She tried to dodge. Then her leg was caught, held fast, pulled. *No!* The earth slammed hard against her, a weight pressed down on her body, someone with his knee in her back. *Oh, Carlos! Not this!* Her arms were drawn back and a thong wrapped tightly around her wrists.

She pulled up her face from the earth. There was dirt in her mouth. She turned her head, looking back, and saw the knee of the man who straddled her, deerskin leggings with a beaded fringe. Beyond, still on her feet, Ana was caught between two men, her face wild as they bound her. And through the leaves of the trees the rain began to fall.

Part Two

CAROLINA

1704–1705

CHAPTER TWENTY

The Jamaica sky was bright blue, the air hot and humid as the coach carrying Isaac Bull rolled out of Kingston into the green countryside. Perspiration trickled down his skin beneath his clothes, soaking into his linen shirt to the very ruffles that hung limply from the wide sleeves of his full-skirted coat. He took off the coat, folded it, and laid it on the seat beside him. Even his cravat, stylishly twisted with its ends stuck through a buttonhole of his embroidered waistcoat, felt damp and heavy. He shed the waistcoat and then fumbled through the pockets of his folded coat and found a lace handkerchief and wiped his face. His periwig was like a stifling blanket. It would take time to become accustomed to this new climate. There was never a May so hot as this in England.

Isaac settled back and closed his eyes, exhausted from his long sea journey. He had expected to spend this night in Kingston waiting for his cousin to receive notification of his arrival and send a coach for him. But he had barely set foot on land when a helpful stranger, impressed at meeting a kinsman of Theophilus Swade, offered his own coach and driver to take him straightway to Swade Hall. The man had even sent a messenger ahead by fast horse to alert Swade of his arrival. Isaac might be far from the land of his birth, but at least here in this place he would have the connections he needed to reestablish his position in life. Though who could ever have imagined that the time would come when a kinsman by marriage would have greater regard for his interests than did the brother of his own blood.

Isaac's thoughts grew dim, and he slept in the heavy heat. When he awoke again, daylight was fading and the air had cooled a little. Looking out the window of the coach, he saw green fields of cane turning golden in the Jamaican twilight. Mountains loomed ahead like a towering wall, their slopes dark green with the lushness of forest. The high peaks, visible only when Isaac craned his neck almost out of the window, were fading from blue to purple. The cooler air was a welcome relief.

Sitting on the edge of his seat, Isaac gave his attention to the world outside and tried to absorb all that was new to him. He especially watched the slaves in the fields, men and women naked to the waist, their faces lost in the fading light so that all he saw was their bodies, starkly black against the golden cane, and the slicing of their long knives, a continuous motion, never pausing, like some bizarre machine. In all his life until this day, Isaac Bull had seen perhaps five slaves, liveried black men in exotic turbans ornamenting wealthy drawing rooms in London. He had never seen anything like this slavery in Jamaica and he studied it closely.

As the coach rounded a curve in the road, the coachman called out to him that Swade Hall lay ahead. Then his cousin's estate came into view, and Isaac smiled slightly and sat back, shaking his head at the size of the house. Its corner towers made it look like a castle. Stretching between the towers were arched balconies atop arched terraces, like double-tiered aqueducts. Here was what a modest investment and good management could earn in the Indies. A man could right his fortune in a place like this and reclaim lost advantages.

The coach pulled up in front of Swade Hall, and Theophilus Swade came out to meet it, his paunch and his periwig bouncing with his buoyant stride as he called out a welcome to Isaac and threw open the door of the coach to draw him into his rummy embrace.

"Look at you, you're a full-grown man," laughed Swade, holding Isaac by his shoulders and pushing him out to arms length. "But then, every boy who lives long enough turns into one."

Isaac laughed. This was the Swade he remembered, the jocular, affectionate husband of his mother's favorite cousin.

"I'd hoped you'd not forgotten me," he said.

"Forgotten you?" said Swade, turning to walk to the house with his arm about Isaac's shoulder. "I only wish Anne were alive to see you. I can hear her now going on about Molly's younger boy. She never thought that much of Robert, you know. She could smell the devil in him."

"We were grieved at her death," said Isaac, sidestepping the subject of his brother for the moment. "She was like a sister to Mother. We mourned her that way."

"I've not married again," said Swade as he ushered Isaac into the great hall of his house where dozens of chairs lined the walls beneath rich hangings. A liveried footman stood by, a middle-aged black man. "It's all too hard to hold a wife in the Indies. Death stalks them. But I have a few good women in the quarters. Black as the devil and sweet as molasses."

Isaac nodded, only half paying attention. This hall alone was almost as large as the entire townhouse Swade had owned in London. To think that his fortune had grown so large.

"I am impressed, Cousin Swade."

"With my women or my house?"

"Your house. I expected it to be more like the one you had in London."

"That little mouse-hole," Swade laughed, waving his hand. "Rude beginnings, Cousin Isaac. Are you hungry? We can have our supper now, or if you'd rather, you can settle in a bit first. Whichever you choose, we'll do it with a bowl of punch."

"Then I'll take food," said Isaac. "Settle my stomach first."

Swade looked over at the footman. "Tell the kitchen we're ready, Apollo."

The black man nodded and left the hall at a pace that was almost, but not quite, leisurely.

"Apollo?" Isaac said with a smile.

Swade laughed. "Named for the god himself. Can't you see him sipping nectar with Zeus? Well, perhaps not nectar, but he could gnaw a ham bone with Zeus and give the other gods a laugh or two." He steered Isaac toward the long dining table in the center of the hall. "I apologize for not having other guests to keep you company tonight. Tomorrow I'll fill the hall. But tonight there is too much to talk about. England, friends, and family. Your own position and your future. And your voyage—my God! Let's not forget you've just come off the perilous seas."

"I've certainly not forgotten," said Isaac, exaggerating the rolling gait he had brought with him from the ship. "I still have my sea legs."

"What about privateers? Those Frenchmen are a plague upon us. It takes the grace of God to get about the seas these days."

Two slave boys entered to stand behind the chairs of two places already set at one end of the long table. Swade seated himself at the head of the table and Isaac sat at his right, while Apollo brought in a silver bowl of punch—rum mixed with water, lime juice, sugar, and nutmeg. Two silver cups were filled and Swade proposed a toast.

"To you, my dear cousin, and your new life in the colonies."

Isaac smiled, nodded, and took a sip from his cup, while Swade drank down a hearty draught. Then Isaac toasted Swade's health and long life, and Swade drained his cup and refilled it from the bowl.

"Tell me about your adventures with the privateers," said Swade as they settled back in their chairs.

"There were none," said Isaac. "The French were napping, or off chasing some bigger prize. We met no enemy but the weather, and God sided with us in that engagement and brought us through."

"With masts intact?"

"We came through sound."

"Then that was no storm," said Swade. "That was just a little wind and rain. You've not known fear, Cousin Isaac, until you've seen your main and mizzen masts break away. Dear Jesus, you've not prayed until the ship rolls over and the piss runs down your legs before it rights again. God above, I hate ships." He made a motion with his hand to Apollo, and the footman went out and returned immediately with a heavily-laden tray and began setting out the food—roast duck, a roast of fresh pork, pickled peppers, minced meat pie, orange slices, olives, salted fish, a dish of cut pieces of a pale yellow fruit that Isaac could not identify, custard, and candied sweet-meats of still another strange fruit.

"I hope this is enough," said Swade, rising to his feet and taking up a knife to carve the meat. "If not, I'll send to the kitchen for more."

"No, this is quite enough," said Isaac. "More than I can do justice to. Tell me about these fruits, Cousin. Some of them are new to me."

"Try this one," said Swade, pointing with his knife to the yellow fruit. "I'll wager you've had it in England in sweetmeats."

Isaac reached out and picked up a piece and put it in his mouth, a smile breaking over his face. "Pineapple." He chewed it slowly, savoring the sweet flavor, his memory drifting to the shops of London. But in that return to days past, his mood clouded. "I remember it from the days when I could still afford sweetmeats," he said grimly.

Swade had finished his artful carving of the duck and pushed the platter toward Isaac before turning his attention to the pork. "So Robert managed to take everything," said Swade. "It would be of interest to know how he did it."

"He did it first by being the oldest and second by being a thief."

"You have no doubt that your mother left a will?"

"None whatsoever," Isaac said bitterly. He put down the piece of duck he had been lifting to his mouth and felt again the injustice, the wound still raw after more than a year. "She told me of it. She never showed me the will itself, but she showed me the chest, the small blue one in which she kept her papers. She patted it with her hand and told me the will was inside and that it finished the plan that she and Father had for us. When Father died, his estate went to Robert, of course. As first-born, he was the legitimate heir, and I never begrudged him his birthright. My own annuity was but a hundred pounds because I was to inherit Mother's patrimony. Not that her estate would measure up to what Robert had, but at least with that I would have the means to live according to the station in which I was raised. It was all in the little blue chest, she said, and she held it in her lap and patted it."

"But when they opened the chest, the will was not to be found?" asked Swade, pushing the pork toward Isaac and sitting down.

"There was no chest," said Isaac, his voice rising at the outrage, as if it were new again. "I was in London when she died. Two days passed before I reached home. Everything was in order, Robert told me. She had some few papers in her desk, he said, but no will. They had turned the house over looking for one. They had contacted friends and attorneys.

"The blue chest, I told him. Look in her blue chest.

"What blue chest? he said." Isaac banged his hand on the table, sitting forward in a fury. "He looked me squarely in the eye and asked, *What* blue chest? As if he had never seen it, as if we two had not grown up sharing our place at her knee with that blue chest. It was always in her chamber, and when she traveled she never failed to take it with her. And yet he looked into my eyes, my own brother, and said, *What* blue chest?" Isaac sat back in his chair, silenced by his anger and pain.

"May he rot in hell," said Swade, reaching for the custard. "And undoubtedly he will. So in the absence of a will, you received only half your due, and you were left to survive on that and your modest annuity."

"Which was scarcely possible. As soon as my creditors heard about the settlement, they called in all my debts, some of them considerable, and refused to advance me any others. It seems that my entire position was based upon two assumptions that had suddenly been proven false—namely, that I would inherit the whole of my mother's estate, and that my brother would back me in a pinch. So there I was, cut off. The woman I was to marry would not see me anymore. I had to lie in my bed at night and worry whether my scant possessions could be sold for enough to keep me out of debtors' prison. I, who had been raised in comfort on my father's estate, was reduced to a single suit of clothing and a chest of books. A friend, God bless him in heaven, for he's dead now, paid for my passage to Jamaica. If there be a chance in the world to repair my fortunes, he told me, it will be in a place like this."

"But perhaps not in this very place," said Swade, looking at him over his cup of rum. "I would, however, like to see your brother come here to settle."

Isaac gave him a startled look.

"Do you know why I say that?" Swade asked.

"No, I do not," said Isaac, anger in his voice.

"Because Jamaica is a pesthouse," said Swade, leaning forward. "If Robert came here, he could very well be dead in a year, or in five years. Ten years at the most. We have a hundred ways to kill him. A fever would be most likely, chills that would shake him to pieces, sweats that would damn near drown him. Perhaps he'd get the bloody flux, a pretty way to die, blood gushing out both ends. If he lived through that, by God, we'd have other snares for him, and we'd get him before long. Like as not, he'd drink himself to death with the worry of it. We bury them every day, twenty-five, thirty years old, all of them rich, young, and dead. Christ's blood, Cousin, when they get to be twenty, we call them middle-aged and make them judges. I'm forty-one, and they say I'm an old man."

Isaac helped himself to the minced meat pie and then to the custard, relieved that Swade at least was on his side. "People die in England," he said.

"But not like they do here," said Swade, emptying the punch bowl and handing it to the serving boy to be refilled. "I don't want you to settle here, Cousin Isaac. You were a favorite of Anne's and mine. I don't want to take you under my wing and smother away your life."

"I have no means to go elsewhere," said Isaac, sitting back uneasily in his chair. "I will never return to England. It may be I must live as a poor man, but I shan't do it in the land where I once was rich."

"Don't mistake me, Cousin, I do mean to help you. Your hundred pounds a year, well managed, is a sound enough base to build upon. But I think Carolina would be the place for you. It's not the most healthful colony in America, but it's a great improvement over the islands. And it's newly planted, that's the thing. Barely thirty years. Long enough to be established, but not so long that the best opportunities have all been taken up. There's room there for a man in your position."

"Carolina," said Isaac, his brow furrowing as he tried to recall what he knew about the place. "Do they grow sugar there?"

"The climate's not so well-suited for it as here," said Swade. He picked a sweetmeat from the dish and ate it, licking his fingers. "They've not been able to compete with the islands in that. Nor with Virginia in tobacco. It seems that rice will be the crop for Carolina. They ship out more and more of it every year."

"I'd not know where to start," said Isaac. "Here I could learn from you. I have no connections in Carolina."

"But I do. A fellow named Hawkins, a merchant friend. That's the way for you to start—in trade. Improve your capital. You can't get into rice until you have the means to buy the slaves."

"You think this Hawkins will take me on?"

"He will if he can. If he has no place for you, he'll find someone who does. I've done business with John Hawkins for ten years. If I give you a letter, he'll take it to heart."

Isaac stared across the room and let his mind circle, like a sea bird, slowly descending until it came to rest on this new idea—Carolina. He smiled a little. "Would that I had known to pay attention when I heard the name

Carolina spoken in England. I never had the least notion of living there.
Does Spain not press against the place?"

"Carolina presses Spain," said Swade. "There's recent news on that.
Came in on one of Hawkins' ships, from Boston by way of Carolina, Captain Pitts." He turned to Apollo. "Fetch me my *Boston News*. You'll find it
on the table in my chamber." The slave left the hall. "You've not come to
the ends of the earth, Cousin. We have a newspaper in the colonies now.
Out of Boston. Brand new. Captain Pitts brought me the first two copies."

"I'll be interested to see it," said Isaac.

They let the conversation lapse and watched the punch in their cups until
Apollo returned and handed Swade several printed sheets. Swade leafed
through them.

"Here we are. Not a month old. Printed April 24, 1704. The headline
reads, An Account of the Command of Colonel Moore in his Expedition
Last Winter Against the Spaniards and Spanish Indians. In a Letter From
him to the Governor of Carolina." Swade looked at Isaac. "Would you wish
to hear it read?"

"By all means," said Isaac, settling back in his chair.

"Very well, then. This is what it says." Swade cleared his throat. "May it
please your honor to accept of this short narrative of what I with the army
under my command have been doing since my departure from the Ocmulgee on the nineteenth December. On the fourteenth January we came
to a town and strong and almost regular fort, about sun rising, called Ayubale. At our first approach the Indians fired guns and shot arrows at us
briskly, from which we sheltered ourselves under the side of a great mud-
walled house till we could take a view of the fort and consider the best way
of assaulting it—which we concluded to be by breaking down the church
door, which made a part of the fort, with axes. . . ."

Isaac closed his eyes to listen. While Swade read the report with growing
drama in his voice, Isaac pictured in his mind the storming and taking of
Ayubale, the ensuing surrender of Ivitachuco, and the destruction of almost the entire province of Apalachee.

". . . Apalachee is now reduced to such a feeble and low condition, that
it can neither support Saint Augustine with provision or disturb, endamage
or frighten us or our Indians living between us and Apalachee and the
French. In short, we have made Carolina as safe as the conquest of Apalachee can make it. If I had not so many men wounded in our storming of
Ayubale, I would have assaulted Saint Lewis Fort.

"On Sabbath the 23d instant, I came out of Apalachee and am now about
thirty miles on my way home. The number of free Apalachee Indians which

are now under my protection and bound with me to Carolina are thirteen hundred. And one hundred for slaves. Dated in the woods fifty miles north of Apalachee."

Swade put the paper on the table and looked up at Isaac. "I would say that Carolina is far more of a problem to Spain than Spain is to Carolina."

Isaac smiled. "It certainly seems so."

Swade ladled more punch into the silver cups. Then he sent Apollo to fetch tobacco pipes.

"Captain Pitt brought me three of those Apalachee slaves in his cargo," he said, settling back in his chair.

"I've heard it said that Indians make poor slaves," said Isaac.

"They do. They die like children. Too melancholic." Swade took the pipe Apollo offered and let his serving boy light it with a hot coal held in smoking tongs. "Niggers are bad enough at getting sick and dying, but Indians are worse. Yet they're cheap, you see. Only half the price of a nigger. So you get a year's work from an Indian and he's dead. But your new nigger might be dead, too, and that nigger's grave will cost you twice as much. Forty pounds to twenty. It's worth the risk, I say. I take an Indian when I can get one. God knows, you must bow to economy where you can. A planter's greatest cost is his slaves. To keep a hundred slaves, you have to buy six new ones every year. Now figure that. What is it? Every sixteen, seventeen years, you replace them all. They live no longer than that on the average, sixteen or seventeen years." He shook his head.

"I would have thought it the opposite," said Isaac. "If a man had a herd of cattle as large, he'd soon have a great many more through natural increase."

"Niggers don't have the hardiness of other brutes. Far more pickaninnies die then ever live to take up a hoe."

"But at least they die in a Christian land with a chance of seeing God."

"Niggers don't go to God," said Swade, pushing back his chair to make room to stretch out his legs. He folded his hands over his round belly and eyed Isaac narrowly. "They're not Christians."

Isaac reached for a sweetmeat as he considered his response. He knew this debate from the coffee houses of London, but it was different now at the table of a sugar planter whose help he desperately needed. He glanced at Apollo, well-dressed in matching coat and breeches, silk stockings and buckled shoes. Obviously he was a man, the same workmanship of God in slave as in master. Conscience demanded an acknowledgement.

"Surely with the benefit of instruction they could become Christians," he said, keeping his tone carefully dispassionate. "Surely God would be pleased by it."

Swade laughed. "If you knew slaves, you'd know better what you're saying." He sat up suddenly. "Come with me. We'll take a walk, stir up our
blood a bit. I'll show you a sugar plantation."

"In the dark?" asked Isaac.

Swade got to his feet. "Fetch us a lantern, Apollo."

✳ The night air was cool and refreshing. The moonlight spread wide
across the heavens, blotting out the stars and spilling down upon the land-
scape in a silvery half-light beyond the golden glow of the lantern. Black
forms slipped silently through the far edge of the lantern light. Isaac found
it eerie to be in the midst of so many dark and silent people. He felt himself
an intruder among them with his white skin and powdered periwig. But
master, too. His skin, his civility, his superior birth, placed him above these
dark men and women.

"This is one of my mills," said Swade, holding the lantern higher in a
vain attempt to throw light on the large building before them. The open
door and windows were dimly illuminated, and the steady noise of machinery, which earlier had been vague and distant, was now concentrated and
insistent.

"It's water-powered," said Swade, leading Isaac to the doorway.

The two men stood for a moment in silence while Isaac looked in at the
strange scene: machinery and black men and piles of cut cane, all poorly
illuminated by a bright straw fire in a great fireplace on one side of the
room. The fire tender was a naked black boy, perhaps ten years old, his
body glistening with sweat in the yellow light.

"We keep it running around the clock," said Swade. "It's only a matter
of hours, you see, before the juice spoils in the cane. Every piece of cane
cut today will be milled by morning. The juice crushed out here runs into
a pipe that carries it out of this building and into the boiling house. I'd give
you a closer look, but I don't want to disturb my niggers. Feeding the mill
is a tricky business, especially at night. Catch a finger in those rollers and
there's no stopping it until the whole man is crushed through like a stick
of cane."

"My God," said Isaac. He watched the black forms of the workers stooping in the dim light to take up the cane, rising to feed it into the rollers,
stooping again, rhythmic, like the cutting in the fields, never pausing, like
the unrelenting machine.

Swade withdrew his light, and Isaac turned and followed him out through
the moonlight to the adjacent boiling house, lit as the mill-house had been
by firelight. Swade led the way inside. Here it was incredibly hot and stink-

ing. Isaac took out his handkerchief to mop his brow, wishing he could be rid of his periwig. The noise from the mill in the other building faded, like wind in the trees, almost the same as silence. The sounds of the boiling house were quieter and more varied, the plopping sound of thick boiling syrup, the dull metallic rap of a ladle against the lip of a copper cauldron, the humming voices of the two black men who sweated before the row of steaming coppers in the weirdly flickering firelight. Isaac was not sure if the voices were singing or speaking. At times they seemed almost to moan.

"There are four coppers, you see," said Swade, holding up his lantern to throw more light. "The juice comes into the cistern there from the mill-house. Quashee ladles it into the largest copper. They boil it down, moving it from one copper to another until it reaches that small one where Sam is working. He's the one who has to know when to strike it, when to damp the fire and let it cool to crystals. There's no sure way to tell when the time is right to strike. He just has to know. These boys are some of the best niggers I own. But I'll tell you, Cousin, it's like training horses. You can teach them tricks, but you can't raise them from their brutish state and make them Christians. It would be a mockery of Jesus Christ to say he died for creatures like this."

Isaac felt his pulse rise. He had argued this issue in London and felt strongly about it. Christ died for all men, and these were men, however low their station.

"I cannot help but think they have souls," he said tightly. The scene was affecting him, the heat and the stench, the darkness and the firelight, the sweat-drenched black men, the humming, and that moaning sound, strange, not like speech or song.

"They are incapable of understanding Christian precepts," Swade insisted. "You have some things to learn. You'd best be careful where you speak your London views. They'll not be well received in Carolina. A slave-holder must protect his property. There's a question whether the law will ultimately sustain the enslavement of Christians. We all know that. But niggers are heathens, you see, and lack the faculties for conversion. I will never argue from any other position, and if you intend to join the planting class, you'd best start trying it out yourself."

Isaac said nothing, knowing he should not disagree. The silence lengthened as Swade waited for a response. "I understand," Isaac said at last.

"But you don't agree," said Swade. He turned to leave, and as the lantern light swept the boiling house, an image of a man, dark and grotesque, appeared in one corner and then fell back into darkness as the light passed by. Isaac was stunned by the sight and looked hard at the dark form, still faintly visible, a man with his arms strung up above his head. The moaning came from him.

"What is that?" he said, putting a hand on Swade's arm to draw back the lantern light. Swade held the lamp toward the corner, illuminating a black man hanging from his thumbs bound together, his toes barely touching the packed earth floor. He was naked. His back, turned toward them, was raw and bleeding from his neck to his feet, the flesh lashed open into a single wound. His low moaning was almost beyond hearing.

"Mingo," said Swade. "Damn his black hide. Tried to take to the mountains." He drew the lantern away and moved on toward the door. Isaac followed, looking back in horrified fascination.

The air outside was cool and sweet. Isaac breathed deeply and tried to forget what he had seen. Such punishment was as necessary to slavery, he told himself, as the stocks and pillory were necessary to government. He would learn this in time, grow accustomed to it. These things were not so cruel as they might seem to someone unused to them.

"You see those mountains there?" said Swade, raising his hand to the dark wall that blocked out the stars above the horizon. "The whole interior of the island is filled with them. A vast area empty of Englishmen. If a runaway escapes the dogs and gets free of us, we never see him again. There are whole towns of escaped slaves up there. Maroons we call them. Savage people. It's not safe for a white man to venture up there with anything less than an army around him. They're the bane of the island, those mountains."

"So Mingo was caught by the dogs," said Isaac.

"They chased him all night, treed him this morning. And a pity it is. He's trained as a carpenter, but now I'll have to put him in the fields. Such a beating takes twenty pounds off his value, but in the fields we can watch him. He'll wear chains on his legs from now on." Swade shook his head. "He couldn't appreciate the good life he had."

Isaac said nothing. The slaves were pitiful. It was hard for him to believe their lot was beyond improvement.

"I think you are ready for a glass of madeira," said Swade. "Tomorrow I want you to walk about the place. Inquire freely of the niggers anything you wish to know. I'll send a boy with you to help you talk to them. Most of them speak gibberish. Incomprehensible to an Englishman."

Isaac turned with relief to follow Swade back along the road to the house. The night air now seemed stifling. He wished to sit still in a comfortable chair, to take off his periwig and stretch out his legs. But Swade was diverging from the route they had followed before, taking a different way.

"I have one more stop for you," said Swade. "You'll not be sorry."

Isaac followed wearily along, wishing for an end to the lessons. A cluster of small houses appeared before them in the darkness, neat cabins of wood with thatched roofs.

"It's here I keep my house niggers and my women," said Swade. "Mulatto women. Lovely creatures. There's one I want to show you, for your own pleasure."

Isaac's interest began to rise. He looked around, noting his whereabouts more carefully. They passed by two cabins and stopped at the third one. The door was open and it was dark inside until Swade entered with his lantern. On a rude bedstead built against a wall, a young woman stirred, rustling the straw mattress beneath her slender brown body, which was half covered by a linen sheet. She opened her eyes, squinting and holding up her hand against the light. Her breasts were plump and firm with wide, dark nipples. She was little more than a girl, perhaps sixteen.

"Evening, Master," she said sleepily, smiling up at Swade and then glancing at Isaac.

Swade reached out and lifted back the sheet to reveal the whole of her naked body. She turned onto her side, propping herself up on one elbow and running her fingers over the curve of her raised hip. Swade looked at Isaac and smiled, then dropped the sheet back over her.

Isaac felt himself aroused and glanced about the room for distraction, noticing the neatness of it. It was furnished with a table and stool, a wooden cup and bowl. The floor was cleanly swept. She lived in luxury compared to the rude straw huts of the field slaves that he had seen from the window of the coach.

"Her name is Penelope," said Swade. "Visit her whenever you please. She's free of disease. I guarantee it."

Isaac nodded, somewhat embarrassed but not displeased.

"Mr. Bull may return later tonight," Swade said to Penelope as he turned and started toward the door.

Isaac followed.

"I'd like that, Master Swade," Penelope said softly as they went out the door into the night.

※ The parlor of Swade Hall was furnished with finely crafted chairs, chests, and small tables, all imported from England. But most sumptuous of all the furnishings was the parlor bed with its rich brocade hangings drawn closed. Swade had had Isaac's chest brought to this room, along with a decanter of madeira wine and two cut-crystal goblets. Now he filled the goblets and handed one of them to Isaac and took up the other for himself.

"A toast, Cousin Isaac," he said grandly, holding up his glass. "My heart is full tonight and I fain would give words to it. I am alone in Jamaica, without kith or kin. My wife is dead. My son and daughter I've sent to England so they might live long enough to inherit my fortune. And I live with the knowledge that when they do inherit it, some coarse overseer will move his creole wife and brats into Swade Hall and drive my estate into ruin by his larcenous management. I know not why I stay here all alone, except that I fear the sea. And I love what I have built here. I would not rest easy in London knowing it was falling into neglect. So I am resigned to my loneliness, taking refuge in the friends I have around me. But now a kinsman comes, seeking me out above all others in his distress."

Isaac nodded.

"A kinsman," Swade repeated, savoring the word. "With a kinsman comes all the links of blood and marriage, all the memories of days and faces passed away. Those lovely summers in England on your father's estate, your mother and my wife linked in happy cousinhood, and you, companionable boy that you were, accompanying your father and me on a hunt or on business about the place. I feared all my links of kin were broken by the wide ocean. But here you've come, remembering those days, turning in your desperate hour to your Cousin Theophilus. I am moved. If only I loved you less, I would keep you with me. But I'll take comfort in the nearness of Carolina. I have a scheme for you, dear Cousin. Let us drink first to kinship."

"May it always be held dear," said Isaac, raising his glass.

They seated themselves then in two of the parlor chairs, and Swade leaned back, his elbows on the arms of his chair, his wine goblet enclosed in both hands before his chin.

"I'm going to outfit a ship. I normally stay away from shipping and work instead through agents in Kingston. Pay them to take the risks. But this war with France has driven the risks so high, and the fees in proportion, that there's scarcely any profit left when I'm done with shipping costs. So I propose to outfit my own ship, fill the hold with rum and sugar, put you aboard as my agent, and send you to Charles Town in Carolina. You've shown luck in evading privateers. Perhaps it will hold. In Charles Town you can work with John Hawkins to gather a return cargo for me. You collect the commission on my outgoing shipment and on a share of my incoming, and there you have something to start with in Carolina."

"Well," said Isaac, looking into his wine glass and searching for appropriate words. "God bless you, Cousin. I never expected such kindness."

"Kindness? You may very well be hauled into Martinico by a Frenchman. I'm employing you to share my risk. You risk your life and I risk my money. This is a business venture."

"Very well," said Isaac, looking up and raising his glass. "To business."

Swade drained his goblet and set it down in a gesture of satisfaction. "Shall we spend the night drinking toasts, or retire for a bit of sleep before morning comes?"

"You've given me much to lie abed and think about," said Isaac.

"Not the least of which is Penelope," said Swade, bending toward him with a chuckle as he rose to his feet.

"She is lovely," said Isaac, rising after him. He went with Swade to the door of the parlor and stood for a moment watching him walk away across the dimly lit hall. Then he turned back to the curtained parlor bed, which was more splendidly furnished than any other in which he had ever slept.

Isaac made his way in silence through the darkness of Swade Hall. He shrouded his lantern with his coat so that he could barely see beyond each step. He was ashamed of his stealth. He knew he should go boldly with the lantern fully bright, unabashed at his passion. The last woman he had was a chambermaid in England. Yet he was not desperate. He felt he was in control of himself. It was only that the memory of Penelope was so fresh, the sheet turned back, her naked body long and brown, her fingers moving tantalizingly along her flesh.

He uncovered the lantern by degrees, gaining boldness as he moved through the entryway toward the outer door. He opened the door soundlessly and slipped out into the night. Combining passion with stealth was too old a habit to shed in a single night.

A dog came out from beneath the house and greeted him with wagging tail, then moved before him down the road, checking over his shoulder from time to time to make sure his man-friend was following. Isaac watched him as he trotted in the furthest light of the lantern, and he wondered if this were one of the same dogs who only last night had gone crashing through the forest in pursuit of Mingo. The image of that other naked body he had seen that night intruded into his mind, the black man hanging by up-stretched arms in the boiling house, his open back raw and glistening in the firelight. Even now he was hanging there.

And Penelope. Was she not a slave like Mingo? Might she someday be hung by her thumbs? Isaac's passion began to fade. He tried to forget the dismal scene in the boiling house, but it would not be pushed away. Could he lose himself with Penelope after all he had seen this day? Knowing she was less free than the dog that trotted before him? He stopped and stood for a long time in the warm, humid night, undecided. Then, with a weary sigh, he turned around and went back to the bed in the parlor.

CHAPTER TWENTY-ONE

Isaac left Jamaica in December on the sloop Fair Hope, her hold filled with sugar and rum. It was a small vessel and he was the only passenger aboard. He shared the captain's cabin. As they sailed north past Cuba and then up the long eastern coast of Florida, the air gradually cooled until at last, as they drew near Carolina, they felt the chill of winter. Isaac rejoiced in the cold weather as he stood on the deck and watched the coast grow larger. This new land had seasons closer to the ones he had known in England. A small part, at least, of what he had lost in leaving his native land had been given back to him.

As they came into Charles Town harbor, the sky was pale blue, the cold air growing warmer in the late morning sun. Gulls soared and swooped above them, their creaking voices pleasant on the breeze, heightening the peacefulness of the winter day. The harbor was still. Only two other sloops and a brigantine rode quietly on the water along with fishing boats and periagos and canoes from inland river plantations. Fair Hope dropped her anchor out in the bay, and Isaac was rowed ashore in a skiff.

For a little while Isaac walked about the streets of Charles Town, enthralled with how raw it was. Rough-timbered warehouses stood side by side with more finely constructed counting houses, shops, taverns, and homes. Among the people on the streets he saw an occasional gentleman in powdered wig and silk stockings, and behind the curtains of a sedan chair that went by on the shoulders of strong black men he glimpsed a richly dressed woman, as fashionable as any London lady of quality. Yet most of the people were dressed in ill-matched combinations of homespun and cheap English cloth, some of the men in leather breeches, many wigless, their scrawny hair hanging lank beneath their hats. There were stockingless, barefooted black men in ragged breeches and tattered shirts, and black women in thin dresses, keeping to the sun-warmed side of the streets as they went about their business. And he saw Indians: a woman sitting in the sun selling Indian pottery in forms that imitated European tableware; another peddling a basket of herbs; and lounging near the water were Indian men in bright loincloths and leather leggings, some with English shirts worn loose. Both men and women wore blankets about their shoulders, red, blue, or dirty white with a stripe of red about the border. They were a swarthy people, with jet black hair and exotic faces, some of them marked with strange tattoos. Isaac took it all in, happy that his life had brought him to this new place, to this toehold of settled land at the edge of a new world, where civilized Christians mingled with heathen savages from the jungles of Africa and the forests of America.

He soon found John Hawkins' counting house, next door to the sign of the Indian Queen, just as the captain of his sloop had directed him. A young clerk showed him into Hawkins' private office.

"A Mr. Bull to see you, sir," said the clerk. "Just arrived on Captain Bradley."

The clerk withdrew, leaving Isaac alone with the stout gentleman who sat before the fire, an open ledger on his lap. He had a pleasant, ruddy face with striking blue eyes. John Hawkins set the book on a table beside his chair and rose with some difficulty, extending his hand to Isaac. "So you've come from Jamaica," he said. "Obviously you escaped the French."

"By God's providence," said Isaac. "It was an uneasy voyage. I'm glad to be ashore." He reached into the pocket of his coat and brought out a sealed packet and offered it to Hawkins. "I'm sent by Mr. Theophilus Swade. You'll find here the invoices pertaining to the cargo on the Fair Hope and also a letter of introduction that Mr. Swade most kindly undertook to write on my behalf."

"Have a seat, Mr. Bull," said John Hawkins, taking the packet and then motioning with it to a chair on the other side of the hearth from his own. He resettled himself, easing down gingerly and groaning lightly. "Gout," he said, shaking his head.

Isaac took the chair offered him and settled back, gazing about the room as Hawkins inspected the contents of Swade's packet. When Hawkins came to the letter of introduction, he quit shuffling the papers and became still as he read. Only the crackle of the fire broke the silence. At last John Hawkins lowered the letter to his lap, took off his spectacles and put them on the table.

"Welcome to Carolina, Mr. Bull," he said warmly. "It is an honor to be counted the first of the many friends you'll soon have in the province. Would it be agreeable to you if I send to have your baggage directed to my home?"

"That's by no means necessary," Isaac said. "My intention is to take a room in a tavern until I find more permanent lodgings."

"Of course it is. But I won't hear of it. You'll lodge with me for now. It's the least I can do for a kinsman of Theophilus Swade. Why don't we step over to the Indian Queen for a drink. You must tell me all about my old friend, what he's been up to this past while. That'd best be done over a mug of flip, don't you agree?"

"That would certainly be pleasant," said Isaac, rising to his feet as Haw-

kins rose. He was feeling bright and clear, challenged by his new situation.
Here was a new beginning in a land where none had ever known him and could not hold him to what he had been before.

They made their way slowly from the counting house, John Hawkins leaning on a silver-headed cane, favoring his gout-ridden leg, stepping gingerly. As they mounted the steps of the tavern, Isaac studied the sign above the door, a rather awkward painting of an Indian queen, bare of breast and foot, wearing a short skirt of blue trade cloth tucked around her waist, a crown of red feathers on her head. He followed Hawkins inside toward a hum of voices and laughter, into a smokey room dimly lit by daylight filtering in through small windows. The smell was of ale and rum, of burning pine in the great fireplace, of tobacco smoke from long-stemmed pipes, and beneath it all the musty smell of human bodies unwashed since the last warm weather. There were two men drinking together in the high-backed settle beside the fire. In the rest of the small room more than half the tables were filled by men and women of all stations, some of quality, some tradesmen, some of the lower sort.

As John Hawkins moved toward an empty table, a gentleman rose from the company of his fellows and came over to him. "Tom!" said John Hawkins, reaching out with obvious warmth to shake the man's hand in both of his. "They said you were back."

"Soaking up the comforts of civilization," the other man said with a smile. He was a middle-aged gentleman with a pleasant face and intelligent eyes. He glanced curiously at Isaac.

"This is Mr. Isaac Bull," said John Hawkins. "Just arrived from London by way of Jamaica. Came in on Captain Bradley with a commission from Theophilus Swade. Mr. Bull, this is Thomas Nairne, one of the finest men to draw breath in Carolina. He's a planter to the south in Colleton County and an Indian trader of considerable repute."

"It is an honor to make your acquaintance," said Isaac.

"Don't listen to John Hawkins," Nairne said with a smile. "He's a master of flattery when there is something he wants."

"I only want your company, Tom, only your company. Come join us in a mug of flip. Help me acquaint this young man with the peculiar land he's chosen for his home."

"Then you've come to settle?" said Nairne, moving with them to an empty table.

"I have indeed," said Isaac. "I intend to make my life here, come what may."

A boy walked over to serve them and Hawkins ordered flip all around. He turned to Nairne as the boy left. "Tell us your latest adventure. Did you meet with success?" Then to Isaac he explained, "Mr. Nairne has just re-turned from Florida. For a man with an adventurous spirit, there's money to be made there in slaves. Spain's Indians are free game, you know. Tom goes raiding with our Creek Indians, and he gets a nice share of the booty."

Nairne shook his head. "It's hardly worth my time anymore, there are so few Spanish Indians left in that land. None at all in the missions. We have to go far down the cape chasing the wild ones, but even those are getting scarce. Florida is all but empty."

"Spain is finished in Florida," John Hawkins said confidently.

"Not altogether," said Nairne. "They can hold out forever in that fortress at Saint Augustine. But they hold the land only so far as their guns can cover it from the parapets. I say, leave the Spaniards in their fort. It's the French we should be campaigning against while they've naught but a toe-hold on the country. I went to the governor yesterday and offered again to lead an assault against Mobile, but he still won't hear of it from me. Says he has men working on that plan." He lowered his voice and leaned forward. "And they'll be working till judgement day. If the French were pushed out, the governor and his men would lose the secret trade they carry on with those papist devils. Never mind that our Queen Anne is at war with them. Never mind that they contrive to woo our Indians from us and break up our trade."

"But in truth the French lack the goods to win over our Indians," said John Hawkins. "Manufacturing in France lags too far behind. They can't compete with our prices."

"It's English goods they would use in their trade," said Nairne, keeping his voice low. "Our esteemed governor would gladly supply them if it meant the rest of us were cut out and he alone engrossed the traffic."

"As much as I despise the man," said John Hawkins, "I find it difficult to believe he would try anything so blatant as that."

"Blatant?" said Nairne with a scoff. "This governor does nothing that is not blatant." He fell silent as the boy approached the table with their flip — molasses-sweetened beer fortified with rum and stirred hot and foamy with a red-hot poker from the fire.

The door of the tavern opened, and Nairne and Hawkins both glanced over at the two fashionably dressed gentlemen who were coming in. Nairne cleared his throat, while Hawkins reached for his flip.

"Our friends," John Hawkins said quietly to Isaac, sarcasm in his voice.

The two men made their way among the tables, exchanging greetings here and there, then ambled over to speak to Nairne.

"Welcome home, Thomas," said one of them, reaching out to shake Nairne's hand, which Nairne offered without rising.

"Thank you, James." Nairne's voice was pleasant enough, though Isaac detected a relative lack of cordiality.

Hawkins put a hand on Isaac's shoulder. "Allow me to make an introduction, gentlemen. We have a new settler among us, Mr. Isaac Bull of London. This is his first day on the soil of Carolina."

Isaac rose politely to his feet, nodding to the two men.

"Colonel James Moore," said Hawkins, and Moore reached out to shake Isaac's hand. "And Mr. Thomas Broughton, son-in-law of our beloved Governor Johnson." Isaac shook hands with the tall, lean gentleman. "Mr. Broughton has a considerable interest in the Indian trade," said Hawkins.

"It's a fascinating realm of commerce, from all I've heard," said Isaac.

Broughton smiled stiffly.

"Colonel Moore is a former governor of Carolina," said Hawkins. "Though his real reputation is in soldiering." He leaned back in his chair and folded his hands over his rotund belly, looking up at Moore with a smile that had the devil in it. "It was two years past he led one of the opening salvos in Queen Anne's war. Took our army against Saint Augustine. The city was destroyed and the fortress besieged, but unfortunately it could not be taken. Then just a year ago he led another of his great campaigns. This time it was Apalachee he went against."

Isaac nodded, remembering the newspaper account Swade had read to him.

"He laid waste the province. Spared none but a strong blockhouse and a single town where the papist savages came out and purchased their lives with the silver from their church. It's said that Colonel Moore's family will not eat their fried pork anymore unless it be served on church silver."

Hawkins watched Moore with twinkling eyes, while Nairne smiled down at his mug of flip. Broughton stood stiff and unamused, but Moore's manner was easy as he slowly scratched his arm and chuckled.

"You've only got the story partly right, John. It's true enough we eat off of papist silver, but we only do it on holy days." He laughed loudly and slapped Hawkins on the back.

Isaac joined the laughter and took his seat again.

"Tell us about *your* ventures," Broughton said, turning to Nairne. "You've just come in from a Florida campaign of your own, a success from all I hear. Four slaves for yourself, I believe, for which you can thank the governor's generosity in granting you the commission."

"Your information is not correct," Nairne said coldly. "My share of the slaves was but three."

"After the governor's present, I presume," said Broughton.

"Not a difficult presumption, is it? I deposited a healthy young lad in the governor's slave pen this morning. I am twenty pounds poorer. Your father-in-law is twenty pounds richer."

"Only his due, Mr. Nairne, the just rewards of his office."

Nairne said nothing.

"Well, good day to you, gentlemen," said Moore, nodding pleasantly. "We must go speak with some other fellows over here. Welcome to Carolina, Mr. Bull. Take care to watch your step. Our streets are slippery with dung."

Isaac nodded cordially.

Nairne smiled, shaking his head as the two men moved away. "James Moore is a shrewd old bastard," he said softly. "He's been here for thirty years, almost as long as the colony itself. He's seen it all. It's a pity we can't win him to our side." He paused to drain his mug. "I've got to get on with business," he said, pushing back his chair. He looked at John Hawkins. "I hear your brother Abraham has come down to sit out the Boston winter in a more pleasant climate."

"It's as much to give his daughter a change of scenery as anything," said Hawkins. "Her mother died this past year and she's taking it rather badly. But the change seems to be doing her good. Come join us for dinner. We're on our way now."

"I wish I were able," said Nairne, rising to his feet. "I'll come another time, if the invitation holds."

"Tomorrow, then."

"Splendid," said Nairne, nodding to Hawkins and then to Isaac. "We'll be seeing more of each other, Mr. Bull. Welcome to Carolina." He glanced over at James Moore. "Colonel Moore's advice is sound. You would do well to watch your step."

"I intend to, Mr. Nairne," Isaac said warmly, and he raised his mug in salute.

﹡ John Hawkins' home was newly built of brick with green shutters and shining brass hardware. Standing before the front door, Isaac turned and looked back down the spacious avenue to the pleasant view of the harbor where the three sloops and the brigantine rode at anchor and a periago was moving out on its oars against the wind. Hawkins pushed open the door, and as Isaac turned back, a black man appeared, dressed in what seemed to be the cast-off clothes and ill-fitting wig of his master. He ushered them inside with mumbled greetings and reached out solicitously to take their hats and gloves. Isaac followed Hawkins into the sitting room where cushioned chairs were arranged pleasantly about the hearth. Two men, one older and one younger, rose to greet them.

"Mr. Isaac Bull, please make the acquaintance of my brother, Mr. Abraham Hawkins, down from Boston on a visit," said John Hawkins, indicating with a gesture a gentleman whose body was leaner than his brother's, but with the same ruddy skin and blue eyes. Abraham had a prominent aquiline nose and an intelligent face framed by a full-flowing wig that was somewhat out of fashion.

"And my son Henry," said John Hawkins.

Isaac shook the hand of Henry Hawkins, whom he judged to be only slightly older than himself, still carrying the leanness of youth, though he was beginning to show a trace of a paunch beneath his embroidered waistcoat.

As the black man brought in mugs of ale, Isaac looked around at the furnishings, at the handsome cupboard with silver porringers shining in the open shelves and at the mahogany table laid with pewter for the dinner hour. Isaac found it more to his liking than the ostentatious manner of living at Swade Hall where nothing but gold or silver had touched his lips. He settled himself into the comfortable arm chair that was urged upon him, and John Hawkins briefly explained to the others the circumstances of Isaac's coming among them.

"So you were cheated out of your inheritance," said Abraham Hawkins, settling into his chair. As he spoke, he laid his finger alongside his large nose in what seemed to be an habitual gesture, as if its size kept him ever conscious of it. He stretched out his feet toward the fire. He alone had declined the offer of ale. "Your brother is not only a thief but a fool. There's never a more reliable partner for business affairs than a man's own brother. He should have clasped you to his bosom."

"As Abraham did me," said John Hawkins. "Our father's estate was modest. Abraham was the heir, his right by birth. I could have been left to get my own living without any cause for complaint. But Abraham offered to share everything with me."

"And look what we have done with it," said Abraham. "Our mercantile house has offices now in Boston and Charles Town. We have agents in most of the sugar islands, in London, and in Africa. Our combined efforts have far surpassed anything that could have been accomplished by either of us alone. And here is the best of it." He leaned forward and looked meaningfully at Isaac. "Always we can rest at night in the knowledge that each of our interests is being guarded by the other."

Isaac nodded, thinking of the treachery of his own brother.

"It has been a good partnership," said John Hawkins. "Together we have been able to cover the colonies. That is the key to commerce, Mr. Bull—to have access to all of its parts." He took up a long-stemmed porcelain pipe from a table near his chair and, favoring his gouty leg, he leaned forward to tap out the ashes into the fireplace. The black man, who had been standing unobtrusively in the background, came forward with a box of tobacco from which John Hawkins drew enough to refill his pipe. Replacing the box on a shelf beside the hearth, the slave took up a pair of slender tongs and plucked a small coal from the fire and lit his master's pipe. Hawkins exhaled a cloud of fragrant white smoke. He expounded: "Boston is our home office. We started there. But the trouble with New England is that it lacks exports. The real profits are to be made in the plantation colonies. A warm climate and the labor of slaves, those are the two prerequisites. You've seen them with their sugar in Jamaica, Mr. Bull. You understand what I say."

Isaac nodded.

"Here in Carolina we are putting our hope in rice," said young Henry Hawkins. He handed his empty mug to the slave to be refilled.

"There's yet a part for New England merchants in this," said Abraham.

John Hawkins smiled, drawing his pipe from his mouth just far enough to speak. "For Abraham there is nothing but New England. The purity of spirit in that region suits him. This is a man who never smokes tobacco and rarely drinks rum. All the other colonies are disappointing to him. No matter the riches to be gained from them, they lack refinement. Nothing good can come of them, except of course all the money that he makes from tobacco and rum."

"And what is it that New England gives for the money?" asked Isaac. "Her shipping?"

"For the most part," said Abraham. "Primarily shipping. We carry Africans to the plantation colonies, as well as our own fish and flour and beer. And we carry away their sugar and rice and tobacco. It's a lucrative commerce."

Isaac was feeling the effects of the ale atop the earlier flip he had drunk. The black man, who had left the room unnoticed, now returned with food, assisted by a black boy about twelve years of age, who wore nothing but a homespun shirt that hung to just above his knees. They set dishes of steaming food on the table and were heading back to the kitchen when they stopped before the doorway to let a young woman enter the room. Isaac glanced toward her, then stared, struck by the beauty of her youthful figure, her breasts high and round, her waist slender. She had a delicate face with pale blue eyes that fell shyly to the floor at the moment they brushed over him and perceived a stranger in the room. He rose to his feet, the other gentlemen following suit. Abraham Hawkins stepped forward to offer her his arm.

"My daughter Charity, Mr. Bull," said the New Englander.

Charity curtsied, her brown curls falling gently forward from the black ribbon that tied them behind. Isaac bowed deeply, his eyes tracing over her as he lowered his head and then raised it again. The ale was warm within him.

They all stood about for a few moments, conversing lightly while the slaves finished bringing in the food. Then Henry Hawkins gave his arm to his cousin Charity and escorted her to the narrow table where she seated herself at the end of one of the cushioned benches. Isaac moved with pretended inattention toward the place opposite her and was relieved when no one interfered with his design by offering him a different place. He noticed that Henry, with a detectable air of possession, had seated himself beside Charity.

Abraham Hawkins prayed for divine blessing and the food was passed. Isaac took little for his plate, his hunger having first been mitigated by the generous portion of ale he had consumed and now destroyed completely by the disarming presence of this beautifully delicate young woman. He ate without tasting and drank without noticing whether he had filled his cup with cider, wine, or beer.

"Perhaps you are wondering about the stew, Mr. Bull," said John Hawkins from the head of the table. "I would be surprised if you have tasted the like before."

Isaac looked at his plate. He was sober enough at least to distinguish his stew from his pudding, but though it appeared he had eaten generously of it, he had no recollection of it.

"It's not beef with dumplings?" he said. "I thought at first it was that."

"The meat is venison," said John Hawkins. "And those dumplings are no such thing. It's hominy you're eating. I've an Indian cook in the kitchen. Bella is her name. She's been a slave of mine for seventeen years. For the first ten of those years my wife was alive and tried to teach her to cook for an Englishman's family. She learned well enough, and yet many's the time an Indian dish appears among the rest. We've come to have a taste for most of them." He reached for the dish of stew.

"It's the same with Doll, our Guinea woman in Boston," said Charity. "We don't know how she does it. She takes meat and vegetables that are perfectly English and puts them together in the most startling ways. Often it can be quite a treat, but other times it is not at all to our taste. Mother used to try to correct her, but never to good effect." For a moment Charity looked away sadly, her thumb reaching across the palm of her hand to caress a gold mourning ring that bore a death's head in black enamel. But then she caught herself. She glanced at her father and smiled reassuringly. "I wonder how Burnaby is faring in the house with her," she said. "It's a real question who would be master, my brother or black Doll." She laughed lightly, and her eyes flickered over Isaac. She blushed.

Isaac felt a sweet sting of desire. Here was a woman he would pursue if he could. But his brother had ruined him not only in finance but in love. He could not compete with the likes of Henry Hawkins. The convenience of a match between these two cousins was obvious. Henry clearly had it in mind, and the two fathers would undoubtedly promote it. But as Isaac finished his meal, turning his eyes to Charity at every opportunity, he could not dispel the notion that it was his own presence rather than Henry's that was causing her to set aside the memory of her dead mother and enjoy the company that was around her.

As the meal drew to a close, Isaac engaged her more determinedly in conversation, hoping to delay the moment when she would excuse herself and leave the men to their madeira. But at last she patted her lips with her napkin, and then, after making a small, almost imperceptible adjustment in the soft lace that lined the low square neckline of her gown, she begged her uncle to excuse her and rose from the table. Isaac and Henry both rose with her, while her father and uncle nodded to her from their seats.

"You should think of getting out this afternoon," Abraham said to his daughter. "Mistress Bellinger is anxious for you to call. She warns me that it's unhealthy for you to stay alone in your chamber so much."

Charity smiled. "My health is in no danger, I assure you, Father. But I would enjoy going abroad today. I'll have Cajoe summon a chair to take me."

"Then give my regards to Mistress Bellinger," said her uncle, stirring in his chair to make his leg more comfortable.

"And mine," said Henry, taking his seat again.

Isaac still remained on his feet.

Charity looked at him. "Will we be seeing more of you, Mr. Bull?"

He smiled. "Perhaps more than you would wish. Your uncle has invited me to stay here until I find other lodgings."

"Then you must not hurry in your search," said Charity.

He bowed slightly.

She turned and walked briskly from the hall.

As Isaac returned to his seat, Henry was pressing tobacco into the bowl of his pipe and looking irritably toward the empty doorway.

"Damn those niggers," he said, setting the pipe down roughly and getting up to fetch a coal from the fire. "They're never here when you need them." He fished up a coal with the smoking tongs and then stood for a moment watching the door again. "Jack!" he called loudly. He came back to the table and lit everyone's pipe, ending with his own. As he was taking his seat, the black man entered the room.

Henry glared at him and held out the tongs with the coal that had now cooled. Jack hurried forward to take them.

"Sorry, Master," he murmured. "Miss Charity sent me to fetch Cajoe. He be clear back to the woodshed. I . . ."

"That's enough, Jack," said John Hawkins, waving him away.

The black man stepped silently back to the shadows.

"They always have excuses." said Henry. "At least my plantation niggers don't give me excuses. They can scarcely speak a word of English." He laughed.

"You're a rice planter, then?" said Isaac.

"Someday it will be rice. I only took up the land this autumn past. It's covered with pines at the moment. There's pitch and tar to be harvested for the next few years, and as the land is cleared, I'll run cattle on it. Rice is my goal, Mr. Bull, but that's yet down the road. Perhaps ten years."

"Until now Henry has managed our firm's interest in the Indian trade," said John Hawkins, puffing on his pipe. "That's a profitable realm, Mr. Bull. There's a great demand in England for deerskins, for which God be praised. Carolina would have failed without it."

"I thought rice was the mainstay," said Isaac.

"Only now is it coming to be," said young Henry. "In the beginning no one knew how to cultivate it. Or once cultivated, how to thresh it."

"At first all our hopes were in other commodities," said John Hawkins. "Silk, olives, wine. All of them failed. We would have had nothing to trade with England in those early days had not the Indians been willing to bring us packloads of dressed deerskins to exchange for guns and cheap cloth. And even now, with rice on the rise, a planter starting out is likely to have more interest in the Indian trade than in the working of his land, for in the trade he can raise the capital to buy his slaves."

John Hawkins took a draught from his pipe, savored it, and then exhaled into the smoky haze above the table. "Slaves are everything in a plantation colony, Mr. Bull. The getting of slaves consumes the interests of men. Carolina traders swarm among the Indians beyond our settlements. There are so many traders, they stumble over one another. They've gone a thousand miles into this land in search of yet more trade. Our government is in perpetual turmoil because of the conflicts between the trading factions. All because deerskins mean money, and money means slaves."

"And slaves mean rice," said Henry. "And rice means more money and more slaves."

Abraham Hawkins laughed, touching his finger to his nose. "This morning in the Indian Queen I was engaged in conversation by a man who had just bought his first slave. He was in the best of spirits, full of optimism for the future. He had paid thirty pounds for the slave and was estimating that the slave would turn him a profit of thirty pounds in a year. If he reinvested that profit in another slave, he said, then at the end of the second year, the profit from the two slaves would allow him to buy two more, and from those four slaves would come profit enough to buy four more, and by virtue of mathematical progression he reasoned he would own a thousand slaves in ten years."

The others laughed.

"We should already be kings by his theory," said John Hawkins.

"And I could be one myself in a mere ten years by investing my poor stake in a slave," said Isaac, setting down his pipe, which had gone out. He took a sip of madeira.

"And how *do* you intend to invest your stake?" asked John Hawkins, leveling his gaze at Isaac.

"In the Indian trade, Mr. Hawkins," Isaac said evenly, meeting his eyes.

John Hawkins nodded. "My advice to you is this. Take Swade's commission in trade goods. I'll put you with a man of mine, Sam Clutterbuck by name, and he'll take you with him into Indian country. With luck you'll double or triple your stake in a few months' time."

"That is the kind of advice I need," said Isaac. "I thank you for it, and for the use of your man. You will consider me at your service, of course."

John Hawkins smiled slightly and nodded, but said nothing as he watched Isaac and puffed thoughtfully on his pipe. Isaac knew an agreement was forming between them, only partly spoken, a decision by both of them that their interests would henceforth lie together. Isaac raised his cup in a silent toast. John Hawkins raised his own in return.

CHAPTER TWENTY-TWO

The trail could scarcely be seen on the littered floor of the great pine forest, and Henry Hawkins had strayed from it more than once. Now, as before, Hawkins pulled slowly to a halt because the next blaze-marked tree had failed to appear. Behind him Isaac Bull reined in his horse and turned about his two packhorses with their jingling bells and led the way back to the last blaze mark, where Henry stopped for a moment to study the situation and then chose another course, one that soon led to the next blaze.

From Charles Town they had taken the Dorchester Road that paralleled the eastern side of the Ashley River. After going about ten miles inland, they had forded the Ashley and struck out northwest to the Edisto River, for

a more difficult crossing, and then continued northward, looping around
to miss the worst of the small, irksome headwaters of the Ashepoo River.
They had already reached the headwaters of Black Creek and then Boggy
Gut Creek, and now they were headed toward the Combahee River.

"Does Clutterbuck ever use this trail?" asked Isaac. "I could not have
found my way alone."

"He never does," said Henry over his shoulder. "He uses the river,
though it's more than a mile from his house to his landing. Had we not
needed to bring in new horses, we would have come by periago ourselves.
Though I admit I like to get out on the land."

It did appear to Isaac that Henry was at home in the forest. He rode his
horse easily, with no sign of the discomfort that Isaac was feeling after a
little more than two days in the saddle. They had covered nearly forty miles
since leaving Charles Town, stopping in at plantations that were only to be
found by leaving the rough main trail and taking smaller and even more
difficult trails down to the lower land near the rivers. No planter could
survive who had to carry his produce to market over these swamp-infested
trails. The rivers were the real highways of Carolina.

"It's not far now," said Henry. "Not an hour if I be right about where
we are."

"How often have you come this way?" asked Isaac, raising himself
slightly in the saddle to relieve his backside.

"Twice," said Henry, "but only once since Clutterbuck's been living
here. I came the first time with a surveyor. This is my land he's squatting on."

Isaac looked about in surprise. "This is your plantation?"

Henry laughed. "Not here. I bought this tract for speculation. I intend it
only for resale. My place lies yonder six or seven miles." He waved his hand
to the left. "Down the river."

"And you have no objection to Clutterbuck settling himself on your
land?"

"None. He's a rare man among traders, Sam Clutterbuck is. They're most
of them a scabby parcel of thieves. When we find a trader like Sam who
stays up with his debts, we try to keep him with us. And anyway, this is
sorry land up here in the piney woods. He was smart enough to stay away
from a river tract that would like as not be sold out from under him before
too many years."

They rode along in silence then, and Isaac let his thoughts drift back to
Charles Town and the days he had passed in John Hawkins' house enjoying
the company of Charity. She had not kept so much to her chamber while
he was there, but had come down often to sit with him by the fire or walk

in the garden, pleasantly passing the time. It was only when Henry's courtesy began to cool that Isaac had finally made the effort to find other lodgings. Once Isaac was out of the house and away from Charity, Henry's cordiality returned. All was easy between them now.

As they rode on, the trail became gradually more distinct, showing signs of use, and Isaac began to watch more sharply ahead until at last he glimpsed a wisp of smoke above the treetops. In the next moment came the barking of dogs.

The clearing they came into was surprisingly small, no more than three acres of corn stubble, and nowhere was it free of stumps, not even in the dooryard where a woman stood staring with surprise as she watched them ride out of the forest. Two young children clung to her skirts and a third, a boy of perhaps six years, peered around the corner of the rough log house, poised like a deer for flight.

A man came out of the house, strode past the woman and out through the rough field to greet them, the dogs running barking before him. He was hatless, his brown hair straggling down to his collar. His shirt was of rough homespun, his coat and breeches of deerskin. His shoes were moccasins in the Indian fashion. He reached up to shake the hand of Henry Hawkins and then turned and called sharply to the dogs to stop their barking. They ignored him, keeping up such a clamor that speech was impossible. Only when the man grabbed up a stick did the dogs fall silent and slink away. Then he looked at Isaac and his two packhorses.

"I'm damned if you ain't come to go trading," he said, holding out his hand. "Sam Clutterbuck's my name."

"Isaac Bull," said Isaac, reaching down to shake his hand.

"My father wishes you to teach Mr. Bull the Indian trade," said Henry. "He's just come new into the country."

Isaac shifted uncomfortably. Sam Clutterbuck had his eyes glued to him, boldly studying him and seeming not altogether pleased with what he saw. Isaac could scarcely blame him. In all his life he had known no greater wilderness than the well-kept park on his father's estate in England. Clutterbuck was no fool. He could see Isaac for what he was. It was all well enough to entertain lofty ideas of getting into the Indian trade, but there was undoubtedly much to learn before a profit could be made. Isaac nodded toward the packhorses. "These goods are mine outright. I have no debts to clear. Everything I get for them in trade will be my own. I'm offering you a quarter of what I take in."

Henry turned quickly and looked at him. "There's no need for that," he said curtly. "Sam works for us. He does what we ask."

"It's the truth," said Clutterbuck. "I ask nothing of you, Mr. Bull."

"The offer stands," said Isaac, and he lowered himself gingerly from his horse. "I have much to learn, Mr. Clutterbuck, and I expect you to teach me well." He rubbed his backside. "My ignorance of this country is exceeded only by the soreness of my ass."

Clutterbuck laughed. Then he looked down at the ground and pushed up a clod of soil with his moccasined toe, turning the matter over in his mind. He looked up at Isaac again. "Suppose we settle for ten percent?"

"Fifteen," said Isaac.

"It's a bargain, then, and the fairest I ever struck." Clutterbuck glanced up at Henry Hawkins. "You heard the way of it, Mr. Hawkins. It weren't none of my asking."

Henry shrugged. "I heard, and I've nothing more to say about it. It's his own money he's giving away."

"I mean to give him a fair return," said Clutterbuck. Then he turned and looked across the clearing to the dooryard, where the woman was no longer to be seen. "Come along now and see Bess," he said. "She was beside herself when she seen you coming. It's been more'n a year since any Englishman's come up this way." He started toward the house, Henry following, still mounted, and Isaac walking behind with his horses.

Sam Clutterbuck's house was a single-room, windowless log cabin with no light inside except from the open door. Bess stood just inside the doorway, hurriedly tying back her hair with a fresh new ribbon and looking out at Sam with tears in her haggard eyes. She might have been a young woman, scarcely older than Isaac, but her face was so worn it was difficult to tell.

"Get 'em out," she said softly to Sam.

Sam made no response, and her voice rose. "Get 'em out!" she cried. "I tried to tell 'em to go! Now you get 'em out!"

Isaac and Henry both stopped in surprise and stepped back from the door. Sam went inside.

"There now," he said soothingly, taking her arm. "They're all right. Let 'em stay."

"No!" she cried, snatching away her arm and brushing furious tears from her face. "I ain't having 'em. There's company come, and I ain't having 'em. You get 'em out, Sam."

Sam turned and looked over his shoulder and saw Isaac and Henry hanging back. He laughed.

"Come on in," he said. "It ain't the twain of you she's speaking of." He turned back to his wife. "Look, Bess, they're afraid to come in. You're scaring 'em off."

"There now, Sam, look what you done," Bess said angrily and pushed past him to the door. "Don't you go away," she said to Isaac and Henry.

"I've beer and bread set out for you. It's not much, I well know, but it's all I have. I've a bit of jam I been saving all this time, keeping it hid from the babes, saving it for company. Now come in. God knows you're welcome. It's them I want out." She pointed into the dimness of the room.

Isaac moved toward the door and craned his neck to look inside. Four Indian men were squatting before the fire. They wore breechcloths of blue stroud and leggings and moccasins of deerskin. In the warmth from the fire they had dropped away their mantles of duffield cloth, revealing geometric tatoos on their chests and arms. They were passing a pipe among themselves and paying small attention to the commotion at the door.

"I've Christian company, Sam," pleaded Bess, turning back to her husband. "How am I to entertain them with my house full of savages?"

"They care not a whit, Bess. Henry and Isaac are in the trading business, same as me. They keep company with Indians the same as I do. Now, I asked these Yamasee fellows to come up here to pack my goods down to the river and man my boat and do my hunting for me as I go, and they've come, and I ain't a'turning 'em out. So there's an end to it. Let the gentlemen come in."

She turned back to Isaac and Henry. "I never meant to keep you waiting," she said softly. She reached out and grabbed both of Isaac's hands and squeezed them tightly in her own, her eyes filling with tears again. "Bess is my name. I'm so honored to meet you, sir. I pray you'll tarry with us a long while." Then the smile left her face, though she still clung to his hands. She looked over at her husband. "You'll be taking him away in the morning, won't you, Sam?" she said bitterly. "You'll load him up in the boat and take him away with you. And Mr. Hawkins there will take the horses, and away he'll ride, won't he, Sam? And here I'll be alone again, Bess and her poor little babes and not another Christian soul to give her comfort." She turned back to Isaac. "He leaves me here with none to help me but two heathen slaves. One of 'em's naught but a lazy wench and the other a boy that ain't hardly a boy anymore. I vow he's getting old enough to be wondering what I got beneath my skirts, but Sam still leaves me alone with him."

"That'll do, Bess," Sam said sternly. "Let Mr. Hawkins in and give us some beer."

Bess looked out the door at Henry, who was still standing in the yard. "Mr. Hawkins," she said, smoothing her hair nervously once again. She held out her hand to him, and he came forward and took it politely. The tears in her eyes welled up. "I wish you'd come a'visiting more often. Perhaps you've taken a wife since I seen you last."

Henry smiled stiffly and shook his head, easing his hand from her grip.

"It's a pity," Bess said, brushing her hands across her cheeks. "I've prayed that you'd marry and settle a wife on your plantation. It's a far distance to walk, I know, but I'd make the journey every week, I swear I would, to share the company of another Christian woman." She fell silent and stared out the door across the stump-filled clearing to the high forest of pines. Then she turned back to Henry and Isaac. "Don't neither of you know what lonesome is," she said quietly. "I can see it plain in your faces. You're just like Sam. He don't understand how alone a woman can be."

"I understand, Bess," Sam said wearily. "It's just that there's naught I can do about it. But look on it, you got company for a night, at least. Show us that beer and that jam you've been saving. Let's have a merry time." He looked over at Isaac and Henry. "A day later and you'd have missed me. I'm setting out in the morning."

Bess looked at him, then turned abruptly away and walked stiffly to a high shelf on the far wall and reached up to take down a small stoneware jar. She came back to the wide board table set up on its trestles in the center of the room and set the jar down hard beside the wooden pitcher of beer and the loaf of cold cornbread.

"A'setting out in the morning, he is," she muttered bitterly. "Leaving Bess and her poor little babes." She looked over at the one bed in the cabin, where the two smallest children sat huddled, dumbstruck, watching the strangers. The older child, who had earlier been at the corner of the cabin outside, was nowhere to be seen. "A'setting out in the morning," she repeated. "He never stays but a fortnight and off he goes again." She lifted the top from the jar.

"Bedamned!" she cried, grabbing up the jar and peering into it. "It's empty!" She burst into angry tears. "Somebody's eaten the bloody jam!" She turned and hurled the jar with all her strength toward the four Yamasee men, one of whom flung himself onto another to avoid being hit. The jar crashed onto the hearth, and Bess ran sobbing from the house.

For a moment there was silence. Then the two children began to cry and the Yamasee men began to laugh. Sam smiled and said something to the men in their language, and they nodded and laughed harder.

Sam turned to Isaac and Henry and shrugged. "I'll wager my oldest son got into that jam. But I'll let her blame these fellows and spare the tyke. Let's have this beer now and settle down. I promise we'll be out of here in the morning." He stood silent for a moment, looking out the empty door. "Poor old Bess," he said quietly. Then he turned back to the table and reached for the beer.

 The periago, a simple flat-bottomed boat, loaded with Isaac and Sam and their trading goods and manned by the four hired Yamasees, descended the Combahee River in less than a day and wound southward through the coastal marshes, past Port Royal Island with its rich plantations, past the Yamasee settlements on the mainland, and on the second day entered the mouth of the Savannah River. It was Isaac's first journey into Indian country, and he felt himself returned to his boyhood, where flights of fancy were little different from life itself, where all was wondrous and the beauty of sky and grass and trees was not separate from himself, where he was one with the earth, touching up against it, his hands at home with the feel of a tree and his knees with the give of the ground as he knelt upon it, where his face knew the warmth of the sun on a cool day at the verge of spring, where his ears were familiar with wind in the trees, with the sound of a river's current, with bird song, with the rattle in the breeze of last summer's leaves, dead and brown, still clinging this last little while to airy branches against the sky.

It was on the great Savannah River that the reverie truly began as the tattooed boatmen rowed steadily against the unrelenting current, and day after day the land gently rose, the moss-draped swamps giving way to spacious pine forests, to broad canebrakes and wide meadows. The river gradually narrowed, but still remained a broad waterway. Occasionally periagos and canoes went by, their occupants waving and hallooing in their speedy descent, and when they passed from sight, all fell back into silence except for the dip of the oars and the murmur of the river.

A fortnight after leaving Port Royal they began to see more traffic on the river, especially more Indian dugout canoes. Swarthy hunters in breechcloths and fringed leggings appeared more frequently on the forested bluffs above the river. In the days that followed, the land grew more hilly and cornfields began to appear in the bottoms, some fields brown with last year's stubble, others blackened by recent burnings in preparation for spring planting. Dwellings appeared, widely scattered at first, small clusters of rough huts with dogs and chickens in the yards and black-haired, tawny-skinned children playing among frames of stretched deerskins. The homesteads occurred with increasing frequency, interspersed with cornfields, until at last, on the east side of the river, a high bluff appeared, a sheer wall of layered, many-colored clays. On the high shoulder of the bluff was a stockaded English trading house and beyond that was an Indian town with English colors flying over a council house at the edge of an open plaza. Across the river were cornfields and another town and yet another trading house. Pulled up on both shores were more periagos and canoes than Isaac had seen since leaving Charles Town harbor.

Just upstream, he was told, the shoals began, and large boats could go no further. Here was the end of the river road, the staging area for the great inland trade. It was called Savano Town after the Indians who were the most numerous of the people living in the town on the bluff. But settlements stretched along both sides of the river for several miles, and the people living in them were from a number of Indian nations, all newly arrived in the last twenty years, all settled here to be close to the English traders.

Sam Clutterbuck directed the Yamasee boatmen to put the periago in at the western bank, across from the bluff, and to unload it. He paid the Yamasees in stroud cloth and gunpowder and hired eight new bearers for the westward journey overland. These new men were Apalachees, the same people who but a year ago had consented to come with James Moore from the Spanish missions of Florida, thus avoiding being made slaves like so many of their kinsmen. Several of the bearers had anglicized Spanish names, Christian names like Lewis, Peter, and Emmanuel, though the popery into which they had been baptized was considered by the traders to be little better than heathendom itself.

The overland journey from Savano Town deep into Creek country took seven days, a steady fifteen to twenty miles a day on a clear trail through rolling, fertile hills. Compared to these interior lands, the settled parts of Carolina were but fens and mires. On these gentle hills stood a lofty forest of oak, hickory, and pine scattered through with magnolia, wild cherry, dogwood, and persimmon. In places the forest gave way to open savannah—grassland with trees widely scattered. In the bottomlands wide canebrakes and spreading meadows bordered creeks and rivers rushing swiftly over rocky beds. The topsoil was rich and dark and deep. The water was clear and sweet, and the air held none of the miasma of the swampy coastal lands.

Five days out of Savano Town they reached the settlement of the Oconees, a spacious town along a wide river. The Indians were burning their fields that day, and the smoke rose up from the fertile bottomland for as far upstream as the eye could see. Isaac and Sam were entertained that evening in the council house by the leader of the town, a man the traders called the Oconee King. They smoked the king's tobacco, ate the food he provided them, and watched the young people dance. In return, Isaac and Sam handed out small gifts of handkerchiefs, ribbons, and beads to the king and his headmen. At last they excused themselves and retired to sleep in the log strong-house of the principal trader of the town.

On their second day out of Oconee Town, they began fording the tributary creeks of the upper Ocmulgee River, where towns and fields of the Creek Indians filled the bottomlands. These people, too, like the ones at Savano Town, had lived here but a short time. They had moved eastward from the Chattahoochee River to be closer to the English, with whom they were trading, and further from the Spaniards, with whom they were at war.

Sam Clutterbuck's trading house was not in one of the larger Creek towns. It was in an out-of-the-way settlement that held scarcely twenty houses, though just as in the larger towns, this village had a plaza, cleanly swept, from the center of which rose a tall pole with a bear skull on top. Beside the plaza was the square ground—four long sheds with open fronts facing each other. And beside the square ground was the council house, more than twice the size of a dwelling house, the broad conical roof rising high above the low, clay-plastered walls. The homes of the people stood in order about the central plaza. Sam's trading house was off to one side, not separate from the town, but not squarely in it.

Sam pulled up short at the sight of it. "Now what have we here?" he said, putting a hand on his hip. "It ain't the first time I seen this sight, but I swear it's going to be the last."

"What is it?" asked Isaac, seeing nothing but a sturdy log house with smoke rising from the stick-and-clay chimney.

"There's smoke from the chimney but the door's closed tight. And no lock put on it—he ain't gone. It's daylight, and he's closed up tight."

Isaac did not understand the significance. He looked at Sam for an explanation.

"I left my man Nate Ramsay here," said Sam. "He ought to have the door open. There ain't no other way to get light, save for his firelight. I've seen it before and I know the meaning. The door's barred, I'll wager. He's got himself in trouble again, and it's the last time. I'm finished with him. I warned him before, and now I'm done with him."

Sam motioned for the bearers to follow him as he turned away from his course toward the trading house and went instead to an Indian house that stood to one side of it. As Sam directed the bearers to deposit their loads against the wall under the broad eaves of the roof, an Indian woman came out and stood in the doorway. She wore a knee-length skirt of red calico and a blue duffel mantle around her shoulders. On her hip was a young child, a boy who, judging by the lightness of his skin and the roundness of his eyes, had a white man for his father. The woman stood quietly waiting, her face happy, as Sam measured out powder as payment to the bearers, and Isaac, following Sam's direction, allotted each a proportionate measure of shot. Then, as the bearers sauntered out of the yard, Sam went over and took the child in his arms and reached out to give the woman a tender stroke on her cheek.

She spoke to him in her Muskogee language and he answered. He said something more and glanced toward Isaac, and she looked over at him and smiled shyly.

Isaac nodded in return.

Then the woman and Sam entered into a long and serious conversation during which the woman made animated gestures and pointed several times toward the trading house. Isaac could understand nothing that was said except the name Nate, which was frequently mentioned.

At last Sam handed back the child and said something to the woman about his goods piled beside her house. Then he went over and rummaged about in them for a few moments, pulling out a gun, a large bundle of stroud, and two ruffled shirts. He measured out generous portions of powder and shot. Then he handed the bundle of stroud to Isaac. Gathering up the gun, the ammunition, and the shirts, he motioned for Isaac to follow him, and they headed out of the yard. "We're off to pay court to the king," said Sam. "We've some patching up to do."

"What has happened?" asked Isaac. "I gather you were right about your man Nate Ramsay."

"Curse his bloody soul to hell," muttered Sam. "He near beat a woman to death in a fit of jealousy. She lies abed yet, though they say now she'll live. There was a question of it at first. And if that ain't enough, he went out that same night and beat up a man named Hitchifapa, Tobacco-eater. Beat the fellow until he handed over forty deerskins to pay off a rum debt owed to Nate by one of Tobacco-eater's kinsmen, who had died. Now I got to go make amends with the woman's kin, with Tobacco-eater, with the king, and to top it off, the bloody emperor's come down from Coweta Town and I got to deal with him."

"The emperor?" said Isaac. "They have an emperor?"

"He's the king of Coweta Town. It ain't that he rules the other kings, but they all of 'em listen to him, and more often than not they follow his lead. His name is Brims. Emperor Brims, we call him. He wastes little love on the traders."

Isaac glanced about uncomfortably. He was not yet accustomed to the crowd of children who always came flocking in Indian towns when any Englishman arrived. With all this trouble at the trading house, he would rather be less conspicuous. In the yards outside the houses women milling hominy corn paused, their long pestles resting in log mortars as they watched them pass. Blanket-wrapped men in groups of two or three stood silently about their outside fires, following the traders with sullen eyes.

"There's many a man like Nate Ramsay in the towns out here," Sam said soberly. "Who can blame old Brims for feeling ill against us? I don't blame him a whit. If he could get along without the trade, he'd throw us out in the blink of an eye, and there'd be justice in it."

"They once got along without the trade."

"But that was before any mother's son of 'em owned a gun. Now, can't one group give up their guns unless the rest of 'em do. And that they never will. They're as divided amongst themselves as the nations of Europe are divided one against another."

"All to the good for us," said Isaac.

"That's right," Sam said grimly. "It's all to the good. While they're a'cutting each others' throats, we don't have to worry about ours."

The king's house was little different from any of the others in the town, except that it was seated close by the council house. There were dogs and children in the yard, an outside fire burned down to ash-covered coals, a mortar and pestle standing idle, and drying frames holding stretched deerskins. The king himself came out to greet them, a man with steady eyes and a self-assured manner. His breechcloth was of blue stroud and his deerskin leggings had brass tinkers fastened in the fringe. He had on a ruffled linen shirt cut open down the front and worn loose like the gown of a judge, though it reached only to his thighs. His hair was unadorned, but the rims of his ears had been slit and stretched, hooplike, as was the fashion among these men, and wrapped with brass wire and decorated with tufted white feathers. The king greeted Sam with noticeable reserve, yet with the decorum that was always present when Indians met under conditions of peace, no matter how strained that peace might be.

Exactly how strained their peace was with this king, Isaac could not determine. He understood not a word of the Muskogee language that Sam seemed to speak as eloquently as his mother tongue. Isaac shook hands with the king and followed Sam inside the house, where four other men, including the visiting emperor, sat on mats spread about the fire. The two traders were offered places, and as they sat down, cross-legged, a pleasant-faced woman came forward with a dish of food for them to share. There was silence as they ate and more silence as a pipe was passed around. This was usual with the Indians at the beginning of any gathering. It seemed to Isaac to be a time for everyone to settle down and collect his thoughts.

Isaac knew without being told which of the men about the fire was Emperor Brims. The distinction was not in the man's dress or ornamentation. It was in his manner, in the intelligence of his eyes, and in the deference paid him by the others, including the king. When the silence was at last broken, it was Brims himself who opened the discussion with a lengthy talk in which he gestured much, his tone scornful and angry. Sam listened impassively, and Isaac did likewise, though he understood nothing. When the emperor had finished, the king took up the talk, and again there were gestures, and now the name of Nate Ramsay began to be mentioned. When the king had finished, he called over his wife and whispered something to her and she left the house.

The pipe was passed around again, this time with Sam supplying the pouch of tobacco. The atmosphere was solemn. No words were spoken. At last the king's wife returned, and with her were three people—an elderly woman, a man of middle years, and a younger man with a battered face. They did not come to the fire, but stood quietly just inside the door.

Then Sam began his talk. His tone was earnest and his manner open and honest. He seemed distressed at what had gone on in his absence, but there was no fear in him. At the end of his talk he picked up the trade gun he had brought in with him and held it out toward the little group that had lately arrived. The younger of the two men came forward and took it and waited patiently while Sam measured out powder and shot. Then, unfolding the bundle of stroud cloth, Sam measured out a yard's length along his arm, cut it and gave it to the man. With his new gun, ammunition, and cloth, the man retired from the house, seemingly mollified. Isaac assumed he was the one named Tobacco-eater and that the goods were compensation for the beating and for the forty deerskins extorted from him by Ramsey.

Sam then measured out the rest of the stroud, counting off the yards as he stretched them one after another along his arm. Then he folded it all up again and offered it to the man and woman who still stood by the door, evidently kinspeople of the beaten woman. The two talked together in low voices and there seemed at first to be some disagreement between them. But at last they reached an accord, and the man came forward and accepted the cloth as payment to their clan for damages. Then he and the old woman went out.

Now Sam offered one of the ruffled shirts to the king, who accepted it solemnly, handing it to his wife without inspection. Sam offered the other shirt to Emperor Brims.

Brims refused it. Launching into another talk more heated than the first, he railed against Sam, his gestures sweeping even to Isaac, and several times during the course of his talk the other Indians around the fire murmured their agreement.

Sam listened attentively. Then he, too, made a further talk, deliberate, reasoned, free of anger. At last he took up the gunpowder and shot that remained and offered it with the shirt to Brims. There was a moment of silence during which Brims looked squarely at Sam, his eyes seeking something that he must have found, for he reached out and took the gift. There was a noticeable relaxation about the fire. Sam proceeded to give handkerchiefs to the other men and a ribbon to the king's wife.

It was over. Goodwill had been restored. They all got to their feet and sauntered out into the yard where for a time they stood exchanging small talk, letting the people of the town see that they had come to an accord. Then Sam and Isaac took their leave.

Now Sam went directly back to the trading house. Isaac trailed along after him and stood by while Sam banged loudly on the door, to no avail. He finally roused Nate Ramsay from his drunken sleep by firing a gun in the air, which was quite humorous to the townspeople who had gathered to watch. Ramsay unbarred the door and opened it, standing there for a moment blinking into the light, barefooted, with his shirt hanging loose.

"Sam, ye've come back," he said groggily.

"And a fine welcome it's been," muttered Sam. He pushed the door open and stalked inside and began gathering up Ramsay's belongings and throwing them out the door.

"Easy, Sam," said Ramsay, still somewhat stupefied. "Y'ain't heard my side yet."

"I don't need to," said Sam. He picked up a fifty-pound pack of deerskins and tossed it out the door. "That's more than you deserve, you bloody bastard. Now get out of my territory. I'll protect you no longer."

Ramsay made no further protest. He went out sullenly and put on his boots and rolled up his gear in a blanket. Then, hiring one of the Apalachee bearers to carry his pack of skins, he left the town without so much as a backward glance.

"Now there's an end to it," Sam said to Isaac with an air of relief. "Let's move our goods into the store. Then we can settle down and enjoy ourselves."

Enjoyment for Sam was the company of his woman in the house next door. For Isaac it was the bed in the trading house among the packs of deerskins, bundles of trade goods, and kegs of salted meat. Sam offered to send a woman to him, but Isaac in his weariness declined, and barring the door, he soon fell into a deep sleep.

It was from the depth of that sleep that Sam dragged him with a pounding on the door. Isaac opened his eyes to darkness and at first could not place himself. Then, as Sam called his name, his memory cleared, and he got up and made his way through the darkness to lift the bar and swing open the door. It was as dark outside as in.

"It's still night," said Isaac. "Is there trouble?"

"Trouble, but not danger," said Sam, coming in and crossing the small room to the hearth. He stirred coals up from the ashes and dropped on some splinters of heart pine. Flames sprang up and dimly lit the room. "It's almost morning, in truth. At least we got a little sleep before starting out again."

"Starting out?" Isaac went back to his bed to find his boots. "Where are we going?"

"It's Ramsay again. My woman Anahki just thought to tell me that he was waiting for some slave-catchers to come in here with Indian slaves from the Spanish country. He outfitted these men, you see, gave them credit from the store to the value of two slaves. They're to come back here and pay their debt by giving us two of the slaves they've captured, provided they've captured any. The value of two slaves is no small amount, the same value as four hundred deerskins. Close to a year's trading for a single trader."

"So Ramsay paid these Indians in advance to go down into Spanish country and make a capture of slaves? Was he supposed to do that?"

"Giving credit's a common practice," said Sam. "We all of us do it to get the trade. There are so bloody many of us, and only so many deerskins and slaves being brought in. To obligate an Indian to bring his to you is the secret of the trade. So for Ramsay to advance the price was all to the good if the fellows should meet with success and bring the slaves back to me. Those were my goods he gave 'em, don't forget. But now I'll wager my life he's taken the trail south to meet 'em, and you can be sure he'll not bother to inform 'em that he's no longer working for me. They'll clear their debt in good faith, he'll take the slaves to Charles Town to sell 'em, and I'll be left here like a man whose house has been robbed."

"Unless we catch up with him," said Isaac, rolling up his gear in his blanket.

"And we will. I've hired Anahki's brother to guard the store while we're gone."

Isaac followed Sam to the door and then paused for a moment, turning to look back into the trading house, which was now slipping back into darkness as the pine splinters burned away. "It's a pity to be leaving so soon," he said. "I was taking a liking to the place."

"You'll be back," said Sam. "In truth, you'd best plan to settle in for a few years. It takes that long to learn the language and the ways of these people. You can't move among 'em without knowing their ways."

"Does Nate Ramsay know their ways?" asked Isaac.

"He knows. But he don't give a merry damn."

✳ On the third day of travel, having kept up a relentless pace, Sam and Isaac came upon Nate Ramsay in the early afternoon. Had they lagged but a few hours behind, they would have been too late, for Ramsay had met up with the Creeks he sought and was passing his pipe among them. At his feet was a small keg of rum, as yet untapped. The Creek men had four slaves in their custody, three women and a boy. Nate Ramsay's attention was so much on these captives that he did not notice the approach of Sam and

Isaac until they were almost upon him, though the Creeks had long since spied them.

"Sam!" Ramsay said with a start. He rose quickly to his feet with a stiff smile of pretended pleasure and held out his hand.

Clutterback ignored him, stepping past him to shake hands and exchange words of greeting with the Creek men, all of whom were known to him. Then he turned back to Ramsay.

"Ain't you the trader, Nate. Turned in your skins for a keg of rum and with that you meant to buy two slaves more while stealing the two of mine."

"Easy, Sam," said Ramsay, glancing nervously at the Creeks. "These fellows understand a bit of English, you know."

"I'm only saying you're a master trader. You know your business, Nate. Just pass the keg around, get 'em a little drunk, and they'll sell their own mothers to get the rest of that rum. And when they wake up from their drunk, empty-handed and mad as hornets, you'll be halfway to Charles Town with their slaves, claiming in all righteousness that you bought 'em."

"In the name of God," said Ramsay, hurriedly taking up his keg beneath his arm. "You'll cost me my life if you keep it up." He picked up his gun in his free hand and straightened up, glancing at the Creek men who watched him with stony faces. He said something to them in their language, but they gave no reply. One of them spat and turned away.

"If there's trouble, Sam," Ramsay said grimly, "I'll lay the blame on you." He turned and headed back along the path back toward the north.

"Your trouble is all your own making," Sam called after him.

The Creek men laughed and one of them said something to Sam.

Sam smiled and made a reply in their language. Then he said something further to them, nodding toward Isaac. "It'd be a kindness," he added in English.

"I speak for all," said one of the Creek men. "My brothers understand your tongue but speak it little."

Sam turned to Isaac. "This here is Kacha Fiksiko. That means Heartless Panther in Muskogee. The traders just call him The Panther. He used to live with a trader in the Yamasee settlements. Learned a little English there. He says he's willing to speak English for your benefit."

"I thank you, my friend," said Isaac, holding out his hand to The Panther, who shook it warmly. Isaac then shook hands with the others.

Sam took out his tobacco pouch and offered it to The Panther, then turned and looked at the four slaves who sat huddled together under the watchful eye of their captors. "Two of 'em are mine," Sam said. "What about the others?"

"If you want buy, we sell," said The Panther. "We take full price."

"You was about to take a keg of rum for the twain of 'em," said Sam.

"You send rum away," said The Panther. "If you want cheat, you keep rum here."

"I ain't out to cheat you, you know that."

The Panther nodded. "You good trader. We never burn your trading house. We never rob you. We pass by others, bring trade to you. We take full price. For two slaves, we take price of four hundred skins."

The Panther's companions nodded.

Sam looked at Isaac. "Does it interest you? It's near the mark for the goods you brought in."

"I had thought to be dealing in skins," said Isaac. "I'd not considered slaves."

"You'll find it easier and cheaper to lead two slaves to market than to hire a dozen bearers to carry your deerskins. Even better, we have the slaves in hand. There's no guarantee you could get the skins. The season's at a close. Most hunters have already come in. If it was me, I'd take the slaves if they're healthy, and count myself a lucky man."

"And how do we determine their health?" asked Isaac, finding fewer qualms with the notion of slave-trading than he would have expected, now that he was coming face to face with it.

"We study 'em," said Sam. "No sensible man buys a slave without studying him first. Ain't much different from buying a horse." He walked over to the slaves.

Isaac followed, turning his attention to the three women and the boy, all sitting close together, silent and afraid. As Isaac looked them over, he was surprised at how coolly he appraised them. He was able to put pity aside and think only of how to strike a good bargain, how to discover the worth of these creatures and pay no more than their value. He could see immediately that their quality and value differed. One especially would bring more than the others. She was the youngest of the women, fair of face, the strongest and most fertile years of her life just beginning. If she had the value of two hundred deerskins, then the woman beside her, who looked old enough to be her mother, must necessarily be worth less. Isaac made up his mind that he would not pay equally for them.

"We'd just as well start with the prettiest," said Sam, reaching down to take the arm of the young woman and lift her to her feet. She was as tall as he was, her face drawn, though not cowed, as if she were resolved to be strong. Reaching down, he pulled away the belt that held up her skirt of Spanish cloth so that it fell away, leaving her naked before them.

"Good God, Sam," muttered Isaac as the woman closed her eyes in shame, her hands reaching down to cover herself.

"This ain't no time to be polite," said Sam, beginning an inspection of her limbs, manipulating them as he would those of a horse, feeling her muscle tone, checking her joints. He looked into her mouth, examined her armpits, and forced away her hands to inspect her private parts.

"Some say it was the Spaniards brought the French pox to Europe," he said as he gave the young woman back her skirt. "But she's clean of it to all appearances, and of all else as far as I can see." He stood watching her, waiting as she tied the belt in place with shaking hands. Then he spoke a single word to her in an Indian language.

She raised her eyes to look questioningly at him.

As he repeated the word, he jumped in place and motioned for her to do likewise. With a look of confusion she made a small jump. Sam nodded and stood back, repeating the command and motioning for her to jump higher. She did as she was bid, jumping again and again, higher and higher, until Sam at last was satisfied. He spoke a different word and she stopped, and he waved her back to the others.

"She's prime," he said to Isaac. "Strong and healthy. I ain't forgot your generosity to me. I'll let you take this one. She'll bring you a good price. But you'll have to pay full for her."

"What language did you speak to her?" asked Isaac.

"Apalachee."

"Like the bearers we hired?"

"The same," said Sam. "And it can make trouble for us, too. There's several hundred of 'em in Savano Town and others amongst the Creeks. When I take Apalachees down to market, I find it best to avoid the towns, lest someone recognize his kin and raise a storm."

"But we've our goods back at the trading house and more trading to do."

"No need for us both to go back," said Sam. "I'm thinking I'll send The Panther with you to take the slaves on down to Charles Town. I'll go back with the others and pay 'em off for your slaves and sell the rest of what we brought up, if I can find any hunters still out. When I've finished, I'll come down to Charles Town with the deerskins. You go ahead and put the slaves on the market when you get to town. Take not a farthing less than twenty-five pounds for that woman."

"And for the others?" said Isaac.

Sam shrugged. "Twenty, maybe less. We'll look 'em over and see what we've got. You try your hand now. Pick out your second slave."

Isaac hesitated, his eyes sweeping the dazed faces of the four. It did seem a pity that some must be slaves and others masters. Yet Christ himself had not condemned slavery. Isaac drew in his breath, putting himself in mind of his experience at buying horses. He walked boldly over and took one of the older women by her arm and raised her to her feet.

CHAPTER TWENTY-THREE

Lucia turned her head away and would not watch while they did to Ana what they had just done to her. Trying not to listen as they told Ana to jump, she looked down at the ground, pulling at the new green grass and breaking it off in her fingers. The woman Margarita moved closer to her and put a hand on her knee. Margarita herself would be next after Ana, and her hand, though trembling, was meant to give comfort. She was older than Lucia and had a half-grown son named Pablo, a thin, sad little boy who had gone out with his mother that day at San Augustín to help her gather wood before the storm. They too had gotten lost. They too had been found by the slave-catchers.

Ana was coming back now, breathing hard from her exertion, and as she sat down beside Lucia, the Englishman who could only speak his own language drew the boy Pablo to his feet, and the other Englishman, the one who could speak Indian languages, motioned for Margarita to come stand before him. As Margarita rose to her feet, Lucia put an arm around Ana. Ana leaned against her, trembling and breathing in short, quick breaths.

For more than a moon now they had been forced to trudge north from San Augustín through a desolate country of swampy creeks and rivers and then up into a higher land of rolling hills. At night they would lie linked together by a rope knotted about each of their necks while one of the warriors sat up by a small fire to guard them. By day the rope was removed and they were free as they traveled—free of each other but not of the warriors who watched them closely, never relaxing their guard.

Yet Lucia would not lose hope or think of herself as a slave. She thought only of Carlos, of being free again, of finding him. She imagined how it must have been for him on the day she was taken, how he must have heard the news that slave-catchers had struck and that three women and a boy had been taken. And how he must have walked a little faster, trying not to worry, only to reach the hut and find it empty. She imagined how he must have gone to Teresa's hut to look for them, and how Teresa would have been the one who told him as she held her crying baby in her arms. How did he feel when he heard? She could only imagine. Strong on the outside, torn with pain and helplessness on the inside. He would have wanted to rush out and bring her back, but of course he could not, and he would have known that, too, from the first moment.

So what did he do? Did he leave right away to come north to the Creeks? Did he travel on the very trail she had traveled, or were there other ways to go? A man alone could have traveled faster than the warriors with their captives. If he had come on the same trail, he would have caught up with them by now, and if he had, she would have surely known it, somehow. He would never have passed by them off the trail and gone on. So he must have gone another way. But where was he now? How would she ever find him again?

She was hoping to be taken to a Creek trading town. There were Apalachees in Creek towns and she might have a chance to speak to someone, to tell who she was and where she was from. And maybe Carlos, if he ever came that way, would hear of it and find her, somehow, maybe follow her into the English settlement. But what could he do if he found her, one man against the power of the English? If only she could stay in the Creek country, escape her captors and find him in the trading towns. But how to escape? She had thought about it for all this time, every day, every night, watching for a chance, for one single moment when she could break away and be free. But the moment had never come. And now there were Englishmen buying them on this trail in the middle of nowhere, and maybe they would not even be going to a Creek town, and then there would be no way for Carlos ever to hear of her. Perhaps she would never see him again.

But no. She would escape. Her chance would come if she watched for it, if she never slept. A single moment was all she needed. She would make it happen somehow.

☀ Lucia had seen that a sale had been made, but she was not sure of its terms. Had these two Englishmen bought all of them together, or were they to be divided between them? The sale had been sealed with a pipe of tobacco passed all around, and then the entire party followed the trail northward. Before evening the Englishman who could speak Indian languages and three of the warriors split off from the rest, leaving the other Englishman and the Creek warrior they called The Panther to go on alone with the four captives, whom The Panther tied together because there were now only these two men left to guard them. Lucia despaired at first, the rope making everything seem hopeless. Her hands were free, but in the night as she tried to loosen the knotted rope around her neck, she found it could not be done, not with the others tied to it.

Then on the morning of their second day of traveling in the rope, they crossed a creek that had a waist-high bank on the far side. The stream had a swiftly moving current, with grassy areas on either side. It was a clear spring morning, the sun warm in a blue sky with clouds high and scattered. The cold water felt good as Lucia waded through it, and she reached down quickly and scooped up some to drink. Then on the far side she stood close beside the bank, giving Ana enough slack in the rope to climb up before her. As she waited there, she noticed something protruding from the face of the bank, a piece of flint hardly wider than her thumb and flatter than a stone should be, perhaps a point for an arrow or a spear. With her finger she pushed away the earth and felt the stone's sharp edge and then quickly dug it out, looking away from it as she did. As she climbed up the bank, she kept it hidden in her hand, pressing it against her palm with her thumb, taking care that all her movements were natural so that no one would notice.

Early in the afternoon they stopped to rest, the boy Pablo lying back in the grass, the women sitting close together but not talking. The Englishman lounged back on one elbow looking up into the trees at the newly emerging, lacy green leaves. Only The Panther seemed to have no need of rest. He paced impatiently as if he were anxious to finish the journey and be off to other things. Lucia sometimes wondered if he had a wife, a woman in the trading towns who was waiting for him to come home. He seemed the kind of man with whom a woman could be happy, not especially hard or cruel. And yet he was a slave-catcher. What could be more cruel than that?

She was not watching him directly, but she was aware of his every movement, and she knew when he turned away to scan the forest around them. She touched her hand quickly against Ana's knee. Ana looked at her. Again Lucia touched her knee so that Ana looked down, and Lucia opened her hand to show her the flint. Then, with The Panther still looking away and the Englishman almost asleep in the afternoon sun, Lucia pretended to adjust the waist of her skirt, tucking in the flint around toward the back, rolling the edge of the skirt around it to make a little pouch. Then she looked again at Ana and put her hand on the rope that lay between them, closing her fingers around it. She sawed her thumb slowly across it.

"Tonight," she said softly, hardly louder than breathing.

Ana looked at her with dull eyes, then glanced down at the rope in Lucia's hand and gave a slight, almost imperceptible nod. But did she understand? Would she leap up and run into the night when Lucia cut them free? Lucia let go of the rope and touched Ana's knee and then her own knee, and then, letting her hand lie on the ground between them, she made a motion with her fingers like running, only very slowly to avoid being noticed, then she touched each of their knees again. She looked into Ana's face, and again Ana gave a little nod. Her eyes were not so dull anymore. Relieved, Lucia looked away, but when she did, she saw that The Panther was watching them. Her eyes passed quickly over him, afraid to linger. She was not sure how long he had been watching, but his manner was unchanged and she doubted he had seen anything. Leaning back on her elbows, she tilted her face to the sky and closed her eyes. There was a chance it would work. In the darkness, with only two men to give chase, it might work. If they were lucky. If everything went just right.

✷ The camp that The Panther chose for the night was close by a stream, and this encouraged Lucia, for the sound of the water would cover the sound of her flint as she sawed the rope in the darkness. At dusk The Panther had shot a turkey, singed off the feathers, gutted it, and cut it into six pieces. It was roasting now, impaled on six sticks stuck into the ground at an angle to the fire. They all sat close around to catch the heat of the fire in the evening chill as they watched the meat cook, the captives on one side of the fire, the two men on the other. Lucia looked out into the fading light, studying the land, trying to decide which way they would run in the dark of the night.

Ana was showing more life than she had in all the days since their capture. From time to time she leaned forward to help The Panther turn the pieces of turkey. She was almost cheerful.

When the meat was finally done, The Panther pulled up the sticks from the ground and handed them around, one piece to each. It was too much meat and Lucia's appetite was weak, but she stuffed in all she could, thinking of the strength she would need in the days ahead and the uncertainty of finding food.

When they finished eating, they sat for a time watching the fire. Lucia was feeling increasingly tense, and her stomach was souring from the food. She wished that things would hurry along, that they would all lie down to sleep so that she could wait with her face turned away from the fire. The Panther had been looking at her, glancing at her over his turkey as he ate, watching her more than usual, she thought. She wondered what it was he had seen. The change in Ana? The amount of meat she herself had eaten? Or maybe earlier he had seen her fingers when they made their running motion through the grass. She would not look at him. She watched the fire and waited.

The Panther was taking his time, picking his turkey bones clean, cracking them open and sucking out the marrow. As he finished each one, he tossed it into the fire, until finally he tossed the last one away. Then he got to his feet and walked out of the circle of firelight to relieve himself. They could hear the sound of his water.

When he came back, he squatted beside the Englishman and said some-

thing to him. The Englishman turned and gave the captives a narrow, scru-
tinizing look, and fear jolted into Lucia. Rising to his feet, The Panther
reached into the leather pouch that hung from his belt and brought out a
small bundle that Lucia could not see clearly in the darkness. He picked at
it for a moment, then pulled away the end of a leather thong, unwinding it
with slow deliberation until it came free and dangled from his hand. She
glanced at Ana and saw that her heart was falling, her eyes going dull again.

The Panther walked over, motioning for them all to stand up. Lucia
could hardly breathe now. He went first to Ana and pulled her hands together in front of her and quickly wrapped the thong around them. Then
he pulled loose another thong. Lucia looked away and did not watch as he
pulled her arms together. She felt the thong being wrapped tightly about
her wrists, once, twice, three times, and tied. Then The Panther walked all
the way around her, looking her up and down. Suddenly he stopped and
took her roughly by her arm and turned her so that her back was to the
firelight. She felt his fingers at the waist of her skirt, working at the fold she
had made, turning out the flint blade. He looked at it for a moment in the
light, then tossed it across the fire to the Englishman, who reached up and
caught it with one hand. The two men said nothing. The Panther moved
on to Margarita, taking out another thong. Margarita was puzzled by it all,
and Lucia would not look at her as The Panther bound her. He tied the boy
and then went over and sat down in the firelight away from everyone else.
His knees were drawn up and he rested his forearms on them, his fingers
turning a small twig as he looked over his hands into the fire.

Ana sighed and sat down, the others following, though it was awkward,
and hard to sit comfortably with their hands bound. The thongs were tight
and painful.

"What was it?" Margarita asked quietly.

Lucia shook her head, unable to speak. She closed her eyes and dropped
her head, making a slight rocking motion of despair. It was over. They
would be kept like this, hands bound, necks bound, until they reached the
English settlement. There would be no other chance for her. She knew
now that there never had been a chance. The Panther had seen everything.
Maybe not the flint, he had seemed surprised by that. But he had noticed
every little change in them, their small communications, Ana's buoyed
spirit, maybe even a change in Lucia of which she herself was not aware.
He had seen it all, and why would he not? How many slaves had he carried
to market? It was his business, and he knew it well.

She opened her eyes and saw him watching her. He looked away and
threw the twig into the fire.

CHAPTER TWENTY-FOUR

The trip downriver to Charles Town from the backcountry went much faster than had the earlier, upriver journey. In little more than a week Isaac and The Panther were paddling their canoeload of slaves into the bay at Charles Town. This was no longer the quiet harbor into which Isaac had sailed when he had first arrived in Carolina in the dead of winter. A number of ships now lay at anchor in the roadstead, and periagos lined the wharves, rocking in the spring winds as their cargoes of deerskins and slaves were unloaded. The Panther deftly maneuvered the dugout canoe into a narrow space between two larger vessels. Isaac was glad to find a place to unload, but uneasy about its safety, and he was relieved when all four slaves were secure upon the wharf. With The Panther's help he began herding them along, winding through stacks of deerskins, edging past grimy traders and their servants and slaves, both Indian and black.

Isaac's slaves were so dazed by the bustling scene that there was no need to bind them anymore. The boy clung to his mother, and the young woman and the older one stayed close together, following The Panther simply because there was nothing else for them to do.

They had hardly left the wharf and set foot on the solid earth of Bay Street when The Panther came suddenly to a halt. "Nate Ramsay," he said to Isaac in a low voice.

"Where?" said Isaac. "The man's no concern of mine. He's the one who should dread to show his face."

"Nate Ramsay not afraid," said The Panther.

Isaac looked in the direction toward which The Panther was looking and saw Ramsay coming boldly toward them. At Ramsey's side was a gentleman of quality, a tall, lean man whom Isaac had met before, though it took him a moment to recall who he was. Then he remembered Thomas Broughton, the son-in-law of the governor.

"So you've made it down with your slaves," said Ramsay, a sneer in his voice as he stopped directly before Isaac and planted his feet to block his way.

Isaac glanced from Ramsay to Broughton. The two seemed to be acting in concert, though Broughton's manner was more refined. "I see you've wasted no time finding new employment," Isaac said to Ramsay. He turned and tipped his hat to Broughton and made an attempt to be on his way.

Ramsay fixed himself the firmer. "You're forgetting something," he said in an unpleasant tone.

"And what is that?" asked Isaac, his anger beginning to rise.

"The governor's tariff," said Ramsay with a smile. "If you mean to trade in Carolina, you have to stay square with the governor." He looked over the slaves. "I think the governor would settle for that one." He nodded toward the youngest of the women. "What do you think, Colonel Broughton?"

Broughton nodded. "She will do."

"She belongs to me," Isaac said coldly. "As does the boy." He endeavored to stay calm and keep his wits about him. These slaves were his entire fortune. To lose one would set him back to where he was when he first arrived from Jamaica, nothing gained for all his effort. "The other two belong to Sam Clutterbuck, and they're none of the governor's. They're bought and paid for in legitimate trade."

Ramsay looked down and spat a stream of tobacco juice that splattered against the side of Isaac's boot.

"Well, that may be the way it seems to you, Mr. Bull," he said, raising his eyes and fixing them directly on Isaac's. "But when we tell that to the governor, he's still going to be wanting his due."

"Tell him whatever you wish," Isaac said curtly. "If he has any grievance against us, he can bring it to the counting house of John Hawkins and we'll answer it there. Now excuse me, gentlemen." Again he made a move to leave, but Ramsay and Broughton stood firm.

"You're new to Carolina, Mr. Bull," said Broughton. "You lack familiarity with our laws. The simple fact is that any war expedition commissioned by the governor that results in the taking of slaves brings into play the governor's right to a consideration. A return for his commission."

"Commission?" said Isaac. "There was no commission. It was The Panther who led the war party, and Indians from the Ocmulgee Creeks who followed him. No Englishman was involved in it. Does the governor hand out his commissions to savages?"

"Of course not," said Broughton. "But if what you say is true, it raises a more serious question than before. For if no Englishman witnessed the taking of the slaves, Mr. Bull, you may well be in illegal possession of friendly Indians. It's a sad abuse by our traders that they encourage our loyal Indian nations to kidnap from one another and pass off their victims as legitimate slaves gotten from the enemy."

"From all I hear, that's an abuse you know well," Isaac said hotly. "Your men are the ones who practice it, and it's more than an abuse, it's a danger to the province to goad our friendly Indians and tempt them into war against us. You have no grounds to accost me, Colonel Broughton. None whatever. These are Spanish Indians and no doubt about it. It's all within the law and no concern of yours."

Broughton looked at him narrowly. "You lack prudence, Mr. Bull. It may be you're not planning to stay in the Charles Town trade, but if you are, you'd best learn how things are done. What we have here are four slaves who may well be English allies."

"Indeed they are not," said Isaac.

"You have no proof of it."

"He has none at all," Ramsay said testily. "And I do believe, Colonel Broughton, that I've seen 'em all before. In the Apalachee settlements in the Savano towns. They're all of 'em loyal Indians. I'll swear to it."

"That's a lie!" said Isaac.

"So these are not slaves at all," said Broughton. "You know, of course, that the law forbids the enslavement of friendly Indians. But no doubt you've paid a large price for them. If we were to confiscate all of them, you would be hard pressed to recover your losses. We understand that. It's the governor's desire to promote the cause of commerce in the province. He would not wish to be the ruin of any man. Indeed, he might look the other way on this matter for a small consideration. It would be a penalty, you understand, a warning against the future, and though it might go hard with you, still you must admit that to lose one and keep three is not so grievous an outcome as to lose all four."

"We'll take this one, then," said Ramsay, stepping past Isaac to seize the young woman by the wrist.

"You'll not!" said Isaac, grabbing his arm.

Ramsay shoved roughly at Isaac, still keeping his hold on the woman.

"You're interfering with the execution of the law, Mr. Bull," said Broughton.

"Devil your law," muttered Isaac, struggling to break Ramsay's grip on his slave. "This is bloody robbery."

Ramsay jabbed his elbow hard into Isaac's stomach. Isaac staggered back, his breath gone out of him. But he regained himself, and in a fury now, he threw a punch against Ramsay's jaw with all the force he could give it. Ramsay reeled and fell to one knee, the young woman pulling free from his grasp and moving back with the other slaves. As Ramsay tried to get up, Isaac gave him a shove with his foot and sent him sprawling against the legs of Broughton, who staggered and all but fell trying to extricate himself from the tangle.

Isaac turned to The Panther and motioned for him to go on with the slaves. Ramsay struggled to right himself. Isaac watched him, waiting, ready

to punch him again. But Broughton put a hand on Ramsay's shoulder to
stay him, and without a word Isaac stepped around the two and followed
after his cargo.

He glanced back several times and saw no one following, but only when
the slaves were secure in the pen in the rear of John Hawkins' counting
house did he begin to breathe easily again. Hawkins was not in the office,
and Isaac went out to find him, leaving the clerk to measure out The Panther's payment in ammunition and cloth.

On the stoop of the counting house, Isaac paused for a moment and took
in the bustle of Bay Street: the caravans of horses with jingling bells, the
long trains of Indian bearers with packs of deerskins on their shoulders,
the huddled groups of newly captured slaves, the traders and their helpers,
leather-clad, unshaven, carousing and hallooing, enjoying what for many
was their sole visit to civilization in the course of an entire year. Isaac made
a point of remaining there for some time, serene in his manner, making a
show to Broughton, or to any of his men who happened to know of the
fracas, that he was unafraid, that he had acted within his rights and expected no further trouble—although in truth, he knew not what to expect.
When he felt his point had been made well enough—if indeed anyone at
all had been watching—he went down the steps and along the street to the
Indian Queen.

Though it was yet morning, the tavern was already crowded and loud
with drunken revelry. Isaac made his way among the rooms, searching the
faces of the patrons in the dim light until at last he spied John Hawkins
sitting with his brother Abraham at a table in a corner. The two merchants
failed to notice him until he came up to them, but then they greeted him
warmly and called for a bowl of punch.

"So you've been to Indian country and lived to tell the tale," John Hawkins said amiably.

"I've a tale to tell, all right," said Isaac. "But it's set as much at the Charles
Town waterfront as in the backcountry. Do you know a man named Nate
Ramsay?"

John Hawkins nodded as the serving boy came with the punch. "Not a
very dependable fellow. Clutterbuck has hired him a time or two when he
could find none better."

"He'll not be hiring him anymore," said Isaac. As he downed some
punch, he warmed to his storytelling and had soon related the entire matter of the firing of Nate Ramsay, the getting of the slaves, and finally what
he was beginning to see as his triumph over Ramsay and Broughton at
the wharf.

The Hawkins brothers found entertainment in it. "You're one of us now," John Hawkins said merrily, pounding Isaac on the back. "You'll have nothing but grief from that crew from this point forward, I'll warrant you, but it's no more nor less than the rest of us have. It puts you in good company, I'd say."

"You'd do well to ship those slaves out of the province as soon as you can arrange it," said Abraham. "An incident like this can go on for years, them hacking away at you, charging that the slaves, if they're still about, are not truly slaves but freemen. But if the slaves are gone, there can be no call to free them, and the thing dies away."

"Then all is well enough," said Isaac. "I was planning to send them to Swade in his return cargo. I'm no expert yet in the business of slaves, but I believe he will be pleased with these. He claims he'd rather dig a grave for an Indian that cost him twenty pounds than for a Negro that cost him forty."

Abraham Hawkins shook his head, overtaken for a moment by his New England sensibilities. "It's a sad fate for a slave in the sugar islands. Seems a pity sometimes when one stops to reflect."

"It does indeed," said Isaac. "All for a bit of sweetening."

"And for the rum you're drinking," said John Hawkins, refusing to join them in their high-minded excursion. "And for the commission you were paid for delivering a cargo of that sweetening. And for half the business of our shipping firm, which is to say for the very clothes we are wearing and the next meal we shall eat. Shall we call it quits, then? Reduce ourselves to paupers and send the wretches back to their pagan haunts?"

"I'd say not, on the balance of it," said Abraham, rubbing his finger against his nose. He pushed back his chair. "Why don't we go take a look at these new wretches and see how well Isaac has done for himself."

"Good," said Isaac. "I'd value your opinion. It's the only way I'll learn the trade."

The slave-tender, a ragged fellow named Cobb, negotiated the several locks and bolts of the gate in the high board fence, swung it open, and stepped back to let Isaac and the Hawkins brothers go in before him. The three of them stood in the empty yard and waited while Cobb secured the gate and crossed over to the door that led into the back of the counting house. Here he lifted a bar, removed a padlock, and pushed open the door, calling out a command into the dim interior while motioning with his hand for the occupants to come out into the light.

The slaves came out slowly, blinking and squinting at the sunlight. There were seven in all. Besides the four Indians Isaac had brought in, there were

three blacks—two men and a woman—fresh from the Guinea coast by
way of Barbados, where they had been traded and moved from one ship to
another without setting foot on land. Cobb brought the entire group of
them to a halt in the middle of the yard and spread them out into a line.

"They appear sound enough at first sight," said John Hawkins of the four
Indians. "Though that one may be past her prime." He pointed to the oldest of the women.

"But that one," said Abraham, nodding toward the youngest woman.
"What a fine creature she is." He walked over to her and reached out and
pushed her black hair back from her face. "She looks to be about the age of
Charity." He stepped back and scrutinized her. "Tall and strong."

"She'll fetch a handsome price," John Hawkins agreed. "As much as
thirty pounds. But for the old one, scarce fifteen, I'd say."

"She's not so very old," said Isaac.

"But the good has gone out of her," said John Hawkins. "She'll age ten
years for every year of plantation work. Unless Swade keeps her in his
house. But I suspect he'd prefer the young beauty for that."

"By God, I'm taking a liking to the young one myself," said Abraham,
making a slow circle about her, inspecting her closely. "Not for a bedfellow,
mind you. I've the fear of God in me, a sentiment Theophilus Swade sorely
lacks. I've never bedded servant nor slave, nor do I intend to. But she would
be a pleasure to have about the place, now wouldn't she?" He came back to
stand beside his brother, rubbing his finger slowly against his nose as he
watched the young woman, who bore all of this with a stiff face, her eyes
looking deliberately past them. "Charity does need a maid for her chamber.
I've given up on white servants. The last one I had I would have kicked
bodily out the door and into the street had not my dignity prevented me."

John Hawkins nodded, leaning heavily on his cane to relieve the pain he
was suffering from standing about on his gouty leg. "It's a sad truth about
white servants in the colonies that they are completely worthless. Where
does their arrogance come from? Always balking at the lightest duty, argu-
ing and running away. There's hardly a master in Carolina who will have
one. We all of us prefer slaves."

Abraham moved his hand to his chin, still watching Lucia, but shaking
his head. "Thirty pounds. I could almost buy a black for that."

"Only a raw one like that one there," said John Hawkins, nodding toward the black woman. "If you want a black slave trained to civilization,
you'll have to pay dearly. These Spanish Indians can oft times be a bargain."

"That is true," said Abraham. "Some of my acquaintances in Boston
own Carolina Indians and profess satisfaction in them. One fellow ex-
cepted—his Indian wench ran away and was never found. But for the rest,

they've given good reports. It's crucial, they say, to get one who has come under the influence of the Spanish Church. Though it be popish nonsense in their heads, yet it serves to civilize them halfway."

"This one might well be a papist," said Isaac. "She comes from Saint Augustine. Though I mean not to lean on you. It's no matter to me whether I sell to you or to Swade, so long as I get my thirty pounds." He rocked back on his heels with satisfaction. Sam Clutterbuck had told him to take no less than twenty-five, and here he had the prospect of doing better.

"The question, then," said John Hawkins, "is whether she was baptized by a single pass of a priest through a pagan village or whether she lived in a mission and learned the ways of civilization."

"We could settle it by trying her Spanish," said Isaac. "Does anyone here know the tongue?"

"Not I," said John Hawkins.

"Nor I," said Abraham. "No more than a word or two. What about Cobb?"

"Not me, sir," said Cobb. "But I can find you a sailor quick enough, if that's what you want. There's many a Spaniard that ships on our vessels, and more than a few of our boys learn to speak to 'em. I'll fetch you one if you wish it."

"Good, Cobb," said John Hawkins. "Do that. We'll wait."

As Cobb hurried away, Abraham walked back over to the young slave woman. She was standing close to the older woman now. He reached out and drew her away from the others. For a moment there was a spark of anger in her eyes, but then she looked past him into the distance. John Hawkins walked over to inspect her more closely, Isaac following after him.

"She has no pockmarks," said Abraham, shaking his head regretfully. "I'd be a fool to buy her. The next sweep of smallpox would take her away."

"That's true," said John Hawkins. "It must be considered."

Yet Abraham still looked her over, feeling up and down her arms, turning her several times about.

"Sam Clutterbuck examined her closely," said Isaac. "He found her sound."

"She's not sickened in the meantime?" said Abraham.

"Not to my knowledge."

"Have her run for you," said John Hawkins. "That's the way to determine it. See if she has stamina."

Abraham gave her over to Isaac, who took her arm and began to lead her in a circle in the yard.

"Run!" said Isaac, stepping back from her and waving his hands, as if shooing a chicken before him. She stared blankly at him, seeming not to understand. He began leading her again, taking her arm as he broke into a jog, forcing her to run with him. He took her faster, circling around the little group of slaves and the two men in their silk coats and full wigs. As he started around with her a second time, he let go of her and slowed his pace, pushing her on ahead of him.

"Run!" he said again, waving his hands at her. She continued running alone while he, puffing slightly, walked over to stand with the Hawkins brothers. She kept a good pace, her face closed, revealing nothing of what she was thinking. Her breasts bounced with her stride, her short skirt giving glimpses of her thighs.

"Damn, look at her," murmured John Hawkins. "It makes my balls ache."

"It's her health we're supposed to be judging," said Abraham. "She seems strong enough."

"Is that all you see?" asked his brother with a smile.

"It's all I'll own up to," said Abraham. "Let's stop her now, Isaac, before John forgets himself and ravishes her in the dirt before our very eyes."

Isaac laughed. "That would be a pretty spectacle," he said, stepping out to intercept the woman.

The gate of the yard swung open and Cobb came in with a sailor he had found, a rough-looking fellow dressed in loose pantaloons and a tattered shirt.

"He says he speaks fair Spanish," said Cobb, bringing him over to the place where Isaac and the Hawkins brothers were standing with the young slave woman, who was breathing hard from her run.

"We want you to speak to her," Abraham said to the sailor.

"What is it I'm to say?"

"We want to know whether she's a true papist," said Abraham. "Whether she lived in a mission town. We reason that if she understands what you say and speaks back to you in Spanish, that will tell us enough. Say anything to her that you wish."

"Do you want to know her name?" asked the sailor.

Abraham shrugged. "You might ask her that."

"Where she comes from?"

"Anything," Abraham said impatiently. "Ask her anything at all."

The sailor looked down at the ground for a moment, considering, then he looked back at the woman and began to speak slowly to her in Spanish.

As the sailor spoke, Isaac watched her eyes and saw in them a light of recognition. She nodded slightly and made an answer to him, a few words quietly spoken.

The sailor turned to Abraham. "She says her name is Lucia, and she comes from Apalachee. She says there was a priest in her town, so I'd say she's civilized, all right."

"Do you think she tells the truth?" asked John Hawkins.

The sailor shrugged. "She speaks better Spanish than me. And she says the priest is dead. Why would she say it if it ain't true?"

"I believe her," said Abraham. He moved away a few paces and stood looking at her, his arms crossed. Then he looked at his brother. "I like her, John. I'm going to buy her and give her to Charity."

"You could do worse," said John Hawkins. "She might make you a good slave."

"I believe she will."

"Take time to consider it, if you wish," said Isaac. "There's no hurry."

"Is that any way to make a sale?" Abraham asked good-naturedly. "You should have your hand out to take my money."

Isaac smiled. "Were you a stranger, I'd do it right enough. But I've an interest in staying on the good side of you, and I don't mind saying it."

"Then sell me this slave," said Abraham. "If I live to regret it, I'll blame none but myself."

"Thirty pounds, then?"

Abraham nodded. "Thirty pounds. And we'll take her right along. I'll present her to Charity tonight. It will be just the thing."

"You must join us for the evening, Isaac," said John Hawkins. "We've a gathering planned in Charity's honor. She comes out of mourning tonight."

"I'd be pleased to attend," said Isaac, bowing slightly.

"Cobb," said John Hawkins, motioning to his man, who was standing a little apart beside the sailor. "Bring this one to the gate. We're taking her with us."

"You want her bound, sir?" asked Cobb.

"No, we'll walk her along between us. She's too new yet to try to run."

Cobb went over and took Lucia by her arm and began leading her toward the gate, Isaac and the Hawkins brothers following.

"She's going easy enough," said John Hawkins.

But Lucia was beginning to look around now, distress coming into her face. She looked ahead to the gate and then behind to the wigged Englishmen, and then back across the yard to the older woman, who watched her with lips parted and fear in her eyes. Lucia stopped suddenly and pulled back against Cobb's grip, but Cobb held her tightly. She turned to the three English gentlemen and said something in her language, which was incomprehensible to them.

"Move her along," John Hawkins said sharply to Cobb.

Cobb pulled at her, but she was resisting now, and she was strong. Cobb began to curse.

Struggling, she looked for the sailor, and seeing him near the gate, she

called out to him in Spanish, speaking quickly, fighting against Cobb, motioning back across the yard toward the other woman.

"She says that woman there is her aunt," said the sailor. "She don't want to be taken without her."

"There's always something," said John Hawkins. "You can't listen to them. Move her on, Cobb."

"I'm trying, sir," said Cobb, attempting to catch both her arms to keep her from fighting. "She's a strong one. You'd do well to bind her."

"She'll be all right once she's out," said John Hawkins. "You," he said to the sailor. "Come lend a hand. Help Cobb get her out of here."

The sailor stood motionless, watching Lucia as she struggled and pleaded in words that only he could understand. He shook his head. "It's none of my affair, and I'll have no part in it." He turned his back to them, waiting for the gate to be unlocked.

Isaac stepped forward reluctantly to give Cobb a hand. This was the most unpleasant moment he had yet encountered in his new profession, worse than the fracas with Ramsay, and he wished he could do as the sailor was doing and stay out of it. But she was his slave, he had sold her, and he went now and took hold of her free arm. Together with Cobb they moved her on toward the gate, almost carrying her while she still struggled and made her pleas to the sailor. The sailor would not look at her now, and as soon as the gate was open, he slipped out and was gone.

Isaac and Cobb brought Lucia out into the alley, John Hawkins and Abraham following, the gate pushed to and locked. She turned and looked back at the high board fence, tears in her eyes. But she ceased her struggle. Her shoulders slumped, and when Cobb released her, Isaac led her with little trouble down the alley and out into the bustle of Bay Street.

CHAPTER TWENTY-FIVE

Lucia made herself pay attention to her surroundings as they walked along. She noted the buildings they passed and the turns they made away from the street that fronted the bay. She noted alleys and places where there were people who appeared to be poor, some of them white-skinned, others swarthy, a mixture of bloods. Such people might hide a runaway, just as in San Augustín such people would trade with Carlos for his stolen goods. But they might just as likely turn in a runaway to claim the reward. She would have to be careful, wait, take time to learn the place.

This town where she had been bought as a slave was not so very far from

Creek country. Her hope of escape was strong. But she was in pain over Ana. Her heart dragged the ground because of that, and her mind was so distracted by it that she had to force herself to pay attention to where they were taking her, past wooden houses that were handsome and substantial compared to the poverty of San Augustín. And now they had come to a house made of brick, and they were turning her from the street and taking her through the yard of this place, around to the back where there was a kitchen separate from the house, and peach trees in bloom, and a garden green with spring vegetables, and a stable and sheds and chickens scratching in the yard. They led her to the kitchen. The Englishman who had brought her from Creek country and the tall Englishman with the big nose stood back while the stout Englishman with the cane took her just inside the door. They blocked the light as they stood there, and for a moment she could see nothing but the silhouette of someone across the room in front of the fire, a woman, who turned toward them, wiping her arm over her face. As Lucia's eyes adjusted to the dim light, she could see that the woman was an Indian, Ana's age or a little younger.

The man spoke to the woman in English, Lucia understanding nothing of what was being said. The woman looked at Lucia and nodded and again rubbed her arm across her face, wiping perspiration away. Now the Englishman spoke at length, the woman nodding, glancing now and then at Lucia. The woman said something, and the Englishman answered her and then turned and went out, leaving Lucia standing in the doorway.

The woman looked at her a moment. Then she said, "He says you are from Apalachee." Lucia was surprised to hear words she could understand. The woman was speaking Spanish.

Lucia nodded. "From Ivitachuco."

The woman shrugged. "I do not know that country. I am from Guale."

"I have heard of Guale," said Lucia. "The coastal land north of San Augustín."

"The beautiful islands," said the woman, shaking her head wistfully. "Still at night I dream of that place."

"Were there priests in Guale?"

"When I was there, yes," said the woman. "Now there are no priests, and no Indians either. The English emptied the land with their slaving. Some of my people went to San Augustín with the priests, but most came north to live near the English. Here they call us Yamasees and do not enslave us anymore."

"But you are a slave," said Lucia.

"Because I was taken before the peace. Just as you will always be a slave no matter what peace they make with other Apalachees."

"No, that is not true for me. I will get away. I have a husband in the
Creek country."

The woman looked at her a moment and said nothing. Then she said, "Come sit. I will find something for you to eat."

"I am not hungry."

"Come inside anyway," said the woman. "I have my work to do. There is to be an entertainment tonight. For two days I have been cooking for it and doing my other work besides, and now they give me you to look after."

Lucia followed her across the room and sat down on the floor where the woman directed her to sit, leaning back against an open barrel of cornmeal. The kitchen smelled of wood smoke and baked bread and roasting meat.

"Master John says you are called Lucia," said the woman. She had spread flour on a table beneath a small open window and was now turning bread dough onto it from a large wooden bowl. She scattered flour over the dough and began to knead it. "Here I am called Bella," she said. "In Guale I was Isabel."

"That is my grandmother's name," said Lucia. She closed her eyes for a moment, leaning her head against the barrel, her thoughts going back to Isabel. She wondered if she were still alive. But then it was Ana she was thinking of, Ana at the friary, Ana in the slave yard.

"I had a husband, too," said Bella. "And a little girl. All I could think of when they first brought me here was how to get free, how to get back to them. I could not eat or do anything but sit in a corner and grieve. Finally they whipped me to try to make me eat. So I slipped away and ran, and for two days I was free. But it was horrible. I did not know where to go. The country was strange, and I could only travel at night. If I tried to go off the roads I got lost in the swamps. But on the roads there was danger of being seen, and I did not know which road to follow. Finally I came to an Indian house at the edge of some woods on a white man's plantation. I thought, here was someone who could help me and tell me how to go. So I hid and watched that little house, and when daylight began to rise, an Indian woman came out to get firewood. I went up to her and told her I was hungry. She took me into her house and I ate with her and her husband. They were Cussoes. This country around here used to belong to the Cusso people. I did not tell them who I was. I was not sure I could trust them. But they knew. The word had been spread, you see, a runaway slave, a young Yamasee woman. They said nothing to me about it, but after we had eaten, the man went out, and in a little while he came back with a white man, and before I could get to my feet, I was a slave again. The white man paid the Cussoes some money and brought me back to Master John." She paused and then added, "You can still see where he whipped me when he got me home again." She brought her flour-covered fingers to the front of her soiled bodice and unfastened it, slipping it down from her shoulders as she turned her back to Lucia. The scars were plain to see, welts that covered her back entirely.

"I am sorry," Lucia said quietly.

"They almost killed me," Bella said matter-of-factly, dressing herself again.

"How long ago did this happen?" asked Lucia.

"I was no older than you are. If my daughter still lives, she is grown now. And my husband would be an old man, probably with another wife growing old beside him."

"Did you never try again to run away? If you had known more, you might have made it."

Bella shook her head. "I know more now. I know how hopeless it is. Even in the Creek country a runaway slave is not safe. English traders are everywhere, and always there is someone who will turn you over to the traders for a bottle of rum."

"How do they know you are a runaway?"

"They know."

"How?"

"By the way you act. And by scars like these."

"I have nothing like that," said Lucia.

"You will if you try to run away."

"No, I will wait and plan it out. They will not catch me."

"They catch everyone."

"Not everyone. There were black people at San Augustín who had escaped from here."

"How many?"

"I am not sure."

"Ten?"

"More than that."

"A hundred?"

"Not that many."

"But which is closer, ten or a hundred?"

"Ten, I guess. But more."

"The runaways they have caught are more than a hundred. Many more. It is hopeless to run away. You should listen to me when I tell you this. You must forget that husband of yours. For you, he is a dead man. You will never see him again."

"You are wrong," said Lucia, looking away toward the open doorway and the bright sunlight, blinking back tears that sprang into her eyes.

"They are taking you to Boston," said Bella.

Lucia looked sharply at her. "Where?"

"To Boston."

"Where is that?" Her heart began to pound, panic rising.

"I do not know. But it is far away. You have to go on a ship."

"A ship?" Lucia stared at her. Not a ship. Not the sea. She could never get back.

"You belong to Miss Charity Hawkins," said Bella. "She visits here, but she lives in Boston. It is for her they are having the company tonight. They will be giving you to her as a present in the middle of it all. They want me to see that you are well dressed. Master John said they would be sending out some clothes."

Lucia was not listening. "I cannot go to Boston," she said.

"You had better forget that husband of yours," Bella warned.

"I will not!" Lucia said fiercely, her eyes filling with tears as she glared at Bella. "I will get back to him. They will not take me to Boston. I will run away before they can take me away from here."

Putting out a floured hand to quiet her, Bella looked over toward the door where there now stood a slender black woman, younger than Bella but older than Lucia, her face hard and drawn. She carried a bundle in her arms, holding it to her chest with large-knuckled, bony hands. Coming into the kitchen, she dropped it in front of Lucia and then stood there without saying a word. Lucia looked at the fallen bundle—a red woolen blanket and several garments, unidentifiable in the heap they were in.

"This is Venus," said Bella as she came over to inspect the pile, wiping her hands on her dress. "That is her slave name. Her basket name, her real name, is Beneba, because she was born on a Tuesday."

Lucia nodded to the woman, but Venus made no acknowledgement.

"These are your things," said Bella. She leaned down and picked up the blanket, refolded it, and put it on Lucia's lap.

Lucia spread her hand on it and stared at the thick wool, remembering the red blanket Carlos had worn in Ivitachuco, how the wind would catch it and billow it out.

"Look here," said Bella, reaching down to bring up a garment of white linen. "They are giving you a shift." She spoke brightly, trying to lift Lucia's spirits. "They mean to treat you well. Better than I am treated. Look, I have only this petticoat, no shift beneath." She pulled up her skirt to show her bare legs. "Venus does not have one either." She glanced at the black woman, but seeing the stoniness of her face, she let that go and turned back to the clothing. "Here, stand up," she said to Lucia. "Let us see how it fits."

Lucia looked at her but did not rise. It seemed more than she could do to go on with this, to let them dress her as they wished, drawing her ever more deeply into this place where she did not want to be. "I would rather stay dressed as I am," she said. Venus scoffed bitterly, and Lucia glanced at her and then away.

"They are making you a lady's maid," said Bella. "They are taking you into the house tonight and presenting you to Miss Charity in front of all those people. Do you think you can go in there looking like a wild thing? Master John told me to dress you up. Now, I have enough to do without you making trouble for me."

Lucia looked at her a moment longer, then stood up with resignation and began slipping off her deerskin skirt. "I want to keep this," she said, laying the skirt carefully on the barrel of cornmeal.

"No need to do that," said Bella. "You will not be wearing it again."

"Yes, I will," Lucia said firmly. "When I leave this place."

"You should be careful how you talk," Bella said quietly. Taking up a basin, she went over to a barrel by the door and dipped up some water and brought it back, giving it to Lucia with a rag. "Wash yourself," she said.

Bella waited in silence while she bathed. Then she lifted the shift over Lucia's head and smoothed it down for her. Bella leaned down and picked up the other two garments and held them up, looking at them with admiration. "Not just a petticoat for you. They have sent out a gown as well. And these are not old things. Miss Charity brought them from Boston to wear herself." She gave Lucia the blue and white striped petticoat to put on and then helped her fasten the waist. "It is too short," said Bella, stepping back to look. "I can see your ankles."

Lucia said nothing, not caring.

"But it will have to do," said Bella. Now she held open the bright blue gown for Lucia to put her arms through. It had a low square neckline and full, wide-cuffed sleeves that fell just below the elbow. Bella helped her fasten the gown snugly at the waist and lace up the bodice, and then she pulled back the open skirt, fastening it up into billows over either hip to reveal the striped petticoat beneath.

"Now," Bella said, standing back to admire the effect. She looked at Venus. "Did you ever see such a change?"

Venus spoke sharply in English and turned around and left.

"What did she say?" asked Lucia.

"She's jealous," said Bella. "While Miss Charity has been here, Venus has been serving her. She thinks they would have given her these clothes if you had not come. But she is wrong. They are dressing you up to surprise Miss Charity. They never would have given these to Venus."

"She can have them when I leave," said Lucia.

Bella gave her a hard look. "Listen to me," she said sternly. "Do not keep saying such things. Do you think you can trust these others just because they are slaves like you? A slave can trust no one—*no one*—do you hear? And she the least." Bella jerked her head toward the door where Venus had gone out. "Already she has heard too much."

"She does not speak Spanish," said Lucia.

"But she understands a little of it, and so do some of the others around here. A single word repeated to the master can get you a whipping." Bella went back to the bread dough, kneaded it halfheartedly for a moment, and then covered it with a cloth. She looked at Lucia. "Maybe I should not tell you this, but I will. It is possible you will not have to go to Boston."

"What do you mean?" Lucia tried to step toward her, but the skirts were heavy around her legs. It was like walking in water.

"Master John and Master Abraham are trying to arrange a marriage. If they have their way, Miss Charity will be staying in Carolina."

"I do not understand," said Lucia.

"They want Miss Charity to marry Master Henry. He's Master John's son. If she marries him, she will go with him to live on his plantation."

"Near this place?"

"West of here, toward Indian country."

Lucia smiled, putting her hand against her heart as if to keep it from collapsing in relief. "Then let her marry him. Do you think she will?"

"No one knows. She seems not to care for him. But her father wants it very much." Bella shook her head. "You yourself should not want it. I know your heart, how it beats for your husband, but I have already told you that you cannot get away. If Miss Charity weds Master Henry, then he becomes your master, and you do not want that man to own you. He is a bad one, worse than Master John and much worse than Master Abraham. There is not one of us here who would not tremble at the thought of being taken to his plantation. It is bad enough for us when he is here at his father's house."

"I understand what you are saying," Lucia said soberly. "But I would rather be his slave than be taken away on a ship. I hope she marries him."

"I knew you would feel that way," said Bella. She stood for a moment looking thoughtfully at Lucia. Then she turned away and began kneading the bread again, and for a time there was silence in the room. At last Bella said quietly, "Did you meet anyone from Guale when you were at San Augustín?"

"No," said Lucia. "It was a bad time. We did not know many people."

Bella kept on with her work. "I often think about my people. My husband and my little child. My mother, my sister, my brothers. I do not know what happened to any of them."

"Were you alone when you were captured?"

Bella nodded. "I was at the spring. It was daylight. It seemed safe. My mother was watching my daughter for me."

"I was not alone," said Lucia. "My aunt was with me. We were taken together. There was that comfort, at least, that we would have each other. But then today they left her there." She spoke softly, her arms crossed tightly over her stomach. She had not squarely faced this yet, her sorrow for Ana. She wanted to sit down, but the dress was in her way. She could neither sit nor walk comfortably.

"Where did they leave her?" asked Bella.

"Wherever we were. I do not know. The Englishmen came, your Master John and the others. They looked me over and then took me away. She is still there, shut up in a dark room." Lucia hunched over her folded arms. "What do you think they will do with her?"

"Sell her," said Bella. She covered the dough again and brushed the flour from her hands. "We will see what we can learn. I will send Cajoe to ask after her."

"Who is Cajoe?"

"Venus' boy. He works at the waterfront sometimes, helps out at Master John's storehouse. Maybe he will be able to find out what happens to her."

"You have been very good to me," Lucia said quietly.

"It is putting me behind in my work," said Bella. "You have to learn to walk in that dress. Try to do it yourself. I have too much to do to stop and teach you."

"Do not worry about me," said Lucia. "I can manage. And I can help you with your work."

"Not in that dress," said Bella. "Just stay out of my way. That is how you can help me most."

"I would rather be busy."

Bella looked at her. "You are not the same as I was when they first made me a slave. You are not huddling in a corner, full of grief."

"Because I know I will not be a slave for long."

Bella put her hands to her ears. "Stop saying that! I do not want to hear it anymore!"

"Then you will not," said Lucia. Turning away from her, she lifted her skirts a little and began to practice walking in a sea of cloth.

CHAPTER TWENTY-SIX

Isaac Bull wandered through the gathering of bewigged men and richly-dressed women who milled about in the candlelight of John Hawkins' hall. He felt serene, warmed by the brandy he had downed, and he smiled amiably as he paused at the edges of conversations, pretending to listen while his eyes returned continually to the group of young ladies across the room where Charity Hawkins was talking and laughing, playing hostess in her uncle's home. Her drab mourning garb had been put aside for a gown of emerald silk, her light brown hair tied prettily with a matching ribbon. Isaac was especially struck tonight by how fair she was, by the delicious whiteness of her skin above the low neckline of her gown. Earlier in the evening the slave woman Lucia had been brought in and presented to her, and Isaac had watched them together, both near the same age, both in fine attire, but Charity so startlingly fair beside the swarthiness of the slave woman. The more brandy Isaac imbibed, the more his eyes lingered on her beauty. Yet he knew he had no chance with her. He could no more win her hand without a fortune than he could cross the sea without a ship, and not even the brandy could make him lose sight of that truth. He watched now as Henry Hawkins broke away from the segregated company of the men and made his way over to Charity's group. It seemed to Isaac that some of the life left her eyes when she saw him coming, although she greeted her cousin amiably enough and made some comment to her companions that elicited their laughter. Other gentlemen, following the lead of their host, drifted over to mix with the ladies, Isaac among them, steering a course toward Charity. But by the time he got near her, Henry had already edged her from the company, as a herding dog cuts out a sheep. As Isaac turned to leave, Charity looked over Henry's shoulder and caught his eye. Smiling, she put a hand on Henry's arm and moved him to one side.

"Mr. Bull," she said, her tone inviting him to join them.

Henry's face clouded. He had the disordered look of one who had drunk too much. But he caught himself and put on a seeming civility that took effect everywhere except in his eyes. Had Isaac himself been more sober, he might have declined the invitation, but instead he let Charity's smile draw him in.

"Henry is entertaining me with talk of his Fairmeadow," Charity said to

Isaac. "You yourself have just returned from those parts. Is his plantation as fine as he claims it to be?"

"I'm sure that it is," Isaac said graciously. "Though in truth I've not seen it. I do know, however, that the country is full of promise, no doubt of that." He glanced away, unable to look her squarely in the eye as he remembered the misery of Sam Clutterbuck's wife in the midst of those swamps and forests.

"Then you would recommend it?" she asked, her tone serious and direct, her gaiety put aside.

Isaac looked back at her and felt the giddiness of the brandy leaving him. "I hope to have my own estate in that country someday," he said. "But my advice to anyone proposing to settle there would be to go to the place first and have a look at it. That is the only sensible course whether one proposes to settle in Carolina or Lincolnshire."

"So you see, he recommends it," said Henry, his voice loud from drink. "He's been there and found it to his liking. And who'd not love so fair a place? Is that not what you say, my friend?" Henry put a hand on Isaac's shoulder and shook it hard.

"Indeed," Isaac said amiably. "I wish Fairmeadow were my own."

"Of course you do," Henry said, and then he leaned toward Charity. "It is so fair a place, it excites the envy of my fellows."

"So it seems," said Charity, stepping back slightly to keep a distance between them. She looked beyond the two men into the crowded room. "Here comes Father," she said, relief in her voice.

Isaac and Henry both turned to see Abraham Hawkins approach, his abstention from drink giving him a steady step, though his manner was jovial enough. Abraham nodded to Isaac and then put one hand on Charity's arm and the other on Henry's. "I thought you two had gone out to walk in the garden," he said without subtlety. The blood rose in Charity's face.

"I've been trying to come around to that," said Henry, leaning toward Abraham with a knowing smile.

Isaac shifted uncomfortably, turning slightly away from them.

"I fear I'm not up to a walk," said Charity. "I'd been hoping for a word with you, Father, to ask you to make excuses for me to the company. I've a dreadful headache. I've done my best to hide it, but it's like a hammer in my head and getting worse by the moment. There's nothing for it but to retire to my chamber. Would you forgive me for that?"

Abraham sighed. "I suppose this has been too much for one night. Your first appearance out of mourning, and the new chambermaid atop that. Do you like your Indian woman, my dear?"

"She's lovely," said Charity, kissing her father's cheek. "What a sweet surprise she is. I hated so to send her back to the kitchen. She'll be good company in my chamber, once Bella has taught her enough English to get along."

"I'm sure she'll learn quickly," said Abraham. "Her transformation in a single day has been amazing. If you had seen her this morning when I bought her, you'd scarce believe the progress. Don't you agree, Isaac?"

"It's true," said Isaac. "This morning she was naught but a savage, and tonight a lady's maid. It was marvelous to see the change."

"So you had a hand in obtaining her?" Charity said to Isaac.

"She was one of the slaves I brought down from the backcountry."

"It's sad to think of the business of slaving," Charity said quietly. She put her fingers against her temples. "You will make excuses for me, won't you, Father? And bid the company good night for me when they leave? Let me slip out now without raising a fuss. I'd hate to cast a pall over things." Without giving Abraham a chance to respond, she made a curtsy to the three of them and moved toward the door, stopping here and there to exchange brief pleasantries, until at last she disappeared from the room.

"She inherited those headaches from me," Abraham said to Henry with a note of apology. "There are times when they pound my skull so that I cannot even stand, and nothing will do but to go to bed and draw the curtains around me."

Henry said nothing. Isaac felt uncomfortable again. They seemed to have forgotten him. As he began to move away, he saw Abraham lean close to Henry.

"Give her time," the older man said quietly. "She's young, you know."

Isaac wandered among the milling guests, edging close to several conversations, but nothing engaged his interest now except the increasing fullness of his bladder. Finally, he made his way out of the crowded room, glad to be free of the company, and went out the back door of the house into the pleasant air of the spring evening. Crossing the lantern-lit yard, he strolled out into the darkness of the garden and relieved himself. Then he stood for a time and watched the stars.

As he was returning to the house, he came around the corner of the kitchen and glimpsed the skirt of a woman's gown disappearing through the kitchen door, a flash of emerald in the lanternlight. Stopping for a moment, he watched the doorway, listening to the soft voices within. He knew he should not be doing this. Glancing toward the house with its bright candlelight streaming through the windows and the sounds of laughter floating out into the evening, he tried to tell himself to go back in and rejoin the company. But something in him would not listen. He stayed where he was, waiting, until at last he heard a rustle of silk in the narrow kitchen doorway and Charity appeared before him.

"Miss Hawkins," he said, bowing low. "Your headache has improved, I trust?"

"Why no!" said Charity, clearly startled. Then recognizing him, she smiled. "In truth, it is somewhat better, Mr. Bull."

"Perhaps the night air improves it," said Isaac. "The garden is pleasant this evening. Have you tried it?"

Charity glanced uncertainly toward the garden and then back at the house again. Isaac watched her in the dim light, his eyes lingering on her breasts pressed tightly against her close-fitting bodice, rising and falling with her breathing. She looked back at him. "I really should go in."

"Of course," he said. "But if the night air recruits you, it would be sensible to take a turn about the garden first."

Charity smiled. "Perhaps a short turn. A very short turn."

Isaac held out his arm to her, and they walked together onto the garden path.

"I was taking some oranges to my new Indian woman," said Charity.

"I'm sure she was grateful."

Charity shook her head. "I cannot know. It is impossible to read anything in her face. I pity her."

"But you should not. What better fate could befall her? What kinder mistress? I myself would trade places with her in an instant, were it offered."

"Mr. Bull!" Charity stopped short and pulled her hand free of his arm.

"A thousand apologies," Isaac said quickly, bowing low before her. "Believe me, I meant no disrespect. It was a poor choice of words. I'd as soon take my own life as offend you."

"There," said Charity, a smile stealing over her face. "It's not worth dying over, that's for certain. You are forgiven. Your words, if taken innocently, were quite sweet." She reached out and took his arm again.

"I meant them no other way, I assure you." They walked in silence now, and he steered a course toward the darker part of the garden, waiting to feel her resistance to it. But her fingers only tightened on his arm. "When do you return to Boston?" he asked.

She shook her head. "Were it for me to decide, I would be in Boston today. But my father has his own ideas."

"I suppose his business delays him."

"You might say so," said Charity, a touch of bitterness in her voice. She looked up at the stars in the moonless sky, her throat softly white in their

dim light. "These stars must appear so very tame to you here," she said
quietly, "after so many nights in the wild."

They slowed to a stop, she still looking away at the heavens. He made no reply, but only watched her, scarcely able to keep himself from reaching out to touch her.

She gave a barely audible sigh. "My father has plans for me, and he'll not return to Boston until he has seen them through. I'm afraid he intends to return there alone."

"And leave you here with Henry?"

She nodded.

"It would be a fine match," Isaac said diplomatically.

"Devil a fine match!" said Charity. "It would be a fine match for business, all right. But a pox on business. If I marry a man, it will be for love."

"They say there's no sorrier reason to marry than that," said Isaac. "If I believed otherwise, I would court you myself."

She turned her face away so that he could not see it—but this time her hand stayed in his arm. He ached to hold her.

"I pray I have not offended you," he said softly.

She shook her head.

He reached out and put his fingers lightly against her neck. She did not pull away. "Had I a fortune, I would court you with every ounce of my being. I'd not rest till I'd gained your consent to be mine."

For a long moment she was silent, still looking away. "And it may be you would have it," she whispered at last. She turned and looked at him.

He reached for her and pulled her to him and held her trembling in his arms, her breasts soft against his chest.

"You would not marry for love?" she asked softly.

"I would not marry with nothing to offer. But in a few years, my dear—in a few years I will be in a position to take a wife. And then it will surely be love that I seek, not fortune."

Charity was still for a moment, but then she began to pull gently away from him. "I have quite forgotten myself," she said shakily, reaching up to smooth her hair. "I don't know what you must think of me, Mr. Bull. This is not my normal practice with gentlemen, I assure you."

"I'm sure it is not."

"I am ashamed to have behaved so badly."

"No," said Isaac. "It was my own misconduct to press myself upon you. I had no right to do it. I am unworthy even to be here in your company."

"You are certainly worthy," said Charity. "You are beyond doubt a gentleman and you are entertained as such by my uncle."

"But I have no position in society. I have nothing to my name but the worth of two slaves and an annuity of a mere hundred pounds."

"You are no pauper, then," said Charity, her eyes smiling up at him in the starlight.

"That is debatable. Your father, I think, would take the other side. Especially if I sought to court you."

"But what if I wished it?" There suddenly was anger in her voice. "How could he refuse us if he loves me?" She looked away, close to tears.

"On the contrary," said Isaac, "how could he not if he loves you? The responsibility for your future lies entirely upon him. It is his duty as a father to arrange it to your greatest advantage."

"To the advantage of my brother Burnaby, you mean. He is the heir to my father's entire share of the company, save my own small portion. If I am united with Henry, all stays intact, even as it is now. Burnaby and Henry will work in partnership as Father and Uncle have always done. They mean to keep my share from going out of it. Otherwise they would encourage me to entertain other suitors. But Henry is the only one they will consider. It must be Henry or none."

"Surely you overstate the case," said Isaac. "I scarcely believe they would turn away a well-heeled gentleman of good family."

"They *would*, Isaac," Charity said earnestly. She reached out and took his hand and placed it against her cheek. "Feel my blush," she said softly. "It is too dark to see it, but I'd not have you think I could say such a thing without shame."

"There is no cause for shame," he whispered, drawing her into his arms again, savoring the warmth of her flesh, the sweet scent of the fragrance that she wore. He would give his life to have a taste of her. Bending his head, he put his lips against her hair, but she did not raise her face to him, and he carried it no further. "We must not be swept away," he said quietly. "I am not a gentleman of means. We cannot expect your father to entertain my suit."

"But you come from a good family," said Charity, pulling back and looking up at him again. "Your fortune is on the rise."

"We must face the truth. I have almost nothing. I do have hopes for the future, but those very hopes are our undoing, for they ride upon the patronage of your father and uncle and upon the good graces of Henry himself. If I were to press my suit, my hopes of fortune would be dashed and I'd have nothing at all to offer you."

"You would have your annuity," Charity said stubbornly, "and I my marriage portion."

"But how much of a portion would your father allow if you defy him
and insist on such a heedless match?"

"Is it hopeless, then?"

"Perhaps not. If you can put off Henry and go home to Boston. And
then in a little while, perhaps in two years, or three, if you can wait so long."

"I can wait," she said firmly.

"No," said Isaac. "Do not promise me that. The time will seem longer
than you can now imagine, and you will not be seeing me at all. Your
friends will be marrying, and suitors with good prospects will come calling.
I cannot ask you to wait for me. But if perchance you are yet unwed when
I have gained a suitable position, then I will come and put my case before
your father and endeavor with all honor and respect to win your hand."

"You are kind to speak of honor after I have conducted myself so shame-
lessly with you. I have thrown away all claim to honor in this last hour. I
fear when you reflect upon it, you will look elsewhere for a wife. I would
not blame you if you did."

Isaac smiled at her. "You have no idea what you are talking about. Believe
me, I have known shameless women. They have not the hundredth part of
your modesty. Your own innocence causes you to misjudge yourself."

Charity looked at him, searching his face, and then returned his smile.
"How could I ever marry Henry after coming to know you, Isaac? I will
make Father take me home to Boston. And I will wait for you, no matter
how long it takes."

"I ask no promise from you," Isaac repeated. "And I will take none. But
I am overwhelmed that you would consider me at all."

"I, too, am overwhelmed," said Charity. "This has come upon us so
suddenly." She turned and looked anxiously toward the house. "I should
go back before I am missed."

Isaac gave her his arm again and they started back through the garden.
"I wish I could come calling on you while you are still here," he said. "But
I take Henry to be the jealous sort. It would not require much provoca-
tion, I think, for him to throw me out on the street with no prospects
whatsoever."

"Then we will keep on as we were before," said Charity. "Mere friends
to all appearance."

"Which is all we should be for the moment. You owe me no obligation.
You must always consider what is best for your future, and if another suitor
intervenes to win your heart, I will count myself an unlucky man, but I will
hold you blameless for my bad luck."

"I cannot imagine that would happen," said Charity.

"But you must not rule it out."

"Very well. If you wish me to say it, I will not rule it out. But I cannot imagine it."

They stopped now at the edge of the garden. Beyond was the lanternlight of the dooryard. Isaac looked at her, wanting to hold her again, but hesitating, aware of the proximity of the house and the danger of being seen.

"I will not sleep tonight," he said softly.

"Nor I," she whispered.

He looked at her face, so soft and fair, her eyes intent on his, her lips slightly parted. He bent his head and kissed her, tasting her sweetness. For a moment she returned the kiss, and then she pulled away.

"Forgive me," he said quietly.

She made no reply, but lingered there beside him. Then she whispered, "Good night," and turned and walked quickly across the yard to the house.

Isaac watched her until she was out of sight. Then he followed her across the yard. As he passed by the kitchen, he noticed the Indian cook standing silently in the doorway.

CHAPTER TWENTY-SEVEN

Lucia drew the brush through Charity's hair, concentrating on making the crown smooth without destroying the curl beneath, trying to do it as she had seen Venus do it. Charity was paying little attention in the mirror, but Venus was standing by watching intently, waiting for the slightest excuse to criticize. Lucia pinned the hair carefully at the nape of Charity's neck, then reached for the blue ribbon on the dressing table. Venus shifted slightly, and Lucia stiffened. She stood for a moment, holding the ribbon, studying the job she had done so far. Unable to see anything wrong with it, she slipped the ribbon beneath the curls and tied it in a careful bow. Then she looked into the mirror at Charity.

"You like?" she asked in her faltering English.

Charity turned her head slightly one way and then another, inspecting herself in the mirror.

"It's very neat, Lucia."

Venus shook her head contemptuously. "If you could see the back, Miss Charity." Venus' English had a Jamaican lilt, rich with African intonations. She stepped up brusquely and untied the ribbon and pulled out the pins. "Let me do it over. Best make Lucia a kitchen slave. She's never gonna learn how to take care of you."

"You should have let me see it, Venus, before you took it down. I'll be the one to judge her progress."

"It was nothing but a mess, Miss Charity. Take my word."

Lucia stood back with her lips tight. Venus was supposed to be her teacher but everything she learned was in spite of the woman. And Lucia wanted to learn. She wanted them to think her a good slave. She wanted to be trusted and sent out into the streets on errands. At night she pestered Bella to help her with her English. Charity was impressed with her progress, and Lucia herself was pleased, for she knew she would need to be able to speak English in order to make her way back to Carlos. She could only pass through the settlement if she appeared to be a free Indian, perhaps a basketmaker like those she had seen selling their wares at the waterfront.

"There now," said Venus, stepping back to admire what she had done with Charity's hair. It was no different from Lucia's work. Venus picked up a lace headdress from the dressing table, but Charity reached out and took it from her.

"Let Lucia do it. You have to let her practice or she'll never learn a thing."

"And everything takes twice as long," grumbled Venus, stepping back out of the way.

As Lucia worked with the headdress, smoothing it in place, there came a knock at the chamber door. Venus stood sullenly while Lucia went over and opened the door to Abraham Hawkins, who was dressed in a morning gown with a silk turban on his shaved head in place of his cumbersome wig.

"May I come in?" His tone was stiff.

"Certainly, Father," Charity answered, she, too, keeping a distance in her voice.

The tension was an old one now, as familiar to the slaves as to the family. Charity's defiant refusal of the proposed match with Henry had gone on for more than two months.

Abraham came in and stood just inside the door. "I've a message from Captain Little," he said coldly.

Charity looked at him, her face grim. It pained her to be the cause of her father's displeasure.

"He plans to set sail on the twentieth of this month," said Abraham. "Wind and weather permitting."

Charity nodded but said nothing.

"That gives you little more than two weeks to come to your senses, Daughter."

Lucia strained to comprehend what Abraham was saying, wishing he would speak more slowly. She thought it had to do with the ship. Did he say two weeks? Did she have only half a moon to finish her plan for escape? That was hardly time enough.

"My mind is quite made up, Father," Charity said quietly. "I am sorry that this grieves you so, I truly am. But I wish you would consider my happiness in the matter."

"That is my consideration entirely," Abraham said irritably. "You are not so very far from spinsterhood, you know. Women younger than yourself are married every day. And here you turn down a fine offer, the best a woman could ask for, a large plantation, a half-interest in a lucrative trading company. I cannot understand you at all."

"Understand that I do not love Henry and you will understand everything."

"Love!" Abraham said fiercely, his face turning red and his voice rising. *"Love!"* He glared at her, trembling with anger. *"Love be damned!"* he shouted, stamping his foot so hard the whole room shuddered. Then he turned and went out, slamming the door with all his might.

Charity stared after him, stricken, tears welling up in her eyes. "Go on," she said weakly, waving Lucia and Venus from the room. As they left her, she put her head down on the dressing table and wept.

✸ Bella stood at the table in the kitchen chopping onions, blinking away the tears they caused.

"We heard him all the way out here," she said to Lucia.

"Love be damned!" mocked Cajoe, trying to make his voice deep like a man's. He was sitting against the wall by the kitchen door, his knees up, the tail of his long white shirt pulled down between his legs in a careless attempt at modesty. Beside him the waiting man Jack squatted on his heels to keep from dirtying his suit of clothes. As he laughed, his wig slipped a little more askew, for it had once belonged to John Hawkins, whose head was larger—fatter—than Jack's, so that it never sat exactly straight on the black man's head.

"She might change her mind now," Lucia said hopefully, speaking to Bella in Spanish. "She was crying."

"She will not change her mind," said Bella. "I am certain of it, for the reason I told you before."

"What reason?" asked Jack in English.

Bella waved her hand at him. "See?" she said in Spanish to Lucia. "You cannot say anything around here. They understand too much." She looked over at Jack. "Never mind," she said in English. "It is not for you to know. It is only for me, because I saw it, and for Lucia."

"Why Lucia?"

"Because it is her business."

"No more her business than mine," said Jack. "Who been with this family longer? Even Cajoe been here longer than she has."

"For you two it is nothing but gossip," said Bella. "For Lucia it means going away on a ship. I'll say no more."

"Love be damned!" Cajoe said again and laughed, poking Jack with his elbow.

"You two get out!" snapped Bella. "Go on, you're in my way." They got up, still laughing, and left the kitchen. Bella waited until they were gone and then she said quietly to Lucia, "It makes no difference what Master Abraham says. Isaac Bull is in her heart. I saw how they kissed on that night you first came here. And the next day she tells Master Abraham she'll not have Master Henry for a husband and that she wants to go home to Boston. And they spend all this time waiting, trying to turn her around, but she stays fast. And now the ship is about to sail." Bella shook her head. "She'll not change her mind. She's almost won."

Lucia walked over and stood in the doorway of the kitchen looking out. It was too soon to put her plan into action. She could not yet be certain of the people she had chosen: an Indian woman who sold pottery on Bay Street and a black boy who worked in a stable on the south side of town. There would be danger in approaching them. She had nothing to offer them, and they had no reason to keep her confidence. But time was growing short. Another week, no more than that, and she would have to speak forthrightly to them.

"Are you still thinking of running away?" asked Bella, her voice so low it was almost inaudible, as if she expected unfriendly ears to be pressed all around the kitchen walls.

"No," said Lucia, looking out toward the garden.

Bella scraped the chopped onions into an iron pot and said nothing more.

※ The family was at table for their midday meal when the news of Burnaby came. The meal had been tense enough until then, Charity picking at her food, still in pain over her father's outburst earlier in the morning. And to make things worse, Henry was there, silent, scowling over his food, though he ate with a hearty appetite. Abraham had not said a word since he shouted at Charity. He was drinking more than eating. No longer the temperate Puritan, he had gone through almost an entire tankard of ale. Only John Hawkins attempted conversation. Charity made polite answers. Abraham and Henry kept their stubborn silences.

Then the news came, a letter from the ship of Captain Markley, just arrived in port within the hour. Jack brought it in and handed it to Abraham. It was bordered with black.

"Brother!" Charity cried when she saw it and slumped forward against the table, weeping, overturning her wine. Later they all wondered, as did she herself, how she had known it was Burnaby while the letter was yet sealed.

Burnaby Hawkins had gone down to his death on a company ship that was bound by way of England for the African coast. The vessel had made it safely to the west coast of England, but there a storm had caught it and blown it across to Ireland, where it sank within sight of land. Seven of the crew survived, which made Burnaby's death seem even more bitter.

Charity could not walk to her bed. Henry carried her and she remembered little of it except clinging to his neck and weeping while they were going up the stairs. Lucia was there to help her off with her gown and tuck her into bed, but then there was no one to comfort her except Lucia herself, who sat on the bed beside her and held her hand and spoke softly to her with soothing words, mixing both Spanish and Apalachee into her English. Finally Mistress Bellinger, a family friend, rushed into the room and gathered Charity into her arms, rocking her against her bosom, giving her the comfort of a woman of her own kind.

When Charity finally came to her senses, she asked about her father and was told he was in the garden and could not be consoled. She insisted on going to him, but when she tried to stand, her legs gave way, and Lucia and Mistress Bellinger put her back into bed.

When Charity awoke the next morning, Mistress Bellinger was gone and Henry was sitting in a chair beside her bed. He looked like Burnaby. The resemblance of one to the other had always been there, faintly, but she could see it more clearly now. Her eyes filled with tears.

"How is my father?" she asked softly.

"Still in the garden," said Henry.

"All night?"

Henry nodded.

Charity turned her face into her pillow and began weeping anew. Henry reached over and awkwardly patted her shoulder.

Later he brought her up some hot tea and slices of freshly baked bread with butter and peach preserves. He carried the tray himself and set it on her lap and sat beside her, encouraging her to eat and saying comforting things to her. Her father had finally come out of the garden, he told her, and seemed to be somewhat better. They had helped him to his bed and he was sleeping now. Surely he would come to Charity when he awoke.

But it would be two more days before Charity saw her father. The burden of his willful absence from her added immensely to her sorrow.

✳ Charity was sitting up in her bed reading old letters from Burnaby
when Abraham finally appeared at her door. When she looked up and saw
him there, his face haggard and changed, she began to cry, not only for the
sorrow that the two of them shared, but also with a kind of remorse, as if
she herself were partly to blame for breaking his heart. He came to her and
sat on the bed beside her, and she wept for a long time in his arms.

At last she collected herself and sat back, wiping her hands hard against
her face, blowing her nose on a linen towel.

"How can we bear it?" she said softly. "First mother and now Burnaby.
He should have lived to marry and have children. He should have lived to
be an old man."

"And to bury his father," said Abraham. "It is not right for a man to
bury his only son." They were silent for a moment, remembering that there
would be no burial, Burnaby's body lost in the sea, dragged by currents,
eaten by fish. Abraham looked down at his hands, slowly opening them,
turning them, inspecting the wrinkles, the age spots. "You are the heir now,"
he said. "My only living child."

Charity nodded. She knew it, but she had not yet come to grips with the
implications. "I should have been the one who died," she said. "The daughter instead of the son."

"No, no," said Abraham, laying a hand upon her knee. But he did not
look at her. "God works His will upon us. There is nothing for it but to
submit to His plan."

Again there was silence.

"Of course, now you will marry Henry," said Abraham.

Charity looked quickly at his face. His eyes were red-rimmed, older by
ten years in the last few days.

"Please, Father," she said, feeling herself near tears again. "We must not
speak of that, not until we have both regained ourselves a little. It only
deepens our pain."

"The deepest pain is already here," he said, putting his fist to his heart.
"The thought that half the trading company might leave our family's hands.
After my entire life has been given to it."

"But I *am* your family," murmured Charity, tears welling up and spilling
down her cheeks.

"But you are a woman. Your husband will have your share. His children
will be the heirs."

"My children, too," she whispered, looking at him helplessly. Then she
began to sob, burying her face in the towel.

"But if Henry were your husband," said Abraham, ignoring her tears, "it
would be a fusing of the company rather than a dividing of it. Think of it,
Daughter. It would pass from you and Henry to but a single heir. Had

Burnaby lived there would have been two heirs, his and yours. God's plan for us is obvious, even in this terrible loss. No matter that I die from the grief of it, all is now in place for the future. I can find some comfort in that." He looked down at his hands, folded now in his lap, and slowly stroked one upon the other.

Charity regained control of herself, stopping her weeping; but she would not look at him. She absently twisted the towel in her hands. "You must give me time to think upon it. I am not myself yet. I cannot think."

"The ship sails in little more than a week," said Abraham.

"But we do not have to be on it. We could take a later passage."

Abraham shook his head. "I must return to Boston. There is much to be attended to now, so many affairs left hanging. I myself will be sailing with that ship. That's one certainty you can depend upon, Daughter."

Charity stared down at the linen towel, twisted almost to a rope. "This has all come so suddenly," she said.

"Often as not death comes suddenly," said Abraham.

They were silent a moment, and in the silence they could hear footsteps on the stairs and then the shuffle of Jack's step in his ill-fitting shoes.

"Master Abraham," said the black man, stopping at the door.

"What is it, Jack?"

"Master Bull come to call, sir, to pay his respects. Master John want to know will you come down?"

Abraham drew in a long sigh, then nodded his head. "Tell them I will be down presently. And then come to my chamber and help me dress. Or send Cajoe."

"Yes, Master. I'll send Cajoe to you."

Abraham rose slowly to his feet and stood for a moment looking down at Charity. "You must consider it very carefully, Daughter. An heir has responsibilities to the family and to the future. It is easier to be a younger child. But those days are over for you. I suggest you address the matter in prayer and listen to what the Almighty tells you to do."

"I shall," she said softly.

She watched him leave the room. When he had pulled the door closed behind him, she sank back into the pillows, pressing her hands against her cheeks. Isaac downstairs! If only she could speak to him.

She sat up suddenly, pushing back the covers. When she got up, her legs swayed, weakened by three days in bed. She held onto the bedpost and stood for a moment, gathering her strength, trying to think of what she was about. She wanted to dress and go downstairs, but how could she, bedridden as she had been and no one having bid her to come down or even thought of doing so? She went to her door and opened it and turned her car toward the stairwell, listening. She could hear their voices clearly enough, her uncle's, mainly, sometimes Henry's. They were speaking of Burnaby, of all his good qualities, of the promise everyone had seen in him. She waited and then there was Isaac's voice, just briefly, a sympathetic word, and then John Hawkins was talking again.

Charity came back into the room and paced nervously. She considered ringing for Lucia to come dress her. But instead she went to the window and looked out onto the street and tried to think. Was her father right? Must the family come first? Was she living for Burnaby now, his life in hers? Might she know better what to do if she were older? If she were a man instead of a woman? Certainly her father had no doubts.

She went back to the door and listened again. Now Abraham was downstairs, speaking in a subdued voice. There was a lull. Then came Isaac's voice. She strained to listen and heard her own name spoken. He was asking about her. And it was Henry who answered, explaining that her grief was keeping her abed, but that he would relay Isaac's condolences to her.

There it was, then. She could not go down. She went back and sat on the edge of her bed and held her hands tightly in her lap and tried to think, but felt lost in a hopeless muddle. Why did it have to happen this way? She had it all in hand before. Bad as it was, her father would have gotten over it. But now everything had changed.

She heard Isaac taking his leave, the front door opening and then closing behind him. She got up and went to the window and watched him as he walked away. At that distance he seemed almost a stranger to her. If only she could speak to him, be with him again as she had been that night in the garden. It all seemed so remote now, almost as if it had never happened.

She stood for a long time staring out the window, watching the people in the street, the children playing, the horsemen trotting by, a pig rooting for garbage in the shade of a moss-draped oak. At last she turned back into the room and sat down on the bed with her writing box on her lap. Taking out paper, quill, and ink, she wrote a note to Isaac asking him to meet her in the garden that night at eleven o'clock by the watchman's call. She sealed it and wrote his name on it. Then she rang for Lucia, and when the slave woman came, Charity explained to her in slow and careful words where to find Isaac's lodgings.

☀ Lucia walked along the street by the bay looking for the Indian woman who sold pottery. Charity's letter to Isaac was in her pocket, but she was tending her own business now. The pottery woman was nowhere in sight. Lucia began to look for her down the alleys and up the side streets, but still there was no sign of her. How many more chances would she have to come out? Hardly a week, and the ship would sail. But the woman clearly was not here today, and at last Lucia stopped searching and stood thinking for a moment. She could go to the stable south of town and speak to the black boy whose acquaintance she had made, arrange that part of her plan at least. But she did not trust the boy as much as she did the woman. He was younger, and she had seen less of him. She could too easily imagine him going to his master and telling all for a reward. And his master would go to John or Abraham Hawkins, and that would be the end of any hope for her. They would whip her and keep her under guard, perhaps even sell her away to some far off land, just as they did to Ana.

It was more than a month since Ana's ship had sailed. Lucia had been unable to leave the house, but Cajoe had come down to the waterfront and watched it go. It was taking Ana to a place called Jamaica, a sugar island, Cajoe had called it, as if he really knew what that meant. Boston was not a sugar island, he said, though it did not matter to her what Boston was. All that mattered was that they would take her there on a ship, which meant she could never get back to Carlos again.

She went on now, looking for the place where Charity was sending her. Maybe she would wait a little longer—a few more days—before she searched out the boy at the stable. She turned down a side street and began to watch the houses that she passed, looking for the one that had been described to her, two stories high and unpainted except for shutters that were blue. When she found it, she went up and knocked on the door.

A woman answered.

"Letter," said Lucia in her rough English, taking the letter from her pocket. "Mr. Bull."

"I'll take it up to him," said the woman, holding out her hand.

Lucia shook her head.

"No, dearie, you don't understand," said the woman, speaking loudly, as if that would help Lucia comprehend her words. She pointed to herself. "I am his landlady. I will take it up to him." She made a motion with her hands as if taking the letter from Lucia and carrying it back into the house.

"Mr. Bull here now?"

"He is in his chamber. And I will go up the stairs and take it to him." She held out her hand for the letter, and Lucia handed it to her.

"There now, you're a good servant," the woman said kindly, patting Lucia's shoulder. "Someone is training you up very well. You can tell your master or mistress that the letter has been delivered to Mr. Bull."

Lucia nodded, only half understanding the woman's words. She bowed and turned away. As she walked back up the street, she began looking again for the pottery woman.

✻ The landlady closed the door as Lucia left and went upstairs with the letter. The door to Isaac Bull's chamber was closed. She knocked, expecting an answer. But there was none and she knocked again.

"Mr. Bull?" she called. But only silence came back.

"Well, bless me," she muttered. "I thought he was here." And putting the letter into her apron pocket, she turned and went back down the stairs.

CHAPTER TWENTY-EIGHT

Charity came into the parlor of her uncle's house and curtsied before the Reverend Jonathan Clark, minister of the Presbyterian church that she and her father attended when they visited Charles Town.

"How good of you to call, Brother Clark," she said. Glancing over her shoulder, she saw that her father, who had ushered her downstairs, had not come with her into the room. "I'm sure Father will join us in a moment. He told you, did he not, that Uncle and Cousin Henry are out for the afternoon?"

"Seeing to business at the counting house, I believe," said Clark, nodding pleasantly as they both seated themselves. He was a thin man of middle years, plainly dressed with no wig. The crown of his head was almost bald and what hair remained to him was combed up elaborately to cover it.

"Business must go on," Charity said quietly.

"Indeed," said Clark. He rested his elbows on the arms of his chair and looked at her with so much seriousness that she had to look away. "It pleases me to see you are recovering," he said.

"Thank you," she said, forcing a smile. "I left my bed yesterday and began moving about, repairing my strength. I had supper with the family, and later in the evening I walked alone in the garden." She glanced at him and then down at her hands. "I suppose in time the wound will heal."

"With God's help."

"Of course," she said, nodding. There was silence, and she wished for her father to come. Her mind was too numb to make conversation. She was tired, no sleep last night after Isaac had failed to appear in the garden, leaving her to wait and wait until finally she had returned to her chamber and rung for Lucia to ask her if she were certain she had delivered the letter directly to him. Lucia had assured her that she had.

"It is an awesome burden that has fallen on you," said Brother Clark.

Charity looked at him, uncertain what he meant.

"A man is more suitable to carry it," said Clark. "But a woman is capable of it, if she seeks advice. Many a woman has managed, and some very well."

"An estate, you mean?"

"And such an estate as you will inherit. So prosperous a company."

"I never expected it to come to me," said Charity. "I have not prepared myself for it."

"But there still is time."

"Of course," said Charity, smiling a little. "My father is very much alive, for which God be praised."

Clark nodded. "Abraham can train you up to your duties, if you but listen to him."

Charity looked at him a moment and then away. She now understood that her father had arranged this. "So he has spoken to you of the difficulty between us," she said quietly.

"He told me a little of it."

Charity still looked away. She said nothing.

"Henry is a fine fellow," said Clark. "A gentleman of substance. Good family. And rather handsome, I believe, in the eyes of the ladies."

"I am aware of his qualities," said Charity. "He is my cousin."

"Then why you refuse a match with him is beyond my understanding. It is certainly not pleasing in the eyes of God. Your father wills it for your own benefit, and yet you disobey him. What of the Fifth Commandment, child? Honor thy father?"

Charity was silent again. She was thinking of Isaac, remembering the shame she had felt as she waited alone in the garden, listening into the night until the watch called out the midnight hour.

"If only I could be given more time," she said. "A year, perhaps, to better know my mind."

"Would you put your father in his grave?" Clark asked soberly.

Charity looked at him, and he met her eyes and held them.

"You think he is that much affected?" she asked.

"I know he is. Never have I seen a man so changed."

"Because his only son has just died."

Clark shook his head. "That is not all that troubles him, and you know it very well. You double his burden with your stubbornness, and he is sinking under it."

Rising to her feet, Charity walked to the window and leaned against it, looking out into the street. Her life seemed to be out of her hands. She was helpless. It would be Henry. And why should it be otherwise? It was Henry who had sat by her in her grief, who had consoled her and waited upon her with his own hands, while Isaac had refused to come to her at all. She had been foolish, and cruel to her father. Could Burnaby's death have been God's judgement upon her? She shook her head, unable to bear that thought.

"I am a poor sinner," she murmured.

The Reverend Clark rose from his chair and came to her. "Let us pray together."

Without looking at him, Charity dropped to her knees, resting her head on her hands as she gripped the window sill. Clark knelt beside her and began to pray. She gave herself to the words he uttered, drawing them into her heart, clinging to them, believing them. And when it was over, she rose to her feet and turned and saw her father standing in the doorway, his eyes glistening with tears. She walked over and knelt before him.

"Your blessing, Father."

Abraham put both his hands on her head. "God bless you, Daughter," he said with emotion and then drew her up and embraced her.

Brother Clark resumed his seat, and Charity and Abraham came over and sat down as well. Abraham looked happily from one to the other. "So it's settled, is it?"

"I suppose it is," said Charity, relieved to be at peace with him again.

"It will be a pleasure to have you a resident of Carolina," Clark said to her.

"I only wish Charles Town were to be our home," said Charity. "I fear I'll be lonesome at Fairmeadow, and uneasy, too, so close to the Indian country."

"The Indians should be of no concern to you," said Clark. "They're all of them loyal to us. Addicted to our trading goods, they are."

"Yet loneliness is a real consideration," said Abraham. "It has given me some unease, thinking on it. How would it be if you had your old Doll with you, and Timboe as well?"

"Oh, Father, would you consider it?" Charity reached out and put an earnest hand on his arm. "It would make all the difference to have them by me."

"Then it's done. I'll send them down to you from Boston on the first ship." He looked over at Clark and explained. "Doll is our old cook. And she was Charity's nurse as well. A Guinea slave. Timboe is her son, the same age as Charity. Doll nursed them together, the black babe on one breast and the white one on the other."

"It would be wise to send them," said Clark. "Especially that fellow Timboe. That will give her a man among the slaves whom she can trust."

"I thought so myself," said Abraham. He smiled and patted Charity's hand, which still rested on his arm. "And you'll have your Lucia with you. And John has spoken of sending Cajoe down to Fairmeadow, so you'll have a boy already trained to the house. Is the prospect improving, my dear?"

"Yes," said Charity, nodding.

"When Henry comes home we will close the affair," said Abraham. "Have done with it."

"Close it?" said Charity, drawing her hand away.

"If Brother Clark will stay with us a while longer," said Abraham, looking over at the minister.

"Certainly," said Clark.

"I'll ring up some tea, then, while we wait," said Abraham.

"Close it?" Charity repeated, her tone more insistent.

Abraham looked at her. "Do you mean to marry Henry or not?"

"Yes, I do. But not today."

"Why not today?"

"It's too soon."

"Too soon? We've been wading through this swamp near half a year. It's time we reached the other side. Not a moment too soon, I'd say. My ship sails in less than a week. I'd like to see you settled into married life before I take my leave."

"Then perhaps tomorrow, Father. But not today."

"And what is the difference, tomorrow or today?"

"I need time to reflect. And time alone with Henry. We've not even spoken of this, he and I."

"What do you mean, not spoken of it? He pled his case to you long ago."

"But it was all quite formal. And I was not receptive at the time."

"You'll have all your life to talk to Henry. But if you think you must have pause before we go ahead, we can delay until tonight. Marry by candlelight if you wish. If Brother Clark can return to us then."

"I could arrange it," said Clark.

"Then what say you, Daughter?"

Charity took in a long breath and slowly let it out again. "You promise to send Doll to me?"

"It's as good as done. I'll give you written title to her this very day if you wish. And to Timboe as well."

"Very well then," she said quietly. She looked down at the rug.

"Tonight?" said Abraham.

She nodded.

He leaned forward exultantly and put a hand on her shoulder. "Are you happy, Daughter?"

She shrugged and smiled weakly.

"It's natural to feel a bit of fright," said Abraham. "But you'll learn the ways of a wife soon enough, and then you'll be happy, I'm sure of it. This is a good marriage you're making. A fine, sensible marriage."

"Indeed," said Charity. She rose to her feet, and excusing herself, she left them and went upstairs to her chamber.

CHAPTER TWENTY-NINE

Isaac Bull was met by his landlady as he came into his lodging house. He was perspiring heavily from the noon heat, his shirt clinging to his body, his waistcoat soaked through.

"Mr. Bull," she said, taking the letter from her pocket, a trace of chagrin on her face. "This letter," she said hesitantly. "It came two days ago. I put it into my apron pocket, you see. It was my intention to give it to you when you came in, you see, but you were late and I was sleeping. And the next day I put on a fresh apron, as I always do."

Taking the letter, Isaac looked at his name on the outside. He did not recognize the handwriting.

"It was only today when I was putting the apron in the wash," said the woman, still trying to explain.

"No harm, I'm sure," said Isaac, putting the letter in his pocket. He smiled at her and she relaxed a bit.

"And there's more," she said. "You've a man waiting for you. Claims to be a friend of yours, said he'd wait in your chamber. I trust I did the right thing to let him stay there. The door was unlocked, you know."

"Did he give his name?" asked Isaac.

"A Mr. Clutterbuck."

Isaac smiled. "He is a friend. It's good you let him stay."

"Then that's a relief," said the woman. "It's hard to know what's best to do when a stranger asks a favor. Do you wish any refreshment, Mr. Bull? A little ale sent up?"

"Yes, that would be good. Just the thing."

Isaac went up the stairs with a bounce in his step and threw open the door of his room. Sam Clutterbuck was asleep on Isaac's bed, though he awoke at the sound of the door being opened and sat bolt upright as if he were in the danger of the woods.

"Too cheap to get your own lodgings?" said Isaac, going over to shake his hand.

"The door was open," said Sam.

"I'm afraid it always is," said Isaac. "It's the mark of a poor man that he leaves his room unlocked." He took off his waistcoat and threw it over the end of the bed, then pulled off his periwig, replacing it with a cool silk turban.

"What do you mean poor?" said Sam. "I thought you had the worth of two slaves to your credit."

"That and little else. But I don't keep my money here. It's locked in John Hawkins' counting house, most of it. The rest I took with me today, looking to buy a horse."

"A horse?" said Sam. "And what good'll a horse be to you? A perfect waste of your money."

A boy brought in a tankard of ale and set it on a table beneath the window and went out again.

"A man on horseback cuts a better figure than a man afoot," said Isaac. "More opportunities come his way." He poured some of the ale into the one pewter mug he had in the room, keeping that for himself and giving the large tankard to Sam. "To good company," he said, raising his mug. Sam raised the tankard and they drank.

"A horse'll not do you much good in Indian country," said Sam, leaning back against the headboard of the bed. "Nobody there cares what figure a fellow cuts. A horse is good for packing, true enough, but Indians hire cheaper."

"I've been thinking of staying in town a while longer," said Isaac, sitting down on the edge of the bed. "I want to see if I can raise my stake a little before I go back up to trade."

Sam shook his head. "You ought to be going back with me. There's things you need to learn up there. You'll not be a trader until you speak the Creek language and know how things are done amongst those people."

"But if I've nothing to trade, what's the use?"

"You've got the worth of those two slaves you sold. Another year of trading and you can double your money. And the next year double it again. Providing you live close. If you don't go buying horses. Next thing I'll hear, you'll have bought a coach, and not a road in Carolina you can drive it on."

"I've not bought the horse yet," said Isaac.

"But you went looking."

"I heard a fellow out west of town had one for sale. But I worked up a sweat for nothing. It was the sorriest horse I've ever seen. I'd heard it was a good one, too."

"You're bringing London standards to Carolina, I allow."

Isaac smiled and drank down the last of his ale and held out the mug for Sam to refill it from the tankard. "What news do you bring?" asked Isaac. "Has Ramsay been back to plague you?"

"All's quiet up there," said Sam. "I heard the biggest news here today at the Indian Queen."

"What news is that?"

"Y'aint been out taking in the gossip today?"

"I was at the Indian Queen last night. What news do you mean? It may be old to me."

"Not this," said Sam. "Fresh out of the mill. Seems Henry Hawkins has taken a wife of a sudden. Last night it was, like as not while you sat at your supper in the Indian Queen."

Isaac stared at him. "A wife?"

"You look like you been knocked in the head," said Sam. "He ain't dead, just married is all. To that pretty cousin of his."

"God in heaven," murmured Isaac, and he lay back across the bed.

Sam reached out and took away the mug of ale before he could spill it. "Now you look as though I shot you," he said. "You've got a concern in this, I think."

Isaac made no reply. He closed his eyes, pressing the palm of his hand against his forehead. Then he sat up suddenly and reached for his waistcoat and took the letter from the pocket. Breaking the seal, he quickly read it— only a few short lines asking him to meet her in the garden. He pushed the letter under his waistcoat and lay back again. So she had meant to tell him about it beforehand. He was just as glad to have missed that scene. He closed his eyes again.

"It ain't no business of mine," said Sam, taking a long drink of ale. "Though I hate to see you suffer so. She always was Henry's, you know. There weren't never any question of that."

"No," said Isaac without opening his eyes. "There never was."

"It would have taken a gentleman of means to have courted her away from him. Not that you're no gentleman. I ain't saying that. You're more a gentleman than Henry, if you want to cut it that way. But if you don't mind my saying so, you ain't got the money to back it up. Not that you're a poor man. God knows, you got more than me. But then that ain't saying much. I ain't got a pot to piss in. Just that scrubby little farm on another man's land."

Isaac opened his eyes. "You don't have to say anything, Sam."

"But you look in so much pain. I hate to see you suffer so when there's no cause for it. She always was Henry's." He looked at Isaac. "Unless there was something 'twixt the two of you I never knowed about. Not that I'm asking, you understand. It ain't no business of mine."

"No, there was nothing," said Isaac. He lay still for a moment staring up at the ceiling. "But wasn't she a lovely thing?"

"That she was," said Sam. "And still is, I'm sure. Marriage makes women go to fat, I know, but she ain't been wed but a day."

Isaac sat up and drew in a long, deep breath. "I believe I'll go back to Indian country with you, Sam, stay at your trading house if you'll have me. You told me once that it takes two or three years to learn all there is to know."

"Not even I know all there is to know," said Sam. "But three years'll make a trader of you, I promise you that. And there ain't nobody I'd rather have in my trading house. You can forget all these other troubles. I'll fix you up with a pretty little Indian woman."

Isaac nodded, but said nothing.

"They make good wives," said Sam. "Better than any white woman."

Isaac looked around for his mug. "Let's change the subject."

Sam handed him back his mug, and Isaac took a long drink. They sat in silence until finally Sam shook his head. "Damned if it ain't hard to think of something else when you got on a woman your mind."

"What about horses?" said Isaac.

"You're not buying one?"

"Not now. But one of these days, when I get a little ahead."

So they settled back and spoke of horses and then of the Indian trade. And whenever the tankard of ale got low, Isaac rang the landlady for another.

CHAPTER THIRTY

Lucia worked contentedly, folding gowns and petticoats, packing them away in a wooden trunk. For almost a month now she had been in good spirits, patient and full of hope. The ship had sailed away to Boston with no one aboard from this house except Abraham, and now in a few days' time Henry would be taking Charity and Lucia and Cajoe to his plantation near the Indian country. They would travel the same course Lucia had traveled when brought to Charles Town, in a boat that would weave its way through the marshy waterways among the coastal islands. She had asked very carefully about this. The vessel would be larger than the canoe she had come in. It had sails that were sometimes run up when the wind was favorable. But it was not a ship, and they would not go out on the open sea. It would take them along the coast to the Combahee River and then up that river to Henry's plantation. It was the same river, Bella had told her, that marked the boundary of the English settlement. On the far side of it was the country of the Yamasees, Bella's own people. And beyond the Yamasees were the Creek trading towns. There was nothing but time now, time to know the country, time to plan the escape. She would not attempt it until she was certain of success, for if ever they were to put the scars of a whipping on her back, she could never go freely among the Indian towns. There would always be someone, Bella kept telling her, who would see her for a runaway and turn her in to the traders for a reward.

She finished folding Charity's gown of green silk and laid it in the trunk, pressing it down to make it fit. "It's full," she said to Charity, who was standing by the bed, sorting through a pile of linen garments. Henry Hawkins was stretched out on the bed, leaning back lazily against the headboard as he watched the progress.

Charity came over to inspect the trunk, pushing down on the clothes to see if more room could be found in it. "Tight as can be," Charity said. She looked around at the clothing that still lay in piles on the bed and on the floor. Only one empty trunk remained. "I'm down to my last chest," she said to Henry. "I fear I've too much to go into it. I'll need another."

Henry shrugged. "Send out for one. It's a small enough expense."

"I could leave some things behind."

"Bring it every last bit. I want you to feel you lack for nothing at Fairmeadow. Especially at first, while the house is still rough. You must be prepared for that, you know. You'll find it a rude place. A bit small. But it was never meant to be the main house forever. When you see the foundation I've laid for the new one, you'll be heartened."

Charity smiled. "So long as it's more than a cabin you're taking me to."

"I'd not call it a cabin. It's made of lumber, not logs. And the rooms are spacious. Two up and two down. That's no cabin by any measure."

"I'm sure it will please me," said Charity. "You've given me fair warning. I'm ready to find beauty in it at first sight."

Henry smiled. "If I show you the slave cabins first, the house will seem a palace."

Lucia glanced up at him. She still could not understand everything that was being said, but she knew they were talking about Fairmeadow, something about the house there, and something about slaves. Henry had more than thirty slaves at Fairmeadow, Bella had told her. Most were from Africa and could speak English no better than Lucia could, and perhaps not as well, for they worked outside, not in the house, and they had not had someone like Bella to teach them. She turned back to her work, smoothing and folding, packing things into the last trunk. She did not hear Venus come into the chamber, and she looked up in surprise at her voice.

"Master Henry," said Venus. The black woman stood meekly just inside the doorway, her head slightly bowed, her voice full of supplication.

"What is it?" Henry asked irritably.

"Master Henry, my heart be breaking all apart. You taking my Cajoe away."

Henry and Charity exchanged glances. Lucia kept on with her work. She understood all that was said, for Venus was speaking slowly and simply.

"He'll still be in the family, Venus," Charity said. "Whenever we come back here to visit, Cajoe can come along."

"But he my baby boy," said Venus, her hands twisting nervously at her petticoat. "He be all I have in this world. My little baby boy." Her voice trembled.

"Don't you cry," ordered Henry.

"He's no baby," said Charity. "He's twelve years old, more than old enough to be put out. I don't know what more you could want. If we bring him with us when we come back to visit, you'll see him as often as Henry sees his own father."

"But I want to see him every day," said Venus. "Take me to Fairmeadow. That's what I come to ask you. Buy me from Master John and take me to Fairmeadow with my boy."

Charity looked at Henry as if they might consider it, but Henry shook his head. "We don't need her. Don't need her, don't want her."

Charity gave a little sigh. "We can't use you at Fairmeadow, Venus. We have Lucia, you know."

There was silence then, and Lucia glanced up and saw Venus glaring at her, hatred in her eyes.

"You better watch that Lucia," Venus said in a low voice.

"What do you mean?" said Henry.

"Go on out, Venus," said Charity, waving her hand impatiently to dismiss her. "Don't try to make trouble."

Lucia sat back on her heels, her hands gripping the edge of the open trunk. She looked directly at Venus, but Venus would not meet her eyes.

"She means to run away," said Venus. "It's all she been thinking since the day she come, wanting to get down to Fairmeadow and run away. She just biding her time."

"Why do you say that?" asked Henry, sitting up a little. "Has she spoken to you about it?"

"Not to me. But I heard her saying it to Bella. She got a husband in the Indian towns."

Charity turned and looked at Lucia, surprised that she might have a husband somewhere, another life beyond this one.

"Are you lying to me?" asked Henry.

"No, sir," said Venus. "You call Bella in and ask her. That Lucia couldn't talk about nothing but staying off that ship to Boston. She wanted to go to Fairmeadow where she could run away."

Henry looked over at Lucia. "Is that true, Lucia?" he asked coldly.

She met his eyes. "No, sir," she said, making her voice strong. "She lies."

Then she went back to her work, smoothing a petticoat that was already packed, already smooth.

"Do you have a husband in the trading towns?"

"No, Sir."

"She be the one lying," said Venus. "You want me to tell Bella to come up?"

"No," said Henry. "I believe you, Venus. You can go now. But send Jack up to me. And ask Master John to come."

"Yes, Sir," said Venus, and she bowed to him and left the room.

Lucia's hands were trembling now as she went on with her work.

"Build us a fire, Lucia," Henry ordered.

Lucia looked up at him in surprise.

"A fire?" said Charity. "It's the middle of summer, Henry. You'll run us out with the heat."

"Go ahead," Henry said to Lucia. "Build us a fire. A small one."

Lucia still hesitated.

"Go on!" Henry ordered again, roughly this time. Lucia got up and went to the fireplace. There was kindling in the box, and she took it and began to arrange it on the hearth, moving slowly, uneasily.

"Has it to do with what Venus said?" asked Charity. "We don't know whether to believe her or not."

"I believe her," said Henry. "I've known Venus long enough to know when she's lying and when she's telling the truth."

Lucia took the tinderbox from the mantle and stood for a moment trying to collect herself. But the trembling in her hands would not stop. She did not know what would happen next, what to prepare for. Kneeling down, she worked awkwardly with the steel and flint to light the fire. She could hear Jack coming down the hall, shuffling in his clumsy shoes. The spark caught the tinder, and she laid splinters on it, nursing it up, and then pushed the burning tinder beneath the kindling. Jack was in the room now.

"Bring me the small mahogany box," Henry said to him. "You packed it yesterday in one of the trunks."

"Yes, sir, I know where it is," said Jack, and he went out again.

"What are you going to do, Henry?" asked Charity.

Henry made no reply.

Lucia remained kneeling by the fire, watching the flames move up into the kindling. She reached out and shifted the pieces of wood, and the flame intensified. It was hot in the room and her face began to perspire from the heat of the fire, but she stayed there with it, dreading to turn back into the room. Jack returned, and in another moment John Hawkins came in.

Lucia moved back a bit from the fire and glanced over at Henry, who stood by the bed, leaning over a little wooden chest, searching through the contents. Then he found what he was looking for and brought it out, a small iron instrument, long, something like a fork, but not a fork at all. Lucia could not tell what it was.

"What do you mean to do with that?" asked John Hawkins.

"What is it?" asked Charity. "Let me see."

Henry handed it to her, an iron rod with a wooden handle on one end and on the other, attached at a right angle to the rod, the form of the letter H.

"Oh, Henry," Charity said in dismay, handing it quickly back to him as if she did not want it in her hand. "You don't mean to use that on her?"

"It will take the running away right out of her," said Henry. He looked at his father. "Venus tells us our Indian wench intends to give us the slip."

"Then that's what she needs, all right," said John Hawkins, nodding soberly at the iron brand. "She'll never get a mile beyond Fairmeadow without someone fetching her back to you."

"It's too harsh," said Charity. "I don't want you to do it, Henry."

Lucia still knelt on the floor, watching them, uncertain, yet gaining a growing notion of what they were saying, her breath quickening, dread like a weight in her: the fire, the iron tool—they meant to mark her, scar her so she could never get away. She glanced away from them toward the door. Then suddenly she was up and running, out into the hallway, flying toward the stairwell, people shouting. And then a violent jerk, her skirt snapping back against her legs, Henry's voice close, loud and commanding. She threw herself forward, trying to tear away, but he had her now, his arms encircling her as she fought against him.

"Jack!" His voice was in her ear. "God damn your black ass! Come help me or I'll whip you to shreds!"

"I'm here, Master Henry," said Jack, taking hold of one of Lucia's arms and pulling it down to her side.

"Where were you before?" muttered Henry.

Jack made no answer, and they pulled her back into the bed chamber as she struggled to get free. John Hawkins came forward and took Henry's place, helping Jack hold her.

Charity was in tears. "Henry," she pleaded, grabbing his arm.

He turned angrily to her, pulling his arm free. "Get out!" he commanded, pointing toward the door. "If you can't watch it, get out."

"Henry!"

"Get out, God damn it!" he shouted and gave Charity a shove. She stumbled out of the room, weeping, her face in her hands.

Lucia stared a moment at the empty door, then looked around at Henry. He had the brand in his hands and was taking it to the fire. She pulled against the men who held her. They gripped her tightly, no hope of escape, but still she struggled, watching the brand in the fire, Henry squatting on his heels before it, patiently waiting for it to get hot.

Then after a while, he picked up the brand and rose to his feet and came toward her. She whimpered, pulling back from him. Jack held both her arms now, pulling them hard behind her. John Hawkins took her head in his hands and turned one side of her face toward Henry.

"Be still," Jack said softly to her. "Be still now."

Then pain. Her body jerked against it, but she did not cry out. She closed her eyes and knew nothing but the fire searing into her cheek. She did not feel her head being turned. Jack was talking to her, words of comfort. Then pain again, the other cheek afire. She no longer struggled. Her head fell back against Jack's shoulder and he held her, rocking her in his arms.

Part Three

FAIRMEADOW

1714–1715

CHAPTER THIRTY-ONE

Kneeling before the fireplace, Lucia opened the little cloth bundle and looked for a moment at the four herbal medicines that were inside it, then blew her breath on them and dropped them into the kettle of simmering water.

"Why did you do that?" asked Grace Hawkins. The girl stood beside Lucia, watching, asking the questions of an eight-year-old.

"To bring the medicine into the water," said Lucia. "So Abe can drink it."

"No, why did you blow on it?"

Lucia turned and looked at her. The girl had her mother's light brown hair, though not her fine features; her face was round, her lips full like Henry's.

"To tell you that, I would have to tell you so much more. You would have to fast for four days before I could even start."

"Not eat for four whole days?"

Lucia nodded.

"I don't want to do that."

"I thought not," said Lucia and she turned back to the kettle, stirring it with a wooden spoon.

"I know why you did it," said Grace.

"Why?" said Lucia, hardly paying attention.

"It's what witches do, that's why."

Lucia looked at her again. "Do you think I am a witch?"

Grace nodded soberly.

"Then why do you stand here? Aren't you afraid?"

"No."

Lucia lifted the simmering pot from the fire. "If I am a witch, you should be afraid."

"Sheba says she's not afraid."

"So it's Sheba who tells you these things."

"And Tickey."

Lucia shook her head. Her accusers were the nurse and the houseboy, neither hardly more than a child.

"Ask Cajoe what he thinks about it," said Lucia. "He's old enough to know a few things."

"I did ask him. He says you are a doctor, not a witch."

"Don't you believe him?"

Grace shrugged. "I do a little bit."

"What about the next time you get sick? Will you want me to take care of you like I always have before?"

Grace nodded. "I don't think you're a bad witch, Lucia."

"It lifts my heart to hear it," Lucia said flatly. She dipped a silver cup into the medicine and then dried the outside of the cup with her apron. "You don't mind, then, if I give some medicine to your little brother?" She got up and walked over to the bed where Abraham, just two years old, sat playing with a small block of wood, moving it so it rocked along like a horse over the crumpled sheets. "Here, Abe," she said, sitting down on the bed beside him. She put her finger into the reddish liquid to make sure it was not too hot for him and then held it while he drank, making him keep on when he tried to turn his head away.

"There," she said when he had finished. She set the empty cup on a table by his bed and put her hand against his forehead.

"How is he?" asked Grace.

"Better," said Lucia. "Not much fever today."

Grace got onto the bed. "You're better, Abe." She picked up his horse and galloped it over his legs. He laughed and reached for it.

"Give me," he said. "My horse, Gracie."

She held it away from him and then galloped it over his head so that he fell back on the bed laughing.

Lucia got up and took the cup back to the mantle. Sheba came into the room followed by Robin, the middle Hawkins child, who ran to join his brother and sister on the bed. Robin was the heir, the oldest son.

"Miss Charity want you," said Sheba in her rough English. She was young, scarcely past her first menses, raised in the quarters and only recently brought to the house as a nurse.

"Try to make Abe take a rest," said Lucia. "His fever is down today. Tomorrow he'll be out of bed, I think."

"But if he don't want no rest?" asked Sheba. "I can't make that boy be still."

"Try telling him some of your witch stories," Lucia said cooly.

Sheba looked quickly at her and then away.

Lucia picked up the pot of medicine and left the room, crossing the hallway past the head of the stairs and going into the other upstairs chamber. Charity was sitting in a chair by the window, her feet resting on a cushioned stool. She was thinner and paler than in her maiden days, a chronic sufferer of the climate's intermittent fever and chills—the seasoning, they called it, the country fever, the fall fever, fever and ague.

"Here is some medicine for you," said Lucia, taking the kettle over and setting it down on the hearth.

"I don't need any today," said Charity. "I chewed some Jesuit bark and that seemed to be enough. I'd like to dress and go downstairs and sit in the parlor. It's hot up here. Too hot for October."

"Much too hot," Lucia agreed. "It makes the fever season drag on." She began laying out clothes for Charity, a gown and a petticoat and a clean linen shift.

"At least we've had a dry year," said Charity, getting up slowly from her chair. "Less miasma from the swamps. There have been worse years for sickness than this one." She reached up suddenly and slapped lightly at her cheek, then looked at her hand, at the spot of blood from the crushed mosquito. "It will be relief to see cold weather come. As much to be rid of the mosquitoes as the fever."

Lucia began helping her to dress.

"I heard you tell Sheba that Abe is better," said Charity.

"Yes. His fever is almost gone."

"I thought so last night," said Charity. "He was livelier. He told me he wanted to eat cinnamon rolls. I meant to tell Doll to make some up for him. But it quite went by me when I spoke to her."

"I will go tell her," said Lucia.

"Yes, do that. And stay and visit with her if you wish. I'll not be needing you for a while."

Lucia went out, started down the stairs, and then stopped, her bare feet silent on the painted wood. On the bottom step sat Henry Hawkins, tugging to pull off one of his boots. His wig was slightly askew, his clothes rumpled. He had not come in the night before but had stayed at the overseer's house, drinking, no doubt, as he often did.

Lucia stood near the top of the stairs waiting to see if he would leave, but he seemed settled there, pulling ineffectually at his boot, and so she went on down, moving close to the rail, hoping to slip quickly past him. When she reached the last few steps behind him, he turned and saw her and smiled that smile of his that she hated so much. He reached back with his arm and caught her about her skirted legs, pulling her against him, his face brushing her thighs.

"Lucia," he growled in a low, playful voice.

She tried to pull free, putting out her hand to push him away. "Shall I tell Miss Charity you've come in?" she asked coldly. He released her and she moved past, but then he reached out and caught the hem of her skirt.

"Tell her nothing," he said, keeping his voice low. "I'm about to leave again. Going downriver today. But I've got a damned stone in my boot. Pull it off for me, Lucia."

"I'll call Cajoe," said Lucia, tugging at her skirt with her hand. He kept it tightly in his grip.

"No need for Cajoe. You can do it." He held out his leg toward her. She looked at it, not wanting to touch him, knowing that for him it would be more than just her taking off his boot. For him there would be pleasure in having her lean over him, her hands on him, pulling at the boot. Probably he would curl his toes to make it harder for her. She glanced up the empty stairwell and then away. Were it not for Charity's threats to him, he would have had his way with her long ago. But Charity would not have him do his whoring on her own chambermaid. So he toyed with her, always hoping to soften her, wanting her to come to him willingly and never tell his wife. But Lucia only grew more repelled by him as his drinking worsened year after year.

"Let me call Cajoe," she said again, giving a fierce tug at her skirt to free it. But he held it tightly and motioned her to him with his head.

"Come on," he said, wiggling his foot. "Be a good girl, Lucia."

Lucia looked again up the stairwell. "Miss Charity!" she called. "Master Henry's here."

"Henry?" Charity's voice came down from above.

"Pox on you," Henry muttered irritably and let go of her skirt.

She drew in a breath of relief and moved away through the short hallway that divided the house, one room on each side upstairs and down. At each end of the hallway was a door to the outside, the front door facing the river and the boat landing, the back leading out toward the kitchen. As Lucia headed toward the back door, she glanced into the sitting room and saw Cajoe setting the table for dinner. The boy Tickey was helping him, dressed in nothing but a white shirt, the way Cajoe used to be dressed before he became a waiting man and gained the privilege of Henry's old clothing.

Cajoe looked up and saw her. "You going to the kitchen?" he asked. "There's company out there."

"Who?" asked Lucia, a little surprised. It was rare to get visitors in the kitchen unless white people had come to the big house, bringing their servants with them.

"An Indian woman," said the boy Tickey.

"Another witch?" said Lucia.

Tickey looked at her and grinned, but then, seeing the sternness in her face, he stopped smiling and shrugged as if he did not understand what she meant. He turned from her and went back to his work.

"I never seen her before," said Cajoe, ignoring her exchange with Tickey. "She say she come from downriver. Somewhere around Port Royal. She's selling herbs."

"We've no need of herbs," said Lucia. She went on out into the autumn morning. The sun, half risen in the sky, was already hot, even in the shade of the moss-draped trees. Lucia crossed the yard to the kitchen and went inside, into the dimness and the heat. Doll was at the great fireplace, her small black figure bending, lifting, straining as she rearranged kettles on their pot hooks, moving them to cooler or hotter places over the fire. The visitor, who sat by an open window, trying to catch a breeze, was an older woman, the age that Ana might be were she still alive somewhere. She was dressed in English clothing, a simple frock of coarse cloth and an apron. She nodded at Lucia without saying anything, and they both waited for Doll to turn around.

The black woman straightened up from the hearth and wiped her face with her apron as she turned back toward her guest, unaware yet that Lucia had come in. Doll was small and slender, close in age to the visitor. A white kerchief was tied about her hair and on her aging face could still be plainly seen her country marks, the decorative, patterned scarring she had received in her Ibo homeland in Africa to mark her entry into womanhood.

Seeing Lucia, she motioned her in with her head as she wiped her hands on her apron. "This is Elizabeth Birdfeather," she said of the Indian woman. "She has come to visit you."

Lucia nodded to the visitor. "You have come," she said politely in the Indian way.

"I have come," replied Elizabeth Birdfeather.

Lucia looked over at Doll. "Miss Charity wants cinnamon rolls for Abe," she said.

"Not for dinner?" said Doll. "It's too late for that."

"Any time will do. Just so he has them today." Lucia went over and sat on a split-cane mat that was spread against the wall near Elizabeth Birdfeather. "I am Lucia," she said to the woman.

"Yes," said Elizabeth Birdfeather. "From Apalachee."

Lucia smiled. "Doll has been talking about me."

The woman shook her head. "This I know already."

Lucia looked at her, her heart slowing. Could she have come from the Creek towns? "You are Yamasee?" she asked, afraid to assume too much. The Yamasee towns were close by, the Creek towns much farther away.

"No," said Elizabeth Birdfeather.

Lucia leaned back against the wall and braced herself, hardly breathing. Was she Creek then?

"I am Cusso," said the woman, naming the people whose land had once been where Charles Town now stood.

Lucia let out her breath, her hopes retreating to that dark room from which they so seldom ventured. Ten years had gone by. Carlos might be dead now. Or living with another wife. "You are a little way from home," she said quietly.

Elizabeth Birdfeather shrugged. "I travel. Sometimes Charles Town. Sometimes Goose Creek. Sometimes Port Royal. Sell herbs to white people. I am curer, like you."

"Doll has told you this about me?" Lucia said again.

"I told her naught but that you live here," said Doll, who was busy now mixing up the dough for the rolls. "And that she already knew."

"Why I come," said Elizabeth Birdfeather. "Hear talk on plantations. In kitchens. People say Lucia at Fairmeadow best curer on Combahee River. Say she speaks to Sun. Calls her Mother."

Lucia shrugged. "I sing a song to the Sun in the mornings. It is the old Apalachee way."

"No other Apalachees do that," said Elizabeth Birdfeather.

Lucia looked at her. "Do you know Apalachee people?"

"In Yamasee towns."

"Do you go there? To the Yamasee towns?"

"Sometimes. Too many white people here. I go there. Get away. But now too many white people there. English planters south of Combahee River. And traders. Too many traders in Yamasee towns. Too much bully to Indian people. Too much rum. Yamasee country no good now."

"But you know Apalachees there?"

"Some."

"Have you ever met a man, or heard of him perhaps, a man named Carlos? An Apalachee? A big man, tall?" Lucia raised up her hand to indicate his height, and sitting there on the floor she remembered how it used to be to look up and see him towering above her. "Like a tree," she said quietly.

But Elizabeth Birdfeather was shaking her head. "I know Carlos," she said. "But not large man. Not even tall as me."

"No," said Lucia. "That would not be him." She looked down at the floor, raising her hand absently to touch one of the H-shaped scars on her cheeks.

"That Carlos was her husband," said Doll. "Before the slave-catchers took her from Florida. That was before Miss Charity married Master Henry and brought me down here from Boston. A long time ago. But she'll have no other man."

Elizabeth Birdfeather nodded. "They say Sun Woman sleeps alone."

Lucia looked up and smiled a little. "Do they call me Sun Woman?"

"Yes. You speak to Sun. Call her your mother. Other Indians call her Grandmother. But to you, Mother."

"It's an old way with the Apalachees that some few call her Mother. I did not seek it for myself. I was born to it."

"She is the only one who sings that song," said Doll, looking around from the fire. "The only one in all the world."

"Unless my grandmother is still in This World," said Lucia. "But I think she must be gone by now. She was old when I last saw her, and that was long ago."

As she spoke there came the sound of voices from the main house—hurried, excited talk and then silence. Then Timboe was at the kitchen door, Doll's son, a strongly built, handsome man. His face was anxious as he looked from Elizabeth Birdfeather to Doll. He did not notice Lucia sitting in the shadows.

"Where's Lucia?" he asked.

"I'm here," she said, rising to her feet.

"It's Daphne," he said. "The baby's trying to come!"

"Too soon!" exclaimed Doll, wiping her hands on her apron. But then she looked forlornly around the kitchen, realizing she could not leave so near the dinner hour, even though Daphne was her own son's wife.

"It was Colley driving her too hard," Timboe said angrily. "I warned him of it. I warned him this very morning."

Timboe was a cooper who spent his days making barrels to hold the tar and pitch and turpentine that were the main products of Fairmeadow. But while he worked in the cooper's shed, his wife Daphne was out in the woods with the rest of the hands cutting the sides of the pine trees to make the turpentine flow. Daphne could swing a box ax or a hatchet as well as any man. She was tall, a Fulani woman. Not only was she skilled at cutting boxes in the bases of pine trees, but she could reach up to a greater height than could some of the men to cut the streaks in the pines that made the gum flow. But now she was big with child and should not be driven like a man.

"Be easy," Lucia said to Timboe. "The trouble might pass if she rests and keeps still."

"No," said Timboe. "Her water's broke."

Lucia glanced at Doll, who shook her head, resigning herself to misfortune. Then, as Lucia started from the kitchen after Timboe, she stopped and looked around at Elizabeth Birdfeather. "Come with us, if you wish," she said to the Cusso woman. "Perhaps your knowledge will help us."

"I come," said Elizabeth Birdfeather, rising to her feet and following them out toward the quarters.

✳ It was a month at least before Daphne was due to deliver, and her labor was too weak to push down the baby. Night came, and her soft moaning mingled with the cricket song in the warm darkness and with the quiet talk of the workers who had come dragging home to the quarters just after dusk. Elizabeth Birdfeather was still there, and Doll came in from the kitchen, giving Lucia a chance to get out of the cabin for a few moments to rest near the firelight where the people were gathered.

The slave quarters consisted of seven small cabins facing each other in two rows across a sandy wagon track. More than thirty people lived there. Close by, but a little apart, was the overseer's house, though it was dark tonight, Dudley Price having gone off that morning with Henry Hawkins, the two of them heading down the Combahee in the large cypress canoe, with two black men manning the paddles. A fire of pine knots burned in the street between the cabins, the light dancing on the twisted limbs of moss-draped oaks that spread out overhead. Lucia sat a little away from the others and listened to their talk and watched their faces in the firelight. Timboe was the quietest among them, his face closed with worry.

"Colley done it," said Basey, an older man, one of the first slaves Henry had brought to Fairmeadow. As he spoke, Lucia glanced down the street toward the black driver's cabin. Colley was staying inside tonight. "Colley drive hard-hard," said Basey, speaking the pidgin they could all understand, a limited but common language that bridged their varied languages from so many different lands. "Colley say we gotta please Massa Henry. I say, 'Whoa, now. How come do that?' But Colley got whip in hand. We go chop-chop. Keep ahead that whip."

"Hot," said Juba, holding up her hand to feel the air. She was Basey's wife, a turpentine worker the same as he and most of the others. "Hot-hot today. Massa Henry tell Colley go round again. Hurry-hurry."

Then Juba waved her hand, frustrated with the limits of the pidgin, and began to speak rapidly in her native Wolof, explaining more fully what she meant to say. Some of the others who shared that language, or at least understood it, nodded as she spoke.

Lucia did not understand it but knew what was being said. She had heard it from others, that Henry had decided that with the weather so warm there was time for an extra dipping of turpentine from the boxes, if they hurried, chopping the fresh channels in the bark, coming back to dip up the sticky gum, each worker tending fifty acres of trees in a race against the cold

weather that could come at any time and stop the flow of the gum. Henry
wanted another dipping, but how many extra barrels of turpentine would
he need to pay for the life of Daphne's baby, and perhaps for Daphne's life
as well?

Lucia got up and walked away from the fire, passing along the row of
cabins until she came to the end, where a boy and a girl were playing in the
darkness outside a cabin door. "Little Will," she said. The boy looked up at
her. "Go to the big house and tell Sheba to give you my sleeping mat. Bring
it to me at Daphne's cabin."

"That baby come yet?" asked Little Will, getting to his feet.

"Not yet," said Lucia. She turned from him and looked at Colley's cabin
directly across the sandy road. The driver was there, leaning against the
doorway. She could not see his face in the darkness.

"That baby gonna die," said the girl who had been playing with Little
Will. The boy was leaving now, trudging off beneath the trees toward the
big house.

"You better go home," Lucia said to the girl, putting a hand on her back
and giving her a little shove toward her parents' cabin down the way. The
child ran on ahead, and Lucia glanced once more at Colley and then started
back along the row of cabins. She went inside to Daphne without stopping
again at the fire.

The cabin was a small, bare place, no furnishings except split-cane mats
on the dirt floor and a single low stool beside the mud-and-stick fireplace.
A small fire burned in the hearth, casting a dim light onto the dark figures
in the room. Daphne lay on a mat in the corner, no one attending her now,
for there was little that could be done except to wait. Lucia went over and
knelt beside her, putting her hands on her swollen belly, waiting to feel the
strength of her contractions. Daphne had the light copper skin of the Fulani
people, narrow nose and thin lips, straight hair. Her pale face was glistening
with sweat, her eyes closed in weariness and pain. Lucia's hands moved over
her, pressing to feel the position of the child. It was unchanged from before,
and Daphne's contractions were weaker.

Doll came over and stood beside Lucia. "I will kill Colley myself if she
dies," Doll said in a low voice. "I'll kill him to keep Timboe from doing it."

"Lucia kill Colley," said Chany, a Yoruba woman who could speak no
other English but the pidgin. "Nobody know. Colley sick-sick. Then dead."
She mimed the driver's death as she spoke.

Lucia turned and looked at her—short, solidly built, her country scars
on her face. She was the mother of Sheba and probably was the source of
the witch talk in the big house.

"I do not kill people," said Lucia.

Chany shrugged, obviously unconvinced.

Lucia got to her feet and walked over to the door and stood looking out into the night, at the people near the fire, at Timboe with his face closed and dark. She was glad Henry Hawkins was not home to see him. Henry always looked for the worst in Timboe, treating him more harshly than the others. Timboe was Charity's favorite, her own slave brought down from Boston, where the two had grown up together in the same house.

Lucia became aware that someone had come up to stand beside her. She turned and saw Elizabeth Birdfeather looking out into the night, as if she too were interested in the people, in Timboe himself.

"I have strong medicine," the Cusso woman said very softly.

For a moment Lucia made no reply, uncertain what was being offered, whether it was something to save Daphne's life or to end Colley's. "What is it?" she said at last.

"Root," said Elizabeth Birdfeather, speaking so no one else could hear. "Bring baby. Not alive."

"The baby will die anyway," Lucia said quietly. "Do you have it with you?"

"In basket."

"I will see you are paid for it," said Lucia. "Miss Charity will pay you."

Elizabeth Birdfeather shook her head. "I give it. Tomorrow we go out. I show you where it grows. Then always you have it."

"My heart is full," said Lucia. "I will give you something in return, if I have anything you need."

"I hear song to Sun," said Elizabeth Birdfeather.

Lucia shook her head regretfully. "That cannot be passed like a medicine from one curer to another."

"I watch you sing," said Elizabeth Birdfeather. "No more. When people speak of Sun Woman, I tell them I see her. Hear her song."

"Your medicine is stronger than mine," said Lucia. "You should tell them that."

Elizabeth Birdfeather shook her head. "I know Cusso root. I am Cusso. But I am granddaughter of Sun. You are her daughter, and so you are mother to me. Mother to all who walk This World."

Lucia was embarrassed to be regarded in this way. "It is only a song that I sing. An old way of the Apalachees."

They were silent for a little time, watching the night. Then Elizabeth Birdfeather said, more quietly than before, "I have something for Colley. Something strong."

Lucia shook her head. "I already have medicine like that," she said softly. "If I need it."

CHAPTER THIRTY-TWO

Isaac Bull awoke with the first faint light of dawn and for a moment could not recall where he was. Then he knew. He was in the parlor bed at Fairmeadow, his back aching from the sag of the feather mattress. He had lost his liking for this way of sleeping, having grown accustomed over the years to a hard cane bed in the Indian fashion with mats and skins spread on it. He sat up, rubbing his back with both hands. There was enough light to make out the shapes of things. He got up and found his clothes where he had laid them on a chair and pulled them on in the darkness. Then he hunched his shoulders, stretching the aching muscles, and walked quietly out into the hallway, where Cajoe and Tickey were still asleep on their split-cane mats on the floor. He stepped by them and went out the front door, certain he was waking them with the sound of its opening, but not looking back as he pulled the door quietly closed behind him.

Dawn was coming rapidly, darkness lifting to gray. He strolled down toward the river, feeling the welcome coolness in the air, the promise that winter would be coming after all. Walking out onto the landing, he checked the mooring of his canoe and then sat down on the rough planking and watched the river flow past. Another trading season was beginning. He was anxious to be on his way, but he had only come to Fairmeadow last night and would have to stay another day at least, paying obligatory homage to Henry, who was sole owner of the company now, old John having died last year and Abraham dead even longer. Not that Henry had moved to take charge of the company. He was addicted to plantation life and left his commercial affairs in the hands of others, agents in Charles Town and Boston who oversaw the shipping operations, while Isaac handled his Indian trade. But Henry liked to think he maintained control, and he insisted that Isaac bide awhile in his comings and goings. They must talk business together, Henry would say, though all they talked about was turpentine, tar, and pitch. And cattle. And slaves.

A fish jumped. Isaac looked toward the sound and saw the spreading rings. Perhaps if Charity were not here he could enjoy the laziness of these visits — cards and dice, fishing, rum punch constantly flowing. But all those pleasures were overbalanced by the discomfort of her presence, the politeness and formality between them, her misery in this place so plain to be seen, his antipathy for Henry because of it. He should quit this Indian trade. He often thought of quitting, now that he had enough money to start a plantation of his own. But he did not want anything so rough as this—not cattle and turpentine. He had enough for this, but not for what he wanted. His plantation would produce rice, and his would be a gentleman's life with all the refinements he had enjoyed in his youth before his brother's betrayal. Rice required more slaves than did turpentine and cattle. And a gentleman's life required a wife of a better sort than his Indian woman in the backcountry. Not that she would come out with him if he asked her—she had a low opinion of life in Carolina.

Isaac heard the front door of the house open and close, and looking over his shoulder, he saw the slave woman Lucia coming down toward the river. The sun was almost up now, its light pushing into the eastern sky in streaks of red and purple. Seeing Isaac at the landing, Lucia veered away from the path and went to the river a little way downstream, where she disappeared into the dense growth along the bank. A few moments of silence passed, and then, as the sun appeared above the horizon, Isaac heard the soft sound of Indian song. He stayed there watching the sunlight spread across the water until at last Lucia came away from the river bank and returned to the house. Then he too got up and started back.

Smoke was rising from both chimneys now. The house had come to life, the hallway clear of sleeping mats and slaves. Grace and Robin, dressed in their nightshirts, played on the stairs. Isaac went into the sitting room where the boy Tickey was readying the table for breakfast. He took a seat by the fire and watched the resinous fatwood. As its pungent tar was drawn to the surface by the heat, he thought he could see it bubbling out just before the voracious flames consumed it.

Overhead were footsteps, the heavy ones of Henry and the light ones of Charity. Then Henry's came out into the hallway and down the stairs, and overhead only the sound of Charity remained. Isaac started to rise as Henry came into the room, but Henry waved him back to his seat.

"What was it we drank last night?" asked Henry, putting his hand to his silk-turbaned head. He sat down heavily on a chair beside Isaac.

"Madeira," said Isaac.

Henry slumped further down in the chair, his fingers pressed against his temples. "How much did I have?"

"Too much," said Isaac with a smile.

"God knows it's true," said Henry. He stared away into the fire, keeping his head still as if to slow the flow of blood and ease the pounding.

"I've been sitting here watching the tar drip from the pine," said Isaac. "It must be the influence of Fairmeadow working upon me."

"You can't see any tar there," said Henry, keeping his head perfectly still. "It's all going up in smoke."

"It seems to me I can see it come to the surface," said Isaac. "Just before the flames get it."

"That's all you'll see in a fire that high. Takes the half-smothered fire of a kiln to draw it out without burning it."

"I've never yet seen a tar kiln fired," said Isaac.

"You've not?" Henry forgot his head and turned to look at him. "How could you be all these years in Carolina and never see a tar kiln?"

"I've seen kilns aplenty," said Isaac. "But I've never seen one fired. It's mostly done in winter, when I'm in the backcountry."

"Well, today you will see it, then. That settles how the morning will go. My people are starting up a kiln in the woods. I'll send Tickey with you to guide the way. Charity can ride along on the horse with you to entertain you, and I'll go back to bed. I've got to get this headache off me before I can make anything of the day."

"I'm sure Charity would find no pleasure in that," said Isaac. "I'll go alone with the boy."

"No, no, let her go with you. Her health is returning with the cool weather and she needs to get out. Do it as a favor to me. She stays so melancholy, dragging about the house."

For a moment Isaac did not reply, but listened to the small sound of her movements overhead. He did not at all want to go riding out with her seated behind him on the horse, her hands holding onto his waist. "We will leave it to her," Isaac said at last. "I'm sure she would not enjoy it."

"If I left it to her she would lie abed all day every day," said Henry. He turned to the slave boy who was still dawdling around the table. "Tickey!"

"Yes, Master Henry," said the boy.

"Go to the stable and tell Smart to saddle up Jupiter. And tell him to put the pillion behind the saddle for Miss Charity."

"And a horse for me?" said the boy.

"You can walk. You've got two legs."

"But they short little legs."

"Tickey!"

"Yes, Sir," said Tickey and went out.

Henry closed his eyes to quiet the pounding blood in his head, while Isaac looked away into the fire, his lips drawn tight.

✳ Isaac and Charity rode in silence through a ghost forest of dead and rotting pines. The towering trees had seen their last year of turpentining and were waiting for the storms of next spring to bring them down. Once the trees were down and had further rotted on the ground, the slaves would come among them again, the same slaves who had hacked away their bark to make the tall white faces and carved deep boxes into the sapwood at their bases to collect the oozing gum. This time the harvest would be the hearts of the trees, heavy with resin, which would be hauled to the kilns to be burned down for tar.

The boy Tickey trotted along before the horse, leading the way along the cart track that wound through the dead forest. Isaac could feel Charity behind him as she tried not to lean against him, her hands holding to his waist as loosely as she could. She had paled when she was told of the outing, and Isaac had tried again to avoid the situation. But Henry had insisted, fairly shoving the two of them out the door, and now they were both trying to make the best of it, exchanging pleasantries as they rode along. But the way was far and the pines monotonous, and their silences grew longer.

"It's dismal with the trees dying all around," said Isaac.

Charity made no reply and he regretted having said it. She did not need to be told what was dismal in this place. The silence was uncomfortable now.

"All of it is dismal, dead trees or no," Charity said at last. As she spoke, he felt her hands tighten ever so slightly on his waist. "I never hear the name Fairmeadow without wishing to laugh aloud," she said bitterly.

"Fairmeadow will come up to its name someday," said Isaac. "When the trees are gone and the rice is planted."

"There will never be rice here," said Charity. "Henry put fifty acres in rice for one year, and then he turned that land into pasture for some of his cattle."

"I remember that," said Isaac. It was a sorry field of rice Henry had planted.

"There was too much management in planting rice," said Charity. "He had to stay home and look after it instead of coming and going as he pleased. So that little trial brought an end to the matter. I'll never see rice on this place any more than I'll see that house he started. The foundation of it is so covered over with vines that it's no longer even visible. Trees are growing up in the middle of it."

"I don't understand him," said Isaac. "It's not money he lacks."

"He's happy with all as it is and cares not to make any changes. Never mind that we've three children packed into that little house. If more come I don't know where we'll put them, but you can be sure he'll not worry himself about it. He'll break open a bottle of rum and go off down the river to carouse with his friends and leave me and Fairmeadow to shift for ourselves, the same as we always do."

There was nothing to say to that, and Isaac did not try. Ahead he could see a clearing and a roof of some kind. As they drew nearer he saw it was a cooper's shed, great piles of staves and finished barrels stacked high. And near it was the tar kiln, though no smoke was rising from it. Two black men were at work making barrels. The clearing, littered with fallen timber, stretched on for many acres. Beyond it was a green forest of living pines.

The black men looked up in surprise as Isaac and Charity rode into the clearing. One of them strode forward to meet them.

"We've come for nothing, I think," said Charity, looking around Isaac at the cold tar kiln. "Timboe," she said to the black man as he came up to them. "We thought you were firing the kiln."

"Not today," said Timboe, reaching up with strong arms to help her down from the horse. Isaac dismounted after her. Timboe nodded to him, "Good day to you, sir."

Isaac returned the nod, surprised to find a black man so mannered and well spoken here in the pine woods of Fairmeadow. He handed the reins of the horse to Tickey.

"Was there not supposed to be a firing?" said Charity. "Henry said there was."

"It's the weather," said Timboe. "Too dry."

"And what difference does the dryness of the air make?" asked Isaac, walking over to look at the kiln, which had the appearance of a large earthen oven set on a low mound.

"If the air's too dry, there's the risk of it blowing," said Timboe.

"Exploding?" asked Isaac.

"Blowing us to pieces," said the other slave, still at work on the barrels. He was young, hardly more than a boy, of slighter build than Timboe, cheerful in his countenance. "Barrel staves be on the roof of the big house," he said, laughing. The boy Tickey laughed too, though Timboe remained sober.

"It's not to be made a joke of, Moon," said Charity. Then to Isaac she said, "That's a real danger, the kilns exploding. We had a man killed by it once and others burned. It was horrible."

"These barrels be little splinters floating down the river," said Moon. "And me, I be gone 'fore I ever learned to hoop one tight."

"You've learned well enough," said Timboe. Then to Charity he said, "He's a smart boy. Learns fast. You tell Master Henry that he's got a good man in Moon."

Charity smiled. "I'll tell him."

"And tell him something else for me, Miss Charity." There was a change in his voice. Isaac looked closely at him.

"What is it, Timboe?" Charity said with concern.

"You tell him," said Timboe, speaking slowly and deliberately, "that if Dudley Price kills my woman, there will be hell to pay on this plantation."

"Whoo!" said Moon and turned his back to them, returning to his work.

"I can't tell him that," said Charity. "What do you mean by it? I thought Daphne was coming along very well."

"So well that Dudley Price has put her back to work."

"Today?"

"Today." He jerked his head toward the pine forest in the distance. "She's out there now dipping turpentine, and not two weeks since she almost died with that dead baby."

"God help us," Charity said wearily, looking out toward the forest. She shook her head. "What can we do?"

"Ride out there," said Timboe. "Tell Price to send her back to the quarters."

"I can't do that," said Charity. "Henry'll not have his overseer crossed. He would not even do that himself in front of the slaves."

"Then you tell Master Henry what I told you," Timboe said angrily, turning away from them abruptly and going back to work.

"It doesn't help to get angry," said Charity.

"Nothing helps," said Timboe, banging with his hammer on the barrel he was making.

"Moon," said Charity, turning to the younger man.

"I ain't said a thing," said Moon. "I ain't in this."

"I want you to go out where they're working," said Charity. "Tell Dudley Price I'm concerned about Daphne. Tell him I'm asking him to work her lightly for a few days, let her rest when she needs to."

"*Asking* him," Timboe said sarcastically.

"You watch yourself," Isaac said sharply, taking a step in Timboe's direction.

"It's all right," said Charity, putting a hand on Isaac's arm.

"I've never heard so impudent a slave," said Isaac, keeping his eyes on the sullen cooper.

"Timboe and I have known each other a long time," she said.

Timboe went on with his work, not looking at either of them.

Charity looked over at Moon. "Go on," she said sharply. "Do what I told you."

"Yes, Missus," said Moon. He turned and started out across the clearing.

Timboe looked up from his work. "Moon!" he called.

Moon stopped and looked back.

"Tell him not to make her fill that dip bucket to the top. Let her empty it in the barrel before it's full."

Moon looked at Charity and she nodded. "Yes," she said. "Ask him to do that."

"Those buckets are *heavy* when they're full," muttered Timboe, turning back to the barrel. "Even if he doesn't kill her, she'll end up like Juba with her womb fallen out."

Charity reddened. "Timboe!"

Isaac glanced at her and then away, standing awkwardly in the silence. "Let's go back," he said.

They mounted the horse in silence, and with Tickey following along behind them, they rode out of the clearing and back through the brown forest of dead pines.

✹ It was dusk and Lucia was in the kitchen helping Doll clean up after supper. Little Will appeared breathlessly at the kitchen door.

"Timboe say for Lucia to come!" he said, and then he was gone again.

"What's happened now?" said Doll. Drying her hands, she left the kitchen as it was and went out with Lucia into the deepening twilight.

They found Daphne prostrate on her mat, the firelit cabin crowded with people.

"They had to carry her home," Timboe said, his voice low and angry.

"I be all right," Daphne said weakly, making a little wave of her hand at him. "Tired-tired. Let me rest. I be all right."

Lucia knelt beside her. Daphne was sticky with gum, sand and bits of forest litter clinging to her skin. Lucia put her fingers on her lower abdomen and pressed in. "Does this hurt?" she asked.

Daphne shook her head. "Nothing hurts. Just tired."

Lucia felt the beat of the woman's heart and then sat back and watched her breathe. She seemed all right, just weak and tired.

Lucia stood up. "She's worn out. Let her sleep."

"She whip," said Basey, and the others nodded, letting him speak for them, for he had been at Fairmeadow longer than anyone else.

"Whipped?" said Timboe, and at once he was down beside Daphne, turning her over to look at her back, Daphne struggling without effect to stop him from seeing the red welts on her light-colored skin. Timboe let go of her and she rolled back, silent and afraid, her eyes on his face.

"Colley," said Basey, making a whipping motion with his arm.

"Dudley Price made Colley do it," said a man named Peter, Carolina-born. "He say, 'Colley, keep her moving.' I hear him. He say, 'Whip her if she need it. There's gum to dip.'"

Timboe stood up. "Did Moon come out to where you were working?"

"I went out," Moon said defensively. He lived in the cabin with Daphne and Timboe and was sitting on his mat on the floor.

"Moon come," said Basey.

"Did he talk to Dudley Price?" asked Timboe.

"He talk," said Basey. "I see." He pointed to his eye to make himself clear. "Talk-talk. Price—," Basey heaved up his chest and put on a mean face, "he angry."

Timboe started toward the door, pushing people out of his way.

"Timboe!" Daphne called to him. Lucia stepped toward him, but it was Doll who moved quickly enough to stop him at the door.

"What you going to do?" Doll demanded.

"Talk to Henry Hawkins."

"Talk how?"

"Humble," Timboe said sarcastically, hanging his head and letting his shoulders droop. "Like this. I'll say, please, Massa Henry, please good sir, don't let your hell hounds kill my wife."

Doll jerked his arm roughly. "Don't you do it," she said sharply.

Timboe reached up and rubbed his face. He took a deep breath and let it out again. "I won't say it like that," he said in a calmer voice. "But I mean to speak to him. Can't anybody but Henry Hawkins tell Dudley Price what to do. I'll be easy. I'll be humble. I'll tell him my wife is still weak from childbed, and please, Master Henry, won't you help her."

Doll let go of his arm. "Do it that way," she said, nodding. "Make him think he's all the master. Let him think he's God Almighty sitting over you."

"I'll pray to him," said Timboe.

"Yes," said Doll. "That's the way he likes it."

Timboe stepped out into the darkness, and Doll stood in the doorway watching him go.

For a moment the cabin was silent. Then the Yoruba woman Chany started talking in her own language.

"What's she talking about?" Doll asked irritably.

"She say Dudley Price too mean to change," said Peter, who was Chany's husband. "She say somebody with powers ought to put an end to Dudley Price. And Colley, too."

Several people looked at Lucia, but she ignored them and went back over to sit with Daphne.

Chany had more to say.

"Some people think they be too good to help the poor tar hands," Peter translated. "Some people come doctor us when we be whip, but what we need is an end to that whip."

Lucia glanced up at Chany, who stood with her arms folded, looking down at her.

"No one here can do that," Doll said from the doorway. The finality with which she spoke brought the matter to a close.

Isaac Bull sat before the fireplace in the sitting room, Henry Hawkins on one side of him, Dudley Price on the other. A bowl of rum punch was on the hearth in front of them. Dudley Price leaned forward in his chair and refilled his cup.

"There's not so much punch to be had in Indian country, aye, Mr. Bull?" said Price.

"Not so much," said Isaac, speaking deliberately, as if the subject were of great importance. "We've rum aplenty. But we lack lemons."

"There can be no punch without lemons," said Price, his words slurring a bit. He sat back nursing his cup.

Isaac felt himself a little too far gone with the rum, the firelight more mesmerizing than it should have been, the company more companionable. The day had been miserable, that ride with Charity, seeing her unhappiness more clearly than he had ever wanted to see it. And then an afternoon with Henry shut up in the parlor with an accounting book that was never opened, Henry slowly getting drunk, talking of his dead father, complaining of Charity's health, bragging of the women, black and white, he had bedded on his jaunts about the countryside. And then a melancholy evening meal, Charity angry with Henry because he was drunk. She left the table before the meal was over, excusing herself with a headache and retiring to her chamber. Henry was relieved to see her go and sent Tickey to fetch Dudley Price to join the company.

"Tomorrow we'll go down to Stanfield," said Henry, referring to the next plantation down the river. "Find some entertainment there."

"Tomorrow I'll go on my way," said Isaac.

"But we've not talked business yet."

"We've talked it aplenty. I've got it all here." He patted the pocket of his coat as if there were papers in it.

"You have what there?" asked Henry.

"Your orders. I wrote 'em all down."

"When'd I give you orders?'

"Today. Last night. And good ones they are. I've got 'em all here." He patted his pocket again.

Henry looked at him a moment and then nodded. "Good," he said. "I'm pleased you got 'em down." He leaned over and dipped his cup into the punch bowl.

Cajoe came in from the hallway. "Master Henry," he said quietly.

Henry sat back with his punch and took a long, leisurely drink. Then, without looking toward Cajoe, he said, "What is it?"

"Timboe come to talk to you," said Cajoe.

"Timboe?"

"Yes, sir. He be at the back door."

"What's he want?"

"Don't know."

"Go ask him what he wants."

"Yes, sir," said Cajoe and went out again.

"Timboe," Henry said contemptuously, staring over his cup into the fire. "I've had my fill of that nigger."

"He's a bad one, all right," said Dudley Price.

"Thinks he's the one should be master, and white men his slaves," said Henry.

"Master Henry," said Cajoe, back in the doorway. "He say he only tell it to you."

"Well, you tell him I'll talk to him tomorrow. I've got company here."

"Yes, sir," said Cajoe, and he was gone again.

"If not for Charity I'd have sold him by now," said Henry. "I swear, I don't know what she sees in that black son of a whore. To hear her defend him you'd think she was speaking of her own brother. Or worse."

Isaac turned and looked at him. Henry smiled a little and made a slight raise of his cup. "Be glad she's no wife of yours," Henry said. He looked back into the fire and then added, "At least she brought a fortune with her."

"I'd count myself lucky to have such a wife," said Isaac. "Fortune or no."

There came the sound of voices from the hall, Cajoe's voice low and agitated, and then the sound of scuffling. Then Timboe was there, standing just inside the doorway, almost invisible beyond the circle of firelight.

"Master Henry," he said.

"What are you doing in here?" demanded Henry. He put down his cup and pushed around his chair to face the door.

"It's my wife, Master Henry." Timboe spoke softly and humbly, not at all the way Isaac had heard him earlier in the day. "She's lying in the cabin, Master Henry, all whipped down."

"Not again," said Dudley Price, and he, too, set his cup on the floor. "I've heard enough of this woman for one day. They all conspire with her, helping her feign some mortal illness. He sent Moon out to me today, had him claim Mrs. Hawkins sent him."

"She did send him," said Isaac. "I heard her do so."

"What?" said Henry, turning to Isaac. "What did she do?"

"She sent to ask Mr. Price to use Timboe's wife with mercy."

"Yes, sir," Timboe said quietly. "That's what she did."

"Mercy?" said Dudley Price. "I never saw a faker like that Daphne. She's fit enough when she's in the quarters, but she's near dead in the woods. She can't have it both ways. Either she's up and well or she's down and sick."

"Well, she's down and sick right now," said Timboe. "Whipped down. And I'm begging you, let her be for a while. Let her rest and get her strength. She's a good worker, Master Henry. You don't want to lose such a good worker."

Henry looked at Isaac again. "How did Charity get mixed up in this?" he asked angrily. "What does she think she's doing giving orders to my overseer?"

"She gave no orders," said Isaac.

"You said she did."

"She asked Mr. Price to show mercy to the woman, to let her rest when needed and to spare her heavy loads."

"She gave him orders, then."

"No, not orders." Isaac looked away. He wished he had not drunk so much so that his mind could be clearer.

"She asked for mercy," said Timboe. "And I'm asking for mercy, Master Henry. I'm praying to you for mercy for my wife."

"What do you mean, mercy?" demanded Henry. "What do you want? Say it clearly."

"I want you to tell Mr. Price to let Daphne lie in until she's strong enough to work." An edge had come into his voice, the humility giving way.

"Are you saying Mr. Price does not know his business?"

"No, sir, I'm not saying that," said Timboe, struggling to dampen his tone. "He knows his business. Yes, sir, he does."

"Then get your black ass out of my house," said Henry. He turned his chair back toward the fire and leaned down and picked up his rum.

There was silence. The fire popped, a shower of sparks flaring up.

"But you'll tell him," Timboe said in a low voice.

"He'll work the slaves as he sees best," said Henry. "That's what I pay him for."

"And if he kills my wife, it's I who will pay him," said Timboe, the humility completely gone now.

"You'll what?" said Henry, jerking around to look at him.

"I'll kill him," Timboe said.

"God damn you to hell!" shouted Henry, and there was a clatter of pewter cups on the floor as he and Dudley Price jumped to their feet, Isaac rising more slowly, watching as the two rushed at Timboe, pinning his arms, shoving him out into the hallway and toward the back door. Timboe did not resist. Isaac followed and saw Charity on the stairs, but he would not look at her nor pause to answer the questions she called after them as they went out into the night.

"Cajoe!" called Henry. He had to call twice more before Cajoe appeared. "Bring the cowhide! And a lantern." Then he and Dudley Price went on, moving rapidly, pushing Timboe toward the blacksmith shop that lay midway between the house and the quarters. Nothing was said. Everyone understood what had happened and what would happen next.

A tall sturdy post stood in the yard of the blacksmith shop, an iron ring attached to the top of it, rawhide thongs hanging down from the ring. Henry and Price tied Timboe to it, his wrists bound together, arms above his head. Then they waited for Cajoe, and waited longer until Henry began to swear, and then finally Cajoe arrived, a pool of lantern light moving toward them in the darkness. Cajoe handed the rawhide whip to Dudley Price without looking squarely at him.

Price walked over and prodded Timboe roughly in the back with the butt of the whip. "Now tell us again what you said, nigger?"

"You heard what I said," answered Timboe, his voice low and defiant.

"I'll hear you beg for your life," said Price, and he stepped back, flexing his arm.

Timboe made no reply. There was silence, no sound but the breathing of men. And then the sharp crack of the whip.

☀ Lucia was sitting with Doll in the doorway of the cabin when the sound of the whip came through the darkness. Doll stiffened, reaching out to grip the door frame. Behind them in the cabin Daphne cried out. There was a commotion as Chany sought to keep her from rising, and then there was stillness and the sound of her weeping. Basey left the cabin, Lucia shifting to one side to let him go by. He went out into the darkness, down the row of cabins toward the blacksmith shop to be the eyes of them all.

Lucia leaned against the doorway. She did not have to be there to see it. Rawhide cutting into flesh. Timboe's flesh. What had he done? What had he said? Things a slave could not say. He could not be husband to his wife, could not protect her and shield her. This was what would happen. This. This. Nothing but this.

Doll was hunched over now, her hands clasped behind her head, her face between her knees as she rocked back and forth, murmuring in her native Ibo words Lucia could not understand. Lucia rose to her feet and went out into the sandy street. Going the opposite direction from the way Basey had gone, she walked the short distance to the overseer's house, dark and still. There in the moonlight, just in front of the doorway, where Dudley Price's footsteps marked the sandy earth, she leaned down and scooped up a handful of that earth and put it in her apron pocket. Then she turned and went back through the quarters, past the dark cabins until she came to Colley's door where again she bent over and scooped up a handful of trodden sand. As she straightened up, putting the sand in her pocket, she saw Colley come to the door and look out at her. But he said nothing and she went on, walking beneath the trees toward the blacksmith shop with its circle of lantern light. She could hear the stroke of the whip. No sound came from Timboe, no moaning or begging for mercy. She would not look to see him hanging there but instead circled the shop in the darkness and went on toward the big house to the dooryard where Henry Hawkins' feet had stepped, and there she picked up another handful of earth.

She went into the kitchen, and by the light of a small pinewood torch she took her medicine basket from the place where it was hidden behind barrels dusty with flour, and from the basket she took a piece of black cloth and a long, white, hollow root of water hemlock, a deadly poison, one small piece of it enough to kill a cow, more than enough to kill a man. She wrapped it in the cloth and put it in her apron pocket. Picking up a wooden spoon, she went out of the kitchen, still carrying the torch, and around to the back, through the weeds to a pile of decaying garbage. Using the spoon, she dug into the moist earth beneath the garbage, holding the torch down close until she had found four earthworms. She opened the black cloth, moved the root aside and laid out the wiggling worms to the Four Ways, making a circle of devouring death. Then she pushed them into the center, and using the spoon, she mashed them into a paste and mixed in some of the sand from her pocket. She scraped this from the cloth and forced it down into the hollow of the poison root. Then she wrapped the root in the cloth again and put out her torch.

She went on by moonlight now, making her way through the trees and then out across a field and into a patch of woods, where she walked with a sure step, familiar with this place, finding her way easily to the foot of a great tall pine, dead in the living woods, its trunk split open by lightning. She pulled away four small splinters of the lightning-struck wood and thrust them, with their power of both the Upper and Under Worlds, down into the paste-filled hollow of the root. Then, kneeling at the base of the tree, she used the spoon to dig into the soft earth, hollowing out a small grave, deep and narrow, patting smooth the sides. Into the bottom she laid the root, and over that she spread the rest of the sand, turning her apron pocket inside out to empty it. Then over the root and the sand she placed the black cloth, carefully smoothing it, and then earth, a handful at a time as she began to sing.

"Hear me now!
I have come to cover over your souls.
Your name is Henry Hawkins.
Your name is Dudley Price.
Your name is Colley.
Your footsteps have I stilled beneath the earth.
Worms have I brought to devour you.
A black cloth have I brought to cover you over.
Toward the Other World your paths are stretching out.
With black earth have I come to cover you.
Your souls are fading.
Your spirits dwindle away, never to reappear.
Hear me now!"

The hole was filled. She smoothed the ground and covered it over with forest litter so that no sign of her work could be seen. Then she got up and retraced her steps back through the woods and across the field. As she passed by the blacksmith shop, there was silence. The whipping was over.

CHAPTER THIRTY-THREE

It was Christmas and the big house was full, a festival for all but the house slaves. From the quarters came the sound of drums and singing, three days free of toil for the hands. In the big house the music came from a fiddle played by a black slave brought along by the Stanhopes from Stanfield Plantation. No holiday for the fiddler, either.

Lucia moved continuously from room to room, attending to the guests. The women were gathered in the parlor, where at night they all slept together in the parlor bed and on pallets on the floor. The men were in the sitting room and the children upstairs in the chamber of the Hawkins children, where Sheba had more to do than she could handle. When Lucia went up to look in on her, she found the girl in tears, undone not only by the mischief of her wards, but also because she was missing the festivities in the quarters. This was Sheba's first Christmas in the big house. Lucia promised to send Tickey up to help her, but when she found Tickey, he was busy bringing food from the kitchen, so Sheba was left to manage on her own.

Lucia went next into the parlor and helped the women dress for dinner. As they were moving from the parlor to the sitting room to take their places at the table, Charity stopped in the hallway and put her hand on Lucia's arm.

"Go take a rest, Lucia," Charity said. "Go out to the quarters and watch the dancing. We'll not need you here for a little time."

"Then Sheba needs me upstairs," said Lucia.

"Sheba can get along. You've earned a rest. Go on. It's Christmas. Enjoy yourself." Charity shook her head and smiled. "Though if my dear father is watching from heaven, you can be sure he's angry at me for all this festivity. He was ever the Puritan. He worked on Christmas day like any other. And if he could see what a medley of guests I have at my table . . ." She lowered her voice. "Bess Clutterbuck, of all people." She laughed.

Lucia smiled absently, unconcerned with the niceties of white society. "I will go down to the quarters then," she said. "If only to see what is happening."

"Wild things, to be sure," Charity said brightly as she walked on toward the sitting room. She was happy to have guests in the house.

Lucia went out into the fading afternoon light. The days were at their shortest, the air cold. She pulled her woolen shawl more snugly about her shoulders and walked down the path toward the quarters. As she neared the blacksmith shop, she slowed her step at the sound of someone urinating. It came from behind the wide trunk of a live oak tree, and she stopped and waited until the sound had ceased before she went on past the tree. It was Henry Hawkins she found there, fumbling with the buttons of his breeches. "They are serving dinner now," she said to him without slowing her pace.

Stepping toward her, Henry grabbed her arm and pulled her to him, the smell of brandy strong on his breath. "Lucia," he said with a drunken smile.

"You'll be late," she said, trying to pull away.

He caught her free arm with his other hand and held her, his fingers tight, hurting her. "Let them start without me. Stay here with me awhile."

"No," she said, struggling to pull free. "Let me go now."

"Beg me," he said in a low voice, his smile giving way to vacant arousal. His fingers tightened and he shook her. "Beg me, you whore."

"Please, Master," she said quietly, not struggling now, for that seemed only to make him worse. "Please let me go."

His eyes moved slowly over her. Then suddenly he shook her hard and pushed her back against the tree. "Why won't you stay with me?" he said fiercely and pressed himself against her, his breath in her face.

"Please, Master Henry."

He leaned forward, forcing his mouth to hers, but she closed her lips tightly and turned her face away, so that at last he pulled back and shook her again, knocking her against the rough trunk of the tree. "God damn you," he hissed. "God damn you to hell!" And he flung her aside.

She kept on her feet and ran a few steps, and then, seeing that he was not pursuing her, she slowed to a fast walk and went on toward the quarters, her arms clasped tightly about herself, her heart beating hard. How long before the medicine would work? His soul should already be fading. Four days it was supposed to have taken, but four days in curing could mean four months, or even four years. Four years would be too long.

The sandy road between the two rows of slave cabins was filled with people milling about, drinking and eating. A bonfire burned at either end of the quarters, and in the center, dancers circled about. The smell of roasted meat was in the air. Henry had given them a cow for their feast. A cow and three kegs of rum. The drinking had started early in the morning.

Lucia wandered through the gathering, marveling at how many people were there. The men who tended the cowpens on the distant reaches of Fairmeadow had come in for the occasion. There were people from other plantations, some having come with the white guests, others on their own. Many of them Lucia did not even know. She looked for familiar faces and finally found Daphne and Timboe among one of the circles of people sitting about. Moon was there, and some others from Fairmeadow, and a woman Lucia did not recognize from behind. But as she moved around the circle to an opening where she could sit, she saw that it was Elizabeth Birdfeather.

"My sister," she said in surprise. "You have come."

"I have come," said Elizabeth Birdfeather, nodding to her. She put her hand on the knee of Daphne, who was beside her. "This one much better now."

"Yes, she has recovered," said Lucia, sitting down.

"Because Timboe stood up for me," said Daphne. She glanced at her husband, giving him an anxious smile which he did not return. He would not look at her nor at any of the others. "They drove me hard-hard. But Timboe stood up."

There was silence then, for the truth was that neither Dudley Price nor Colley had relented at all, and Daphne had gone on tending her fifty acres of trees the same as the others, avoiding the whip by driving herself, until cold weather had set in at last and given her respite. She had recovered her strength in spite of it all. But her spirit was not the same as it once had been. She had lost her baby, and she had lost a part of Timboe. Defeated by his master, he had grown quiet and bitter.

Lucia looked over at Elizabeth Birdfeather. "I heard you had left these parts and gone back to Charles Town."

"Not Charles Town," said Elizabeth Birdfeather. "Go to Yamasee towns." She paused and then she said, "Much talk there."

"What kind of talk?" asked Lucia. She glanced at Timboe. He was still looking away from them, but his face was not so hard now. He was listening.

"Big talk," said the woman. She paused and looked at the others, studying each face in the circle, judging and calculating. Then she asked forthrightly, "Who loves English?"

Timboe gave a short laugh.

"What they ever do to make us love them?" asked Moon.

"They say this in Yamasee country," said Elizabeth Birdfeather. "In Creek country. In every Indian country. Much talk."

"What are they saying?" asked Lucia, intent now on Elizabeth Birdfeather's halting words.

"They say it must end."

"What must end?" asked Timboe.

"English."

There was silence then, all eyes upon her.

"Creek big man, Emperor Brims, talks uprising. Indian people listen more and more. Too many traders. Too much cheating. Too much debt. English planters come across Combahee River. English cattle roam everywhere, ruin Yamasee fields. Brims asks this: Will English people ever stop? Will Indian people ever live in peace?"

"No," Lucia said quietly, shaking her head. "It was never so with the Spaniards. And the English are worse."

Elizabeth Birdfeather looked at her and nodded. "Apalachee people know. Apalachees are strong with Brims."

Lucia nodded. "That is good."

"There is man, his name rises," said Elizabeth Birdfeather, still looking at Lucia. "Apalachee man. Close to Brims. When Apalachee people rise up to follow Brims, this man leads them. They say this in Yamasee towns."

Lucia sat motionless, her eyes locked on Elizabeth Birdfeather's. She knew what was coming, what it had to be.

"He is chief of Apalachee town in Creek country. They call him King Carlos."

Lucia closed her eyes.

"When I hear his name, I think of you," said Elizabeth Birdfeather. "I ask, Is he big man? They say he is big. But they mean strong leader. These Yamasee never see him. They only hear talk."

Lucia nodded. She opened her eyes and glanced at the others and saw them all watching her. "Carlos is a common name," she said.

"Many Spanish Indian name Carlos," said Elizabeth Birdfeather. "But I think, Maybe. So I send message. Apalachee man goes to Creek country. I tell this man, Tell King Carlos his wife Lucia lives on Henry Hawkins' plantation on Combahee River." She shrugged her shoulders. "Maybe message finds him."

Lucia looked away into the fading twilight. The bonfires were growing brighter. The drumming had picked up, the intricate African rhythms shutting out the beating of her heart. *Carlos.* Who else could it be? He was raised to be a chief, trained up to it by the priest. She felt numb, apart from the world, as in a dream. Moving slowly, she rose to her feet.

"I must go back to my work," she said quietly. She turned to Elizabeth Birdfeather. "I thank you, my sister, for thinking of me."

Elizabeth Birdfeather nodded. "Maybe your Carlos."

"No," said Lucia. "I think probably he is not." But as she made her way back through the milling people, her eyes clouded with tears, and her hand trembled as she brushed them away.

☀ The Christmas table was heaped with food, the guests sitting shoulder to shoulder on the benches along either side. Isaac Bull could feel Charity's hip against his own, her arm brushing against his as she raised her spoon to her mouth. And when she was not eating, she would lay her hand in her lap and let her arm rest fully against his, as if their crowding together would not let her do otherwise, though Bess Clutterbuck, sitting on the other side of him, was hardly touching him at all. "I've never sat to a finer feast," he said to Charity.

"Surely in England you have."

"No," he said, shaking his head. "This is the finest." Though in truth he had never known anyone to set a richer table than Theophilus Swade in Jamaica.

"You'd best watch yourself, Isaac," said Sam Clutterbuck, who was sitting across the table.

Isaac looked at him, smiling a little, aware of several things to which the warning might apply. "Watch myself about what?"

"About coming down from the Indian country for Christmas feasts and such. You'll come to the same end as I have—giving up the trading life."

"And how do you find your first year as a planter?" asked Isaac. "Are you settling into it?"

"He's been a'clearing land like he was four men," said Bess. "Our oldest boy's a help to him, now, almost a man. And our Choctaw slave's a better hand than I ever thought he'd be, now that Sam's come home to work him.

In just this first winter, the three of 'em have cleared almost half as much land as all we had cleared before."

"You can see who likes having me at home," said Sam. "But chopping down trees don't put ready money in my pocket. That's the most of what I miss about trading. I can't say I miss the troubles, though."

"We've more of those than ever," said Isaac. "It's why I've come down. Not for the feast, good as it is, but to go on to Charles Town to meet with the Trading Board. They say their aim is to keep the traders in line, but they're not having the least effect from all I can see. I could name you twenty traders who ought right now to be pulled out of the Indian country."

"I could name you forty," said Sam. "Ought to be pulled out and hung."

"Hung?" said Charity. "What have they done?"

"Robbery," said Sam. "Murder. What does it take to deserve hanging? They done it all, lording it over the Indians like they was kings out there." Sam reached out with his knife to a platter of beef and speared a slice and brought it to his plate. "Sooner or later those fellers is going to come to justice. If it ain't done by our own people, it will be the Indians who do it, and we'll not like the shape of it. Once killing starts, it ain't easy to stop it."

Charity looked at Isaac. "Is it so dire as that? Are you in danger?"

Isaac shrugged. "There has always been some danger, and things are more unsettled now than ever. But we'll manage it. I've no doubt of that."

"I praise God Sam's safe out of it," said Bess.

"Safe?" said Sam, laughing as he chewed. "What makes us safe? The Combahee River? You think they've got no canoes? There'd not be a safe place in Carolina, not Charles Town itself, if they rose up against us. If they come together—the Yamasees, the Creeks, the Apalachees, the Cherokees, the Catawbas, the Talapoosas, Choctaws, Chickasaws, and all the rest we've sent traders among—what chance would we have? They outnumber us ten to one."

"Sam," scolded Isaac. "You'll unsettle the ladies with that foolishness. What does it matter where the numbers lie? Our own slaves outnumber us for all of that, and yet we're perfectly safe. We're master of them, and they know it. And so too with the Indians. We master them through the trade. They can't rid themselves of us without losing our trade, and that they'll never do. And besides, they are not capable of combining forces. You yourself once told me they are as divided as the nations of Europe."

"Then why are you going to Charles Town?" asked Sam.

"For just the reason I said."

"Because things in the backcountry have got you worried," said Sam.

"But it's only the safety of our traders that worries me, not that of the settlements. There's where I'm differing with you. I see no danger to any planters unless it be those who have crossed the river and taken up Yamasee land. As to them, they've no business there, and any trouble that comes to them is trouble of their own making."

"I hope there's none that comes to them," said Charity. "I'd sooner have that land settled by Englishmen than roamed by Indians. I wish the Yamasees would move over to the Savannah River. Perhaps we could pay them to do that, cancel their trading debt or some like arrangement."

"They'd not welcome the suggestion," said Isaac. "They consider that debt to be the accumulated swindling of all the traders amongst them. It's a sore point, to say the least. I say it's time we listened to some of their complaints and instituted reforms in the trade. That's the point I mean to press in Charles Town."

"Well, I hope you tarry there a long while," said Charity. "I can't say I like the notion of you returning to the backcountry if there be so much danger there as you say."

"Perhaps I've overstated it," said Isaac. He could feel her warm against him, her arm, her hip, her thigh, and he regretted the effect it was having on him, the awakening of a desire so long mastered and put away. "I'll be in Charles Town a month perhaps. No more than that. I've no worry about going back among the Indians. The situation can only improve once the Trading Board is fully apprised of the problem."

"Will you stop here again on your return?" asked Charity, her voice a little softer now, almost as if they were alone, though many ears were listening.

"Henry will want a report of what transpires in Charles Town," he said. "I'll stop long enough for that."

She nodded and looked down at her plate, and there was a silence that no one attempted to fill. Then suddenly she brightened, becoming social again, and leaned forward to look down the table.

"Where *is* Henry?" she asked. "Did he ever come in?"

"He's right there," said Sam, nodding toward the end of the table. "He came in some little while ago."

"Drunk, I suppose," Charity said gaily.

"He's listing a bit to one side," said Sam. "But he's still sitting up."

"As I see it," said Bess Clutterbuck, "if he ain't under the table, he ain't drunk."

They all laughed, Charity with the rest, leaning a little against Isaac as she did.

CHAPTER THIRTY-FOUR

Lucia sat up suddenly, pushing back the blanket that covered her where she lay on the mat outside the door of Charity's chamber. The house was dark, the shuttered windows closing out the moonlight. Her heart pounded with fright. Her dream had been so vivid that she could still see it—flames shooting up, a sphere of fire with Moon and Basey enclosed in it, silent as they looked at her, surprise on their faces. She rubbed her hand over her face, trying to shake off the dream. Then she lay down again, pulling the blanket back up, and closed her eyes, seeking sleep.

But the sphere of fire was still there, Moon and Basey in it. It was more than a dream. She sat up again and then got up from the mat, pulling the blanket with her and wrapping it about herself against the winter cold. Silently she made her way to the stairs and down, through the lower hallway, past Cajoe and Tickey asleep on the floor, and out the front door to stand in the moonlight and look toward the quarters.

What was she expecting to see? Firelight against the sky, a cabin burning? There was nothing. Her gaze moved out to the river, to the landing where a sloop was moored, loaded with barrels of salted beef and tar, its crew asleep below the deck. Tomorrow it was to ride out with the tide, bound for Jamaica—the same sugar island where Ana had been taken. Lucia looked again toward the quarters. All was quiet. But still she lingered in the cold night air, the dream with her, unease in her heart. More than unease. Fear.

She walked out across the yard, the ground cold through her thin slippers. The path to the quarters showed plainly in the moonlight and she hurried along it, shivering in her blanket, her breath white. The water in the horse trough by the blacksmith shop was frozen on the surface. Above the quarters a haze of smoke hung in the air, the fires in the cabins burning through the night against the cold. She walked quickly down the row to the cabin that Moon shared with Daphne and Timboe and stopped before the door, hesitating, then pushed it open a little way and slipped inside. A fire burned low in the hearth and by its light she could see the dark shapes inside. But where people should have been sleeping there was only empty floor, except in Daphne's corner.

Lucia went to the hearth and added more wood to the fire. The sound awakened Daphne, who rolled over and, upon seeing Lucia, sat up.

"What be wrong?" Daphne asked. "Timboe?"

Lucia shook her head. "It is nothing. I am looking for Moon."

"It be morning?"

"No," said Lucia. "Where is Moon?"

"With Timboe." Daphne got up with her blanket around her and came to stand shivering by the fire. She was taller even than Lucia, her limbs long and lean.

"Where is Timboe, then?"

"At the tar kiln," said Daphne.

Lucia looked at her, startled. "They are firing tonight?"

Daphne nodded. "For the ship. Massa Henry, he want more tar loaded on. He say, fire another kiln. Timboe, he say, let it rain first, air too dry. Massa Henry say, ship pulling out, fire another kiln."

"Who else is there?" asked Lucia. "Besides Timboe and Moon?"

"Basey. He say he better go. Timboe angry, don't want to fire. Dudley Price, Colley, they go make 'em fire it big. Basey, he go hold Timboe down, keep trouble away."

Lucia's hands were gripping her blanket. "Which tar kiln?" she asked quietly.

"By the cooper's shed." Daphne looked at her. "You going out there? Why you want Moon? It be night. Dark-dark."

Lucia looked into the fire, uncertain how to answer. "I had a dream. Probably it is nothing."

"Timboe be in danger?"

Lucia shook her head. "He was not in the dream."

Daphne was silent, looking into the fire. Then she said, "Timboe always be in danger."

"You go back to bed," said Lucia. "I'm sorry I had to wake you."

"Can't sleep now," said Daphne. She pulled a low stool close to the hearth and sat down, wrapping her arms about her knees beneath the blanket. "You going out there for true?"

"Yes," said Lucia.

"Tell Timboe . . ." Daphne stared at the flames, searching for words. "Tell him I be waiting for him."

"I'll tell him," said Lucia. Pulling her blanket close, she turned away and went out of the cabin into the freezing night.

✵ Lucia moved quickly along the track through the woods, keeping warm by the pace that she set. At first she walked without any clear thought except that she must get to the tar kiln, reach Moon and Basey before the dream could reach them. But the dream was fading now, her fright with it, and she began to feel foolish for being out in the night on a mission so hard to explain even to herself. But still she went on, until at last she saw firelight ahead. Coming out of the trees, she stopped at the edge of the clearing, relieved to see that all was as it should be. The men were sitting around a fire for warmth, Moon, Basey, and Timboe on one side, and Colley and Dudley Price on the other. Close by them was the mounded earth of the kiln, smoke rising from the top of it in the moonlight. Timboe saw her dark figure approaching before the others did. Surprised, he rose to his feet and came toward her, peering to see who she was.

"It's Lucia," she said to him, and as she heard her own voice in the night, she felt more foolish than ever and regretted completely that she had come. There were Moon and Basey sitting contentedly by the fire, everything normal and right. She could hardly recall the dream anymore. She stood there at the edge of the trees, not wanting to go forward.

"Who is it?" Dudley Price called out.

"Lucia, Master," Timboe answered, and because she would not come closer to him, he walked out to meet her where she stood.

"Is Daphne ill?" he asked anxiously.

"No," she said and drew in a troubled breath, not knowing what to say to him.

"Then what is it?" he asked, truly puzzled. "Is it Juba? Shall I call Basey?"

"No," said Lucia. Her heart was beating with a strange fright.

"What does she want?" called Dudley Price. The overseer rose to his feet by the fire. Taking a few steps toward the kiln, he reached down and picked up a long piece of cane and stood for a moment leaning on it as if it were a staff. Lucia was watching him, but Timboe was not.

"Don't know, Master," Timboe called over his shoulder. Then he looked hard at Lucia. "Is my mother sick?" he asked in a low voice.

"No," said Lucia, feeling oddly near tears. She watched the overseer, a dark shadow in the firelight as he walked slowly around the kiln, holding the cane horizontally in his hands as if it were a spear and the kiln an animal into which he meant to thrust it. "It's Moon and Basey," she said softly. "Perhaps you should tell them to come over here."

"Why?" asked Timboe, turning to look at them. He saw Price at the kiln. "Don't give it more air, Master!" he called out. "Can't take more air!"

"Who gives the orders here?" Price answered, and he drew back the cane and thrust it through the packed earth of the kiln.

"No!" shouted Timboe, starting toward him. The men at the fire leaped up. Then came a blast of light, the force of it hurling Lucia back into the woods, the ground shaking, trees bent as in a wind, earth coming down like rain. She lay stunned where she fell, silence all around, and only slowly did she begin to feel pain in the shoulder on which she had landed, and just as slowly did the silence give way to the sound of moaning. It was dark now, only moonlight. She raised herself up a little and felt her shoulder, moving her fingers slowly along it, finding no broken bone. Trying it out, she found she could move it. She raised herself further, all her limbs working. She pushed up onto her knees, her legs weak and shaking so that she had to hold onto a tree to pull herself to her feet. For a few moments she could do no more than stand there looking out into the clearing. The tar kiln was gone, and the cooper's shed had collapsed into rubble. No sign of the men. But she could hear moaning and when she felt that her legs would hold her, she let go of the tree and took a few steps into the clearing.

"Timboe," she called into the darkness.

"Here." His voice was low and not far away. It was a separate sound from the moaning.

"Where are you?"

"Here," he said again, and she went toward his voice and then saw him move as he slowly pushed himself up onto his hands and knees and sat back on his heels.

"Are you hurt badly?" she said, coming over to him. She could hear his labored breathing.

"Ribs broken maybe. Some cuts." His voice was unsteady.

She knelt beside him and saw his chest glistening in the moonlight. Putting her hand on it, she felt blood. "Where does that come from?"

"I don't know."

She moved her hand over him, feeling carefully until she found a gash in his right breast. "Lean over," she said pulling his shoulder forward to help close the wound. "Hold it with your hand. Try to press on it. I'll go to the others."

She guided his hand to the wound and felt him press against it, and then she got up and moved toward the moaning sound. She found Basey in the darkness—the moaning was his. Feeling his mangled body, she knew that he was dying. She bent over him, speaking softly to him, but he seemed unaware of her. After a few moments she left him and went to look for the others, though no sounds came from them to guide her. She found Moon's body, and then Colley's. There was no sign of Dudley Price, and when she remembered how close he had been to the kiln, she stopped looking for him. She went back to Basey. His moaning had ceased. He was unconscious and hardly breathing. Knowing there was nothing she could do, she left him and went back to Timboe.

"Dead?" he asked as she knelt down beside him.

"All of them," she answered. She put her hand on his chest. "How is it?"

"I don't know," he said. "I can't see it."

She felt the blood, stickier now. "It's stopping, I think."

"You knew Moon and Basey would die."

"I dreamed it. This very night. It's why I came."

"You should have called them away."

"I didn't know what was going to happen."

"You called me away. You should have called them."

"I never called anyone. You came of your own."

He was silent, realizing it was true. In the silence they heard the sound of voices. Through the trees, torchlight was approaching, many lights bobbing up and down in the hands of people running. It seemed forever that they watched the scattered flames coming closer through the straight black trunks of the pines. Lucia's numbness began to give way to sorrow as the lights came into the clearing, Daphne in the lead, her long legs running, her face wild. When she saw the emptiness of the clearing she stopped and stood still for a moment, stunned. Then she cried out and ran forward again, holding her torch high to throw light ahead as she searched the ground for Timboe.

As Lucia rose to her feet, Daphne saw the movement and turned toward it, and after a few steps her light fell on Timboe. When she saw that he was sitting up, the wildness went out of her face. She stumbled to him, weeping, while Lucia went to look for Basey's wife Juba in the crowd.

Everyone had come, all the people from the quarters. The clearing was filled with them, some standing and watching in silence, others aimlessly milling about, some crying. Lucia saw Doll wandering about in tears and hurried to her. "Don't cry," said Lucia, grasping her arm. "He's all right."

"Where?" asked Doll.

Lucia pointed her toward Timboe and Daphne and went on looking for Juba, hoping to find her before Juba found Basey. But then a cry went up, Juba's voice rising above the chaos. Tears filled Lucia's eyes. There had been nothing she could do, nothing at all. The dream had been useless to her, everything happening just beyond her reach.

The cold of the night came through to her, forgotten until then, and she stood shivering and full of sorrow. She wanted to be away from all this, to lie in a quiet place and be still. Four men dead, and two of them, Colley and Price, she had killed herself with the poison root buried in the woods. But it brought no satisfaction, only a sick, bad feeling, and grief for Moon and Basey who did not deserve to die.

Henry Hawkins rode into the clearing on horseback, Cajoe running before him with a lantern to show the way. Henry had taken time to dress himself fully, bracing himself against the cold with stockings and boots and greatcoat. Now he reined in his horse at the sight before him: the cooper's shed and tar kiln gone, the people mourning.

"What happened?" he demanded in a loud voice. Those who were talking fell silent. There was only the sound of weeping.

"Where is Price?" he demanded, rising up in his stirrups to look for him among the slaves. "Dudley Price! Where are you?"

"Dead," someone said in a low voice.

Henry froze for a moment in that lifted position, his eyes no longer searching. Then he sat back heavily in the saddle. He looked down at Cajoe. "Is that true?"

Cajoe shook his head. "I don't know, Master."

Henry looked out at the others. "Is it true? Is he dead?"

"True," said Chany's husband Peter, daring to speak up.

"What happened?" said Henry. "Is anyone else hurt?"

"Colley. Moon. Basey," said Peter. "All dead."

"Dead?" Henry cried in anger. "God almighty! Dead?" He jumped down from his horse. "God damn this night! How can they all be dead? What about Timboe? He was firing that kiln."

"Timboe be alive," said Peter. "He be cut up, but he alive."

"He did it, then," said Henry, his anger mounting. "Where is that son of a bitch? He did it. He threatened to kill Dudley Price. I heard him myself. Where is he? We should have strung him up then. Where is he?" No one moved. He raised his riding whip threateningly, and the ones in front stepped back a little, but still no one made way for him or showed him where to go.

Henry stepped in among the people, pushing them out of his way, his anger driving him now. He came at last to the place where Timboe still sat on the ground, Daphne kneeling beside him and Doll standing over him. With one hand Henry pushed Doll out of the way and with the other he brought down the whip across Timboe's face. Daphne cried out and threw herself over him, but Henry kicked her and then kicked her again until Timboe himself pushed her away and struggled to get to his feet.

"Stay down, nigger," snarled Henry, beating him down with the whip. "Killed him, did you? Killed him? And three good slaves. You black devil son of a whore. Blew 'em up. God damn you to hell. I'm through with you."

"He didn't do it, Master," cried Doll, grabbing at Henry's arm. Timboe tried again to rise, but it was Daphne now who stopped him, tears on her face as she wrapped her arms around his neck.

"Be good," she said softly. "Be good."

"It was Dudley Price who did it," said Lucia, pushing her way through to them.

Henry Hawkins turned and looked at her. "What the devil do you know about it?"

"I was here," she said. "Dudley Price stuck a cane through the kiln."

"Trying to make it burn faster," said Timboe.

"Timboe tried to stop him," said Lucia.

Henry looked from one of them to the other. Then he gave a bitter laugh. "What kind of fool do you take me for? What would she be doing out here? You all lie for each other." He turned and looked around. "Cajoe!" he called. "Peter! You two come here."

"Lucia tell you the truth, Massa," Daphne said in a quiet voice. "She come to our cabin. Ask for Moon!"

"Shut up," Henry said sharply. "Pox on you all. There's not a truth-teller among you. Cajoe! Damn your ass, where are you?"

"Here, Master," said Cajoe, making his way forward through the crowd.

"Where's Peter?"

"He coming."

"I want the two of you to take Timboe back. Guard him well. If he gets away, I'll ship you out in his place. You hear me now?"

"Shipping him?" said Doll, her voice loud in the sudden stillness.

"Would you rather me hang him, then?" said Henry. "He ought to be hung."

"No, Massa," Daphne said softly. She got to her feet, standing close beside Timboe, her body stiff. "Timboe, he didn't do nothing, Massa Henry."

Henry looked back at Cajoe. "Take him to the blacksmith shop. Tell Will to put irons on him, then put him on the sloop."

"No, Master," said Doll, her voice turning sorrowful and pleading. "Don't do that, Master Henry." She fell on her knees beside Henry Hawkins, her hands on his legs. "Please, Master Henry. Don't ship my son to no sugar island. Please Master Henry. Ship him to Charles Town. To Virginia. Send him back to Boston."

"Get away!" Henry said sharply, stepping back from her. She followed him on her knees.

"Please, Master Henry. Old Doll, she's begging you. Not to no sugar island. They'll kill him there, work him to death. I beg you. I pray to you."

Timboe sat without moving, Daphne standing still as death beside him, her face almost white.

"Bring him on," Henry said to Cajoe and Peter, who were beside him now. He stood and waited while they went to Timboe and took his arms and raised him to his feet. Timboe was trembling—from the cold, from his wounds, from shock and rage. He was weak, his legs unsteady, and the two men had to hold him up as he walked. Daphne stayed with him, silent and stricken, reaching out again and again to touch him.

Henry turned to follow them. "Someone bring my horse," he ordered.

"Master Henry," said Doll and grabbed his ankles. She was weeping now. "Don't do this, please." She pressed her face against his legs, crying.

Henry leaned down and pushed her roughly away. "Leave me alone, woman!" He kicked at her to keep her back. "Touch me again and I'll have you whipped." As he moved away, she stayed where she was, sinking down until her face was against the earth.

✳ Lucia went back with the others along the sandy road through the pines. She walked beside Doll, who clung to her arm, leaning heavily. Morning was coming in the eastern sky, a faint light through the trees. The cold seemed sharper than ever. Lucia's bruised shoulder was stiff.

"Witchcraft." Chany's voice rose above the silence. There was no other sound but the trudging of their feet on the road. No one made any response to her.

"Witch," said Chany. "Kill bad. Kill good. No heart."

"Dudley Price did it," said Doll. "He killed them all. Lucia saw it."

"Lucia see it," Chany said. "Night. Woods. Cold-cold. Lucia go out. Lucia see it. Strange."

No one said anything. Lucia looked straight ahead, too weary and stricken to say anything.

"Colley know," said Chany. "He tell me. Lucia take dirt from his door. Now he dead. Dudley Price dead. Moon dead. Basey dead. Timboe . . ."

"Shut your mouth," Doll said sharply. She leaned against Lucia. "Never mind," Doll said softly. "Never mind what she says."

Lucia said nothing, her heart heavy, knowing the truth. Glancing back over her shoulder, she saw that everyone had fallen back, leaving her to walk alone with no one but Doll beside her.

CHAPTER THIRTY-FIVE

Lucia walked out from the big house to the landing, seeking the warmth of the afternoon sun. Peter and the blacksmith Will and his son, Little Will, were fishing from the riverbank near the wharf. In addition to Sundays the slaves now had Saturday afternoons to themselves, more time for getting their own food, for hunting and fishing and tending their gardens. Sam Clutterbuck had given them that, one of the first changes he made when he became the new overseer of the place. This new freedom was not yet approved by Henry, who had been gone to Charles Town these last few weeks, but it seemed likely that it would be, for Henry would not want to undermine Sam's authority by crossing him on so large a matter.

Lucia walked out onto the landing and sat down, turning her back to catch the full heat of the sun. It was late winter, the air still cold, but in the sunshine she could feel the coming spring. She looked across the Combahee at the treeline that marked the beginning of the Yamasee country. She had never seen a living soul on that side, except people from Fairmeadow, who hunted and fished it as if it belonged as much to Henry as this side did.

Peter and Will drew in their lines and moved further down the bank, away from her. Though she tried not to notice, it pained her that everyone continued to keep clear of her, punishing her for what they believed she had done to Moon and Basey and Timboe. Only Cajoe and Doll did not shun her. Cajoe because he seldom associated with people from the quarters and felt little for them. Doll because she laid the blame elsewhere—on Dudley Price for blowing up the kiln, and on Henry Hawkins for sending Timboe away to Jamaica. But the friendship of Doll and Cajoe was not enough to make up for the ostracism by the others. It was one thing for her to choose solitude, but another to have it forced upon her.

Pulling her knees up against her chest, Lucia rested her chin on her folded arms and watched the trees across the river. Carlos. King Carlos of the Creek country. How long since Elizabeth Birdfeather's message might have reached him? A moon? Two moons? Some hopeful part of her had been waiting for an answer, for word from him delivered by a traveler on the river or by Elizabeth Birdfeather herself. But the weeks were passing and only silence came from that wide country beyond the trees. She had given much thought to how it might be for him, ten years since he had seen her, his grief healed over and his life continuing on. It seemed likely he had taken another wife. Why should he not? A man whose wife is dead takes another. It is the usual thing to do, no matter how much he might have cared for the one who is gone. And now after ten years someone comes and tells him that his first wife is not dead. How would he feel about it as he looked across the fire at the woman who is now his wife? Not happiness. More likely distress. And what could he do, knowing where that first wife is? She is a slave, and it is not in his power to free her. So he would make no response. Of course he would not. He would put this knowledge of her away in a sad part of himself and try not to think of her anymore.

She watched the slow-moving water, dark from the inland swamps that it drained. For ten years she had carried the hope of Carlos. For too long. It was slipping away now, and she knew she should let it go. She should never have lived so long in so much loneliness. She should have taken another man.

At the far bend of the river a canoe came in sight, pushing its way upstream. She raised her head and narrowed her eyes to sharpen her vision. A bewigged Englishman rode in the center, with two boatmen paddling. She thought at first it must be Henry, but as the canoe came closer she could see that the boatmen were not black men but Indians. She watched a few moments longer, and then, recognizing the man who sat between them, she got to her feet and went up to the house to tell Charity that Isaac Bull was arriving.

✳ Isaac was pleased to see Sam Clutterbuck come down to greet him as the cypress dugout came to rest against the wharf.

"Mighty good to see you," said Sam, reaching out to give him a hand. "Welcome back to Fairmeadow."

"I understand you're a part of the place now," said Isaac as he came up to stand beside him.

"You've seen Henry in Charles Town, then," said Sam.

"Drunk as a sailor."

"He was drunk when he left," said Sam. "It cleared the air mightily to have him out of here. I hope he stays gone yet awhile."

"I believe he will. He seemed in no haste to return."

"Did he tell you what happened?" asked Sam.

"He said Dudley Price is dead. Mrs. Hawkins' Timboe blew him up with a tar kiln and took three slaves along with him."

Sam shook his head. "Who knows how it happened? But one thing's for certain. Timboe don't belong to Mrs. Hawkins no more. Henry shipped him out."

"So he told me," Isaac said.

"Made folks mighty unhappy around here," said Sam. "That's why he went to Charles Town. Not even she would speak to him." He nodded toward the house.

They were silent for a moment. Then Isaac said, "What about you? I thought you'd turned planter."

"Couldn't afford to stay at it, not after he offered me this. I go home on Saturday evenings, do a little work there, come back on Sunday evenings.

Bess is content enough with it, better than me going back into the trade."
He glanced toward the river. "I was just making ready to leave for home, if the truth be known."

"Go ahead," said Isaac. "I'll be pulling out myself as soon as I pay my regards to Mrs. Hawkins. I want to see that everything is well, with Henry being gone and all the rest."

"Well, you might as well stay the night," said Sam. "No sense sleeping on the riverbank. I'll stay over if she wants me to. Keep it all proper."

"No, you go on. I'll make it back down to Stanfield tonight. There'll be an early moon to guide me."

Sam shrugged. "However you want it then. But tell me this. How did it go with the Trading Board in Charles Town?"

"Not so well as I had hoped," said Isaac. "They're asking Thomas Nairne to take charge of the situation, to go into the Indian towns and hear their complaints, smooth things over where he can. But I didn't see that they were of a mind to push through any true reform amongst the traders."

"The Trading Board is too distant from the trade," said Sam. "I didn't expect much of 'em. There's nothing for it, I reckon, but to hope Nairne can calm things down for yet another while."

There was silence then, each of them looking away at the wharf or the water, thinking separate thoughts, their conversation at an end. Isaac looked up toward the house and saw Charity standing in the doorway.

"I should go up," he said.

Sam nodded. "I'll wait around a bit, see if she wants me to stay."

"You go home to Bess. I'll be out of here within the hour."

"I do believe you're trying to be rid of me," Sam said with a smile.

Isaac laughed a little as he met his eyes. "Nobody ever questioned *you* being left alone with her."

"And why would they, a scabby dirt farmer like myself?"

Isaac chuckled and clapped him gently on the shoulder. "Take care of yourself, old friend. Give my regards to Bess." He turned and started away.

"And you give mine to Emperor Brims," Sam said after him. "Tell him that whenever he gets to having hard feelings about things, just drink a little rum and sleep it off. It's always worked for me."

"I'll give him your advice," said Isaac, and he went on up to the house.

Charity waited for him at the door, a smile on her face, her movements slightly flustered as she held out her hands to clasp both of his in greeting. Her touch was light and she did not linger in it, pulling her hands free almost immediately and stepping back to let him go ahead of her into the house. He walked in silence to the sitting room, she behind him, no words beyond their first greeting. Cajoe appeared and stood by quietly, waiting to serve them.

"Bring us some ale," Charity said to Cajoe as she sat down in a cushioned chair near the fire. Isaac waited until she was seated and then took the chair opposite her.

"It is good of you to come," she said quietly. "Sam told you, I suppose, that Henry is away."

"I saw Henry in Charles Town," said Isaac.

"Oh, yes. Of course you would have." She looked away into the fire. "I am not thinking very clearly these days."

"I was grieved to hear of the tragedy," said Isaac.

"He made it worse than it needed to be." Charity's voice was resigned in its sadness. "It was bad enough, four men killed. But then to sell Timboe away." She shook her head, her eyes moist as she watched the fire. "I think he did it because Timboe was mine. Because I cared for him."

"You don't believe Timboe caused the explosion?"

"No."

Isaac watched her, pained by her misery, unable to think of anything to say.

Cajoe brought the ale, his footsteps loud in the silence. Isaac took both mugs from him and gave one to Charity. Her face softened a little as she met his eyes.

"To your happiness," he said gently, raising his mug.

Tears sprang into her eyes and overflowed. Looking away from him, she set her ale on the table beside her chair and pressed her hand to her face, her shoulders shaking with silent weeping.

Isaac looked around at Cajoe. "Leave us," he said, and the black man turned away and went out of the room. Isaac leaned forward, resting his elbows on his knees, his head bent as he studied the mug of ale in his hands. He waited for her crying to ease.

"That's not the effect I meant to have," he said quietly.

"I know," she murmured, shaking her head. She lowered her hand from her face and composed herself. "Forgive me, Isaac."

He stared down into his ale, wondering if she realized she had used his Christian name. "I cannot pretend to be blind to your misery," he said.

"And I can no longer hide it. From you the least." She shook her head, raising her hand to her cheek. "I should not have said that." She fell silent, staring away beyond him, until at last she drew in a long sigh. "I think you had best leave and come back another time when Henry is here."

He looked up at her. "Let me take you to Stanfield then. You can visit there for a time. You need to be in company."

She shook her head. "Those are Henry's friends, not mine. He does his whoring there."

There was another silence, Isaac looking down at his ale again. "Then perhaps you should go to Charles Town," he said. "I'm loathe to leave you here, seeing the distress you are in."

"Henry is in Charles Town," she answered, her voice strengthening. "I do not wish to be where he is."

He looked up at her. "Then what am I to do?"

"Leave me as you found me," she said, smiling a little. "I have my children with me, and my slaves. I am presenting too melancholy a picture, I think. It's not so very bad, Isaac. Truly it is not." She paused and her smile wavered as she looked away. For a moment she hesitated, then she added softly, "It is only that I know how much better it might have been."

She tried to keep her smile, but her eyes were filling with tears again. Isaac moved toward her, setting his ale aside. He reached for her and she came to him and he closed his arms around her, smelling her sweet fragrance, feeling her softness against the rough wool of his coat. For a long time he held her, caressing her. Then she pulled back gently, and he released her and moved back to his chair, his eyes on her, looking for a smile. For a moment she looked down at her hands. The smile that he sought was half-formed, a light in her eyes as she held one of her hands in the other and ran her thumb lightly over each of the nails. Then she looked up, the smile blossoming, and he returned it, pleased with her happiness. She nodded a little, then looked away, glancing over at his mug and seeing it almost empty.

"Will you have more?" she asked, looking back at him, the happiness still with her.

He nodded, and as she called for Cajoe, he watched her, his passion stirring. A few moments passed, and then Cajoe came in with a pitcher and refilled both their mugs.

"That will be all," said Charity, and as Cajoe turned to go, she added, "Leave the ale." He put the pitcher on the mantle and went out, pulling the door closed behind him. Charity looked at Isaac and laughed a little, as if pleased at the ease with which she was handling herself now.

"You're feeling better," he said, his eyes intent on her, finding pleasure in her every movement.

"Yes." She tried to hold his gaze, but at last she blushed and glanced away toward the fire. The wood was smoldering, and she got up and went over to stir it.

Isaac rose and followed her, standing behind her as she took the poker and bent forward to shift the logs. Flames rose up around the wood. As she straightened, he put his hands on her waist and turned her toward him, taking the poker from her hand and putting it aside. And then he was holding her again, she pressing against him, his hands moving over her, feeling her, keeping at first to her back and her face and her shoulders, and then at last moving slowly toward her breasts, aching to touch them, fearing she would stop him. But she did not stop him. He kissed her and caressed her until at last she broke away a little, still holding him, and murmered, "The children."

"Hang the children," he said, pulling her close again.

"Isaac, how awful. You would hang my babies?" She laughed softly, pushing him away. "We will lock ourselves in the parlor," she said. And taking his hand she led him across the hallway into the parlor, where she pushed the door closed behind them and turned the key.

✸ Isaac lay in the darkness, the heavy curtains closing in the parlor bed against the cold of the night. Beneath the warm blankets Charity lay beside him, flesh against flesh, her breathing soft as she, too, stared silently into the darkness. He had been at Fairmeadow for three days now. Sam had come back on Sunday night and knew at once what was happening. The house slaves knew. The children did not. Charity was careful of that, making sure she called him Mr. Bull in their presence and coming to his bed only late at night when the children were sleeping. The house slaves could be trusted, she said. He himself knew that Sam was no problem. But still there was danger. Tomorrow he would be on his way.

"Tell me about the Indian country," Charity said softly, snuggling down more deeply in his arm.

"What would you like to know?"

"How it looks."

"That depends on where you are. The Yamasee country is no different from this. But up in the Creek country the land changes. It's more pleasant, in truth. Hills and rivulets. No miasma in the air."

"I wish I lived there, then."

"With the Indians?"

"No," she said, a smile in her voice. "I wish England had a colony there."

"She will have, in time."

"There and on the moon, as well."

"You don't believe me?"

She shook her head. "Where would England find settlers for it? Already we are spread so thin we never see our neighbors. And we're not thirty miles from the sea."

"There are always more settlers," said Isaac. "Look how they are spilling over the Combahee."

"But the Combahee is right here. Indian country stretches hundreds of miles.

"Thousands," said Isaac.

"There," said Charity, as if she had won her point. "It's beyond comprehension."

"Unless you have seen it."

She stroked her hand over his chest. "Have you seen it?"

"I've seen it to the Mississippi River. And they say it goes on as far again on the other side."

"And all of it full of Indians," said Charity. "It's a sobering thought. We are so small, perched here on the edge of such a vast land. Think how quickly all those savages could overwhelm us."

"Only if they were united, and that they will never be. It's not in their nature to think of themselves as one people."

"But there's more danger of it now than once there was. Sam said as much at the Christmas feast. I fear for you going back out there." She reached her arm around his chest to hold him more tightly.

He laughed a little. "It's not so dangerous as staying here, now is it?"

She made no reply, and they lay for a time in silence. Then she said sadly, "Were it not for the children, I would leave him."

"I know you would," he said.

"The law gives them to him if we divorce, and he would surely want to keep them. Especially Robin and Abe. He would never let his sons go. It's not the shame of a divorce that stops me, Isaac. It's the children."

"Shh," he said, putting his fingers to her lips, not wanting to be reminded of the hopelessness of their love. He kissed her hair and her face, trying to make her forget. Tomorrow he would leave, and he was not sure when he would come back to Fairmeadow, or even if he would. It pained him to think of it. He buried his face in her hair, moving his hands over her. She moved against him, wanting him. Reaching his arms around her, he pressed her to him. And slowly he made love to her. And then in a little while again. And then again in the light of early dawn.

CHAPTER THIRTY-SIX

Lucia stood at the corner of the house and watched Henry Hawkins climb out of the boat onto the landing. He was thin, his face hollow and drawn. She thought to herself that he must have spent the entire two months in Charles Town swilling rum and eating no solid food. But he seemed to be sober now, his movements steady and sure. He helped lift his baggage from the periago and then turned and stood looking up toward the house, waiting for some sort of greeting. Grace and Robin burst out of the front door and raced each other down to him. Henry squatted down, opening his arms to them, while still glancing now and again toward the house. But Charity did not appear.

As Henry started up from the landing, Lucia turned and walked back through the yard to the kitchen. The late afternoon sun slanted through the trees, the air warm with early spring. In the field behind the kitchen a pear tree was in bloom.

Doll was hard at work at the great fireplace, her face grim beneath her white kerchief as she shifted two iron pans on their trivets above the coals, making room for another one between them. Sweat glistened on her skin. She looked older these days, worn down with grief and anger.

"Is he drunk?" she asked sharply as Lucia came in.

"He seems to be sober," said Lucia. She walked over to help Doll lift down a boiling kettle from its hook and set it away from the fire. A few moments of silence passed, Doll going about her work.

Then Doll asked, "Did she go out to meet him?"

"No," said Lucia.

"I wish he could know," said Doll, her voice hard. "I wish he could know she's made him a cuckold. Nothing would hurt his pride more than that. I wish he could know."

"But he mustn't," said Lucia, giving her a warning look.

Doll waved an impatient hand at her. "You don't have to tell me that. Do you think I've lost my mind?" She turned back to the fire, angrily stirring one of the pots. "Why didn't he stay away?" she muttered. "I hate breathing his air."

Lucia walked over to the doorway and leaned against it, looking out. By the back door of the house little Abe played unattended, dragging a stick through the dirt as if he were snaking timber from the woods with a team of horses. He was too young yet to know how privileged he was, or to recognize the suffering upon which the comforts of his life were built.

Sheba appeared in the doorway of the house. Seeing Abe, she came out and picked him up. Then she looked toward the kitchen and saw Lucia.

"Missus want you," Sheba called across the yard.

Lucia looked around at Doll. "I'll come back and help you get things ready for the table."

"If you can," said Doll, her voice still gruff.

"Maybe he won't stay," Lucia said. "Maybe he'll go back to Charles Town."

Doll poked at the fire, shaking her head and making no reply.

Lucia crossed the yard and went into the house, going first to the sitting room, but finding it empty. She passed by the parlor, knowing they would not be there, and went upstairs to their bed chamber, where she stopped in the half-open doorway, waiting to be noticed. Charity was standing in the light of the window and Henry in a darker corner near the bed. Both of them seemed agitated and unmindful of her presence.

"Look at me," Henry said to Charity, turning fully to face her, holding his arms open to present himself. "Am I drunk? Do you see the least trace of drunkenness in me? I've not touched a drop of rum in two weeks." He rubbed his hand over his chin. "I'm clean-shaven. My clothes are clean. I'm not swearing. Do you hear me swearing?"

"What of it?" Charity asked coldly. "You've been clean and sober before. What of it?"

"It's what you want of me," he said. "I'm trying to make amends, can't you see?"

"I want nothing of you, Henry." She turned away from him and saw Lucia. "I want you to help me move my things to the parlor," she said to her. "I'll be making that my chamber from now on."

"Don't you do it, Lucia," Henry warned, and Lucia stayed where she was. Charity gave Henry a hard look and then turned away and stared out the window.

"Give me this opportunity, it's all I ask," Henry said to her, his voice softening. "Try me for a few days. Just a few days, and you'll see."

"No," Charity said without turning around.

"How long will you nurse a grievance? I gave you two months free of the sight of me. That should be time enough for any Christian woman to find forgiveness in her heart. It was time enough for me to ponder things anew. You can see the difference in me. I know you can. God knows, I can feel it."

Charity made no reply.

Henry looked over at Lucia. "Go on out," he said. "And shut the door."

Lucia moved out into the hallway, closing the door behind her. Downstairs she could hear the sound of the children playing in the sitting room. She started to go down, but then waited, listening at the door.

"Dearest heart," she heard Henry say, his voice was soft and cajoling. "Come over here to the husband who loves you." There was no reply from Charity, no sound from the room. The silence stretched out. At last Henry said, "Come on now. Don't you hear me?" Some of the softness was gone from his voice.

"I hear you," Charity answered quietly.

For a moment longer there was silence. Then Lucia heard the sound of Henry's footsteps crossing the room. "I don't believe you do hear me," said Henry, his voice growing hard. "I am asking you to come over to the bed."

"And I am declining to do so," said Charity. "Now please keep away from me."

"Who do you think you're speaking to? Am I not your husband? Tell me that? Must a man keep away from his own wife?"

"Henry, stop."

"You're my wife, God damn you. Don't tell me to stop."

"Henry!"

There was a sound of scuffling, then Charity's footsteps running, then Henry's, and more scuffling.

"*Stop!*" Charity screamed suddenly, the sound of her voice filling the house. There was a moment of silence. Then the door was flung open and she came out, tears on her face as she ran to the stairs and down. Lucia backed away toward the children's chamber as Henry came to the doorway, breathing heavily. He looked toward the empty stairwell, his hollow face dark with anger. After a moment he came out into the hallway, and noticing Lucia, he stopped and looked coldly at her.

"What are you staring at?" he demanded.

"Nothing," she said quietly. Turning away she ducked into the childrens' chamber and listened until his footsteps had gone down the stairs and out the front door. She went to the window to see where he would go, hoping it would be down to the landing and into the periago and down the river again. But he walked out past the blacksmith shop toward the quarters—going to Sam Clutterbuck's, she thought, to quiet his mind with rum.

She went downstairs and found Charity sitting alone in the parlor. "Do you need me?" Lucia asked.

Charity rose to her feet. "Yes," she said with a steady voice. "Come help me bring down my things."

✺ It was almost dark by the time Lucia returned to the kitchen. Supper had already been served, though Henry had not come back to the house. Doll had finished her work and was sitting on a mat in the chimney corner.

"Does anyone know where he is?" Lucia asked, warming herself at the fire. The air was growing chill with the setting of the sun.

"Peter says he went to Clutterbuck's cabin and got a bottle of rum and then went and shut himself up in Colley's cabin."

"Colley's cabin?"

Doll shook her head. "Only Henry Hawkins would want to keep company with Colley's ghost. He's the only one mean enough to go in that place."

Lucia made no reply, and the two of them watched the fire for a time, each following her own thoughts. Then Doll said quietly, "I wish I'd never gone out to dig yams that day."

"What day?" said Lucia.

"That day in Africa when the slave-catchers caught me. If I had stayed home that day, Henry Hawkins wouldn't own me now. Wouldn't any man own me. And to think how close I came to not going out." She shook her head. "I woke up that morning feeling sick, my stomach not right, and I thought maybe I would stay in. But then I ate a little something and felt better." She drew up her knees and rested her elbows on them, leaning her head in her hands as she stared at the fire. "I almost didn't go out that day."

Lucia tried to picture her in her African homeland, a distant place that Lucia imagined to be like Apalachee. "Did you have Timboe then?" she asked.

"No," said Doll. "Timboe was born in Jamaica. Born there, and now he's gonna die there."

"Jamaica?" Lucia looked at her in surprise. "You have been in Jamaica? You never told me that."

"Don't like to think about it," said Doll. "That was the first place they carried me. I was there two years. Had a man there, but he died. Timboe's father. They worked him to death, just wore him down. Wore me down, too, but I didn't want to die. I was going to run away. I was all set to do it. But then they picked me up and carried me off to Boston. Timboe was just a babe in arms."

"But how could you have run away?" asked Lucia. "Jamaica is an island. Where could you run?"

"To the mountains," said Doll. "That island is big. The white men only live around the edge of it. The middle of it is full of mountains. Slaves get away to those mountains and there's no catching them. They've got villages hidden away up there. Sometimes they come down and raid the plantations, kill the white people and steal their cows. I was going to join them or die trying. I was working up my courage for it, but then the white people jerked me up and put me on a ship to Boston."

"Was that good or bad?" asked Lucia.

Doll shrugged. "Probably if I had run, the dogs would have caught me. Maybe Boston was better." She fell silent, and for a time they watched the fire. Then Doll said quietly, "But if I had made it to the mountains, wouldn't any man have ever owned me again, and couldn't any man have treated Timboe like Henry Hawkins treated him, whipping the manhood out of him and sending him away to die."

"Maybe not to die," said Lucia. "Maybe he'll be the one to get away to the mountains."

"I hope he tries it," said Doll. "Even if they kill him at it, I hope he tries."

Lucia put more wood on the fire, sparks flying up, then she moved back and sat down against a barrel of flour. Neither of them were talking now, and in the silence they heard footsteps approach the kitchen door. Henry Hawkins appeared in the doorway, and they rose to their feet.

"Lucia," said Henry. "Little Will is feeling ill. Go out to the quarters and see about him."

She looked at him warily. His voice was steady enough, not terribly drunk. He was standing straight without having to lean on anything.

"Did his father ask for me?" she said. "They've not been wanting me to doctor them of late."

"It's not up to Big Will, now is it?" said Henry. "I made that plain to him. I put Little Will in Colley's cabin to get him away from the others, so he can rest. You'd best hurry on and see him. He's in a bit of a fright about ghosts."

Lucia glanced at Doll and saw that she, too, was uneasy.

"I'll come along," said Doll.

"You stay here and serve my supper," said Henry. "I'm ready to eat now." He looked again at Lucia. "Take a lantern. It's almost dark and there's no fire in the cabin."

She nodded and stood for a moment, hoping he would leave, but he stayed where he was, waiting to see his orders carried out. So she took down a lantern from a shelf on the wall and lit it at the fireplace and then went out, leaving Doll moving slowly about the kitchen, putting Henry's food over the fire to warm.

As Lucia started down the path to the quarters, she looked back and saw Henry still standing in the firelit doorway of the kitchen, watching her go. She went on uneasily, worrying that he would follow, but when she looked back again, he had turned away and was crossing the yard to the house.

✱ Colley's cabin was dark and she stood in the doorway for a moment,
listening to the snuffling sound within.

"Little Will?" she said quietly, holding her lantern ahead of her as she moved cautiously inside. It was a tight, neat cabin, better furnished than any other in the quarters, with a straw mattress on a bedstead and a table against one wall. She could see the boy lying very still on the bed, his wide eyes watching her with fear. It seemed foolish for Henry to put him through such a fright for the sake of some supposed benefit that solitude would bring him. But there was nothing she could do about it, no way to countermand the master's orders.

"You're not afraid, are you?" she said, taking care to keep a distance at first, knowing he was as much afraid of her witchcraft as of the ghost of Colley.

Little Will made no answer, and in the lantern light she could see him shivering. "Do you have a chill?" she asked.

Still he was silent.

She set the lantern down on the table and came closer to him. "Tell me what's wrong. How do you feel sick?"

"Ain't sick," said Little Will in a small, tight voice.

She sighed. "You don't have to be afraid of me. I came to help you. But you have to tell me what's wrong."

"Nothing's wrong," he said.

"Will you let me put my hand on your head to see if you're hot?"

"I ain't hot," said Little Will, his voice stronger. He snuffled and rubbed his nose with the back of his hand.

"Does your stomach hurt?"

"Don't nothing hurt."

She put her hand on her hip, beginning to lose patience. "Then why are you lying here in bed if nothing is the matter with you?"

"I'm doing what Massa Henry told me to do."

"What did he tell you to do?"

"Lie in this bed."

"And why would he tell you to do that if you're not sick?"

Little Will shrugged. "Don't know why. He just told me to lie here until he come back."

Her heart skipped. She turned toward the doorway. It was empty, everything quiet outside.

"When did he say he was coming back?"

"He didn't say. He just told me to lie here. He didn't say nothing about me being sick."

"Well, if you're not sick, you don't need me," said Lucia, and she went over to pick up the lantern.

"Don't leave me in the dark," said Little Will. His tone had changed. He was not so afraid of her anymore, though he was still afraid of the ghost.

She smiled at him. "I'll leave the lantern. You bring it back to the kitchen tomorrow."

Will nodded. Then his eyes went past her to the door.

Lucia turned and saw Henry Hawkins come into the room and push the door closed behind him. The hollows of his face were shadowed by the dim lantern light, but she could see that his eyes were on her even as he spoke to the boy. "You can go now, Will. Come on. I'll let you out."

"I did what you told me, Massa," said Little Will. He sat up and swung his legs to the floor.

Lucia put out her hand to the boy. "Don't go," she said softly.

He looked at her, puzzled, and seemed to see her fright. He glanced over at Henry.

"Get out," Henry ordered.

Little Will moved slowly to obey, looking first at Lucia and then back at Henry.

"Go get Miss Charity," Lucia said to him. "Tell her to come out here."

"Don't you dare do that," Henry commanded. "I'll have you whipped, do you hear me? If Miss Charity comes out here, I'll whip you and sell you away. Do you hear me, boy?"

"I hear you, Massa," Little Will said in a frightened voice.

"What are you going to do when you leave here?" asked Henry.

"Go home, Massa Henry."

"What are you going to tell people?"

"I ain't telling 'em nothing."

"Nothing at all?"

"Not nothing," said Little Will, near tears now.

"Then get out," said Henry. He opened the door a little and the boy slipped out, the door closing behind him.

Lucia kept her eyes on Henry, trying to steady herself and think. He was not as drunk as he might be. "Do you think I will not tell her?" she said calmly. "Nothing you can say or do will stop me."

"And what will she do?" asked Henry, his voice hard and sneering. "Stop speaking to me? Move out of my chamber? You can tell her anything you want, once I've done with you. It's only the act I don't want interrupted." Still standing in front of the door he reached over and caught the edge of the table and pulled it toward him, the light from the lantern jumping about the room. He pushed the table firmly against the door and then laid

something on it. A rawhide whip. As she looked at it in the lantern light, a
dull feeling came into her.

"We can leave the whip there," he a said in a low voice, "or we can bring it into the play. It's up you, my dark angel." He took a step toward her, his lips turning up in an ugly smile. "My pretty, dark-skinned whore."

She stood motionless, her heart pounding hard, her eyes fixed on him as she tried to think. The door was unlocked, only the table barring it. If she could get around him—but how fast could she move? The table would slow her and he would be on her. Unless she could hurt him, hit him with something. The lantern. But he was her master—they could hang her for striking him.

He took another step, the smile leaving his face as his eyes moved slowly over her body, claiming it, intent now on taking what was his. She stepped back, edging toward the door, knowing he would have her, sick with the knowledge, certain of it, and yet unwilling to yield as she made her small, hopeless movement away from him.

"Take off your clothes," Henry said in a low voice.

She drew in her breath, steadying herself, trying to keep her mind clear. "Sit down, then, and watch me," she said, nodding toward the bed, her voice surprisingly calm.

He laughed. "And watch you bolt for the door? Do you think I'm a fool?" Then the laughter was gone and he was coming toward her, she backing away. He lunged for her, grabbing her arm and flinging her toward the bed. "Take them off, harlot." He stepped back, reaching for the whip.

She crouched against the bed, watching him, terror overtaking her. He stood and watched her, breathing heavily, holding the whip in one hand, caressing the bulge in his breeches with the other. She raised her fingers to the fastenings of her bodice and fumbled there for a moment, her eyes still on him, sick with the sight of him. But her fingers would not do it, she could not make them, and she dropped her hand away and was still.

He swung the whip slowly, his breath quickening. Then he started toward her, the whip drawn back, his other hand reaching down for the neck of her gown. She tried to make herself be still, let him do what he wanted, let him take her now without the whip. But her hand struck out, knocking his arm away, jarring her whole body as she scrambled to her feet.

"I'd as soon lie with a yellow dog," she hissed. He was too close now to use the whip, but he struck out with the butt of it, hitting the side of her face, knocking her back against the bed. She caught herself with her hands, ducking and pushing out from the bed, lunging around him, trying for the door, knowing she would never make it, he not a step behind her, she reaching for the lantern, and then he had her, his arm around her neck, his terrible strength throwing her to the floor. And then the lash. She heard it coming and raised her arm against it, pain cutting through her.

"Please, Master," she said, drawing herself up to meet the next blow, but not fast enough—it caught her side and her hip, tearing at her gown. She turned her back to him, and the next blow came across it, the force of it flattening her against the floor. As she tried to rise, another lash knocked her flat again.

"Please, Master. I'll be good." Another blow. She had her head ducked down against the floor. "I'll do what you want." Another blow, her gown giving way, the rawhide tearing into her skin. "Stop, Master Henry." She was starting to cry. "Take me now. I'm ready." Another blow. And then another. And another. She raised her head, keeping her arm in front of her face, turning to look up at him, shadowy in the lantern light, his eyes glazed, his arm drawing back the whip and swinging it down with all his might, she closing her eyes against it, crying out with the pain, and then looking up at him again, seeing the open buttons of his breeches, his hand there, and that glazed look in his eyes, and the whip coming down again.

She ducked her head and screamed as the lash tore into her. "*Stop!*" she cried, sobbing now, knowing he would not stop. She lay still, trying not to move, hoping he would find less pleasure in it if she no longer struggled. She stopped her weeping, giving him nothing, only her body jerking involuntarily against the blows. And then by slow degrees she heard a different sound, something that was not the whip, wood knocking against wood. She opened her eyes, raising her head a little, and saw the lantern light leaping about the room, the table moving at the door. The whip stopped and Henry looked around, startled, fumbling with his breeches, but not in time to hide himself from the eyes of Sam Clutterbuck, who stood now in the doorway looking from Henry to Lucia.

"I won't have it, Mr. Hawkins," Sam said in a quiet voice. He reached around and pushed the table back a little further and slipped into the room. "There's bounds." He came over and picked up the whip that Henry had dropped in his hurry to button his breeches. "I ain't gonna have it, Mr. Hawkins. You can whore on your wenches all you want, but I'll not have you beating 'em in the bargain. Not where I can hear." He looked down at Lucia. "Not like this. God almighty."

"Get out!" said Henry, jerking his head toward the door. "Who do you think you are? Get off my plantation. Do you hear me? I'm done with you."

"I figured you would be," said Sam. "But I ain't leaving you here to finish what you started. The law won't support you in this, Mr. Hawkins. There's bounds. I'll turn you in if you touch her again."

Lucia lay still and listened, her face in her arms, her fists clenched against the pain. She could feel blood trickling down her side.

Henry was laughing. "I thought you were a man of the world, Sam. You
think the law will support you? There's not a judge in all of Carolina who's
not whored on his slaves."

"It's one thing to bed 'em and another to beat 'em to death. Never mind
whether the case carries for or against you. The charge is enough. It's not
so pretty a picture, a gentleman of your station beating a woman bloody
with his britches down. It would change the way people think of you. They
never would forget it."

Henry glared at him. "God damn you, Sam. I can do more than dismiss
you. I can throw you off your farm. Have you forgotten that?"

"No," said Sam. "I've not forgotten." He walked over and pulled the
table clear of the door, which he opened fully now. "But if you do that, I'll
have to tell why you done it. The same as I'll have to tell why you dismissed
me. There'll be quite an interest in it, you can be sure. It'll be the idlers'
talk from here to Charles Town. Of course, that's not the kind of thing a
fellow tells on a man he's working for."

"I'll not have any man working for me who fancies himself master over
me," Henry said.

"I never fancied myself that for a minute," said Sam. "You made me your
overseer and put me in charge of your slaves, and here I am, doing my job.
Now, I'll whip 'em when they need it. But I can't have 'em being beat for
no other reason than to give you the pleasure of it. They got to know that
when they do the work I tell 'em to do, they'll not come to any grief." He
nodded toward Lucia. "And this ain't telling 'em that."

Henry stared past him, weighing it, thinking, perhaps, of the trouble it
would be to find another overseer. For a long time there was silence. Then
he reached out in anger and turned over the table, Sam grabbing the lantern before it fell. "Stay then," snarled Henry. "Pox on you. Stay and do
your bloody job."

"I'll stay," said Sam.

Henry turned away abruptly and walked over to the bed. Reaching beneath it, he brought out a half-finished bottle of rum, uncorked it and took
a long drink. Then, still holding some of the rum in his mouth, he turned
and sprayed it out over Lucia. As the alcohol burned into her wounds, she
shuddered and drew up her knees, keeping her face turned away from him.
"I wouldn't fuck her with a dog's dick," he muttered, and jamming the cork
into the bottle, he stalked out of the cabin.

Sam righted the table and put the lantern on it, and then stood in the
doorway and watched Henry go. Outside the slaves had gathered, standing in a huddle at a distance. As Lucia began to slowly push herself up,
Doll came forward from among them. At first Doll came alone, but then
Daphne left the others and followed her, and then Chany and Juba. Sam

moved out of the doorway into the yard, and the women came past him into the lantern-lit room. For a moment longer Sam stood outside. Then he turned and walked slowly away through the quarters to his cabin on the other side.

CHAPTER THIRTY-SEVEN

Lucia lay on a mat in the loft above the kitchen. It was Doll's room, a small space pinched in by the angles of the roof. She lay on her stomach with her arms folded under her head and stared into the dark recesses, her mind drifting slowly from one dreary thought to another. Her back hurt too much to lie on it, but it was not so terribly bad. She had seen worse whippings. Timboe's had been worse, on that night she buried the poison root. She understood more than ever the change in him after that, why he had become so sullen and quiet. It was not the bruised and torn flesh that kept her lying here in the loft, but the lowness of her spirit.

Downstairs she could hear Doll shuffling about the kitchen. Early that morning, before breakfast, Charity had come to the kitchen wanting to know where Lucia was, why she had not slept in the house or come in to help Charity dress. And Doll, without the least hesitation, had told her everything that had happened. Charity had come up into the loft, bringing a candle with her, holding it close to Lucia's back, murmuring over what she saw. Lucia had said very little, nothing coming to her to say, and Charity soon left. Not long after, Lucia heard shouting in the house, Charity's voice and Henry's going back and forth. Then little Abe started crying and the shouting stopped. Everything was quiet now.

Lucia closed her eyes, wanting sleep, but the noise in her mind grew louder and more disturbing and she opened her eyes again to regain her composure. So long as she could see this room, she knew she was not in Colley's cabin. Doll was downstairs, and she was safe. Sam Clutterbuck was out there somewhere in the sunshine that filtered in to her in tiny pricks of light through the wooden shingles. This wooden floor was not the earthen floor of Colley's cabin. The space above her was empty—Henry was not there drawing back his whip, bringing it down on her with all his strength.

But Henry was in the big house, so close she could hear his voice when he raised it. He was still her master. Sam Clutterbuck did not own her. Henry Hawkins did. Sam Clutterbuck could be sent away. Doll could be pushed aside. Henry owned this kitchen, this loft. He could come here any time, do whatever he wanted. She turned her head and looked up. The ceiling was low, no room to stand except in the middle. No room to swing a whip. There was comfort in that. No room in this loft for a whip.

Below she heard Cajoe's voice as he came into the kitchen from the house.

"What was that hollering?" Doll asked him.

"Miss Charity's in a fury," said Cajoe. "I never seen her in such a fury. Told him to go back to Charles Town."

"Is he going?" asked Doll.

"He said he ain't going. So she said *she* be going. She said she be taking the children with her. He said he ain't taking the children, but she said she is, and they shout about that for a while. Finally he said take 'em then, but she ain't busting up his household, she ain't taking no servants away. She said she be taking Lucia, but he said she ain't, and they holler some more, but he never did give in on that."

Lucia put her hand to one of the H's branded on her cheeks. Henry was the one who owned her. Not Charity. Everything that was Charity's became his when they married. He owned Lucia—her life, her body. He could keep her here. She stared into the darkness and tried to divert her thoughts, but they only went to grim things, to the carnage she had seen in Salvador's camp, to the starvation at San Augustín, to the slave-catchers in the forest with the rain coming down, to Ana being left behind in the slave pen, to Carlos with his new wife. Her eyes closed, and she drifted into troubled sleep, then awoke in a fright, someone pounding at the door. No, it was footsteps—soft ones coming up the crude stairs into the loft. She turned her head and Charity appeared, her face lit by the candle that she carried. She came over to Lucia and knelt beside her, setting the candle on the floor.

"Are you feeling any better?" Charity asked.

Lucia shrugged. "I am all right."

"I want to tell you what is happening," said Charity. "I told Henry I'd not live with him anymore. I'm taking the children and going to the house in Charles Town." She paused, searching for the right words. "It's all a bit unsettled now. He says he'll not let me take any servants from Fairmeadow. It was hard enough to make him let the children go. But in a little time he'll come around. I'll send for you. I'll not leave you here forever."

At first Lucia made no reply. There was silence, Charity toying nervously with the rings on her fingers. Then Lucia asked quietly, "Will Mr. Bull join you there?"

"No," said Charity. "I cannot risk seeing him in Charles Town with so many people looking on. Were Henry to hear of it, he'd divorce me and take the children away." She clasped her hands in her lap and gave a tremulous sigh.

Lucia closed her eyes, wishing her gone.

"I've talked to Sam Clutterbuck," Charity said. "He assured me he'll do all he can with Henry—concerning you, I mean. And I do believe he can guard you well. Henry is cruel, but he is weak. I'd not go away and leave you did I not think Sam could protect you. And I'll send for you soon, before summer. I'll send for Doll as well. It's my hope to convince Henry to take Venus and Bella in your places."

Lucia nodded.

"I told Sam that I want you to sleep out here with Doll. I don't want Henry taking you into the house again."

Lucia stared past her. What could Sam Clutterbuck do to stop him?

"I'll be leaving before the day is out," said Charity. "Sheba and Cajoe are helping me pack a few things. The rest I'll have sent after me. You'll hear from me soon. I promise you that, Lucia. I'll send for you."

Lucia nodded again, but still said nothing. Charity remained a moment longer and then, reaching for the candle, she rose to her feet. As she went down into the daylit kitchen, the smell of the smoldering wick of the extinguished candle drifted back up into the loft. Lucia looked up at the roof, searching for the specks of sunlight. She wondered whether Charity had allowed herself to consider the fact that Sam Clutterbuck left Fairmeadow every Saturday evening and stayed away for a night and a day. Who would be here to protect her then?

✸ A misty rain was falling as Isaac Bull climbed out of the cypress dugout onto the Fairmeadow wharf. Sam Clutterbuck came out to meet him, his face ducked down against the rain. As they shook hands, Sam said to him in a low voice, "I'm sorry to say we've had a reversal in things. It's Henry who's alone here now. She's gone to Charles Town."

Isaac glanced toward the house. "When did she leave?"

"Not a week ago. It would take more than a word to tell the whole story."

"Is Henry sober?" asked Isaac.

"I wouldn't say so."

"I'd as soon not see him if I can avoid it," said Isaac. "Can we go to your cabin?"

"Come along." Sam turned and led the way beneath the dripping trees.

Sam's cabin had only one room, though it was a large one with a brick fireplace and a window. It was comfortably furnished with a bed, a table, a bench, and two chairs. Sam had a fire burning against the chill of the spring rain, and they drew the two chairs up close to the hearth and settled down.

"So tell me the story," said Isaac.

Sam shook his head. "I don't know how I get tangled up in these things. There's no end to the complications of it." He told Isaac of Henry's attack on Lucia, his own interference in the matter, and of Charity's departure in its wake. "I don't know what he'll do when he finally sobers up," said Sam. "Send me away for good and all, I reckon."

"But then who would manage Fairmeadow for him?" said Isaac. "There are not so many men to choose from, and none of your worth. I'm sure he knows that, drunk or sober. He can't run the place by himself. It would go to ruin in a fortnight."

"Might be you're right," said Sam. "But it leaves me with another problem."

"What is that?"

"Well, tomorrow is Saturday, time for me to go home to Bess like I always do. But now I hate to leave the place. I got a feeling Henry's been lying up there in the house, nursing his rum, waiting for me to shove off up the river so he can get back to Lucia without anyone to get in his way."

"You can't stand guard over her forever," said Isaac. "She'll not be the first slave wench to be forced by her master. It's common enough."

"So I tell myself," said Sam. He shook his head. "It just seems to me that he forfeited his right to her when he laid into her with that whip. I don't know that I can explain it." He reached down and picked up a chip of wood and tossed it into the fire. "God damn it, I've come this far in the thing and I just can't hardly bear to go off now and let him have her."

Isaac made no reply, and they were silent for a time.

Then Sam said, "Will you be going on to Charles Town after Mrs. Hawkins?"

"No," said Isaac. "It was not to see her that I came. Not specifically, I mean. It was to bring a bit of news up the river."

"What news?"

"More rumor than news, but there's enough to it to cause a stir among the traders. You remember our old friend The Panther?"

"Sure."

"Well, it seems he was sharing a bottle with Sam Warner one night of late. In Savana Town. The Panther got some rum in him and began to feel sentimental toward old Warner. Thought he ought to share a little secret with him. He told him that the Creeks are more unhappy with the traders than they've ever been before, that they've taken their complaints to Charles Town with no effect, and that they've run out of time. They're resolved to action. On the first affront from any of the traders, they'll cut them down one and all. And they'll not stop there."

"They will go on to Charles Town, you mean?"

"So Warner supposed. He's gone to Charles Town to alert the governor."

"I hope the governor listens. It's time to get the thing in hand. We need a strict regulation of the trade, nothing less."

"If it's not too late for reform," said Isaac.

Sam looked at him. "Do you think it is?" he asked soberly.

"I don't know," said Isaac. "But I do know Sam Warner was in a fright. There are some who are shrugging it off, but I'm not one of them. This storm has been brewing too long."

Sam leaned forward toward the fire, propping his elbows on his knees, his shoulders bent over while he thought. Then he straightened again.

"I'd like to ask a favor of you," he said.

"Ask it," said Isaac.

"I'd be in your debt if you would go on up the river and tell Bess some of what you have told me. Don't alarm her more than need be, but tell her to be mindful, keep the gun handy, take it with 'em if they go away from the house, and don't any of 'em go out alone. Bar the door at night. Things of that sort. She'll know what to do."

"Then you're not going home tomorrow?" said Isaac.

"No. Tell her that, too. Tell her there's business keeping me here, and it might be a few weeks before I get up there. But if there's any Indian trouble on the river, I'll be there with her before she even hears about it."

"Unless it strikes there first."

Sam shook his head. "You just have to trust the Lord that some things won't happen. My being there one night a week wouldn't give her much protection anyway."

"Do you want me to tell her why you're staying?"

"No," said Sam. "Just tell her it's business. If she heard the other, she'd not think it reason enough." He stood up and stretched, turning his back to the fire. Then he got his pipe from the mantle and pulled a pouch of tobacco from his pocket. "Share a pipe with me," he said. "And settle in for the night. This rain should clear off by tomorrow."

"That's a fair offer," said Isaac. He reached down and pulled off his boots and then leaned back in the chair, stretching out his stockinged feet toward the fire.

✳ Lucia stepped back a few paces and leaned on her hoe, looking with satisfaction at the little field of corn she had planted. It was Sunday afternoon and the day had been pleasant, the air still cool from Friday's rain, the sun shining down with the gentle warmth of spring. Doll had been right to force her out of the kitchen, putting a hoe in her hand and telling her to go plant a patch of corn for the two of them. It was the first time since Henry's attack that her spirits had lightened, the first time she had cared to feel the warmth of the sun or the coolness of a breeze.

If today was her best day since that night in Colley's cabin, yesterday had been her worst. It was Saturday, time for Clutterbuck to go home. By noon she had retreated to the loft, pulled so low with dread that she had done nothing for the rest of the day but lie there, waiting for the night when he would be gone and Henry would finally come to find her. But when darkness came, Clutterbuck was still at Fairmeadow. Doll sent Tickey to find out what was happening, and Tickey came back and reported that he had seen Clutterbuck through the open door of his cabin, that he had a fire going in the hearth and was lying on his bed with his boots off. From this they knew that he was not planning to leave at all.

Lucia at first had been too numb to rejoice. That day of fearful waiting had exhausted her, and she fell asleep soon after Tickey left and did not awaken until Sunday dawn. She and Doll ate a quiet breakfast, speculating on why Clutterbuck had remained at Fairmeadow, and then Doll sent her out to plant their corn. As the day progressed, her spirits rose, until now, as she stood looking at her day's work, she decided she should speak to Sam Clutterbuck and let him know that she was mindful of the protection he was giving her and grateful for it. She had not spoken to him at all since that night in Colley's cabin.

She went back to the kitchen and found Doll dozing, her kerchiefed head leaning back against the wall where she sat beneath the window. Lucia went quietly to work, taking dried peaches from a cloth sack that hung on the wall, sugar from a small barrel in the corner, flour from a larger barrel. Doll stirred, was still for a moment, and then raised her head and looked at her.

"What are you doing?" Doll asked.

"Making a peach pie."

"No need for that," said Doll, rubbing her hands over her face. "We have pudding from yesterday." She stretched and then got to her feet, staggering a little with the sleep that was still in her. "I'd not waste a pie on him, anyway. He don't deserve anything as good as that."

"This is not for Henry," said Lucia. "It's for Sam Clutterbuck."

Doll opened her eyes a little wider and looked at her. "I'm not sure Clutterbuck deserves it, either. You should not be thinking he's a better man than he is. He still is the overseer of this place."

"He's a better man than Dudley Price," said Lucia.

"And who wouldn't be?"

Lucia made no reply. She mixed the sugar and peaches together in a pan, added some water and set them over the fire. Doll stood for a moment, scratching her back and watching. Then, with a shake of her head, she went over and got the butter and brought it to the table to begin mixing it with flour for the crust.

⁕ Lucia hesitated for a moment in the twilight outside Sam Clutterbuck's cabin. The pie, covered with a cloth, was warm in her hands, its aroma sweet and spicy. She was a little uneasy now, not sure exactly what she would say. The oncoming darkness was bringing her spirits down, and she no longer had the enthusiasm for this that she had felt when she began. But the pie was made, and she had come this far with it, so she went on ahead toward the open doorway. "Mr. Clutterbuck?" she called softly.

There was a sound of movement inside, and then Clutterbuck was in the doorway, looking out to see who was there. He smiled when he saw her. "What's that I smell?" he said.

"Peach pie." She held it out to him. He took it from her, lifting the cloth a little and smelling it more deeply. She smiled at the pleasure he was showing.

"Come in and we'll both have some," he said.

"No," she said quietly, shaking her head. "It's all for you. I must go back to the kitchen."

"What for?" He shifted the pie to one hand and reached out to her with the other, taking her by the shoulder in a friendly manner and drawing her inside. "Doll has none but Mr. Hawkins to cook for. That's not enough to keep one cook busy, let alone two." He went over and put the pie on the table while she stood just inside the doorway, uncertain whether to stay or go.

He was paying little attention to her now. Taking out his knife, he carefully cut the pie in half, then gave the pan a quarter turn and halved one of the halves. There was a wooden trencher on the table and he lifted one of the pieces onto it, then got a spoon and pushed it with the trencher across the table toward Lucia. She still stood watching him, tempted by the pie and by his open manner, but wary, trying to think of what the ramifications would be.

He got another spoon and pulled out the bench from beneath the table and sat down. "I'll eat out of the pan," he said, digging the spoon in without further ado. He nodded toward the trencher. "That one's yours."

Still she stood, uncertain how to accept, but thinking now that maybe she would. She smiled a little. "I'll have some, then." She came over and started to pick up the trencher, intending to take it outside.

"No," he said and patted the bench. "Sit down."

She looked at him. It was not the way things were done, a slave sitting down to eat with a white man. She turned and glanced out the door. Anyone could be watching.

"I couldn't do that," she said. "I would like to taste the pie, though."

"Close the door if it bothers you."

"No, I think I'd best go back," said Lucia, starting to turn away without the pie.

"Wait a minute," said Clutterbuck, putting down the spoon in exasperation and rising to his feet. "For God's sake." He walked by her and pushed the door shut. "All I'm trying to do is get you to sit down and have some pie, here where you're safe, where you don't have to worry about nothing. That's all there is to it. I ain't Henry Hawkins out to set you a trap. Just sit down here and let's have some pie." He took his seat again and looked up at her, waiting. "Sit down," he said, this time speaking the words in Apalachee.

She smiled, hesitated another moment, and then sat down on the bench, keeping a wide distance between them. "I've not heard my language spoken for a very long time," she said.

"I don't know much of it," said Sam. "It's Muskogee I know best. I lived a great while amongst the Creeks." He took a bite of the pie and chewed it slowly, savoring it. "This tastes so good it draws your eye down."

"I'm pleased you like it," said Lucia. "Doll made the crust. She used butter in it, not lard."

Clutterbuck took another bite. "And white flour," he said, shaking his head over the fine flavor. "And white sugar in the peaches. This is a feast for a common fellow like me. I'm used to cornmeal and molasses."

"I am grateful for what you did for me that night in Colley's cabin," Lucia said quietly. She did not look at him as she spoke.

"I'm sure you are," said Clutterbuck. "I never doubted it." He went on eating his pie, and she ate hers, neither of them speaking. When finally he had finished, he pushed away the untouched half of the pie and turned on the bench to face her, drawing one leg to the other side and leaning his elbow on the table. She was still eating.

"You like?" he asked in Apalachee.

She smiled. "Yes, it is good." She said it in her language, and for a moment she closed her eyes with the pleasure of those words in her ears and on her tongue. She looked at him and then self-consciously away, her gaze sweeping to the window beyond him. As her eyes came to rest on a whip hanging coiled on a nail beside the window, her smile left her face. She turned back to the pie, ate another bite and then pushed it away, her appetite gone.

Clutterbuck looked at her for a moment, puzzled, then turned and glanced over his shoulder at the whip hanging behind him.

"That," he said and fell silent. He looked away, pondering.

"I must go," she said, making a move to leave. But he reached out and put his hand on her arm to stop her.

"Give me a minute," he said.

"For what?"

"To sweeten things up again. I don't want you going out of here with that cloud on your face. It was pleasant to have you bring me the pie and smile at me and sit with me. The whip is mine true enough, and I use it on your people, because that's what an overseer has to do. But I ain't Henry Hawkins. I don't enjoy using it. And I wish right now that it weren't mine, not the whip nor the job, and that you were just a friend who stopped by to pass a little time with me."

Lucia made an attempt to smile. "I know you are not Henry Hawkins," she said quietly. "I will try to forget the whip." She paused, remembering the fear that only yesterday had paralyzed her until this man had taken it away by not getting into his boat and going up the river. "I do not know why you stayed here last night," she said softly, "but I was very relieved by it. I had been afraid of what he would do when you were away."

"It worried me, too," said Clutterbuck. "That's why I stayed."

She glanced at him and then looked down at the table, unable to speak, her finger tracing the grain of the wood, her throat tight with emotion. Tears came into her eyes, blurring her vision, and her finger ceased its tracing motion.

"I'm ashamed I ever had a hand in making you a slave," he said quietly. "You ought to be home in your own land."

She turned away from him, rubbing her hands over her face, gathering herself together. "We all of us should," she said in a steady voice. "Doll, Timboe, Daphne, Juba, all of us should be home in our own countries."

"God knows it's true," said Sam. "But that ain't the way of the world. I don't know why everything is set up as it is, but that's the way things are." He got up and walked over to the fireplace and stood leaning against the mantle, looking down at the flames. "Sometimes I think of just getting out of the whole mess, going up into the Indian country to live. I don't mean as a trader, either. There's a woman I used to live with up there. A good woman. God above, I miss her sometimes. My whole goddamned chest gets to aching for wanting to be back with her. But I got my wife and young 'uns here to think of. Anahki has her brothers to hunt for her and take care of her, but Bess don't have another soul but me. I rooted her up from England and brought her over here, promising her a better life, and all she got for the trouble was fever and ague and one hardship after another. So I stay here, and I do what I have to do. And yes, goddamn it, I deal in slaves. I

buy 'em and sell 'em. I work 'em for other men. I got three on my own
farm. I don't like it, but that's the way the world is, and I can't do a thing to
change it. So there's an end to it." He kicked a chip of wood into the fire
and sparks flew up.

Lucia watched him for a moment, and then she rose to her feet. "I have
to go now," she said. He nodded but did not turn around to face her.

"I don't want you to be unhappy because I came here," she said. "I
wanted to thank you for the kindness you have shown to me."

"You did thank me," said Clutterbuck. "The pie was good." But still he
would not turn around.

"You are upset with me," she said.

He shook his head. "Not with you."

"Then I will go."

He nodded.

She went out, closing the door quietly behind her.

Part Four

THE UPRISING

1715–1716

CHAPTER THIRTY-EIGHT

Isaac Bull stood at Yamassee landing and watched Thomas Nairne's periago cross the broad expanse of the Coosaw River from Port Royal Island. The houses and outbuildings of the nearest plantation on the great island were barely visible in the distance, the flat land stretching away in the warm April sun. An osprey dove down to the water's surface near the periago and rose again with a fish in its talons. Isaac felt more at ease than he had in months. Governor Craven had finally been brought to his senses, Sam Warner's warning having been confirmed by yet another warning from another trader whose wife had been told of impending danger by a Yamasee man who was friendly to her family. Thomas Nairne was coming now to make arrangements for a meeting in Savana Town between Governor Craven and all the Indian kings and headmen of all the towns from the Yamasee country to the Ocmulgee River. Last evening Isaac had been across the river at Jack Barnwell's plantation when Nairne came in from Charles Town, relieving the minds of all with news of the governor's decisive action, the complacency of the Trading Board overridden at last. After hearing all that Nairne had to tell, Isaac had come back across to the Yamasee towns, and as he had walked from the landing to John Grissom's trading house where he would spend the night, he had spoken to Indians that he met along the way, putting out word of the governor's visit, letting it be known that Nairne would be coming over today to convey the news formally in council.

The periago was almost across now, and Isaac waved a greeting to Nairne, then stood with his hands on his hips, watching him glide in. Finally he stepped forward to catch the rope that was thrown ashore. "A fine day," he said as Thomas Nairne stepped out of the boat.

"Indeed it is," said Nairne. "And more than the weather is good—it's coming here at last with something of substance to offer. My God, what a relief."

"I let out intimations of the news last night," said Isaac. "Already I sense a growing ease among the Indians. Though perhaps I read too much in things, like a woman looking into her tea leaves."

Nairne smiled. "My wife just this very morning read danger in hers. It alarmed her so, she took a stand against my going away. Never mind the governor's business—the tea leaves were speaking. I couldn't leave her till I had soothed her down. It's why I'm late."

"No matter," said Isaac, leading the way to the two horses that were being held for him by an Indian servant. "The Yamasee kings and headmen began gathering in Pocotaligo this morning. We've got Sam Warner and a few other men there to catch the drift of their talk, but all seems peaceful enough."

They mounted their horses, the Yamasee servant trotting out ahead as they started along the trail on the long ride to Pocotaligo Town, eight miles inland. They rode at a leisurely pace, enjoying the day, and it was well into the afternoon when they arrived at the council house. They dismounted and walked together through the plaza, past Indian men who stood talking in groups, some leaning on their muskets, lifting their eyes to watch the white men pass. Isaac nodded to the ones he knew, taking a reading of their faces, hoping to see the easing tensions he thought he had felt earlier in the day. But now he was not so certain of it. At the door of the council house he paused, letting Nairne go first, and then followed in behind him.

The chamber was dark, smoky, and crowded, every seat filled, though some of the men took up room enough for two, leaning back on their elbows on the wide cane benches, smoking their long tobacco pipes, talking quietly, waiting for the bowl of cassina to come around again. Isaac followed Nairne past the central fire to the far side, where the kings of the Yamasee towns were settled in the east-facing seats, the place of highest honor. The kings made room for the two Englishmen, shifting to one side or another, but seeming at the same time to pay little attention to them. As Isaac sat down, he noticed a man he had not expected to see, one of Brims' men, the leader of an Apalachee town in the Creek country.

"Now there's someone I'd as soon do without," he said quietly to Nairne.

"Who is that?" asked Nairne, turning slightly to look without being obvious about it.

"King Carlos," said Isaac.

"I'm not acquainted with him," said Nairne. "Which one is he?"

"The big one," said Isaac without turning to look again. "Tall. Red blanket. He's in tight with Brims, as tight as any man among the Creeks. Brims' wife is an Apalachee, and she and Carlos are closely allied. Six months ago I'd never heard his name, but now there's scarce a week goes by I don't hear it spoken, most often in the same breath with Brims himself."

"Then it's good he's here," said Nairne. "He can take word of my talk where it most needs to go. If Brims doesn't come to the governor's council

in Savana Town, the governor might as well stay home. There can't be any 323
settling of differences without Brims being there to settle his part."

"True enough," said Isaac, settling back in his seat.

More time went by, at least an hour, as a few more Yamasee headmen
came in from the more distant towns. Nairne spoke and joked with those
about him, but Isaac kept quietly to himself, watching the assembled men,
trying to decide which ones had been stirring up the talk of war. There
were mostly younger men gathering about King Carlos. No surprise in that.
The young men were always the ones most eager to fight.

At last the king of Pocotaligo signaled that the council would begin. Pipes
were put away, and freshly brewed cassina was brought out and drunk in
the ritual way, with strict attention to each man's rank. Then a pipe was
passed with tobacco which Nairne supplied, and this, too, went from the
highest man to the lowest. Isaac noticed that King Carlos received his before all but the oldest of the Yamasee kings.

The Pocotaligo king opened the talk with set phrases of welcome, re-
hearsing the history of the years of peace between the Yamasees and the
English and politely leaving off all mention of the current tensions. But
then it was given to Nairne to speak, and he addressed the complaints of
the Yamasee people forthrightly, admitting the tensions, taking blame for
the English, assuring the Yamasees that they were now being heard, that the
governor himself would come to meet with them and the Creeks in Savana
Town and that all their grievances would be heard with newly opened ears.
Redress would be made and changes put in place. The talk went on and on,
with all the elaboration Nairne had learned from his years of dealing with
Indian councils. He knew how to speak the words and phrases they liked
to hear, how to say things as they would say them. Isaac watched the head
men and kings, trying to assess the impact of the talk. But they guarded
their faces, watching Nairne with passionless eyes, skeptical, perhaps—and
why should they not be?

Nairne finished his speech and sat down. The Pocotaligo king rose to
make the first response, but it was only a general talk, keeping clear of
substance, for he would wait to hear first what the others had to say and
then would speak more pointedly at the end. Asking his fellow kings to tell
what was in their hearts, he sat down and waited. There was silence in the
council house, all the men sitting perfectly still, their faces solemn as they
watched the low-burning fire in the central hearth. Then Yamasee Yahola,
one of the older kings, stood up and spoke with angry words, scolding
Nairne for the transgressions of the traders. Isaac began to lose heart. If the
older men were not with them, the younger ones surely would not be. But
as Yamasee Yahola went on, his tone softened, and he let it be known that

though he was not happy with the English, he still was not in favor of war. He knew the misery that war would bring, the painful loss of so many young men, the suffering of women and children. If the English governor would come among them and listen to them and see with his own eyes and hear with his own ears the problems they endured because of the arrogance and tyranny of so many of the traders, then surely the governor's heart would be moved and he would see to it that these things would not happen anymore. And he would remove the worst of the traders from the Yamasee country and not allow them to return.

Nairne nodded as Yamasee Yahola spoke, and the old man warmed to the cause of peace. The Yamasees and the English were one, he said. And because they were brothers, their differences would always be settled without bloodshed. For this his heart was ever thankful.

The old king sat down, and the room was no longer so still. Men shifted in their seats. There was a question of who would speak next. Isaac hoped it would be another of the older men, to keep the cause of peace rolling forward. But it was King Carlos who rose to his feet, leaving his blanket in a heap on his seat, his tall, muscular frame intimidating in the firelight as his intense eyes swept the room and came to rest on Thomas Nairne. The kings and headmen turned their attention to the Apalachee king, and all was still again, so quiet that the crackling of the fire could be heard.

"You appear to be very pleased to hear yourself called a brother of the Yamasees," King Carlos said to Nairne. He spoke in a loud, oratorical voice, using the Muskogee language of the Creeks, which most of the men in the room, including the Englishmen, could understand. "But this must be a joke you are making. When I myself say that the Yamasees are my brothers, I do not joke. The Apalachees and the Yamasees have walked together on a long and sorrowful path. Together our two peoples have known the tyranny of Spaniards, and when we thought our misery with them could be no greater, you sent your slave-catchers among us to steal our wives and children until we no longer could stand against you. All we could do to save ourselves was to leave our lands and come here to this country to be your hunters and your slave-catchers. And for this you expect us to call you our brother? You come to this council house from your settlement, where our wives and children are your slaves, and you expect us to call you our brother? You say your governor will come and give us a talk. But what difference will your governor make with this talk of his? What power does he have over the traders in our towns? What power does he have over the English planters who already defy him by coming across the Combahee River onto Yamasee lands? I will not have your governor stand before me and give me his lies. If you want us to call you our brother and walk with you in peace, then send home to us those of our people you are holding as your slaves. Move your planters off our lands. Take your traders from our towns and let us come into your settlement to trade. These are the actions we want from you. Do these things and we will begin to believe you. Do these things and we might call you our brother. But give us no more of your fine but empty words. We will listen to no more of your talk."

He sat down abruptly and pulled his red blanket tightly about his shoulders, closing himself to any further discussion.

Isaac glanced at Nairne, who gave away nothing in his impassive face. One of the older headmen was rising to speak, and as Nairne turned his attention to him, Isaac looked back at King Carlos, whose face was closed and set, the men around him as stony as he, deaf, all of them, to the mollifying words of the old headman who was now telling the council that they must not cut off talk with the English. Without talk, the old man said, there must be war. The English governor's offer to come in person and sit in council with them was evidence in itself of good faith, and it should be accepted with the expectation that the real changes of which King Carlos had spoken would follow. The old man sat down and another rose and spoke in the same vein, and that speaker was followed by another, the council dragging on into the evening with the peace faction dominating, until at last the Pocotaligo king made his own talk of reconciliation. The council closed with a consensus for peace. But there were a number of men who had chosen not to speak, and when King Carlos left the council house, all of those men went with him.

"You've not won Brims' people yet," said Isaac as he and Nairne walked outside into the cool April night.

"There's time," said Nairne. "It went well with the Yamasee kings, at least. When Brims hears of that, he'll have to reconsider. He cannot rise against us without the Yamasees."

"There were Yamasees with King Carlos," said Isaac. "They said not a word."

Nairne shrugged. "A few. But the venerable old fellows are with us. We'll have to wait for Brims himself to bring the others around."

"You seem to have little doubt that he will," said Isaac.

Nairne smiled. "It went well today. Better than I had hoped. Yamasee Yahola, the Pocotaligo king, the old beloved men, they all spoke out for peace. This trouble has been long in the making. We cannot expect to clear it up in a single day. But we've made a good beginning, and if I seemed cheered, it's because I can see an end to the thing."

"Then I'll let myself be cheered as well," said Isaac. "God knows, you've been at this business longer than I have."

"And I've seen everything," said Nairne. "There are no surprises left for me. The danger was real, there's no denying it, but that's past us now. The governor is turning his own hand to this, and the Indians know it. We can all sleep easy tonight."

"They'll be glad to hear that at Billy Bray's," said Isaac. "That's where I'm taking my lodging. Some of the traders have been gathering there, waiting for things to settle out. Come along and join us. It breaks in half the journey back."

"I think not," said Nairne. "I'm going to stay here tonight."

"It's hard to sleep in a council house," said Isaac. "It seems there are always a few fellows who talk all the night."

"I've slept through storms at sea," said Nairne. "I like the feel of a council house. It's like sleeping in a church."

"However you want it then," said Isaac. "But if you get lonely for your own kind, come down to Billy Bray's."

"Sam Warner will be here with me," said Nairne. "I'll do well enough. Give my regards to Billy."

"I will." Isaac paused for a moment, looking around the plaza. Most of the people had drifted away except for those whose homes were at a distance and would be staying on to sleep in the council house. "I wonder where our friend King Carlos has gone?"

"Back to Emperor Brims, I hope, to tell him that he's losing the Yamasees."

"Why do you suppose he was here today? It was not to come to this council. We only put out word of it last night."

Nairne shook his head. "Brims has his men everywhere these last few months. I've heard reports of them among the Cherokees, up north with the Catawbas, out west as far as the Chickasaws. But we're beginning now to undo all that work of his. I'm not going to worry about King Carlos. Whatever plans he had, this council has changed them, you can be sure."

Isaac nodded. Then he yawned and reached around to scratch his back. "What are your plans for tomorrow?"

"I'll stay here and solidify the peace faction," said Nairne. "Try to bring the young men over." He paused and then added, "Tomorrow is Good Friday, you know."

"No, I didn't realize that," said Isaac. "I lose track of such things when I'm up in this country. I'm glad you told me, though. It's a season no Christian should pass through unaware." He fell silent, and they stood for a few moments looking up at the stars. "Well," he said at last, "I'll be on my way."

"Sleep well," said Nairne.

"And you the same," said Isaac. He turned away and walked across the
plaza toward the place where his horse was tied.

✳ The men at Billy Bray's stayed up far into the night, talking at first of
the council at Pocotaligo and then of general matters of the trade, and then
hardly talking at all as they sat playing at cards. Isaac lost the value of an
entire pack of deerskins before he pulled out of the game and unrolled his
blanket on the floor. He was asleep as soon as he lay down, but then in a
short time he awoke again, the other four men still at it, talking and laughing. He rolled over, but could not go back to sleep. The candlelight seemed
too bright, his friends' voices too loud. At last he rose to his feet and picked
up his blanket and gun and started toward the door.

"We're not disturbing you, are we, Isaac?" said Billy Bray.

"Not a bit," said Isaac. "Only keeping me from sleeping, that's all."

"Then that's a relief. I feared we were disturbing you."

The men laughed and Isaac smiled and shook his head as he went out
into the night. He walked out behind the trading house until he could no
longer hear their voices and then trampled out a place among the palmettos
and spread his blanket. Crawling in between its folds, he stretched out and
lay for a time looking up at the stars, his thoughts going back to the council
house, to the silence of King Carlos and his men. He turned onto his side,
drowsiness settling over him again. For a moment he thought of Charity,
soft and warm beside him in the parlor bed. Then he drifted into sleep.

✳ Isaac awoke to the sound of footsteps in the palmetto, not twenty feet
away. He thought at first it must be one of the traders come out to urinate,
but then as he awoke more fully he realized that no one would walk out so
far for that. He thought then of an animal, a dog or an opossum, but the
sound was too stealthy, more like that of a man walking carefully. His hand
moved to his gun and he turned himself by slow degrees, looking around.
All was hidden by the night. Then the darkness lifted a bit, as if a lantern
had been lit, and he saw the man who had made the sound, an Indian
painted for war. Isaac ducked back beneath the palmetto, trying to gather
his wits and understand what it was he was seeing. The light, growing
brighter, was a fire somewhere—he could hear the crackle. He raised his
head to take another look and saw flames on the roof of the trading house,
and in the surrounding yard painted warriors, twenty men at least, most of
them clustered near the door. His heart was pounding now, almost shut-

ting out the other sounds. He cocked his gun and looked back over his shoulder to make sure there was no one behind him. Then he cupped one hand to his mouth.

"Billy Bray!" he called out as loudly as he could. "God help you, Billy! They've got you surrounded!"

The warriors whirled toward his voice, several raising their guns. Isaac kept down, taking aim at the man who had passed so close to him. He fired, then sprang to his feet and ran, plunging into the darkness, the sound of gunfire at his back, bullets breaking through the brush around him. He felt something hit his left side, as if he had been struck by a club, and he staggered almost to one knee, dropping his gun, but he regained himself and kept running. Behind him there was more gunfire, the men in the trading house fighting for their lives. Isaac guided himself by the sound of it, keeping it always to his back as he set his course for John Grissom's trading house almost three miles to the south. Only once did he reach down to feel the wound in his side, wet with blood, but his legs weakened when he felt it and so he left it alone, setting his mind on Grissom's place. There would be help for him there and help for Billy Bray. Let his legs keep running and his strength hold until he reached that place.

When he was yet half a mile from Grissom's he saw the light of a fire, a bright glow against the wider, paler light of the dawn. He stopped and stood panting, staring at the sight. Billy Bray's and John Grissom's. Had every trading house in the country been torched? Every trader murdered? Thomas Nairne and Sam Warner in the council house? It was Sam Warner who had first heard the warning that they would cut down the traders and then go on to the plantations.

Isaac walked over to a tree and leaned against it, feeling his wound again, knowing he must care for it now or risk bleeding to death. He probed it with his fingers. In the open flesh he felt a splinter of bone, and his stomach turned. The pain of it was throbbing and insistent. But maybe it would not kill him. Surely he could never have run this far if it were going to kill him. His rib was broken, but as yet no splinter had pierced his lung. Better not to think of that possibility. He could do nothing for it, only for the blood. He pulled off his linen shirt and began tearing it in pieces, fumbling in the gray darkness, his hands trembling. He pressed a wad of cloth against the wound, holding it awkwardly with one arm while he wrapped the rest of the shirt about himself to hold it, tying it firmly but not too tightly, because of the splintered rib. That was all he could do. Either it would be enough or it would not—he would know soon enough. He had to try now to reach the river and cross over to Port Royal to raise the alarm.

He started out again, altering his course to avoid Grissom's place, making himself run, relieved that he could still do it, feeling his life in his legs. How far past Grissom's to the river? Another mile? It was nothing. A mile was a stroll to a neighbor's house. His legs could run that far. They had run further than that from Billy Bray's. A mile was nothing. The pain was nothing. The bandage was stopping the blood. Surely it was. But he did not feel it to make sure.

The mile seemed twenty, and the closer he came to the river, the harder the way became, the land swampy from the spring rains, so that finally he could no longer run but only plunge and heave. But then at last he came to the river's edge and sat down heavily on the bank. Ahead, on the other side of the water, the sunrise was spreading above the flat plantation land. At a distance downstream there was a house, almost hidden in a grove of oaks. If he started here and swam as best he could, the current might carry him to it. He leaned back for a moment and closed his eyes, resting, then opened them again and looked out at the wide water. It would be impossible to swim even halfway across it. He got to his feet and searched the bank until he found a light driftwood log of a size he could manage. This might work. He dragged it into the water, feeling the cold shock as he waded out, shuddering when the water touched his wound, but going on deeper and then shoving off, holding the log, pushing it before him as he kicked along, keeping a slow but steady pace, his mind closed to all danger, to everything but the land on the other side.

※ When Isaac pulled himself from the river, his legs were failing and he could not stand. He lay on the bank, and for a few moments he let himself rest. Then he tried again. This time he made it up and stood there swaying, looking around for the house he had seen from the other side. The current had carried him past it and he was standing now at the edge of a field of young corn. On the other side of the field he saw the rough cabins of the plantation's slave quarters, and he staggered toward them.

The first person to see him was a young black boy who came wandering around the corner of one of the cabins. The boy stood and stared for a moment and then turned and ran back. After a moment the boy reappeared with a woman—perhaps his mother. She stopped near the corner of her cabin and looked out toward Isaac, watching him come.

"Hello," he called weakly, waving her to him.

She came out a few steps and then stopped uncertainly.

"Please," he said, aware of the spectacle he made, shirtless and wet, wrapped in a bloody bandage, bent and staggering like a drunkard who had been in a fight, or a murderer on the run. "Come closer, please," he said, motioning to her. "I'm a friend."

The woman advanced cautiously, the boy a few steps behind her. "You're hurt," she said as she neared him.

"Yes," he said, putting his hand to his wound. "The Yamasees are up in arms." The woman looked at him. Instead of the horror he expected to see, there was a light in her eyes. "They are killing everyone," he said, though it was difficult to speak. "Blacks and whites—everyone. Run tell your master. We must flee. All of us. Your life is in danger. Your son's life. Hurry now."

For a moment longer she stood looking at him, still uncertain, but then she turned and pulled up her skirt and started running across the field toward the big house.

"Go get someone to help me," Isaac said to the boy. "I can't walk much further."

The boy ran ahead but then forgot Isaac as he cried out the news that Indians were coming, that black people were being killed. The place was suddenly in confusion, people coming out of the cabins, talking loudly, mothers gathering up their children, everyone uncertain what to do. No one came to Isaac's aid until he had almost reached the first of the cabins. Then a man saw him and came to him, and Isaac clutched his arm, leaning on him. "I can scarcely walk," he murmured. "Help me to the house."

The man called another to help him, and together they supported him, the rest of the slaves following after them, until halfway to the house the master of the place came running out to meet them.

"What is this?" the man cried to Isaac. "Is it true? Have the Yamasees risen?"

"It's true," Isaac said weakly. He could hardly stand now. The black men were holding him up. "We must flee. Have you a boat large enough for all your people?"

"A sloop at my wharf," the man said breathlessly. His eyes were sweeping his plantation, looking at all he was about to lose.

"Send to your neighbors," Isaac murmured. "Raise the alarm." He closed his eyes, the last of his strength draining away. He felt himself collapsing, the black men gathering him up, one of them taking his legs. He was aware of being carried, of hurried voices all around him, and he wondered again about his lung. He was aware of being lowered into the boat. He felt its rocking and heard the soft lapping of the water against the vessel and the wharf. He lay there without opening his eyes, waiting for the rest of the people, remembering the fire in Billy Bray's roof, the Yamasee men in their war paint, changed and terrible. He tried to stop the images, not wanting

to think of what must have happened to his friends at Billy Bray's. And to
Thomas Nairne and Sam Warner. And to John Grissom. And to twenty
other men he could name. And of what might be happening now to the
planters up and down the river. Even to Sam Clutterbuck and Henry Hawkins. But not to Charity. Thank God in heaven for that. She was safe in
Charles Town. No need to worry about her. Only about his lung. And this
damned boat. Would they sit here all day until the Indians came?

He opened his eyes. There were black people all around him, tightly
packed. He could barely glimpse the sky. He raised his hand and tapped at
a man's leg, but so weakly that he failed to get his attention.

"We should be shoving off," he murmured, too quietly to be heard.
He closed his eyes again, all sound receding, darkness flowing over him
like water.

CHAPTER THIRTY-NINE

A dog barked in the first light of dawn, rousing Lucia from sleep. She rolled
onto her back and opened her eyes. The kitchen loft was dark, only a faint
gray light coming up from below.

"What dog was that?" Doll said from her mat. "Not one of ours."

"Did you hear it, too?" Lucia asked softly, rising up on her elbow. She
had not heard it clearly herself, coming as it had in her sleep, waking her
with only an impression that must have been shaped by her dreaming.

But now it came again, and the sound jolted through her. She had never
expected to hear that sound again.

She sat upright, then rose to her knees, her hand clasped over her mouth.

Doll sat up and looked at her. "What is it?" she demanded.

Lucia shook her head, unable to answer. She rose to her feet. The dog
barked again, and she turned to go toward the stairs. "Carlos," she said
softly. "It is Carlos."

Having said it, she grew calm. She went down into the kitchen, thinking
clearly, going neither too fast nor too slowly. She pulled open the door,
and standing in the doorway in the gray darkness, she cupped her hands
around her mouth and gave the answering call, a barking sound that trailed
off into a tremulous howl, just as she had done at Salvador's camp so many
years before.

Silence followed. Doll came down into the kitchen and stood behind her,
peering out into the darkness.

"Maybe it was only a dog," said Doll. "It sounded like a dog."

Lucia shook her head, waving her hand to silence her. She watched the yard, peering into the shadows of the great oaks with their Spanish moss hanging motionless in the stillness. Then she saw a movement. She stepped forward to see more clearly, a shadow visible for a moment, then gone, then visible again. Then another. He was not alone. She walked slowly into the yard, moving toward the dark shapes of the men. There were others now, many more than she expected. Her head was clear and calm and she tried to think what it meant that so many men were with him. It had to be a war party. What else could it be here in the dawn? And yet she had always imagined that he would come alone and they would run together, just the two of them, to some safe place that he would know.

As the distance closed, she could see the men's faces, contorted and strange because of the paint that was on them, red and black paint, like the slave-catchers in the woods outside San Augustín. She stopped, suddenly afraid, her hands clenched tightly at her sides. She searched for Carlos, her eyes going from one man to another until at last she saw him moving toward her through the trees, his face masked in paint, but his form and his way of walking familiar. She stood and stared, joyless and afraid. Dismayed, she shook her head, unable to speak.

He put out his hand and she reached for it and gripped it, finding it familiar and yet strange. She searched his face, but in the dim light she could not see his eyes. Neither she nor he spoke any words, and now their hands parted. She looked past him at his men, who paused restlessly behind him, guns in their hands and hatchets in their belts.

Doll came up beside her, her breath quick and loud in the stillness. She had tied her white kerchief on her head and was carrying an ax in her hand. "Have they come for war?" Doll asked breathlessly.

"Yes," said Lucia, her eyes returning to Carlos.

"Then tell them to follow me," said Doll.

Lucia turned and looked at her. Even in the darkness she could see the excitement in her face. "You stay out of it," said Lucia, reaching out to take away the ax.

But Doll stepped away from her. "This way," she called softly to the men and started toward the house. Some of the warriors followed.

"No," said Lucia, starting after them.

Carlos gripped her arm and pulled her back. She turned and looked at him. For a moment his eyes moved over her face. Then he said, "Let them go. You wait here."

"No," she said. "Henry will kill her!" She pulled free of him and ran, following after the warriors. In the darkness she saw Doll's white kerchief disappear through the doorway of the house. The men streamed after her, Lucia pushing in among them, straining to reach Doll. But she was losing ground, the warriors blocking her way as they crowded into the hallway and up the stairs. Lucia looked up and saw Doll ascending, ax in hand. Then she was at the top, at the door of Henry Hawkins' chamber. On the stairs Lucia craned to see her, watching as Doll tried the door and then threw herself against it, pushing it open a few inches against some furniture Henry had shoved against it. Lucia gained the last steps. The warriors were at the door now and the furniture blockade was nothing at all to them, the door opening into the chamber where the tall bed stood in the corner with its curtains closed and still.

As she raised her ax, Doll's battle cry filled the air, an African shout ringing out high and shrill. The warriors surged after her into the room, raising their own whoops and cries until Lucia could not hear Doll anymore. But she could see her in her white kerchief, her ax waving. Doll reached for the curtain of the bed and jerked it back, and there was Henry Hawkins on his knees, white-faced, two pistols in his hands.

"Doll!" Lucia screamed. Henry fired and then fired again, and Doll fell toward him, her ax cutting into his shoulder, his eyes wide, and then the warriors were on him, their hatchets chopping, all of them gathered around. There was a pause. Then someone was waving Henry's bloody scalp and the whoops filled the air again as they surged back out of the room. Lucia stood still as they rocked past her and were gone.

She did not hurry to the bed. Doll was lying face down, her kerchief fallen away. Lucia could see her absolute stillness and the blood spreading into the sheets beneath her head. She put her hand on Doll's back, feeling the warmth of her body, and then touched her hair, stroking it, but she did not turn her over. She looked at Henry Hawkins lying in a heap, covered with blood. Then suddenly she remembered Sam Clutterbuck. Wheeling around, she ran down the stairs and out of the house.

Daylight was spreading over Fairmeadow. Lucia raced through the yard toward the quarters, ignoring the Apalachee men who were wandering about the place, investigating the different buildings, gathering up booty. Surely Clutterbuck had slipped away. He would have heard the war cries and made his escape. But if he had not . . . She ran faster, past the blacksmith shop where a knot of frightened slaves had gathered.

"Lucia!" someone called after her. "What should we do?"

"Nothing!" she answered and ran on into the quarters, her bare feet pounding hard against the sandy street, her breath coming short. On the other side of the quarters, the door of Sam's cabin was standing open. She ran in at full speed, catching the doorway as she came through it and swinging to a stop, her eyes sweeping the room, hoping to find it empty. But there were men here, warriors, and Sam was lying face down on the floor.

"Is he dead?" She struggled to catch her breath as she looked about at the men. There was Carlos, leaning against the wall by the window, holding Sam's whip in his hands, toying with it. As her eyes met his, tears sprang up and blurred her vision. "Have you killed him?" she asked in a whisper. "He was my friend."

Carlos shook his head. "We have not killed him."

She brushed her hand over her eyes and looked down at Sam and saw now that his hands were tied behind his back.

"Is he hurt?" she asked, looking back at Carlos, wishing the paint were gone from his face. He was watching her closely, his hands turning the whip.

"No," he said. "He is not hurt."

"What will you do with him?"

"We were discussing it," said Carlos, his voice distant and strange. "What do you say we should do?"

"Let him go."

One of the men laughed.

Carlos looked curiously at Lucia. "He is the overseer, is he not? This is his whip?"

"But he is not a bad man," Lucia said. She turned her eyes away, uncomfortable with the intensity of his gaze. "He protected me. He stopped the master from beating me. He kept him from my bed." She would not look at him, nor at Sam, but stared out the window, seeing nothing, aching with the pain of this day.

"Cut him free," Carlos said.

She looked and saw that he was speaking to the warrior who had been laughing and who now sobered and stood for a long moment without moving. Finally the man drew out his knife and walked over and flicked it through the cord that bound Sam's hands. Then he left the cabin without looking back. The other warriors seemed uneasy.

Sam pushed himself up on his elbows and sat up, surprised that his life had been returned to him. He did not know who Carlos was or why he would listen to Lucia. Sam nodded to her. She returned the nod and then turned around and left the cabin.

Outside the air had filled with smoke. Beyond the quarters she could see flames where the big house was burning. Doll's body burning. She walked a little distance to a pine log and sat down, feeling near tears as she rested her head in her hands. After a moment Carlos came out of the cabin, and as she watched him come toward her, she tried to see beneath the warpaint to the Carlos she had once known. He stopped a short distance from her and stood for a moment in silence. Then he said, "I have come."

"You have come," she answered quietly. "A war leader."

"Yes. And I must keep my distance. My men would leave me if they saw me having too much to do with you. My power would be spoiled, they would say, from being with a woman."

"I understand," she said. "That is a safe distance, I think." She looked down and pulled up a sprig of grass and twirled it slowly in her fingers.

"I do not believe that myself," he said. "But they do. They would leave me."

"So you still have your Spanish mind," she said.

He made no reply and in the silence she toyed with the blade of grass, splitting it down the middle with her thumbnail and then dropping it to the ground. She looked up and saw him watching her. "I wish I could see you without that paint. It is hard to know you like this."

"I have not changed," he said. "Nor have you. I am amazed at how much you are the same."

"But I *have* changed," she said quietly. "And so have you, I think."

"Perhaps. It has been many years."

"I hear you are a chief now."

"Finally," he said, one corner of his mouth turning up in a wry smile.

"They call you king."

"The English do that." He was no longer smiling. "They try to flatter and tame us with empty titles. But today we are cutting them off. We are finished with them."

"This is just beginning, then?"

"Yes, this very day."

"And you are not alone?"

"Not at all alone. The Yamasees are with us. The Cherokees. The Catawbas. The Alabamas. All the others. Everyone. It is the English who are alone now."

"And from here you will go on fighting?"

"Yes."

Lucia looked down and pulled up another blade of grass. "What am I supposed to do?"

"One of my men will take you across the river to the Yamasee country. There are places there in the swamps where the Yamasee women are making camps in which to hide until it is safe to go back to their towns."

"Will you know where I am?"

"Yes, certainly."

She turned the grass blade slowly in her fingers, watching it, thinking.

"That man they killed," she said, nodding toward the smoke from the burning house. "This is his name." She pointed to the scars on her cheeks, one at a time. "I buried a poison root to kill him and now he is dead. But that woman who died with him was someone I loved. This same thing has happened to me before. Now I am afraid of killing. It cannot be controlled."

"Your friend was not afraid," said Carlos. "She knew the danger but was not afraid."

Lucia nodded. "She had the courage of a mother cat when a dog has killed her young."

"We are all like that now," said Carlos.

"I know that is true." She let the grass fall from her fingers and sat for a moment watching the ground. Then she looked up beyond him to the cabin. "What will you do with Sam Clutterbuck?" she asked.

"Is that his name?"

"Yes."

"We will leave him here when we go."

"Your men do not like sparing an Englishman."

"Nor do I," he said. "It surprises me that you would have such feeling for a man who has enslaved you."

"Yes," she said. "It is surprising. But I can remember when you cared for the priest."

"Ana cared for him even more. Was it like that with this man?"

She looked up at him, his eyes intent on her. She wanted to say no, it was not like that. But she only shook her head and looked away.

CHAPTER FORTY

Lucia sat with Daphne and Juba just outside the tiny, bark-shingled lean-to that they shared in the hidden camp of the Yamasee women. Nearby were the shelters of the other Fairmeadow slaves. The mosquitoes from the swamp swarmed thickly in the spring heat, and Lucia concentrated on the basket she was weaving, trying to ignore them.

"No good," said Daphne, brushing the mosquitoes from her face. "This place is no good. How far to Saint Augustine?"

"There are mosquitoes there, too," said Lucia.

"Mosquitoes like this? I never hear that."

"Not like this," said Juba, who was sitting on the other side of Daphne. "If Saint Augustine be like this, we would hear. How far?"

Lucia shook her head. "Ten days. Twenty. Far enough." All that the Fair-

meadow slaves thought of now was how to get to Saint Augustine, the sanc-
tuary they had always dreamed of reaching for as long as they had been in
Carolina. The Spaniards would let them live there in freedom. They would
not be slaves anymore.

"People starve in San Augustín," said Lucia. "Carlos and I almost starved."

"Long time ago," Juba said stubbornly.

Lucia shrugged. It was true. And who could say where they should go?
Maybe they would be safer with the Spaniards than with her own people.
At least San Augustín would always be there—the English could never
overrun the fortress. But her own people might lose their war and the slaves
be taken back again. And she with her scars was as vulnerable as they. Her
skin might as well be black.

"If you truly want to go," said Lucia, "someone will show you the way."

"When?" asked Daphne.

Lucia shook her head. "I don't know that."

"When this war be lost," Juba said bluntly.

Lucia said nothing. It was only a week since the uprising began and already the English militia was advancing toward the river, pressing against
the Yamasee country. The Indian men were trying to turn them back, but
if they failed, the Yamasee country would have to be abandoned. These
lands were too close to the English, too hard to defend. The fight would
have to be carried on from a greater distance, where the English would not
dare to come after them. This, at least, was the talk from the men who came
daily to the camp, a few at a time, bringing plunder, visiting their families,
relaying news. Carlos was never among them, nor were any of his men.
Lucia had heard nothing from him since that morning at Fairmeadow almost a week ago.

"If they lose this war, where you go?" asked Daphne. She rubbed her
hands over her arms, chasing mosquitoes.

"I don't know," said Lucia. "To the Creek country, I suppose."

"Come with us," said Daphne. "We stay together."

"You come with me," said Lucia.

Daphne shook her head. "There be ships in Saint Augustine. Maybe
someday we go home."

Lucia made no reply. In the silence she worked a long piece of split cane
in and out around the growing sides of what was to be a large burden
basket, double woven for strength. She had been working on it for two days
now, ever since she had first heard that the English militia was advancing.

"Will your husband come and tell you where to go?" asked Daphne.

"I don't know," said Lucia, keeping on with her work, her fingers moving
swiftly, her concentration focused there.

"He should come," said Daphne. "How he gonna find you when you leave this place?"

"Maybe he would not wish to find me," she said quietly.

"Not wish it? Your husband?"

"Once my husband. Perhaps not now."

"But he came to Fairmeadow."

"He came to set me free."

"That be all, you think?"

Lucia shrugged. "I don't know."

Daphne was silent for a moment. Then she said, "You think he has another wife?"

"Perhaps."

"A man can have two wives."

"If the first wife allows it," said Lucia. She tucked in the last of the length of split cane and reached for another from the pile beside her.

Again Daphne was silent, unsure whether to press her questions further. But finally she asked, "Would you allow it?"

"I don't know," said Lucia. "I did not share him before."

"Sharing a man be better than being alone."

"I am used to being alone."

Daphne shook her head. "Not me," she said quietly. "I ain't never gonna be used to it."

On the other side of her Juba nodded in agreement.

Lucia said nothing, trying not to think of Carlos, not wanting to feel the emptiness that came whenever she recalled that morning at Fairmeadow, seeing him there after so many years, talking to him while he stood painted and distant, preoccupied with war, so different from what she had always imagined. They had been together in Apalachee for so short a time, not even a year, and she so young. Had she ever known him at all? At so young an age, what does anyone know?

"It's that bird girl," said Juba. "Look here. She comes."

Lucia looked up and smiled to see the little girl they had been watching since the first day they came to the camp. Everyone watched her, a girl so small, hardly three years old, with a great blue heron, taller than she, that followed her everywhere she went. She came toward them very deliberately, paying no attention to the gangly bird loping along at her heels—she was concentrating on a small pottery bowl she carried in both hands. Every now and then she raised her eyes from the bowl without lifting her head and looked ahead at them, smiling a little, half shy and half bold.

"You have come," Lucia said as she approached.

"I brought you this," said the little girl without formality, speaking in

Apalachee instead of Yamasee. She stopped and held out the bowl to Lucia, 339
the heron stopping to wait patiently behind her.

"Is it bear oil?" asked Lucia, looking into the bowl.

The little girl nodded. "My mother told me to bring it. She puts a good smell in it. But mosquitoes don't like it." Her voice had a pretty sing-song tone.

"That is good," said Lucia, nodding gratefully. "We need this. Tell her that she lifts our hearts."

The little girl was not listening. Looking at the unfinished basket, she leaned over to touch it.

"Are you making a basket?" she asked in her lilting voice.

"Yes," said Lucia, holding it up for her to see.

"Why?"

"Because I need one," said Lucia.

"Why?"

"Because I have nothing to carry things in."

"Why?"

Lucia put her hand on her hip and smiled at her, shaking her head. "Do you have the why disease?"

"What?" asked the little girl, not understanding.

"She be a question-asker," said Daphne.

"What did she say?" the girl asked Lucia.

"She said you have the why disease. She said it in English."

"Why?"

"Because she does not speak our language."

"Why?"

"So that you will ask questions," said Lucia. "Where did you get the bird?"

"My father gave him to me."

"When it was little?"

"Like this," said the girl, holding her hand down close to the ground. "He got big." She turned around and looked proudly at the bird.

"What do you feed him?"

"He likes fish."

"Does he have a name?"

"Baby."

Lucia smiled. "That is a good name. What about you? Do you have a name?"

The little girl laughed. "I *have* to have a name."

"Then what is it?"

"Blue Heron's Mother."

"That sounds like a new name."

She shrugged. "A little bit new."

"It is a long name for such a little girl."

"My mother calls me Blue. She likes it shorter."

"So do I," said Lucia. "It suits you better."

"Why?" asked Blue.

Lucia ignored the question. "What do they call your mother?" she asked.

"She used to be called Alap Juana. Now they call her Peeper."

"Like the little peeper frog in spring?"

Blue nodded. "It makes people happy to hear the peepers sing. That's what my father says."

"Your mother must be Apalachee," said Lucia.

"How do you know?"

"Because the name she used to have is Apalachee. And because that is the language you are speaking."

"My mother is Apalachee," said Blue, as if reciting an answer to a question she was often asked, "and my father is Yamasee."

"I thought he might be," said Lucia. "Tell your mother that the bear oil makes us happy. Tell her we would like for her to come visit us."

"Me, too?"

Lucia smiled. "Yes. You must be sure to come back again. And bring Baby with you."

Blue nodded. She stood for a moment looking at Lucia, smiling a little, and then she turned and started away.

"We will see you again," Lucia said after her.

Blue looked back briefly, still smiling. Then she skipped a few steps and began to run, the heron following after her in quick, gawky strides.

Daphne laughed. "I never saw such a thing."

"She calls it Baby," said Lucia. She picked up the bowl of bear oil and offered it to Daphne. "Rub some of this on your skin. It will help with the mosquitoes."

"I need it, then," said Daphne, dipping her fingers into the scented oil.

"That woman was kind to send it," said Lucia. "Her name is Peeper. We will have to find out which one she is."

"She be the only one with a heron standing at her fire," said Juba. "Easy to find."

Lucia laughed. "Easy-easy," she said, handing the bear oil to Juba.

Lucia was deep in sleep when Cajoe's voice came through to her, calling her name. She heard it but did not awaken, drawing the sound of it into her dream where Cajoe was a boy in shirttail, as she had first known him

in the house of John Hawkins in Charles Town. Then a hand was shaking
her shoulder, the dream falling away, and she opened her eyes to see him
leaning over her in the darkness, a glow of firelight behind him. She sat up,
confused, looking from Cajoe to the fire burning brightly in the hearth at
the entrance of the lean-to, the same fire Juba had covered with ashes before they went to sleep.

"Did you stir that up?" she asked.

"Yes. You have to get up."

"What is it?" She came fully awake, pulling her blanket up.

"Something has happened," said Cajoe. "The whole camp is stirring. Go
find out for us what it is."

Daphne and Juba were awake now, sitting up and listening.

Lucia got to her feet and went out. The fires in the camp were all burning
brightly, the people up and moving around. The sky was clear, the nearly-
full moon shining in the west, dawn approaching. She walked quickly
among the crowded shelters to the lean-to that she had been told belonged
to Peeper, the mother of Blue, the bird girl.

"My sister," said Lucia, stopping by the fire and looking in. A young
woman was kneeling on the floor, carefully packing her belongings into a
worn pack basket. When she looked up, Lucia recognized Blue's features in
her face and knew that she was Peeper. There was another, older woman
there, folding a blanket, who looked as if she might be Peeper's mother. A
very old man was sitting by the fire. Blue still slept on her mat, tangled in a
red blanket.

"You have come," said Peeper in a friendly tone. She waved her hand
toward a pot by the fire. "There is sofkee."

"You must tell me what is happening," said Lucia. "No one has told us."

Peeper stopped her work and sat back on her heels. "Some of our men
have just brought word," she said calmly. "The English are coming into the
country. They have divided, some coming by the north, some by the south.
Our warriors tried to stop the northern ones near Salkehatchie River, but
they failed. The ones in the south are not being opposed. We have to get
out while there is time."

Lucia nodded, anxiety tightening in her. She stood in silence, watching
Peeper go back to her work. Then she asked, "Were many killed at Salkehatchie? Many of our men?"

"Some were killed," said Peeper. "I do not know how many."

Again there was silence, Lucia thinking of Carlos—he would have been
there, she was sure. But Peeper must also be worried about her man. All
the people in the camp would be worried.

"Where do you intend to go?" asked Lucia.

"To the Creek towns," said Peeper.

"Is everyone going there?"

"No. Some are going back to the Spaniards."

"That is where the people who are with me wish to go."

Peeper nodded. "They would be welcome, I am sure."

"I will tell them," said Lucia, turning away.

"My sister," said Peeper.

Lucia looked back at her.

"Where will you be going?"

"To the Creek towns," said Lucia.

"Then come and walk with us, if you wish."

"That would please me," said Lucia. "My heart is full."

"And mine," said Peeper with a smile.

☀ In the dim light of early dawn Lucia stood with her friends from Fairmeadow—Daphne and Juba, Cajoe, Chany, Peter, Will, Little Will, Sheba, Tickey, all the others. They talked quietly, laughing a little, trying to hide their fears.

"Cajoe can talk to the Spaniards for you," said Lucia. "And some of these Yamasees speak Spanish. He can talk to them." Her burden basket rested on the ground beside her, the tumpline in her hand.

"I've forgotten how to speak Spanish," said Cajoe.

"Think of those days in Bella's kitchen," said Lucia. "It will come back to you."

The fires in the camp had been extinguished and the people were gradually dividing into two groups. The ones who were going south to the Spaniards were the ones whose hearts were not in the fight. Many of them were older people and they spoke of returning to their homes in Guale, as if the Spaniards could give them any more protection now than they were able to give twenty years ago.

"Those are the ones you are going with," said Lucia, putting her hand on Cajoe's arm and pointing to that group.

Cajoe nodded and adjusted the blanket that he carried in a roll across his back. "Maybe we will see you again," he said.

"Maybe," she said, her fingers pressing gently against his arm. Then she turned to the others, briefly touching them, wishing them well, lingering especially with Daphne and Juba, clasping their hands. Then they began moving away. She turned from them and stooped down to fix the tumpline on her forehead, and when she straightened up with the basket on her back, she was alone.

She went over to the group that was bound for the Creek country and found Peeper among them by spotting the heron first. When she came up to them, Blue was crying. Lucia set her basket on the ground. "What is the matter?" she asked the child, putting a hand on her head.

Blue pulled free of her and would not answer.

Peeper shook her head. "It is the bird. I told her that when he gets tired, we will have to leave him behind. We are going too far for him to follow."

Blue looked up at her mother, misery in her face. "I could carry him," she pleaded.

"You will have to be carried yourself," said Peeper. "We will find you another bird when we get to the Creek country."

Blue shook her head, the tears flowing again. "I want Baby."

"Then I will carry him for you," said Lucia. "When he gets tired I will put him in my basket."

Blue looked at her, brushing her hand hard against her tears, then looked at her mother to see if it really could be true.

Peeper shook her head. "He is such a big bird, my daughter. She has no room to carry him."

"I think I can find room," said Lucia. "We will wrap him in a blanket and stuff him in."

Blue looked at her and smiled. "He will not like it very much."

"We will do it to him anyway, " said Lucia.

Blue nodded. "Even if he cries."

"Let him cry," said Lucia.

"He is just a baby," said Blue. She rubbed her hand over her nose, feeling happy again.

✹ They had traveled for three days, walking at a steady pace, the way getting easier as the land rose and the low coastal swamps were left behind. Every day more warriors came to join them, men who were leaving the fighting to come find their families and see them safely to the new country. As the number of men swelled and the distance from the English settlement grew longer, everyone began to feel easier, until now, on this third night, they dared to light fires at their camping place. On this night, too, they took the trouble to make shelters, for the sky had clouded during the day and rain seemed certain before the night was over.

Lucia made her own small shelter, separate from Peeper, whose husband had finally come in on that day. Lucia had watched their silent reunion and was glad for Peeper's high spirits now that her husband was with her again. But that was all she could bear to see. She could not watch them in the night, their glances of contentment while they ate, their easy conversation by the fire, and then, while Blue and the old people slept, their time together beneath their blanket. Peeper deserved her happiness, and Lucia did not want to be there to begrudge it to her. So she threw up a separate shelter, covering it thickly with boughs, making it just large enough for herself to lie in wrapped in her blanket on a deep, soft bed of leaves and pine straw. She built a small fire on the open side of the shelter and had a pile of wood with which to feed the fire through the night.

It was the first time since the morning Carlos had come to Fairmeadow that she had been truly alone, and she lay awake long after the camp had grown silent, the emptiness that she had felt since that morning slipping now into sadness. Her thoughts drifted over him, trying again and again to see him, to know him in the man that she had seen that day, distant and strange, kindling nothing in her that was old, nothing but an empty feeling. And now sadness. Peeper at the next fire in the arms of her man. She here alone. Always alone from her earliest years. So few times had there ever been others. And always she returned to her loneliness, as now, in her separate shelter, solitary by her fire.

She slept a little while. Then the rain began to fall and she awoke, and for a few moments she lay lost in the darkness, unable to remember where she was until lightning lit the night and showed her the boughs of her shelter and the white ashes of her fire. As thunder rumbled in the darkness, she sat up and stirred the fire, bringing up the still glowing coals and adding more wood. For a little time she sat watching the flames as they moved up into the wood and threw their light into the rain outside. Then she lay down again, shivering a little. She closed her eyes and tried to sleep. But the thunder grew louder, the rain pouring down, until finally she gave up on sleep and turned onto her side to watch the fire, its flames whipping about in the wind.

She was still watching when he came. She had heard voices somewhere in the camp and then silence again. The rain had almost stopped and her eyes were heavy with returning sleep, the fire burning lower now, more serenely, as she watched it. Then he was there beyond the fire, coming out of the darkness, soaked by the rain, stooping to look in at her, uncertain he had found the right place. She rose up soundlessly on one elbow, watching him as he recognized her in the firelight. For a moment he did not move but just looked at her, the rain dripping from his head and shoulders and running down his back. There was no war paint on him and his face was as she had always known it, older but the same. He wore a breechcloth and torn moccasins and carried a dripping blanket beneath his arm. She sat up, and he stooped lower and came into the shelter.

She moved to make a place for him. "I built it small," she said softly. "I was not expecting you."

"It is good," he said and tossed aside his soaked blanket and sat down
on hers. He leaned toward the fire, trembling slightly. She put her hand on
his back.

"You are chilled," she said softly. "So cold."

He nodded, his body tense and shivering.

"Here," she said, reaching down for the blanket. "Get up. We will pull
it over us."

He raised himself and let her pull the blanket free. As he sat down again
she put it over him, watching him now, waiting for him to look at her.
When he did, she smiled.

"Come on," she said, reaching out for him. He came to her, slipping his
arms around her as they sank down into the softness of the bed that she
had made, the blanket over them, she holding him, feeling him cold and
wet against her warmth, his arms so tight about her that they gave her pain,
she saying nothing, only holding him more tightly, her face pressed hard
against him.

CHAPTER FORTY-ONE

It was summer in the Creek country and the war dragged on. Raiding parties were going out continually against the English settlements. Lucia stood
at the edge of the stream in the first light of dawn and sang her song of
greeting to the Sun. Behind her Carlos, home from a raid, sat against a
tree and watched her. The day would be another hot one, the summer past
its solstice now, the heat unrelenting. But toward evening another shower
would come, enough to sustain the corn and cool the air for a little time.
It was a good summer for corn, hardly a day going by without some evening rain.

Lucia finished the song and knelt down beside the stream, dipping up
water to her head and breast, four times, washing herself in the power of
the Under World. Then she sat back on her heels, her hands on her knees
as she watched the morning light fill the world, streaming through the trees
in shafts of yellow mist.

"My mother said I was born in the dawn. Sometimes I almost feel that I
remember it."

"If you want to say you remember it," said Carlos, "I will say I believe you."

She laughed and got to her feet. "And neither of us would be telling the
truth."

He shrugged. "So long as we agree."

"I do not remember it," she said, coming over to him.

He reached up and caught her hand. "What did you see in the water?" he asked.

"Nothing. I do not look there anymore. I no longer want to know the future."

"But when I am out on the war trail, do you look to see if I will come back?"

"No. I hoe my corn and wait. And now here you are, home again and safe."

"But not all of us," Carlos said quietly. "I lost a man."

"And his wife knew he would be lost," said Lucia. "She paid a shaman to look into the water, and he saw that her husband would die in this raid. Her sadness started then, when you had only been gone a day. She should have waited for the future to come find her."

"Are you waiting for that?"

She shook her head. "I do not think about it. This is enough. This time since the spring. It is so much more than I ever expected."

"All you needed was a field of corn," he said, teasing her now as he let go of her hand. "Give a woman a cornfield of her own and she will be happy."

She smiled. "Is that what men say? We need more than that to keep us happy. But come see how my corn has grown while you were away. The second planting has already tasseled."

He got up and went with her, leaving the shade of the riverbank and walking out through the cornfields that filled the fertile floodplain. The early morning sun was warm and pleasant. Overhead two bluejays were chasing a crow, harassing it without mercy, breaking the stillness with their cries.

"That is you," said Lucia, stopping to look up at the jays. "The crow is the Englishman. Watch how they drive him out of their country."

"Is this a reading of the future?" he asked, shielding his eyes from the sun as he watched the birds.

"No," she said quietly. "I am only talking."

✴ The sun was well up when they returned to the town, the heat of the day settling in. Carlos went to the council house and Lucia returned alone to their household beside the plaza. It was a small compound for a chief. There was only the house itself and a granary in the yard, no other store-houses, no dwellings for different wives. Stopping at the outside fire, she put down a basket of squashes she had picked from the vines beneath her corn, and then she went into the house to straighten the mats and blanket on the pole-framed bed and to sweep into a corner the pieces of a pot she had broken the night before when she bumped it against a hearthstone. She was so out of practice in making pottery that this first firing of hers had been a poor one, the pots too fragile. But Peeper had promised to help her next time.

She ate a little sofkee, dipping it from the pot by the door, then gathered up a bundle of dyed split cane and a half-finished mat and went out to the shade of the portico to work. When Carlos had first brought her to this place in the spring, nothing had told her more clearly that he had no other wife than the lack of cane mats in his house. There had been a mat on his bed and one by the hearth that was almost worn out from being moved back and forth from the inside to the outside fire. The walls were bare and ugly, the bed hard and uncomfortable. But all of it had seemed lovely to her, this house where no wife had been living. She never asked to know anything beyond that. There had been other women, surely—it was only reasonable to assume so. But so long as they were gone now, so long as there was no wife to claim him, it was all so much more than she had expected. And so she found a special contentment in weaving the mats, Carlos drifting easily in her mind, weaving through her thoughts like the splits of cane.

Looking up, she saw Peeper coming into the yard.

"My sister," she called cheerfully without getting up. "You have come. There is sofkee inside."

"Thank you," said Peeper, showing no interest in sofkee. She had not come to sit and visit. "It would lift my heart if you would come home with me. The heron is sick."

"How sick?" asked Lucia, putting aside her work.

Peeper shrugged. "How can you know with a bird? He is not himself. He sits alone in a corner and refuses to eat."

"Is Blue upset about it?"

"Not yet. She thinks you can cure him."

"My medicine is not meant for birds," said Lucia. "I hope you told her that."

"I did, but she does not understand."

"Let me get my medicine basket. We will go."

Lucia went inside and got what she thought she might need, and then she and Peeper set out through the town at a leisurely pace, the sun too hot for great exertion. In the shade of the trees the horseflies came buzzing about them, and one followed them out into the sun, diving back and forth until it finally landed on Lucia's back, where Peeper slapped it dead. Lucia pretended to stagger and almost fall beneath the blow and they laughed, walking on toward the edge of the town where the new houses had been built by the people who had come that spring from the Yamasee country.

When they reached the yard of Peeper's house, Peeper's mother stopped pounding corn and followed them inside. Blue sat alone in the middle of the floor, playing with two deerskins and a collection of potsherds. The old man, the uncle of Peeper's mother, sat on the side of his bed smoking his pipe. He nodded to Lucia when she came in, but said nothing.

Blue looked up from her play. "Baby is sick," she announced without any great concern. "You have to give him some medicine, Lucia."

"Where is he?" asked Lucia.

"He is over there," said Blue, waving her hand toward the corner and going back to her make-believe.

Peeper led her over toward a corner where the ends of two beds came almost together and made a little place apart. The bird sat huddled with his legs folded beneath him, his feathers ruffled as if he were cold. He was still as Lucia leaned over him. She looked around at Blue. "He seems very sick," she said bluntly to the girl.

"Give him some medicine," said Blue. "Something from your basket."

"I will try," said Lucia. "But I want you to understand that it might not work."

Blue's face fell. She got up and came over to the heron and stood looking down at it.

"I will see what I can do," said Lucia, putting her hand on the girl's head. Blue leaned against her leg.

Then as Blue watched her every move, Lucia brewed up some medicine and sprinkled it over the heron, singing a song four times, keeping time with a gourd rattle, making a circle of power around the bird.

"That will cure him if anything will," the old uncle said as she finished.

But the bird had shown no change and Lucia did not feel hopeful as she went outside to sit in the shade with Peeper and her mother. After a little while the old uncle came out and beckoned to her. "Come see the bird," he said.

They went in and found Blue asleep and the heron standing by the bed on which she lay. His feathers were still not perfectly smooth, but they were not so ruffled as before. His eyes were closed and he seemed to be resting.

"Look at that," Peeper said quietly, shaking her head in amazement. "I was sure he would die."

"He still looks sick," said Lucia.

"But he is standing up," said Peeper. "He is better."

"I am glad to see it," said the old uncle. He walked slowly back to his bed and sat down, taking out his pipe to refill it.

"I will come back in the morning to give the medicine again," said Lucia. "We should give it to him for four days if we want to be sure."

"I would not have you do so much," said Peeper. "Not for a bird."

"Let her come back," said the old uncle. "The bird is getting better. Let her come back and finish the cure."

"I will come back tomorrow," said Lucia. Picking up her medicine basket she went over to the sleeping child and lightly touched her hair. Then she went out into the midday heat and home to her house by the plaza.

※ In the evening Lucia sat with Carlos by the fire in their yard, the last of the summer sunset fading away, the stars bright in the new darkness. The sound of wailing floated over the town as the wife of the dead warrior mourned his death. Always it was someone, the men forever going out against the English, new widows forever being made.

"When will you go again?" Lucia asked.

"I will stay for a little while," said Carlos. "How could I leave all this good food?" He looked at her playfully from the corner of his eye.

"Is that what keeps you here?"

"You know it is not." He lay down on the mat, resting his head in her lap.

Looking down at him, she watched his face in the firelight. "Have you ever been back to Apalachee?" she asked quietly.

He nodded. "I went there once. There was no one there."

"Did you look at for my grandmother?"

"I went to your mother's homestead, and I could see that your grandmother had been living there. There were some ruins of a hut. And there was a little place she had cleared for corn. But it was growing back up in brush again."

"There was no sign of her? No bones?"

"Maybe beneath the ruins of the hut. I did not look."

"I am glad that you went back there."

"It was strange to see the land so empty. No one in all of Apalachee."

"It is waiting for us," she said. "When we get rid of the English, we can go back again."

"Where would you go?" he asked.

"Home."

"To your mother's homestead?"

"Of course. Where did you think?"

He smiled. "I knew it would be there. You have not changed."

"But I have," she said quietly. There was silence then and they watched the smoke as it curled above the fire and went up into the warm night air.

"Maybe not to my mother's homestead after all," she said at last. "If you are still a chief when we go back, we will need to live in your town."

"But if you would rather have your homestead, I would be satisfied with that. Let someone else be chief."

"No, I can live in a town. Truly. So long as I have my own cornfield. And so long as I do not have to be the White Sun Woman and have everyone drop their eyes to the ground when I walk by."

"Salvador was wrong about that," said Carlos. "It did not help Apalachee at all."

"But the song is good," she said. "There have been times when I felt that if I did not sing it, the Sun would go down and never come back again. Through all those bad years, it seemed to me that my song was the only thing that kept it coming back."

"Then you should keep on singing it. You should never stop."

She brushed her fingers over his hair. "Do you truly believe we can win against the English?"

For a moment he did not answer. Then he said, "If we can stay together, we can win. But in truth, I am worried about the Cherokees."

"They are not with us?

"Not completely. But neither are they against us. Not yet."

"Why do they waver?"

"The trade. They hate to lose it. They do not have so many guns as we have."

"They can get them from the French. And from the Spaniards, even."

"The English have the best trade. Their guns are cheaper. But we should not be talking about this now. The Cherokees are not against us. It is like you said this morning, let the future come find us. We will not go looking for it." He reached up and took her hand and held it against his chest, and for a time they were quiet.

The fire was dying low, the wood collapsing into a heap of glowing coals. Lucia reached over and threw on a fresh piece of wood, and then another. Through the sparks and smoke rolling up, she saw Peeper coming into the yard.

"Here is Peeper," she said quietly to Carlos, giving him a nudge. He sat up slowly, groaning like an old man, and she laughed and pushed him up the last part of the way. "My sister," she said to Peeper, reaching for an

empty mat and pulling it around to a place that was not in the smoke.
"Come sit with us."

Peeper shook her head. "I cannot stay. The bird is dying, truly dying now. I am ashamed to keep bothering you about a thing so small, but if you could come home with me again, just for a moment, to show Blue you cannot save it. I know you are here at your fire and ready to go to sleep, but . . ."

Lucia rose to her feet. "It is all right. I will come."

Carlos came with them. The three walked together through the town, past fires where people sat with family and friends, some joking and laughing, others quietly talking, and others silent as they watched the summer night. At Peeper's house her husband and her mother were by the outside fire. Carlos stopped to talk with them while Lucia went inside.

A pine knot burned in the hearth for light, adding its unwanted heat to the closeness of the room. Blue was sitting in the corner, her legs folded beneath her, her small hand slowly stroking the heron. The old uncle sat on his bed, the smoke from his pipe mixing with the pine smoke, heavy in the air. As Lucia came over to the corner, Blue rose and looked at her imploringly. "Baby needs more medicine," she said. "Sing him your song again."

Lucia looked down at the heron. It was lying on its side, its eyes closed and its beak partly open. Its body heaved with sporadic breathing. Lucia reached down and picked up Blue in her arms.

"Your heron is dying, Blue. I cannot help him."

"You can! You can!" Blue began to cry, and Lucia carried her to the center of the room and stood holding her, the girl's face buried in her shoulder.

"We should take him outside now," said Peeper. "Back to the wild world. She would not let us do it before. But now she knows."

The old uncle got up and walked over to the corner. He stood for a moment looking down at the bird, then nudged it with his foot. "The bird is dead," he said.

Blue lifted her head and looked around at the bird, no longer crying, curious to see the creature dead.

Peeper went over and picked up the limp body. The old man went back to his bed and sat down again with his pipe in his hands. "It is a bad sign that the bird has died," he said. "A bad sign."

"No," said Lucia. "It means nothing."

The old man shrugged and made no reply.

Lucia turned away from him and saw Carlos standing just inside the doorway. For a moment they looked at each other, their faces grim. Then she turned away and set Blue down on her feet again.

CHAPTER FORTY-TWO

Isaac Bull opened his eyes to curtained daylight and pushed back the sheet, seeking relief from the late summer heat. He was in one of the bed chambers of Charity Hawkins' house in Charles Town. The bed was damp from the sweat of his bedfellow, a Combahee River planter suffering from fever and ague. Isaac lay still, reluctant to disturb what little peace the man might be finding in his sleep. His wife and children had been murdered by the Yamasees on the first day of the war, the same day Isaac had suffered his wound.

Isaac gingerly stretched the left side of his body, feeling the tightness of the scar, still tender. The doctor said there was no internal damage, though this conclusion came only after Isaac had proved it by not dying. Charity had been told that he might die, no effort made to cushion the news for her. For all anyone knew, he was just another acquaintance made homeless by the war, taken in by her and given space in a bed. The house was full of such people, and she had only been able to show her personal distress for Isaac's dire condition by covering it with grief for her murdered husband. Isaac's wound had been on the mend now for several months, but they had been miserable months—long tedious days of idleness and waiting.

He looked toward the window, the sun bright beyond the curtains, the morning half gone. He slept for lack of anything better to do. Charles Town was a crowded prison, most of the people from the countryside packed inside the city walls, every bed in every house filled, every pantry strained. And now with the summer waning, the season of sickness was upon them, fever and ague rampant, worsened by the crowded conditions. It seemed everyone was affected by it and grew more languid whether they actually had the fever or not. But Isaac, after so many months of convalescence, was tense with restlessness, anxious to be out of the town and off in pursuit of Indians.

He was waiting for the long campaign into the heart of the enemy country. That was the only way to break the rebellion. The Yamasee country had been cleared, but since then there had been no more English offensives, only the defensive manning of garrisons around a shortened perimeter of the settlement and brief forays against the few ragged groups of northern Indians that remained close by. And so the war dragged on, and Isaac spent his days in the agony of boredom, all his work taken away. The Indian trade was the only occupation in which he had ever been engaged in Carolina,

and there could be no more of that until peace was restored. Nor could he
take up planting until the countryside was safe again. Not that he had any
land to plant. But he thought often of Fairmeadow now, wondering how
much he could do with it if that chance were to come his way, or with some
other place, perhaps closer to town, were money to come into his hands.

But there was no certainty that it would. Charity seemed to have little
time for him here, preoccupied as she was with the demands of the house
guests and now distracted completely by her youngest child, gravely ill with
fever and ague. Isaac could never manage to be alone with her, and he had
begun to be uncertain what that interlude at Fairmeadow had meant. Perhaps now that Henry was dead, things were changing for her in ways he
could not anticipate.

He raised himself slowly to his elbows, glancing at his bedfellow to make
sure he still slept. Then he sat up. The sick man stirred and was still again.
Isaac got up and pulled on his clothes, then picked up his shoes and carried
them into the hallway, where he sat in a chair to put them on. From downstairs he could hear the sound of voices, the house guests gathered in the
sitting room, many of them up since dawn for no other purpose than to
talk the long day through about the same subjects they had been discussing
since they first fled their homes—war, sickness, and death; high prices;
ineptness in the government; the misery of the colony. He would avoid
them this morning by going straight to the kitchen to find his breakfast. As
he rose, the door of Charity's chamber opened and Bess Clutterbuck came
out into the hallway, closing the door quietly behind her.

"Good morning to you, Mrs. Clutterbuck," said Isaac, making her a
slight bow. He liked seeing Bess in this house, thriving in her exile, happier
than she had ever been on that pinewoods farm.

"Morning, Mr. Bull," she said. "Did you sleep well?"

"Off and on."

"Is that all?" She looked him up and down. "It's not your wound still
bothering you, is it?"

"No," said Isaac. "That's healed well enough. Maybe it was the moon—
near full, you know. I don't sleep well when the moon is full. Too much
light."

"It's more than the light," said Bess, nodding knowingly. "There's been
times I felt the full moon a'pulling me as if I were the very tides. It's a
strange effect it has."

"Then you must have felt it last night."

"Well, I did, now that I think of it. I sat up with little Abe, hardly slept
a wink."

"And how is the boy?" asked Isaac, glancing beyond her to the door.

Charity had all her children with her in her chamber to free their own chamber for others.

"A tad improved," said Bess. "Go in and see him, if you want. They're all of them up and about in there."

"I'd not want to disturb them," said Isaac.

"It would be no disturbance, I'm sure." Bess turned back to the door and opened it, putting her head inside. "Mr. Bull's here to see Abe," she said.

There was a moment of silence. Then Charity said, "Tell him to come in."

Bess pushed the door open wide and turned back to Isaac. "There you are," she said, and she reached out and patted his arm as she walked past him toward the stairs that led up to the garret room where she and Sam were staying.

Isaac walked reluctantly to the open doorway. Were Charity alone, he would want to see her, but with her children around her and the little one so ill, nothing could come of it but the awkwardness and uncertainty of things unspoken. Hesitating in the doorway, he looked in and saw her standing by Abe's bed, careworn and plain in her black mourning gown. The two older children, Grace and Robin, were playing on the other bed, stacking pillows like a fortress. Charity looked toward Isaac and gave him a fleeting smile, but it was almost without seeing him, so quickly did her attention return to the sick child.

"Bess tells me he is better," said Isaac, coming a little way into the room. Abe was asleep, looking small and frail, with pale skin and dark circles around his eyes.

"Only a little," she said quietly, shaking her head. "He is still so very sick. The worst he's ever been."

"I'm sure Bess is a good nurse," said Isaac.

"Not as good as Lucia was. I am terrified for him. I cannot sleep at night."

"Nor can I," said Isaac. "It's time we are wasting, perhaps, each of us alone."

She gave him a warning look, making a little nod toward Grace and Robin, as if he might have forgotten their presence. There was a moment of strained silence, and Charity leaned down self-consciously and smoothed Abe's sheet.

"I only wanted to see how the boy was faring," said Isaac. "I'm on my way down to find some breakfast. I've risen late this morning."

"Then you've not heard the news from Saint Paul's Parish?" Charity straightened herself and clasped her elbows nervously.

"What news is that?"

"The Indians have invaded it, burned all those fine houses. Lady Blake was burned out. And so many others." She shook her head and stared past him. "There's no end to it. The Indians are going to press on to the very walls of the town."

Isaac walked over to the window and looked out at the sky to the south. No sign of smoke. The enemy was still far enough away, at least, that no smoke could be seen. How many miles to Lady Blake's? Ten? Twelve?

"At least there was no one there to be killed," he said. "Those plantations have all been emptied."

"They should have been guarded by the men in the garrisons," said Charity. "But the Indians slipped right past them. The guards never saw them."

"What Indians were they? Creeks, I suppose?"

"I've no idea," said Charity. "Bess told me as much as I've told you. She had the story from Sam. We didn't linger over the details. I've no heart for it."

He heard the rustle of her skirts as she sat down on the foot of Abe's bed. He turned and looked at her. She had her hand on the boy's leg, gently caressing it.

"I am sorry for all of your cares," Isaac said quietly.

She shook her head. "I have no more than others have. There is so much suffering." She looked down at Abe, her hand holding his small foot through the sheet. "You used to say the Indians would never unite. But here they are, destroying us."

"Not destroying us," said Isaac. "We will fight our way back."

"And if we do not? If the Indians can keep Carolina?"

"Then we will go elsewhere. To Virginia, perhaps, to plant tobacco instead of rice."

"I have been thinking of Boston. I believe I would go back to Boston."

"That would be sensible," said Isaac, watching her closely, her back turned to him, her eyes on the boy. "The other office of your trading firm is there."

"Yes," she said softly.

He glanced out the window again toward the smoke that could not be seen, then turned and walked to the door. He paused and looked back, wanting to say something more to her, but the girl Grace had stopped her play and was watching him intently, as if his conversation with her mother was of great interest to her. So he said nothing, only bowed and left the room.

✳ The stairway to the garret was narrow and dark. Isaac stood at the bottom and called up to Sam, giving notice of his intrusion.

"Come on up," answered Sam, and Isaac climbed toward the light that streamed in through a small window beneath the roof. The summer heat that collected here made the lower floors seem cool. As Isaac came up onto the attic floor, he unbuttoned his waistcoat.

"I don't see how you stay up here during the day," he said.

"It's hot, but quiet," said Sam, who sat on the edge of the bed, his head almost touching the sloping roof. Bess was moving quickly about the small room, rolling up pallets that the children used for sleeping. The children themselves were nowhere to be seen. "The trick is to keep still," said Sam. "Now Bess there, she's working too hard."

"Oh hush, Sam," said Bess. "I can't let Mr. Bull think we live in a pig sty."

"He's been up here before," said Sam. "He knows we do."

"I know nothing of the kind," said Isaac. "It's always very neat. But God above, Sam, it's hot."

"Sit down, then," said Sam, patting the bed beside him. "You're working too hard at standing up."

"That's right," said Bess. "You sit down, Mr. Bull. I'll go fetch the twain of you some beer."

"That would be good of you," said Isaac, taking a seat and removing his waistcoat. "And perhaps you could find a bit of bread to bring up. I've not had my breakfast this morning."

"I'll speak to the cook," said Bess. "Get some ham to bring with it, if I can."

Isaac smiled at her. "You're too good to me, Mrs. Clutterbuck. The bread would be enough."

"You leave it to me," said Bess. She straightened her apron and smoothed her hair and then started down the stairs. They waited in silence until she was gone.

"She's more content here than she ever was at home," said Sam. "It will be flaming hell to make her go back again."

"There's no worry of that for a while," said Isaac. "The Combahee is distant backcountry now. But what is this I hear about Saint Paul's Parish?"

"The noose tightens," Sam said ominously, pulling on his collar as if it were a hangman's rope. "The devils slipped through our lines. The men in the garrisons never saw 'em."

"That's not so surprising," said Isaac.

"Well, they've seen 'em now," said Sam. "Seen 'em and given chase. But the war parties are still out there, last I heard, tearing everything up. Even burnt a ship Mr. Boone was a'building. I'll wager he hated losing that ship worse than losing his house."

"At least there were no more murders. Everyone is here in town."

"Except them that's too poor to be here."

"There've been deaths, then?"

"A few."

"But not like before? No massacre?"

"I'm sure it seemed a massacre to them that died."

"But only a few?"

"That's all I've heard. Three men killed. We'll know more later."

"Do they know which Indians are maurading?"

"They say Apalachees. King Carlos and his men."

"Your friends," Isaac said wryly.

Sam smiled and shook his head, still amazed by his deliverance at Fair-meadow. "I never expected that of 'em, I tell you. I thought I was a dead man. Worse than a dead man. They had me alive and would've done me like they done poor Nairne, a little at a time."

"Three days of torture," said Isaac, shaking his head.

"I hate that it was ever known," said Sam. "Because of his widow, I mean. He's dead and at peace, but she's got to live with knowing how he went. How much better if the truth had not come out."

"I'm just thankful they didn't string you up the same," said Isaac.

"You ain't near as thankful as I am."

Isaac looked down at the floor, trying to dispel the specter of Nairne's death.

"The hardest thing about being left alive," Sam said, "is that now I have to figure out some way to live. The farm's gone. If they're rampaging as close to us as Saint Paul's Parish, it will be a long time before the Combahee will be safe enough for us to go back. But I don't see how I can stay here much longer. There's no work for hire, not with all the slaves that's been brought in, and if there was any work, I still couldn't live, what with the prices of things. Wartime prices. The merchants are getting rich in this. Drinking our blood, they are."

"But you've no expenses here in this house," said Isaac.

"Oh, but I do," said Sam. "I can't see Mrs. Hawkins feeding me and my brood for all these months with nothing in return. She might be kind enough not to make mention of it, but I know what I owe her. If things don't change before long, I'm going to take my young 'uns and go squat in the countryside, scrape up some sort of living out there."

"It's too late in the season to plant," said Isaac. "You'd starve before spring."

"Then what would you do?" asked Sam.

"Leave your family here and go out with the army. Draw a soldier's pay. I'm to lead a company when we go against the Creeks. Come march with me."

Sam was silent for a moment. "March against the Creeks?" he said, shaking his head. "I can't do that. I've got family amongst 'em. A woman. Children. In-laws, so to speak. And many a friend. I've tried to think my way through to it, but I can't do it. Bess rides me about it. She can't see why I don't go for a soldier. And what can I tell her? Not about Anahki. I remind her that King Carlos gave me my life, and that quiets her a little. But then she thinks of all the families killed and starts in again. One act of mercy, she says, don't make up for all that murder. All I can say is that it does for me. I'm out of the fight."

"I have to say, I see it more as Bess sees it," said Isaac.

"It's all beside the point for the present," said Sam. "How many men can we raise? Five hundred? Against how many thousand Indians? And no way to engage 'em without going way the hell deep into their country. We can't do a thing without some help, but where's it to come from? England don't give a merry damn what happens to us. And Virginia don't seem to either, sending us a handful of consumptives for reinforcements. We got better men from North Carolina, but there ain't that many of 'em. So here we sit. We got enough to quiet the Catawbas, maybe, and those others to the north. But I don't see how we can take on the Creeks and Cherokees. It's too far to go, and too many to go against."

"Unless the Cherokees were on our side."

Sam nodded. "That would do it. But what are the chances?"

"Improving all the time, from what I hear."

"Maybe so," said Sam. "You hear more than I do. I don't get much gossip from the governor's circle."

"I don't know how accurate it is by the time it comes to me," said Isaac. "But from what I hear, the Cherokees are interested in talking. There's hope they will send a delegation here to meet with the governor. If we see that happen, we'll know the tide is turning."

"And then you'll be riding out, I guess. Captain Bull."

Isaac nodded.

Sam said, "I hate the whole bloody business of it. I hate the uprising and the putting down of it. All I want is to be back on my farm raising enough corn to keep my family fed. The bastards probably burned my house to the ground. I was doing all right before this came along. After all those years of struggling, I was finally beginning to do all right."

"There's not a man in Carolina doesn't feel the same," said Isaac. "You might as well let your mind be easy in the matter. You've got a place here to stay and that's a blessing. You'll not be turned out with nowhere to go."

Sam looked at him. "Are you speaking as the master of the place?"

"No," Isaac said flatly. "I am not."

"The soon-to-be master, I mean?"

"Not that, either," said Isaac. He got up and began to button his waistcoat.

"You're not going?" said Sam. "Bess ain't brought us the beer yet."

"I need to get out for some air."

Sam sat in silence and watched him. "It would be a pity," he said, "if she forsook you now after all that's passed between you."

"The uprising has changed things for everyone," said Isaac. "She's free of Henry now, and wealthy in her own right. The past is behind her. She sees her future in her children. At least that is how it seems to me." Without waiting for Sam to make a reply, he turned and went down the narrow stairwell, glad to escape into the cooler air below.

★ It was after midnight when Isaac came out of the Indian Queen tavern and stood for a moment on the stoop before the door, steadying himself for the brief descent to the street. The night air helped to sober him. There was a hint of autumn in it. In the next street the watchman called out the hour: two o'clock. Isaac rubbed the back of his neck, upsetting his wig, which he straightened as best he could. Then he went down the three steps, slowly and carefully, until his feet were safely on the ground. He was drunk, but not reeling. Bed was what he needed. Turning himself very deliberately, he set his course toward the Hawkins house. The walk helped to sober him further.

The house was dark when he arrived, no servant waiting up. And why should there be? He was not the master here, only a house guest among so many, likely not even missed. He found the door open and slipped quietly inside, pulling off his shoes in the entryway and going upstairs in his stockinged feet, feeling his way in the darkness. Once up the stairs, he could see a light beneath Charity's door, and he used it to guide himself to his own chamber, where he could see well enough from the moonlight that streamed in through the window. His bedmate lay on his back, his mouth open, snoring loudly. The air in the room smelled of his sickness.

Isaac pulled off his wig and coat and waistcoat, loosened the buttons of his shirt and breeches, and was just about to crawl into bed when he heard a sound in the hallway, the rustle of skirts. He looked up to see Charity pushing open his door. Only her face was visible in the moonlight, her clothing black against the darkness behind her. She raised her hand and it, too, caught the moonlight as she silently motioned for him to follow her. He quietly crossed the room, fastening up his breeches and then picking up his silk turban and putting it on. As he reached the door, she turned and started down the hallway, silent except for her rustling skirts. He followed, carrying his shoes.

They went down the stairs and out the back door, where they stopped for him to put on his shoes, and then they went on through the moonlight into the garden to a bench hidden away beneath a latticed, vine-covered arch. Isaac brushed some stray leaves and twigs from the bench, and they sat down. It was the same garden in which they had first given voice to their hearts, so long ago.

"How is Abe?" he asked quietly, his head now clear, the effects of the rum almost gone.

"He continues to improve," said Charity. "He is sleeping well tonight."

"God be praised," said Isaac. He reached his arm around her shoulders. "It is good to hear."

She leaned against him and sighed. "It has all been such a turmoil, Isaac. There has been no time for us. After you left my chamber this morning, I felt badly. I worried that you might not understand my melancholy."

"The boy is quite ill," said Isaac. "I understand that."

"But that is not the whole of it. There is Henry, too. That still tears at me. I wanted to be rid of him, but I did not wish him murdered by savages. You understand that, don't you?"

"Yes," Isaac said quietly. The air was warm and fragrant and full of cricket song. He watched the play of moonlight and shadows. "Now that he is gone, what do you intend to do?"

"Then you don't understand. Not if you have to ask me that."

He made no reply. She was right. He did not understand.

She sat up from him a little. "Will you make me be the one to propose our marriage?"

He looked at her, smiling with relief. "I proposed it ten years ago."

"And then you took it back and left me waiting in this very garden."

He sat upright, puzzled. "When did I do that?"

"Never mind," she said, putting her hand lightly against his chest. "I've long ago forgiven you."

"Forgiven me what?"

"You can't have forgotten," said Charity.

He pulled back a little and looked at her. "Do you mean the night before you married Henry?"

"At least you do remember it."

"Your letter never came to me until the day after you were wed. It was only then my landlady put it in my hand. It came too late for me to meet you. But I did think it considerate that you meant to tell me of your marriage beforehand. Truly I did."

"Oh dear," Charity said quietly, leaning her face forward into her hands. She seemed at first about to cry, then she laughed.

He tightened his arm around her. "Was that not why you sent for me?"

"No, it was not. I wanted you to save me from marrying Henry. I wanted you to come to me and give me the strength to fend off my father."

"My poor sweet love," murmured Isaac, pulling her into his embrace. They held each other tightly. "When will you marry me?"

"I should mourn Henry a year, until April."

"That's too long. Marry me at Christmas."

"That would be scandalous," she said.

But he knew that she was smiling. He looked down at her. "A Christmas wedding?"

She nodded. "But a private one, Isaac. We should not make a spectacle of ourselves."

For a moment longer he looked at her. Then he kissed her, hardly able to believe she was his own.

CHAPTER FORTY-THREE

Lucia walked with Peeper and Blue down the path through the winter corn-field. The sky was gray overhead, threatening rain or even snow. Twice already in this season it had snowed, though only once did it stay on the ground long enough to make a wispy whiteness, and then it was gone. Both times the sky had been as it was today, heavy and flat, like a great, extended field turned upside down. They walked with their blankets wrapped snugly against the cold, and the two women carried water jars. Blue ran before them rolling a little wheel from a toy cart that Carlos had brought back to her from a raid he had made into the English settlements soon after the heron died. She had not had the cart long before she left it outside, where it had been stepped on by a horse and broken. But in retrieving the wheels from the wreck, she had seen at once that she now had two toys instead of one. She gave one wheel away and kept the other always with her, sending it rolling out ahead wherever she went, delighting in its leaps over humps of earth and its wild careening on downhill slopes. It was like the chunky stones with which the young men played their games in the plaza, rolling them out and hurling their chunky poles after them.

As Lucia and Peeper caught up with her again, Blue picked up the wheel and sent it rolling, racing after it to scoop it up as it fell. But it hit a stone, spun around in a sharp curve and came back a little way, so that she overran it.

"Did you see that?" she asked, laughing as she turned to come back for it. She picked it up and looked at Lucia. "We need more of these."

"Why?" said Lucia.

Blue was walking along beside them now, carrying the wheel. "For the children," she said, as if she were not a child herself. "They all want to have one."

"Then let them play with yours," said Peeper.

"No, I want to play with it. We need more. Tell Carlos, Lucia."

Lucia shook her head. "He is not raiding like that anymore."

"Why not?" asked Blue.

"Because he needs to stay home. All the warriors need to stay home."

"Why?"

"To keep us safe."

"But Carlos is gone now."

"But not far. Only to Coweta Town."

"Why?"

"For a big council."

"Why?"

"For reasons you are too little to know."

Blue looked up at her. "Why?"

Lucia set down her empty water jar and reached for Blue's wheel. "Let me have that," she said.

Blue handed it to her, and Lucia sent it rolling as fast as she could along the path in front of them. Blue went running after it.

"Good," said Peeper, nodding with approval. "Too many questions."

"Too many," Lucia agreed.

She picked up the water jar and they started down the path again, the trees of the river close ahead now. They walked in silence, not wishing to speak of the questions Blue had raised, but thinking of them, the war closing in, the northern tribes quelled and out of the fight. The English efforts were now turned solely against the Creeks. An army was marching out from the settlements—or so it was rumored. Brims had sent for Carlos and the headmen to come to Coweta Town, and for three days they had been there, a long council on these very grave matters. Their discussions would not be based on mere rumors. When Carlos came back, Lucia would know some things for certain.

They left the cornfield and entered the trees beside the river. Blue was carrying her wheel, afraid she might lose it in the water. "Sing your song," Blue said to Lucia as they stopped by the water's edge.

"That is a morning song," said Lucia, lowering the water jar from her head.

"Is it too late?" said Blue.

"Much too late. The sun is over there." Lucia pointed through the trees to a place halfway down the western sky.

Blue looked up at the bleak grayness. "Where?"

"It is covered by clouds," Peeper said to her daughter. "Look at all the twigs that have dropped from these trees in the wind. Why don't you pick up some kindling for me?"

"What about my wheel?"

"I will keep it for you," said Peeper, taking it from her. "Get busy now. When I have filled my jar with water, I will help you."

"I will pick up some for Lucia, too," said Blue, walking slowly away from them among the trees, her eyes on the ground.

Lucia stood for a moment watching the little girl, thinking of the rumors and of Brims' council at Coweta, of the war closing in, threatening to uproot them again. There would be no heron to carry this time. But it would be another unsettling flight, new houses to build, new mats, new pottery, new fields to clear, everything to be started over again.

Peeper filled her water jar and then set it aside and went over to join Blue in picking up sticks. Lucia stooped beside the water and dipped in her own jar, letting the current flow into it. As she drew up the jar, she saw movement in the underbrush across the narrow river. An animal, she thought. The trees and undergrowth across the river were denser than they were on this side, no fields over there, only swamp that ran along the river for a long distance before giving way to higher ground. The boys of the town hunted there and kept the animals scarce, but still there were a few raccoons and opossums, and several times Lucia had seen turkeys, and once a red fox, beautiful in its winter coat, its tail fluffed as it fled from her view. So now she set her jar aside and watched to see what this one would be.

A moment passed and then another. Whatever it was, it seemed to be gone. That first movement must have been its flight. But just as she was about to rise, she heard, from the other side of the water, rustling in the leaves of a magnolia tree whose branches touched the ground. She looked and saw a tawny head appear—a cougar. It startled her, and she felt a chill as she made herself stay perfectly still, reminding herself that the water made a sufficient barrier of safety. The great cat eased partly out of the green foliage and stood looking across at her, its forelegs and shoulders smooth and muscular. What was it doing here, a creature so shy as this? She sometimes heard the screams of cougars in the night, but hardly ever had she even caught a glimpse of one.

Barely moving her head, she looked for Peeper and Blue, certain that they must be seeing what she was seeing and keeping still as she was, or else the animal would not have come out from its cover. But from the corner of her eye she saw them stooped by a little pile of sticks, busily tying them into a bundle that Blue would carry home on her back. She called Peeper's name very softly. Peeper looked up and Lucia nodded across the river. But the cougar was no longer there. Peeper looked puzzled and started to rise, but Lucia held out a hand and put a finger to her lips. For several moments they remained motionless, looking across the river, though Peeper had no idea why. Then finally Lucia shook her head and got up. "I wish you had seen it," she said quietly, still watching the low branches of the magnolia.

"What was it?" asked Peeper, getting to her feet.

"A cougar."

"A cougar?" said Blue. She jumped up and hurried over to stand close to her mother. "Where is a cougar?"

"Across the river," said Lucia. "But it is gone now."

"Are you sure it was a cougar?" Peeper asked skeptically. "Maybe it was a dog. Or a deer."

"It was a cougar," said Lucia. "I saw it very clearly."

"I want to go home now," said Blue, holding onto her mother's skirt. "Which way did it go, Lucia?"

"I do not know." Lucia was still watching across the river. Finally she shook her head and turned away. "Maybe back to the Under World," she said. She reached down and picked up her water jar and lifted it onto her head.

※ By the time Lucia reached home, rain had begun to fall in a light drizzle, with a little sleet mixed in. She ducked inside and set the water jar in its place near the door. She was cold. Her hair and face and the arm that had balanced the jar had all gotten wet. Pulling her arm inside the blanket and rubbing it dry, she turned to go over to build up the fire. Then suddenly she realized it already was burning with a good flame, new wood added to it. She looked up and saw Carlos on their bed, one arm crooked behind his head as he watched her. His eyes were smiling.

"You have come!" she said with surprise.

"What did you think? Is there someone else who comes while I am gone and builds up your fire for you?"

"No," she said, smiling at him. "I was slow to notice the fire. I was thinking of other things."

"What other things?"

"Cougars," she said and went over to stand by the hearth, opening her blanket to let the heat touch against her. She watched him over the fire, happy to see him again.

"What about cougars?"

"I saw one at the river just now."

He laughed, thinking that she was joking.

"It is true," she said seriously. "There was a cougar just across the river from where I was filling my jar. It came out with no fear at all and stood there and looked at me. I think it must have come from the Under World. No cougar from This World would behave that way. It was a water cougar, I am certain. From the underwater places."

Now he too had grown serious. "What do you think it means?"

She shook her head. "Who can say? With the Under World you never know. Maybe it came to warn us of trouble. Or to bring us trouble."

"We have plenty of trouble already," Carlos said quietly.

Lucia looked at him for a moment, and then suddenly she shuddered with cold. She knelt down and poked the fire, collapsing the burning wood against the coals and adding more. Sitting back on her heels, she felt the heat warm on her face.

"Tell me," she said.

"The things we have been hearing are true," said Carlos. "The Catawbas, the Saponis, all those northern tribes have given up the fight. That frees the English to leave their settlement and come against us. They are already on the march. They are coming."

Lucia still held the stick she had used to stir the fire, and now she put the end of it against the coals and watched it catch fire.

"And they come alone?" she asked. "This far? I am surprised they would do that."

But she already knew the answer. Since summer she had feared it.

"They are coming to join together with the Cherokees," said Carlos in a flat voice. "Alone they are no more than five hundred. With the Cherokees they are five times as strong."

"So the Cherokees intend to come against us?"

"Yes."

"Then it is time for us to leave."

"And go where?"

"To the country along the Chattahoochee River. That is what the Creeks have been saying, back to their old-fields where they lived before the English came. The land there is good, they say, and it is far enough away to be safe from the English."

"It would be safer than here," said Carlos. "But if the English are strong, it will not be safe enough. No place will be."

"Then what?" said Lucia, exasperated. "Has Brims some fine plan to save us? I would like to hear it."

"Then I will tell you," Carlos said calmly. He was quiet for a moment, watching the fire, trying to find the best way to begin. "Let us say," he said slowly, "that the English have arrived in the Cherokee country."

"Have they?"

"Not yet. But let us say they have. They have come to join with the Cherokees to put down the rebellion among the Creeks." He turned and looked at Lucia. "We are the Creeks," he said. "The Apalachees are now part of the Creeks."

"I understand that," said Lucia.

"And so are the Yamasees. We are all together now."

"Yes," she said impatiently. "All this is clear to me."

He looked back at the fire. "But when the English arrive among the Cherokees, they find that the Cherokees have had word from the Creeks. The Creeks are seeking peace."

"So that is the plan," Lucia said quietly. "To surrender." She reached up and touched one of the scars on her cheeks. "When we go back under the English, they will want their slaves returned to them."

"No, that is not the plan," said Carlos. "You have not heard all of it yet." He paused, waiting for her to calm herself and listen. "Imagine that the Creeks have sent word to the Cherokees that they want to come to the Cherokee country to talk to the Cherokees about joining them in their peace with the English. So the English sit down and wait, hoping to win us back without a fight. Then our emissaries arrive and go into council with the Cherokees. And still the English wait. But the Creeks have not really come for peace. Instead they persuade the Cherokees to rise up against the English army that is now camped in the midst of their towns. The Creeks have their own warriors hiding nearby, waiting to come join the battle. And so the English army is caught by surprise and cut down. The Carolina settlement is finished."

Lucia picked up the stick she had toyed with before and put the end of it into the fire again, then lifted it and watched it burn. "So it is only a matter of persuading the Cherokees," she said quietly.

"That is all."

"But they have never been much inclined to be with us."

"But neither have they been against us in this war. Not until now."

"And what will bring them over?"

"The trap we have laid. The certainty of cutting off the English army. If they join with us, they can be sure of victory. That is what will bring them over."

"But if they stay with the English, they can also be sure of victory."

"But we will remind them of what it means to live under the English. We will give them a very good talk."

She looked up sharply at him. "Who will give them this talk? Not you?"

"I will be one. Twelve have been chosen to go, the chiefest men among us."

"No!" Lucia said emphatically, throwing the stick into the fire. "We are leaving this place. The plan is crazy. We are getting out of here." She got up angrily and went over and took down her pack basket from the place where it hung on the wall.

Carlos watched her, not saying anything.

"We will take food and blankets," she said. "That is all we have room for."

"And where will we go?" Carlos asked quietly.

She shook her head, pushing her fingers into her hair in anguish. "I do not know. To the French."

"To live as we did with the Spaniards? The English will never leave us alone there, and the French will make themselves masters over us."

"Then where?" asked Lucia, despair in her voice. Her blanket had dropped away and she stood before him now, her shoulders slumped, the pack basket in one hand. "There must be some place for us."

"There is none," said Carlos. "If there is to be a place, we will have to make it here."

"But not like this," she said weakly. "Not with you walking alone into the midst of our enemies." She stood watching him, thinking of all that time she had lived without him, so many years. Her chin began to tremble.

Reaching out, he caught her hand and pulled her toward him, she letting the basket fall as he drew her down, opening his blanket for her. She crawled in beside him, feeling his warmth, and he closed his arms around her and held her close, kissing her hair. She began to cry. For a long time he held her as she cried against him, the weight of his head resting on hers.

After a time she grew still and wiped her face on the blanket. Then she lay quietly and listened to the sound of his breathing, feeling the rise and fall of it, and within it and beneath it the beat of his heart, insistent and sharp.

"It is a gift," she said softly.

"What is?" he murmured.

"This time I have had with you since the spring. I think it has been the Sun thanking me for her song."

He was still, even his breathing checked, nothing now but the sharp rapping of his heart. Then the breathing again, slow and easy as before. He turned his face and pressed it against her hair, and she felt his breath there, warm on her head.

CHAPTER FORTY-FOUR

In the high hills of the Cherokee country, frigid with the cold of January, Isaac Bull walked against the falling snow, his shoulders hunched, his chin pulled down into the collar of his greatcoat. The snow had brought silence, muffling the sound of footsteps on the path, his own and those of the soldier he followed. They were walking from the small Cherokee town where his company was quartered to the main town of Tugaloo. The countryside through which they traveled was almost empty, though when they had first set out over an hour ago, the snow had not yet begun to fall and there had been more people on the path, most of them hurrying home before the storm. Now, closer to Tugaloo, they began to see English tents in the fields. But none of the soldiers were out on the path, only Isaac and the boy who accompanied him.

Isaac did not know why he was being called to Tugaloo. In the three weeks since the army had been in the Cherokee country, he had only once before been called to headquarters, and that was with all the rest of the captains. Together they had listened to an explanation of why the army must continue to sit and do nothing, though the waiting for the promised arrival of the Creek peace delegation had become tedious and the soldiers were growing restless. But this summons was not the same. From all Isaac could learn from the boy who had been sent for him, no other captains were being called.

They came now into the outskirts of Tugaloo, where the snow was beginning to whiten the rooftops. In the doorways of many of the houses there were people watching the storm, children mostly, though sometimes a man or a woman. Now and then they passed a house full of soldiers, boisterous and loud, the silent snow falling all around.

Isaac's escort began to walk more quickly, his hands shoved deep in his pockets, anxious to get to a warm fire. They came to the plaza and skirted along it, the great round council house looming large at one end with its white peace banner, visible even in the snow, hanging limply from its staff at the peak of the conical roof. The young soldier cut across a corner of the plaza, Isaac following after him, and they came to the house that had been lent to the English command by one of the Cherokee headmen. While the boy ducked inside, Isaac stayed back and waited to be announced. After a moment the boy came back out, motioning for him to come in.

It was warm inside, a fire burning briskly in the hearth. Isaac greeted the two officers, who rose to their feet, Colonel Maurice Moore, the commanding officer, and Captain George Chicken, a friend of Moore's and almost a colonel himself, sure to be promoted when this campaign was over.

"Take off your coat, Captain Bull," said Moore, sitting back down on one of the beds. Chicken also sat down again, pushing himself back to lean against the wall, his legs straight out before him.

"Give Captain Bull some brandy, Hume," Moore said to the lad who had escorted Isaac through the snow. "And take some for yourself."

"Thank you, sir," said Hume. He took out two silver cups from a leather chest and poured them each half full of brandy.

Isaac accepted his gratefully and stood with his back to the fire, facing the two officers. Maurice Moore was the son of old James Moore, now dead, who had fought the Spaniards in Florida.

"We've met before," said Moore.

"Yes, sir," said Isaac. "Briefly."

"And you're aquainted with Captain Chicken?"

"Yes, we've met," said Isaac, nodding to Chicken.

"Wretched weather we have," said Moore.

"Indeed it is," said Isaac. "It puts me in mind of England. We seldom get snow in Charles Town. Nor in the Creek country, either, for that matter."

"It's usual here in the mountains," said Chicken. "It often snows in winter."

"This is my first time in the mountains," said Isaac. "If these foothills can be called the mountains."

"This is their beginning," said Chicken. "They get quite high further up. Higher even than those you can see in the distance."

"Have you been up that far?" asked Isaac.

"Several times," said Chicken. "I've dabbled in the Cherokee trade."

"Perhaps you would like to see more of this land for yourself," said Moore.

"How is that?" Isaac took a sip of brandy, savoring its warmth in his mouth, holding it there for a moment, and then feeling it flow down his throat. They were coming to the reason for calling him in.

"I'm sending Captain Chicken over the hills, to meet with Caesar and his people. Do you know who Caesar is?"

Isaac nodded. "He led the Cherokee delegation that met with the governor in Charles Town."

"The same," said Moore. "And the governor urged him to go to war against the Creeks, promised him arms and support, all of which pleased him greatly. And now it seems he's having a difficult time letting go the idea. He's not happy with this sitting around. He threatens to go to war without us."

Isaac shook his head. "We can't have that. We'd never get our peace with the Creeks."

"Which is why I'm sending Chicken to stop him. I want you to go along to aid him."

Isaac took another drink of the brandy and nodded. "Of course I will go," he said. "But I'm not sure how useful I can be. I know Creeks, not Cherokees. And I must say, I am reluctant to leave my company."

"Your company is going to be sitting on their asses, the same as they've been for all these last three weeks. They'll not be needing you here with 'em, I assure you. And as for the other, it's precisely because of your familiarity with the Creeks that I'm sending you. Caesar will have to be convinced that the Creeks do in fact intend to come in for the peace."

"But I've no idea that they do."

"That makes no difference," said Moore. "I'm certain you can find a way to convince him."

"I'll do the best I can," said Isaac. He looked down into his brandy, swirling the golden liquid against the silver cup, pleased with this turn of events. It would be a relief to go out and do something at last. He looked up at Captain Chicken. "Where exactly are we going?"

"Nacoochee valley," said Chicken. "Over these next hills, thirty miles, give or take. The Cherokee town of Chota is there. From what's been told us, it seems Caesar sent word to all the warriors over the high mountains to gather there at Chota to join with us against the Creeks. Not that we can blame him for it. He was only doing as the governor bid him. None of us expected to arrive here and find the Creeks seeking after peace."

Isaac nodded. "So we have to ease him out of it. Try somehow to let him keep his dignity—all those warriors gathering on his word only to be sent home again." He shook his head.

"We've done the same to ourselves," said Moore, "dragging five hundred men up here to turn around and go home without a fight."

"God willing," said Isaac.

"Indeed," Moore said.

For a few moments they were silent, the conversation played out. Isaac turned around and watched the fire.

"You might as well settle in," said Moore. "I was hoping you would start out for Nacoochee today, but this snow has spoiled that. It appears now it will be morning, and no sooner."

Isaac nodded.

"More brandy?"

"I could use a little more." Isaac gave his cup to Hume to be refilled. Then he went over and sat down on an empty bed, feeling slightly ill at ease. Moore got up and stretched and then walked over to the door and pulled back the blanket to watch the snow.

"Look how it falls," he said. "It makes me miss the comforts of home. Are you a married man, Captain Bull?"

"Yes," said Isaac, smiling a little. "Newly married, I am. I was wed barely a week before I left home."

"Is that so?" said Chicken, shifting with interest on the bed where he sat, holding up his finger as if trying to remember something. "Now, aren't you the one who was said to be marrying Henry Hawkins' widow?"

"Indeed, I am the same. And I count myself a lucky fellow."

"Yes," said Chicken, nodding and smiling at him. "Quite lucky, I would say. She is a charming woman."

And a wealthy one, Isaac knew he was thinking. He raised his cup as if in a toast and took another drink.

✳ Caesar, the Cherokee war leader, reminded Isaac of political men in Carolina. He had found a base of power and meant to hold onto it, come what may. He had been the one who, with all the Indian nations at war against the English, had dared to lead his men to Charles Town to sit down with the English governor. And in return he had been promised guns and ammunition for the war against the Creeks and given assurance of generous exchange for any slaves the Cherokees might capture. This English-Cherokee war against the Creeks would bring wealth to many, and Caesar had been the one to arrange it. But now, just as he was at the peak of his glory, the English had come to ask him to put a stop to it all.

The Chota council house was crowded with warriors. The only white men present were Isaac, George Chicken, and Will Scoggins, a long-time trader among the Cherokees who had come along as interpreter. Caesar had been speaking for a long time, Will Scoggins quietly turning his passionate oration into a monotone of English. Tension in the chamber was high, the warriors murmuring their agreement to all that Caesar was saying. Isaac was perspiring heavily in the hot room.

"I do not understand this talk of peace!" cried Caesar, glaring at the

Englishmen. "Your governor speaks with two tongues. To us he says nothing of peace. Only of war. He tells us that the Creeks are terrible enemies of the English. They murdered your people in their beds. They must be cut off. Nothing will make him happier, he says, than for us to join with you in this. And to this we have agreed. We have gathered our warriors and readied ourselves for war, and we have waited for you to arrive and bring us arms and go with us against our enemies, all as your governor promised. Your governor was a happy man. He shook my hand and promised me these things. And now you come to tell me that it was nothing. I say your governor talks with two tongues. We will go to war without him. We will go without your guns and ammunition. We will fight with our own short knives!" Caesar pulled his knife from its sheath and brandished it in the air. The other warriors did the same, rising to their feet and shouting their support.

Isaac and Chicken stood up, putting up their hands to still them. But the council was disintegrating, the men leaving their seats, heading toward the door, ready to start now on the war trail against the Creeks. Isaac left his seat and walked quickly across the room, pushing his way through the crowd until he could reach out and grip Caesar's arm. Caesar turned to look at him.

"Let me speak," Isaac said firmly, using the Muskogee language of the Creeks, hoping Caesar would understand it. Caesar did understand, though he looked at Isaac for a long moment, disdain on his face. Then he wrenched his arm free of Isaac's grip and said something, a short utterance in his own language that Isaac did not understand. But the noise in the chamber diminished and the men began to move grudgingly to their seats. Isaac nodded grimly to Caesar and returned across the room to his own seat. He waited until all was still again, and then he stood up and began his effort, uncertain what he would say.

"If you are to be an ally of the English," said Isaac, with Scoggins translating beside him, "you must follow us both in war and peace. You cannot go to war on your own, without regard for our interest. It may be that at this very moment the Creek delegation is in Tugaloo making a peace to encompass all our peoples. What treachery would it be if you went out now to fall on the Creek villages, making war at the same moment they themselves are making peace?"

"What peace?" said Caesar, rising to his feet. "No word has come here of peace. Where is that delegation the Creeks have promised? They have no intention of seeking peace. They have sought only to delay you so that they could move their women and children to safety and prepare their de-

fenses against us." He waved his hand in disgust at English gullibility and
sat down again.

"If that is true, it is all the more reason to delay going," said Isaac. "If they have moved their women and children to safety, how will you capture any slaves? Would you spill your blood and gain nothing from it? Would you lose your trade with us as well? For if you go against our friends, you become our enemies. The trade is finished. And then where would you get new guns? Where would you get ammunition for the guns you have? Where would you get blankets and clothing?"

"From the French," Caesar said sullenly from where he sat.

Isaac laughed. "Have you ever had satisfaction in trading with the French? They are poorly supplied. Their goods are shoddy."

"But they speak with one tongue," said Caesar.

"And we, too, speak with one tongue," said Isaac. "You are wrong to think the governor deceived you. He did not know the Creeks would come to us seeking peace. Had he known it, he would not have urged you to war. He always prefers peace to war. He is happiest when he is trading."

"As are we," said Caesar. He rose to his feet again, his passion cooling. "But in order to trade, we must capture slaves, and to get slaves we must have war."

"You can trade also with deerskins."

"Of course we can, and we do. But much time and ammunition are spent in getting a bundle of skins, and for that bundle of skins you will give but a small part of what you will give for a slave. This is why our hearts are set on war. Your governor encouraged us in this, and we intend to go on with it."

"Even if we cease our trade with you?"

"I do not believe you will. I do not believe the Creeks will make a peace." Caesar sat down as if weary of the discussion.

Isaac sat down as well. He could see a chance now for at least a delay. He conferred with Chicken, taking his time, letting passions continue to cool. Then he rose to his feet again.

"Let us take this talk back to Colonel Moore in Tugaloo. He is our leader here in the Cherokee country. We cannot decide these things without him. If the Creeks have not yet come to Tugaloo, we will tell him that you believe they do not intend to come at all. And then he may very well wish to come here and join forces with you, and we will all go out together against the Creeks."

"When will we go?" asked Caesar.

"Very soon. Captain Chicken and I will sleep here tonight and leave tomorrow for Tugaloo. We will reach there the following day and send a message back to you. Colonel Moore himself will send it."

"And what will this message tell me?"

"Whether the Creeks have come. But if they have, you must join us in smoking a pipe of peace."

"And if they have not," said Caesar, "we will go out at once to make war against them."

"You must wait for Colonel Moore," said Isaac.

"If there is no peace, I will wait one day for your colonel," said Caesar. "Then with or without him, I will go."

Isaac nodded. "This I understand," he said soberly. "You have spoken clearly and well."

✴ In the council house at Tugaloo, on a bench that now, after a long evening of negotiations, was serving as a bed, Carlos, leader of the Creek delegation to the Cherokees, sank deeply into sleep. At once he began to dream. He was aware as he slept that this dream was intensely interesting, although at first it came from so deep a place that no clear image or meaning penetrated his consciousness. Then it clarified and he was talking to Father Juan, who was strong and healthy as he had been when Carlos was a boy. The priest told Carlos that he lived in a town nearby, over the next range of hills, and he invited Carlos to come for a visit. Carlos accepted the invitation, curious to see the town. Father Juan showed him the path and they set out on it together.

At once they arrived in a well-ordered Indian town, with cornfields all around. Father Juan led Carlos into the chief's house, which was furnished inside like a Spanish house. In the center of the room was a banquet table spread with a rich feast. All the chairs at the table except two were occupied, and Father Juan took his place in one of those. The shaman Salvador was seated at his right hand, and the two holy men put their heads together in amiable conversation. As he dreamed, Carlos knew they were talking about the mysteries of God. Across the table from Father Juan sat Thomas Nairne, the English Indian agent with whom Carlos had argued in the council house at Pocotaligo and who soon after had been tortured and killed. Here he sat unscathed and full of life, his plate piled high with food. He looked up at Carlos and nodded, and Carlos returned the greeting.

There were others present, but Carlos took no note of them. His attention had turned to the head of the table where a beautiful Apalchee woman, radiant with light, presided over the feast. A fragrance of flowers suffused the air around her, and the very sight of her filled Carlos with peace. He knew she was the Holy Virgin. She smiled at him and motioned toward the remaining empty chair. He started toward it, but then remembered Lucia. She was waiting for him. He could not stay here. And with that realization he awoke.

Carlos knew it was a dream of death, but as he lay looking at the still, dark forms in the council house he was not afraid. The feeling of peace that had come to him in the dream lingered on. Was it a premonition? Would he die in the upcoming battle against the English? He was certain now that there would be a battle. The Cherokee headmen were almost ready to join with the Creeks in their plot against the English. Brims was hiding with his forces not far from the town, awaiting word, while Carlos and his delegation slowly brought the Cherokees around. There was still the Conjurer to be won over, a fast friend of the English, a strong man with a solid following. But after unloosing angry harangues earlier in the day, the Conjurer's faction had grown silent in the evening. Something had changed. The wind had shifted. Perhaps tomorrow the alliance would be sealed, and then, in a united front, the Creeks and Cherokees would spring their trap on the English army.

The Indian alliance would have the advantage of surprise, but even so, the fighting would be fierce. Death would come to many. Perhaps to he himself at long last, after he had eluded it so many times before. At the seige of Ivitachuco. At the battle of San Luís. At the slaughter of Salvador's camp. In the starvation and slave raiding at San Augustín. In the cutthroat world of the backcountry trading towns. And through almost a year of fighting against the English in this war.

Lucia was right. Their time together since their reunion had been a gift. If death came to him now, he would not protest. His life had been long considering everything, and because Lucia had been returned to him, he could even say it was complete.

Carlos listened to the sounds around him, to the snoring of his companions, to the cold rain dripping from the smoke hole high above. His heart was still warm from the dream. It had been good to see Father Juan again, healthy and whole. Good to feel the reconciliation of so much of the conflict of his life. The priest, the shaman, the Englishman. Things Spanish and things Indian. The Christian way and the old way of Apalachee. It was the Virgin herself who seemed to bring all of it together and contain it in her own radiant being. Carlos closed his eyes and slipped back into sleep, remembering his early days in the mission, remembering Lucia as he first saw her there, little more than a girl, legs like a colt . . .

Suddenly he was awake.

Yet his vantage point was strange. Where was he? Up. At the apex of the ceiling of the council house. Curious.

Below him was his own body, his head split open by a tomahawk. The sight did not disturb him. He looked around and saw Cherokee warriors moving among the sleeping forms of his comrades, silently killing them all, sparing none. So the Conjurer's faction had prevailed after all. They had met the Creek plot with a counterplot of their own.

Almost at once Carlos began to lose interest in this scene. He remembered the path Father Juan had shown him that led from this place to the Virgin's town. Immediately as he recalled it, it stretched before him. Turning his back on the struggle in the council house, Carlos set out along the path. He thought of Lucia, regretting that he could not return to her. But even that last regret fell away, and his heart grew ever lighter as he moved toward the town of peace, toward the chief's house and the empty chair at the Virgin's feast.

✳ Isaac and George Chicken were deliberately slow in leaving Chota, rising late, sitting for a long time by the fire in the council house, smoking pipes and eating venison and sofkee, all to give the Creeks a little more time to reach Tugaloo before them. Then finally, when the delay had been extended as long as possible, they sent Will Scoggins out to get the horses. As they waited for him beside the plaza, stamping their feet against the cold, they smiled at each other over the length of time he was taking at the task.

"Perhaps he has managed to lose one," said Isaac. "It might take him all morning to find it."

"I'm not sure Caesar would stand for that," said Chicken.

"Can we be blamed if a horse wanders?"

"He knows we delay."

"But what can he do?"

"Nothing," said Chicken, smiling.

They were silent for a time, looking out at the winter hills around the town. These were still not the highest mountains. From a high place on their journey in, Isaac had seen in the far distance a great blue range stretching across the north.

"He may be right about the Creeks," said Chicken. "They may never have meant to come in for peace."

"But he may be wrong," said Isaac.

"And if we get back to Tugaloo and find they've still not come?"

"Then we should come back and try again to delay him."

"But in truth," said Isaac, "he does not want to lose our trade. Nor his special standing with the governor. The French might choose to set Caesar aside and elevate some other Cherokee warrior. You can be sure he has his rivals here."

"No doubt," said Chicken. He crossed his arms against the cold, hunching up his shoulders. "Scoggins can come ahead with the horses now and it will be all right by me. I'm ready to take my leave."

"And there he comes," said Isaac. From behind one of the houses in the distance Scoggins was just coming into view, leading three horses after him. Isaac and Chicken left the plaza and walked briskly to meet him, warming themselves with the exertion. They had almost come up to the horses when suddenly, from beyond the town to the east, there came a high, wavering cry.

"The war whoop!" said Isaac, running the last steps to take the reins of his horse. All the town was suddenly in motion, warriors grabbing up their weapons and streaming out of the town, filling the path and spilling over the fields on either side, rushing to meet the crier who was bringing the news that war had broken out. The three Englishmen mounted quickly and rode out with the rest and found the messenger already surrounded by a crowd. They pushed their way through with their horses until they could hear what was being said. Isaac sat dumbfounded as Scoggins translated.

At long last the Creek emissaries had come to Tugaloo. But they came seeking war, not peace. All Brims' warriors had gathered in ambush near Tugaloo, waiting for their delegates, led by King Carlos, to incite the Cherokees to rise up against the English army. But their plan had failed. Brims' emissaries had been assassinated, slain by the Cherokees themselves in the Tugaloo council house. It had been done without a stir, the English having no knowledge of it until the king of Tugaloo came and told them. With that the English army began preparing to go out against Brims, hoping to reach him before he could learn that his delegates, all of them kings and headmen, were lying cold and dead.

Isaac turned his horse and rode slowly out of the throng into the surrounding field, where he stopped, trying to absorb it all. War, not peace. The Creeks still enemies. King Carlos dead—that enigmatic Apalachee who had spoken so eloquently against the English in the Pocataligo council house, who had slain Henry Hawkins in his bed, and yet had spared the life of Sam Clutterbuck, for what reason no one knew. The death of that man seemed tragic, even though he was an enemy.

The winter air was cold on Isaac's face and his fingers were stiff as they gripped the reins. He turned and looked for Scoggins and Chicken, but it was Caesar who came striding up to him. The war leader looked up at him with a smile.

"You come with me now?" asked Caesar, speaking in rough Muskogee.

"You come with me to Tugaloo," said Isaac. "We will help them finish Brims."

Caesar shook his head. "You have men enough. I go to the Creek villages. Before their warriors return."

"It would be better for you to come with me," said Isaac. "Let Colonel Moore give you your orders."

"I need no orders from your colonel."

Isaac nodded and looked away. There was no reason to hold him back any longer.

CHAPTER FORTY-FIVE

Lucia lay awake listening to the wolves in the fields beyond the town. Their thin, tremulous howls sounded like grieving. They came every night now, the cold making them so hungry and daring that some had been coming up to the very yards of the houses to nose about for food. They seemed to know the men were gone. She turned over and closed her eyes, pulling her blanket over her head to muffle their wailing. She wanted very much to sleep, to shorten the long night and quiet her gloomy thoughts. She lay absolutely still, her breath warm in the blanket pulled up about her face, her eyes determinedly closed. For a long time she tried to empty her mind, to let it settle and open itself to sleep. But the thoughts would not stop, and finally she pushed aside the blanket and sat up, the wolves still howling like lonesome, hungry things.

Pulling her blanket with her, she got up and went to the fire and put on more wood and then sat down close to the flames, her knees pulled up and her blanket wrapped around her. It had been five days now since Carlos had gone with the others into the town of Tugaloo. Five days by her reckoning, assuming all had gone well on their journey there. But whether it was exactly five days ago or not, the deed was surely done by now. Whatever was going to happen had already happened. Either they had gone into Tugaloo and been successful and the Cherokees had risen up against the English, or else they had gone in and not been successful and . . .

She brought up her hands to her face and tried to stop those thoughts, but they were loose now, like the wolves wailing their grief into the night. If they had not been successful, they were dead. Carlos dead. She shook her head, pushing her fingers into her hair, her eyes closed tight, her throat swelling with grief.

"Stop this!" she told herself suddenly, jerking away her hands and opening her eyes. She looked determinedly about, trying to make herself stop thinking, looking at the mats on the wall, the baskets and pots scattered about, everything as it always was. But her throat still hurt, and as she picked up a stick to poke the fire, the pain swelled unbearably and she dropped the stick and put her hands to her face again and began to cry. In that moment it seemed it would all break loose, all her grief pouring out, as if the news itself had already come. But the news had not come, and little by little she got control of herself, rubbing her face and stopping her tears until finally she sat quietly by the fire, feeling drained, her chest hollow and sore. Her thoughts were stilled now, the gloom lifting.

She got up from the fire and went out into the night where she stood and looked up at the stars and felt the cold winter air on her face. The wolves were like singers at a dance, like old women singing together with their high, wavering voices, shuffle-stepping in a circle around a fire. She smiled. That was better. Dancing women with turtleshell rattles on their legs and merry eyes. She would think of the wolves that way. The cold air made her feel stronger. She stood there a while longer, breathing deeply until the cold was all through her and bed seemed a welcome place. Then she went back in and lay down, her blanket close and warm about her, the fire still burning and quietly crackling. Sleep came softly and pulled her away.

She awoke to gunfire and shouting. Then war whoops, the alarm going up from every side. Terror seized her and she lay stiff for a moment, her heart pounding against her chest. Then she rolled from her bed and ran to the door. In the halflight of dawn people rushed about in confusion, calling to one another, frantic women herding their children, an old man running past her armed with a hatchet, two boys carrying knives. She stepped out and caught one of the boys by his arm.

"What is it?" she said. "Do you know what is happening?"

"The enemy!" the boy shouted as if she were deaf. "The enemy is attacking!"

She let him go and started toward the plaza, half running, looking around to see what was happening, trying to determine where the attack was taking place, with how much strength, and whether it was being countered at all. Perhaps they could make a stand in the council house. Or would that only put them in a trap? There was gunfire all around. Shouting and screaming. Her legs were weakening at the growing sound, her thoughts losing their clarity. And then at the plaza's edge, she stopped and wheeled around and began to run back. They were already there, painted warriors, Cherokees, they had to be Cherokees, and they were everywhere, people sprawled in the plaza, dead and bleeding.

The confusion was terrible, people running in every direction, trying to get away. She stopped and stood against the wall of a house, trying to still her panic and get her bearings. Then she started running again, heading now for the side of the town that lay toward the swamp. Others were going that way and soon she was in a little group of people who moved as one, making the safety of a pack as they surged from house to house. But then, as they rounded a corner, there were screams and shouts, and the pack scattered as painted men with hatchets plunged in among them, dragging out women and children, chopping down old men. Lucia veered away and ran without looking back, her heart pounding, despair welling up. She had to get to the swamp. She passed close by the portico of a house. The enemy had already been here, two old people lying dead, a baby with its head crushed, a woman badly wounded, writhing in her blood. Lucia tried not to look.

"I am sorry, my sister," she murmured and ran on, leaving that carnage behind only to find more, and others like herself running past the dead and dying, crossing through this place where the attack must have started, people muttering and crying as they ran, knowing they could not stop but only keep running to save themselves. Ahead lay the cornfields. Lucia could see them now beyond the houses. Almost there. She dodged around a corpse and then had to leap over another as the people fleeing with her pressed in around her. She was in a pack again, her legs growing fleeter and her hopes rising. Some of them would make it. Some would surely make it through the fields and across the river. They were almost out of the town now, almost away.

And then a sound came to her through all the rest, a high-pitched, screaming cry, a child. It was familiar to her, a voice she knew. She stopped and listened as people ran past her, jostling against her. She listened until she could determine where it was coming from, and then she turned and ran toward it, knowing it was Blue.

She found Blue beside Peeper, who lay covered in blood, her eyes staring lifelessly into the red morning sky, her scalp ripped away, her hand still clutching the hatchet with which she had fought, choosing death over slavery. Blue stood beside her and screamed. Lucia reached down for the child, but Blue pulled away, fighting and screaming.

"Blue!" Lucia said sharply. "Blue!" Reaching out, she caught her and gave her a hard shake. Blue looked at her and fell silent. Lucia grabbed her

up, and then once again she was running toward the cornfield, Blue clinging to her, not making another sound.

There was no pack to surround them now, only a scattering of people running through the fields. Up ahead, the group Lucia had been with be- fore suddenly spread out, and she knew that the enemy was there, cutting them off from the river. She was still far up the field, and she turned and started running parallel to the river, wishing it were summer and the corn high enough to hide her. Blue was heavy and the field was rough and she had a pain in her side. But if she could keep going, and if the enemy would keep busy with those others . . . She turned and looked back and gave a little cry. Two warriors giving chase.

Trying to run faster, she cut down toward the river, the slope of the land increasing her speed. Blue bounced against her and she held her tightly and all she could think now was to save her. There was the river, not far to go. If only her legs would hold up and not buckle. If only those men would stop at the water and not follow her across on such a cold day. She did not look back to see how close they might be.

But now from the corner of her eye she saw one moving out to cut her off from the river. She veered away, still going toward the river, but not so directly. The other remained behind her, his breathing and the quick fall of his running feet almost on her. The one cutting her off was closing in. She could not reach the river. Blue clung to her in silence, weighing her down. She turned aside suddenly and started up into the field again, pushing with all that was in her, panting and desperate, and for a moment longer she eluded them, veering this way and that. But then they were on her, one of them reaching out and grabbing her hair and pulling her to a halt. She gave up then without any more struggle, for she remembered Ayubale and the camp of Salvador, and she knew it had to end this way.

CHAPTER FORTY-SIX

Lucia sat on a bench in the sun, leaning back against a high paling fence, watching Blue as she played with the other children in the slave pen. Three sides of the pen were formed by the walls of surrounding buildings, all with their windows barred, and the fourth side, facing the back alley, was closed in by the fence against which she leaned. The building on the opposite side of the yard from the fence belonged to the merchant who owned the slaves, and the man who tended the slaves for him lived in the upper story, where there was a railed balcony on which the slave tender or his wife or one of their sons would sit to keep watch on the yard below. Today it was the wife who was there with another woman who had come to visit her, both of them sitting with their shawls pulled close, for they did not have the sun on them as Lucia did, and the air was still cold.

But the sun was warm and Lucia was grateful for the pleasant feeling of it on her face and arms. She was grateful, too, for the laughter of Blue as she ran in and out of the sunlight chasing after the other children. Blue's nights were not so carefree as this. Her memories came back to her in the darkness, and she often woke from her dreams in tears. But this laughter was good and this warmth from the sun, and Lucia savored it, looking neither to the future nor the past.

Carlos was dead, assassinated. She had learned about it from the Cherokees during the time that they had held her, though she had known already that he must have been dead, for the Cherokees would never have attacked had his mission been successful. Her grief was not as terrible as it might have been. She was oddly at peace, finding an unexpected release in knowing that this time she was not leaving him behind. Whatever misery she would suffer now, at least it would not be that. The whole of her life would go with her wherever she was taken, and she would live it as it came to her. And when there were moments like this of sunshine and laughter, she would take the pleasure for her own, for these small things were all that she had now and all that would ever be given her. Life had delivered its hardest blow, but she was more at one with herself than she had ever been before. Having let go of her desperate hopes, she found much within to sustain her.

She leaned her head back against the fence and closed her eyes, the sun red against her eyelids. From all around she could hear the sounds of Charles Town, the wagons and carts on the cobbled street along the bay, the calls of the street vendors, the muffled singing from a tavern, and drifting in from the harbor the thin shouts of sailors loading and unloading the ships. That was where she would be before long, she and Blue and all the Indian people in this pen, loaded up and shipped away to the sugar islands. The war had sealed their doom. They were no longer to be trusted to remain in the land in which they had always lived. This was a new day. The Englishmen had triumphed, and Carolina was theirs. They would keep their black slaves to labor in their homes and in their fields, for they were not afraid of a people who had been uprooted from their native land and brought here from across the sea. But the Indian slaves were all to be banished, put on ships and taken away to places from which they could never return. Although today they were not taking her anywhere. Today was the new spring sun.

She let her thoughts grow still. She could hear the sea gulls over the bay. A dog barked in the distance. In the alley behind her, footsteps came crunching softly along on the small bits of shell in the sand. They slowed when they reached the corner of the pen and then stopped for a time, as if someone were looking in through the fence. Then they started again and came on a little way and stopped, another long pause, and then they came on and stopped once more, this time just behind her. She opened her eyes and sat forward a little, waiting for the person to move on.

"I find you," a woman's voice said quietly. It was a familiar voice, though Lucia could not place it. Startled, she turned and looked behind her and saw Elizabeth Birdfeather looking through from the other side of the fence.

"My sister!" she said in surprise. "You have come! What are you doing here?"

Elizabeth Birdfeather shrugged. "Selling herbs. Making cures. I hear in streets you are here. Wife of King Carlos. In slave pen near bay. How my heart falls. Sun Woman, slave again."

"But for a little time I was free," said Lucia, reaching her fingers through the palings to touch the woman's hand. "It was because of you. I will never forget it, my sister. My heart is full."

"And mine," said Elizabeth Birdfeather. "You were with husband again."

Lucia nodded. "It was very good. For almost a year we were together."

"Was there wife?"

"I was the only one."

Elizabeth Birdfeather smiled and shook her head with amazement. "King Carlos big man in many ways."

Lucia nodded.

"My heart fall on ground when I hear he is dead," Elizabeth Birdfeather said softly.

"Yes, it is sad. But do not grieve for me, my sister. You have done . . ."

"You there!" A shout came from the balcony. "What are you doing? Who are you talking to?"

Lucia turned back and looked up at the slave tender's wife. "No one, Mistress. A woman selling herbs."

"We don't want any herbs. Tell her to go away. Hey, you! Root woman! Move along, I say!"

Lucia turned back to Elizabeth Birdfeather. "You must go now." She put her fingers through the palings again and entwined them in the woman's own. There were tears in Elizabeth Birdfeather's eyes. "Do not cry, my sister," said Lucia. "I would not have you cry for me."

"I come back," said Elizabeth Birdfeather.

"Hey, down there!" The slave tender's wife had stood up and was leaning over the railing. "Be on your way or I'll have you taken up! I'll not be warning you again!"

"Go on now," said Lucia, pulling in her fingers. She leaned back against the fence again and listened as Elizabeth Birdfeather's footsteps faded away down the alley.

✳ Isaac Bull propped the deed to his new rice plantation on the mantle, pushing a tobacco jar in front of it to hold it up. Then he sat down in a chair near the fire and stretched out his legs as he looked up at the deed with satisfaction.

"We will have to think of a name," he said to Charity, who was sitting near a window to catch light on her embroidery.

"For the baby or the plantation?" asked Charity.

"The plantation," said Isaac. "There's time enough for the baby." He looked at her and smiled to make sure she took no offense. Her pregnancy had barely begun, her stomach still flat.

"What about Burnaby?" she said. "I have been thinking of that."

"For the plantation?"

"No," she laughed. "For the baby."

"Perhaps," he said, looking back at the deed on the mantle. "But give me a name for a rice plantation."

"Parakeet!" said Abe, who was playing on the floor near his mother, building up a tower out of wooden blocks.

"Parakeet?" Isaac looked over at him with a smile. The child had recovered a great deal since the summer, though he still was thin and sickly. "For a name?"

"Yes," said Abe. "I like parakeets. Green parakeets."

"Perhaps we'll use that name for the baby," said Isaac.

Charity shook her head, smiling.

"Sam suggested Bull Heaven," said Isaac.

Charity laughed. "Clutterbuck Heaven would be nearer the mark. It's no less than his salvation for you to make him overseer of such a place."

"He would rather be back on the Combahee, I think. Were it possible."

"I don't see why," said Charity. "There is no more dismal and lonely a country than that land along the Combahee. I'm for selling away Fairmeadow altogether. This new plantation is so much better, close to town as it is, and the fields cleared, and a fine house already built."

"Then give me a name for it."

"Rice Hope," said Charity.

Isaac did not care for the suggestion, but pretended to consider it for a moment. "I think not," he said, shaking his head. "It's not exactly right."

"That's the best I can do," said Charity.

"No, try again."

"You try."

"There's only one name that's come to me," said Isaac. "Cusso Springs. We have the two springs on the place, you know. And it was the Cussoes who first farmed there."

Charity had stopped sewing. She was turning it over. But she did not look at him.

"You don't care for it," he said.

She shook her head. "It has too much of the Indian in it. I'd like to forget Indians, if I could. They've caused us so much pain."

"Then I've no idea what to call the place."

The old slave Jack came into the room. "Miss Charity," he said quietly.

"What is it?" she answered without looking up.

"There's a woman at the back door wants to speak to you. An Indian woman."

"Who?"

"An Indian woman," said Jack. "I never seen her before."

Charity gave Isaac a puzzled look.

"Go find out what she wants," Isaac said to Jack.

The old man bowed and went out.

"Now who could that be?" said Charity. She moved her sewing from her lap, putting the skeins of colored thread back into her sewing basket.

After a few moments Jack returned to the door, somewhat animated now, his eyes bright with interest. "She say she want to speak to you about Lucia."

"Lucia?" Charity rose to her feet. "What in heaven's name? Lucia?"

Isaac, too, got to his feet, and he followed Charity from the room and out through the hall to the back door. Looking out, he saw that the woman was Elizabeth Birdfeather, the seller of roots and herbs. He had last seen her on Port Royal Island several months before the war broke out.

"Mistress Hawkins," Elizabeth Birdfeather said quietly.

"Bull is my name now," said Charity. "What is it you want?"

"I see your Lucia, Mistress Bull. Slave on waterfront."

"On the waterfront?" said Charity. "Here in Charles Town? How did she get here? She's been gone from us a year."

"Taken up in the Indian country, I'd say," said Isaac.

Elizabeth Birdfeather nodded. "Cherokees. Sell to Mister James Moore. Younger."

"With our brand on her?" Charity was indignant.

Elizabeth Birdfeather shrugged. "I see her in pen. I come tell you."

"Thank you," said Charity. "It was good of you."

Isaac took out his purse and gave the woman a twopence. She took it and walked away.

"Lucia," Charity said quietly, pushing the door closed and leaning back against it. She looked at Isaac. "We must get her back. Go tell Moore he has our slave in his pen. The scoundrel. He has to have known it."

"Perhaps he overlooked the marks on her," said Isaac. "James Moore the younger is no scoundrel. God knows, he's one of the leading men of Carolina. Think of it. His father was governor and fought against the Spaniards. His brother was my commander at Tugaloo, and James himself commanded the entire army. The man is no petty thief."

"I say he's a scoundrel," said Charity. "Lucia is branded as clear as can be." She pointed to her own cheeks as she said it. "Two H's. It could mean no other than Henry Hawkins. He had to have known it."

"If he saw it, my dear," Isaac said soothingly. "I'll go speak to him. But it will have to be handled with delicacy."

"Even if he claims not to have known it, she's ours."

"Yes," said Isaac, "and I'll see to it she's returned to us. Be easy now. Think of the babe."

"I'm quite all right," said Charity, starting down the hall again. "Are you going now?"

"We've not found a name for my rice plantation."

"What about Spring Hope?" she said.

He did not reply.

She stopped at the door of the sitting room and turned to him. "It's a handsome name, I think."

He nodded. "I'm thinking about it. It's not bad."

"Will you go now and see to Lucia?"

"I thought you were weary of Indians," he teased.

She closed her lips and looked perplexed. "I am. But what else can we do but bring her back? I'll not have her sold away to some cruel fate we cannot even imagine."

"I'll go now and get her," said Isaac.

Charity nodded, still without smiling, and turned and went into the sitting room.

☀ James Moore the younger took the key from his pocket and put it into the lock of the door that led into the room where the slaves were kept.

"I seldom come into the office, myself," said Moore. "It's luck you caught me here." He tried without effect to turn the key, pulled it out and looked at it, then put it back and rattled it a bit and turned it with more force. The lock gave way. "If we've one of Hawkins' slaves, I've not seen her. But then I've not seen any of this lot except from the balcony above. Though if there's one branded, my men should have seen it. I'll have harsh words for them if it be true."

"And could be it's not true," said Isaac. "We've naught but the word of an Indian hag. But my wife is concerned. She'd not want this one sold away into misery."

"Well, the sugar islands are misery," said Moore, pushing open the door and leading the way in. "There's no doubt of that."

The room they came into was bare except for blankets spread out on the floor. A door stood open to the yard outside and let the daylight in. There was no one here but a lone woman who lay on one of the blankets with her face to the wall.

"Is that the one?" asked Moore.

"I think not," said Isaac, going over to look at her. The woman kept still and did not look up as he bent over her. He could see that she was large with child. "No," he said. "It's not she."

"The others are in the yard," said Moore. He motioned for Isaac to go before him.

As Isaac went out into the bright sunlight, he saw Lucia at once, standing with a group of women, the tallest of them all. She looked over at him with recognition. He motioned her to him.

"That one?" Moore said with surprise.

"Yes," said Isaac. "It is she."

Lucia started across the yard, then stopped and turned aside and went over to pick up a small girl from among the children.

"My man pointed her out to me before," said Moore. "But not for any brand she might have. He said she was the wife of King Carlos. Or the widow, I should say." Lucia was coming toward them, carrying the child on her hip.

Isaac turned and looked incredulously at Moore. "Did I hear you?"

Moore smiled. "I believe you did from the looks of you."

"King Carlos?"

"That's what they say."

Isaac looked back at Lucia as she came to a halt in front of them. "You are the woman of King Carlos?" he asked bluntly, with no more greeting than that.

She paled for an instant, then boosted the child a little higher on her hip. "I was his wife," she said.

"And I suppose you will try to tell me that this is your child. It has only been a year since you were at Fairmeadow."

"I was his wife before I ever was a slave. And yes, this is my child now. Her first mother is dead. I wish to keep her with me."

Isaac stared at her, still amazed at her connection with Carlos. There was dirt smeared on her face, obscuring the brands. He licked his thumb and reached out and rubbed one of them clean—H.

"I see it," said Moore, thinking Isaac was trying to prove his point. "I believed you even without it. It's obvious from the way she speaks to you. And with such clear English, too. So what will you do with her? Not keep her, I should think."

"My wife would wish that."

"But people are ridding themselves of their Indian slaves, selling them away to other parts. It's too dangerous to have them around anymore. The uprising showed that. Especially this one, the wife of King Carlos, no less. Henry Hawkins had her about his very house. She knew all about him, where he kept his guns, where he slept. Like as not, she was the one who brained him."

"No," Lucia said, shaking her head. "I was not the one." She looked at the child and brushed a strand of dark hair from her face.

"I want to get down," the little girl said in Apalachee, a language Isaac could understand.

Lucia set her down. "Stay close," she said quietly, and the little girl went off a few steps and then stood watching them.

"What would *you* do?" Isaac said to Moore. "Send her on to the sugar islands?"

Moore shrugged. "It's up to you."

"Miss Charity would not want us sent away," said Lucia. "Remember how she grieved for Timboe?"

Isaac looked at her. H H—Henry Hawkins. The brands were all he could see now. Would H H flit about forever in his house, drifting through his chamber, making his bed, dressing his wife? He waved her away. "Go over there," he said. "Let us talk."

"Please, sir," she said softly, reaching out and taking his hand in both of hers. "Please don't send us to the sugar islands." He pulled his hand free. She looked at him for a moment, then turned away and took the child's hand and led her across the yard to a bench beside the fence, where they both sat down together.

Isaac would not look at her now. He shook his head. "The wife of King Carlos," he said. "It's a shock to me. I cannot have her about my house, that's for certain."

"Leave her here," said Moore. "I'll give you what she's worth and then sell her away with the others. Though, God knows, it will make twice that I've bought her."

"I don't know," said Isaac. "I'm sure that would make my wife unhappy. I never saw her so melancholy as when Henry Hawkins sold one of her favorites to Jamaica." He paused and put his hand to his chin, thinking. He glanced around at Lucia and then turned back. "Now here's an idea," he said slowly. He looked at Moore. "I've a cousin in Jamaica who has a liking for handsome slaves. I could send her to him and be sure he would use her well." He paused for a moment, thinking further, and then continued. "Yes, I believe I've found the solution. My wife could be easy knowing she was sent as a house servant to a good master. And I'll buy the child to send with her. That will make it even better."

Moore shrugged. "Whatever you wish to do. She's yours. I'll send her over to your pen. And the child as well, if you wish to buy her."

"Yes, I'll take the child," said Isaac. "But have your man row them out into the bay, if you would, to the sloop Adventure, Captain Rigdon. It's one of our vessels. He's waiting for the wind to change and carry him out, Jamaica bound. I'll give you a letter for him to give to Swade. And I'll pay you well for your trouble. It will lessen your loss in buying a slave that was already owned."

"No need for that," said Moore. "My man should have seen the brands. He'll be the one to pay. And as for my trouble, there's none. I'm glad to be of service. I'd not think of taking a penny for it."

"Then come with me to the Indian Queen," said Isaac. "We can finish this business over a bowl of punch. I'll write my letter there."

"Now that I will accept. It would be a pleasure." Moore turned and led the way back into the building.

Isaac followed after him, aware that Lucia was watching him, but he did not turn back to look at her. Inside the dimly lit room the Indian woman still lay in the same position as before, her face to the wall.

"I met your father once," said Isaac as he waited for Moore to unlock the door that led out to the office. "It was my first day in Carolina. He was recently back from his Apalachee campaign and we joked about some church silver he had taken from a Spanish town down there. I'll never forget it. He was a powerful man. In his person, I mean."

"He was," said Moore, opening the door and letting Isaac go through ahead of him. "I was always in awe of him. To think that he came to this land when there was nothing here at all and shaped it into a place where civilized men could live." Moore shut the door and locked it and put the key in his pocket. "An empty, savage land. I never cease to marvel at it."

"Carolina has been a blessing for me, that's for certain," said Isaac. "I've just got the papers today for a plantation in Saint Paul's Parish. The land is cleared and ready for rice. The previous owner died last fall of the fever."

"Do his slaves come with it?" asked Moore.

"What there are of them. I'll be adding more. I intend to ship a great deal of rice through this harbor."

"And I'm sure you will. What will you be calling your place?"

"Spring Hope," said Isaac, flushing a little with pride. He suddenly felt very happy with himself. He had become a man of substance, with a plantation, a shipping firm, a lovely wife, and a fine town house. How much of it all did he owe to Theophilus Swade for sending him here to Carolina? More than he had ever expressed to the man. He would try to express it now in the letter he would send with the slaves. Indeed, he would send these two slaves to Swade without charge, as tokens of his gratitude. That would be just the thing. It would tie it all up quite neatly.

He looked at Moore with a smile. "You'll have to come pay us a visit at Spring Hope when we've settled in."

"I will," said Moore. "I would like to see your plantation." He picked up his hat and opened the front door, pausing for Isaac to go out before him. Isaac made him a little bow and then led the way out into the street.

CHAPTER FORTY-SEVEN

Dawn rose in a spreading arch above the sea, casting its red light over the brooding surface of the dark water. Lucia sat on the deck of the rolling ship, her blanket wrapped around both herself and the child, who sat between her legs, leaning back against her, slumped down in sleep. As the light rose, Lucia could see the land behind them, a thin strip of darkness barely visible above the western horizon. Her initial fear had subsided, the terror she had felt in the moonlight as the ship had crossed the bar and moved out onto the open sea, the water dark and vast, endlessly moving, the sails taut and billowing with the driving power of the wind, the small ship rising and falling with the sea, and the land lost from sight in the darkness.

She and Blue were the only slaves on the ship. There was a place for them to sleep in the hold, but there was no requirement that they stay down there. They could be on the deck, the captain's mate had told her, so long as they kept out of the way of the sailors. It was better up here, though the wind was cold and blew relentlessly. On deck her stomach did not heave so much with the rolling of the ship and Blue was not so terrified as she had been in the dark closeness of the hold. Blue was finally sleeping now, and that was good. She would awake in daylight and be happy again. The sun would be warm and the sky blue. The sails and ropes would enthrall her, and so would the water splashing by. It was only the nights that were hard for Blue. She was fortunate in that. The ignorance of children protected them from care.

Looking down at the little girl, Lucia stroked her dark hair and then rested a hand on her small, warm head. They were going to Jamaica, the same island where Ana had been sent. Ana would surely be dead after all this time. But Timboe had also been sent there, hardly more than a year ago. Jamaica was a large island, Doll had said. Even though he was probably still alive, she was not likely to see him. Not unless he had escaped to the mountains. She might see him there, in the free towns of the runaway slaves, if she could make her own escape. Though escaping would not be easy. Not with Blue to carry along. But Blue was the reason she would have to try it, no matter what the danger. She would not watch this child grow up into slavery. Not this one. Not Blue Heron's Mother.

The sky was growing brighter, yellow light chasing away the streaks of red. She turned and looked back toward land. It had vanished. Nothing but water and sky. And so her world was gone. Apalachee. Gone forever. She was alone now, except for this child leaning warm against her. And the Sun. The same dawn here as at the moment of her birth. The Sun would always be with her.

She turned toward the light, blinking her eyes against the growing glare on the water. As the Sun raised her face above the waves, Lucia lifted up her hands and sang softly to greet her.

HISTORICAL NOTES

In 1539, at the beginning of his trek though southeastern North America, the Spanish explorer Hernando de Soto wintered in Anhayca, the principal town of Apalachee. At that time the Apalachees were a powerful agricultural chiefdom. Although no generally accepted population estimates exist for aboriginal Apalachee, their numbers must have been many tens of thousands.

In 1565 the Spaniards founded Saint Augustine, and in 1608 Franciscan friars made their first visit to the Apalachee country and estimated the population at that time to be only around 25,000. This sharp population decline in the seventy years since De Soto's entrada had been caused by European diseases, to which Native Americans had little immunity. An epidemic of smallpox, for example, would normally take away at least one-third to one-half of a native population, and often more. Even though some migrants came to Apalachee from devastated Indian societies to the north, the total population fell.

As the Franciscans expanded their mission effort through the seventeenth century, the population of Apalachee continued to decline, the people succumbing to further epidemics and to the harsh conditions of forced labor. At the height of the mission effort in 1675, there were some fourteen missions in Apalachee, with as many as two dozen satellite villages, but only 10,520 Indians, according to Spanish count.

By January of 1704, when James Moore made his attack, there were at most 7,000 Apalachee people in the land. Moore killed and enslaved perhaps a thousand of them. In the months following, about eight hundred of the survivors went west to live near the French at Pensacola and Mobile. Between three and four hundred went east with the Spaniards to Timucua and Saint Augustine. Another thirteen hundred or so resettled among the Yamasees and Creeks near Carolina. Many others moved north into present-day Georgia and Alabama to join the Upper and Lower Creeks. By August of that year, the homeland of the Apalachee people was completely abandoned, and for the first time buffalo roamed freely in their old-fields.

In 1715 came the Yamasee War. More Apalachees died, more were enslaved, and the survivors again emigrated and resettled. A few went south to Saint Augustine, but most went west to the Creek homeland along the Chattahoochee River. With this upheaval the remaining Apalachee people, except for those few around Mobile, were absorbed into the Creek Confederacy and their name receded from history. On September 3, 1763, the descendants of those at Mobile boarded ships and were taken to the village of San Carlos de Chachalacasin Tempoala in Mexico.

Some of the great mounds of precolumbian Apalachee can be seen today at Lake Jackson State Park, a few miles north of Tallahassee, Florida. The archaeological site of mission San Luís is within the city limits of Tallahassee. It has a visitor's center and is open to the public, while excavations there continue.

✳ It is ironic that the Apalachees' name was settled upon the Appalachian Mountains, for they never lived in them. Their homeland was hundreds of miles to the south. It was the French who did the naming. In 1564 France founded Fort Caroline, a doomed colony at the mouth of the Saint John's River on Florida's Atlantic coast. Indians living nearby showed the French some sheets of copper which had come from Apalachee, 200 miles to the west. The French mistakenly assumed that the Apalachees also had supplies of silver and gold. We know now that the Apalachees were getting their copper through a native trade network that ran far into the interior of the South, and they evidently maintained control over that trade in the Florida region. The Indians who showed the copper to the French told them two things: that Apalachee was the only source of it, and that it had originally come from some mountains. The French, who never visited the Apalachees or the mountains, misunderstood, believing the Apalachees themselves to be living in a mountainous region.

Thus, on a 1591 map by Theodore de Bry, the "Apalatci Mountains" first appeared, situated vaguely in the interior, running from east to west, with a notation that here silver and gold could be found. De Bry's mountain range was transferred to subsequent maps drawn by Europeans throughout the seventeenth century. And so when the English founded Carolina in the late seventeenth century and went out to explore the backcountry, they expected to find mountains there, and though the mountains they found ran from northeast to southwest and were the homeland of the Cherokee Indians, yet they continued to call them by the name that had already been fixed on maps for nearly a century—the Appalachian Mountains.

✳ Colonel James Moore's account of the Apalachee campaign did indeed appear in the *Boston News* of April 24, 1704. The excerpts read by Theophilus Swade are verbatim, except for the changing of a few words for clarity.

Along with James Moore the elder, a number of the characters in this story were actual persons living at the time. These are, in order of appearance, Father Juan de Villalva of Ivitachuco; Deputy Governor Manuel Solana; Don Patricio Hinachuba; the slain priest, Father Parga; Solana's slain son Juan; Thomas Nairne; Governor Johnson's son-in-law Thomas Broughton; Emperor Brims; Colonel Maurice Moore; Captain George Chicken; Caesar, the Cherokee war leader; the Conjurer, leader of the pro-English faction of the Cherokees; and General James Moore the younger. Some of their actions are fictionalized. All the other characters are purely fictional, but represent social types in the early eighteenth-century South.

The American South during this period was linguistically diverse, and a modern novel can do no more than hint at this complexity. In this work, Apalachee speakers conversing among themselves in their native language are represented in standard English, with the addition of real Apalachee clan names and a few conventional expressions drawn from Southeastern Indian languages in general. Following the same principle, Spaniards speak among themselves in standard English, with a few Spanish words added for flavor. The same convention holds for Apalachees who were fluent in Spanish, as some were, and for African house slaves who were fluent in English, as some were. Indians who knew only elementary Spanish, English, or other Indian languages are represented speaking "broken" English, with varying degrees of ungrammaticality, depending upon the exposure each has had to the language he is trying to speak. This same convention is used for African slaves who spoke a dialect of English that fell short of the English dialect spoken in the upper stratum of Charles Town society and in the plantation great houses. Some standard elements of black English have been added. The speech of the upper stratum of English colonial society is represented in this novel by standard English embellished with a few eighteenth-century linguistic patterns and devices. Some attempt has been made to represent the English speech of poor, backcountry whites, and the same is true of the English creole language spoken by African field slaves on the Carolina rice and indigo plantations. In fact, the diversity of language and dialect in the early eighteenth-century South was far greater than has been indicated here, and only a linguist of preternatural ability could have spoken intelligibly with all the major players in this colonial world.

FROM THE DOCUMENTS

Testimony of Manuel Solana the younger, son of the deputy governor of Apalachee, given in San Augustín, 1705:

The witness [testified that he] did not go along . . . to fight the battle of Ayubale, but that if things went well he was to carry munitions, and that [along the way] he encountered some retreating Indians and Spaniards and [learned that the enemy] had killed Father Fray Juan de Parga . . . and thrown him in a canebrake . . . and that Juan Solana—a brother of the witness—went to his aid and . . . was killed.

Royal cédula from the King of Spain, May 7, 1700:

Don Patricio Hinachuba, the principal [chief] of the entire province [of Apalachee], and Don Andres, [chief] of the village of San Luís, . . . have written to me . . . of the continuous affronts, vexations, and annoyances which they receive from the [Spanish] families . . . in that province . . . [who oblige] them to work for them without giving them food or otherwise compensating for their labor, by which they are obliged to withdraw to the woods where they do not hear Mass, . . . some even passing to [the English].

Manuel Solana, deputy governor of Apalachee, reporting his defeat in the battle of Patale, July 9, 1704:

I proposed . . . to the Indians [that we fall upon the enemy], and they replied to me that if the Spaniards would fight afoot as they do, they would go, but if the Spaniards went on horses, they did not want to go. I told them we would all go afoot. . . .

Francisco Corcoles y Martinez, governor at San Augustín, in a letter to the King of Spain, 1708:

Nothing . . . has sufficed to prevent the enemy from continuing his constant killings and hostilities. . . . Altogether those they have carried off to sell as slaves must number more than ten or twelve thousand persons.

Nathaniel Johnson, governor of South Carolina, in a report to England, 1708 (paraphrased):

> The number of inhabitants in this province of [South Carolina] . . . are computed to be 9,580 souls, of which there are 2,260 free men and women; 120 white servants; 4,100 Negro slaves; and 1,400 Indian slaves.

Commissioners of the Indian Trade, South Carolina, in instructions to a trader, 1716:

> You are to mark all skins . . . and slaves bought by you C H, to which end we send you a brand.

Francis LeJau, Anglican minister in South Carolina, in a letter to England, 1715:

> I take upon me to acquaint [you] of a very dismal piece of news, an Indian war lately broke out in this province. Dismal in all respects. The province is in danger of being lost.

John Lawson, a surveyor in Carolina, in his book about the province, 1709:

> These [Indians] have abundance of storks and cranes in their [meadows]. They take them before they can fly, and breed 'em as tame and familiar as a dung-hill fowl. They had a tame crane at one of these cabins that was scarce less than six foot in height. . . .

Colonel George Chicken in his journal of the campaign into the Cherokee country, 1716:

> The head warriors were in a great passion and said if they made peace with the other Indians they should have no way in getting of slaves to buy ammunition and clothing and that they were resolved to get ready for war.

Francis Le Jau in a letter to England, 1716:

> As for our Indian war . . . it is affirmed that 2000 Cherokees are marched against the main body of the Creek Indians. . . . God send them good success.

SELECTED BIBLIOGRAPHY

Bartram, William. *The Travels of William Bartram.* Edited by Francis Harper. New Haven, Conn., 1958. Reprint, Athens, Ga., 1999.

Bolton, Herbert E. *The Rim of Christendom: A Biography of Eusebio Francisco Kino.* New York, 1936.

Boyd, Mark F., Hale G. Smith, and John W. Griffin. *Here They Once Stood: The Tragic End of the Apalachee Missions.* Gainesville, Fla., 1951.

Braund, Kathryn E. H. *Deerskins and Duffels: The Creek Indian Trade with Anglo-America, 1685–1815.* Lincoln, Nebraska, 1993.

Colonial Records of South Carolina. *Journals of the Commissioners of the Indian Trade.* Edited by W. L. McDowell. Columbia: South Carolina Archives Department, 1955.

Crane, Verner W. *The Southern Frontier, 1670–1732.* Ann Arbor, Mich., 1929.

Drechsel, Emanuel J. *Mobilian Jargon: Linguistic and Sociohistorical Aspects of a Native American Pidgin.* Oxford, 1997.

Dunn, Richard. *Sugar and Slaves: The Rise of the Planter Class in the English West Indies, 1624–1713.* Chapel Hill, N.C., 1972.

Hann, John H. *Apalachee: The Land Between the Rivers.* Gainesville, Florida, 1988.

Hudson, Charles. *The Southeastern Indians.* Knoxville, Tenn., 1976.

———. *Knights of Spain, Warriors of the Sun: Hernando de Soto and the South's Ancient Chiefdoms.* Athens, Georgia, 1997.

Hudson, Charles and Carmen Chaves Tesser, eds. *The Forgotten Centuries: Indians and Europeans in the American South, 1521–1704.* Athens, Georgia, 1994.

Joyner, Charles. *Down By the River Side: A South Carolina Slave Community.* Urbana, Illinois, 1984.

Le Jau, Francis. *The Carolina Chronicle of Dr. Francis Le Jau.* Edited by Frank J. Klingberg. Berkeley, Calif., 1956.

Lawson, John. *A New Voyage to Carolina.* London, 1709. Republished with introduction and notes by Hugh Talmage Lefler. Chapel Hill, N.C., 1967.

400 Mills, Robert. *Mill's Atlas of the State of South Carolina, 1825.* Easley, S.C., 1980.

McEwan, Bonnie G., ed. *The Spanish Missions of Florida.* Gainesville, Florida, 1993.

Sirmans, M. Eugene. *Colonial South Carolina, A Political History, 1663–1763.* Chapel Hill, N.C., 1966.

Swanton, John R. *Social Organization and Social Usages of the Indians of the Creek Confederacy.* 42nd Annual Report of the Bureau of American Ethnology. Washington, D.C., 1928.

Wood, Peter H. *Black Majority: Negroes in Colonial South Carolina.* New York, 1974.

Worth, John E. *The Timucuan Chiefdoms of Spanish Florida.* Gainesville, Florida: University Press of Florida, 1998. Two volumes.

Wright, Gay Goodman. "Turpentining: An Ethnohistorical Study of a Southern Industry and Way of Life." M.A. thesis, University of Georgia, 1979.

Wright, J. Leitch, Jr. *The Only Land They Knew: The Tragic Story of the American Indians in the Old South.* New York, 1981.